swope's RIDGE

Other Books in the Lije Evans Mysteries Series

Farraday Road (Book 1)

Other Books by Ace Collins

Turn Your Radio On:
The Stories behind Gospel Music's
All-Time Greatest Songs

The Cathedrals:
The Story of America's
Best-Loved Gospel Quartet

Stories Behind the Best-Loved
Songs of Christmas

Stories Behind the Hymns
That Inspire America

Stories Behind the Great
Traditions of Christmas

I Saw Him in Your Eyes:
Everyday People Making
Extraordinary Impact

More Stories Behind the
Best-Loved Songs of Christmas

Stories Behind the
Traditions and Songs of Easter

Stories Behind Women of
Extraordinary Faith

Sticks and Stones:
Using Your Words as a Positive Force

Stories Behind Heroes of Faith

ACE COLLINS

BESTSELLING AUTHOR

swope's RIDGE

Lije Evans Mysteries

ZONDERVAN.com/
AUTHORTRACKER
follow your favorite authors

ZONDERVAN

Swope's Ridge

This title is also available in a Zondervan audio edition.
Visit www.zondervan.fm.

Requests for information should be addressed to:

Zondervan, *Grand Rapids, Michigan 49530*

Library of Congress Cataloging-in-Publication Data

Collins, Ace.
Swope's Ridge / Ace Collins.
p. cm.—(Lije Evans mysteries)
ISBN 978-0-310-27953-2 (pbk.)

1. Lawyers—Fiction. 2. Murder—Investigation—Fiction. I. Title.
PS3553.O47475S96 2009
813'.54—dc22 2009018441

Scriptures are taken from the King James Version of the Bible.

Interior design by Christine Orejuela-Winkelman

Printed in the United States of America

---

09 10 11 12 13 14 15 • 22 21 20 19 18 17 16 15 14 13 12 11 10 9 8 7 6 5 4 3 2 1

To Shalee,
whose life is a model for us all

Previously in the Lije Evans Mysteries Series

On a cold June night, in the pouring rain, small-town lawyer Elijah Evans and his wife, Kaitlyn, are found brutally murdered on Farraday Road. By some miracle, however, Lije Evans is revived and saved; when he wakes up in the hospital and learns of his wife's murder, he vows to find her killer.

His only lead is a piece of property Kaitlyn had purchased only days before the tragic incident: mysterious and beautiful Swope's Ridge, upon which sits a cold and lonely fortress built by a German recluse in the post–World War II era. As Lije investigates the history of this land, he discovers that its past is bathed in obsession and blood.

Lije teams up with Diana Curtis, an agent with the Arkansas Bureau of Investigation, and in the resulting journey they find an innocent man sitting on death row, a corrupt ABI director, and a legend hidden deep within the dirt on Swope's Ridge. And through it all, the murderers watch their every move, until finally Lije faces them down.

Escaping with their lives but with little more information than they had when they started, Lije, Diana, and his associates, Heather and Janie, find themselves inside the stark fortress on Swope's Ridge, staring at Lije's great-aunt's high school yearbook, which they found hidden in the house. The mystery turns out to be deeper and more complicated than anyone had imagined.

As they leave the fortress to investigate more, shots ring out from the logging road on Swope's Ridge.

1

October 11, 2001
Waxahachie, Texas

IT WAS JUST PAST EIGHT AND, AS USUAL, OMAR Jones was running late. As he glanced at the clock, the twenty-eight-year-old computer programmer picked up a half-filled cup of coffee and splashed a last lukewarm gulp down his throat. He heard Charlie Gibson on *Good Morning America* voicing yet another story on the attacks in New York and Washington. Had it already been a month? He still couldn't begin to fathom how anyone could fly a jetliner into the World Trade Center towers or the Pentagon. Why would anyone become a terrorist? Why would anyone choose to die like that?

Jones switched off the TV and set down his coffee. He had thirty minutes to get to work, and traffic was sure to be snarled due to construction around Desoto. Hurrying toward the door, he stopped in front of a mirror to make sure his coal-black hair was neatly combed and his thick mustache showed no sign of the oatmeal he had just eaten. Satisfied, he pushed open the side door of his modest three-bedroom track home.

The scene that met him in the carport nearly caused his heart to stop. There, no more than ten feet in front of him, stood a police officer pointing a gun at his chest, with a dozen other officers—all heavily armed with weapons aimed and ready—spread out behind him.

"Omar Saddam Jones?" A man in a black suit stepped toward him.

Unable to manage a verbal response, Jones simply nodded.

"Put your hands on top of your head. Now."

Jones quickly did as he was told.

Three men rushed up behind him, forcefully pulled his arms behind his back, slapped a pair of cuffs around his wrists, and patted him down. Then he was pushed twenty feet toward a squad car. Only then did Jones speak.

"What's this about?" His voice sounded almost childlike to his ears. "You must have the wrong guy. I've done nothing!"

A large man in a dark suit walked to the car, leaned over, and said, "You know the Klasser family."

Jones nodded. "Sure, they're my neighbors."

"They *were* your neighbors," the man said. "Someone killed them. A month ago. Even the baby was murdered. Where have you been?"

Albert Klasser wasn't just his neighbor; he was a good friend. They played softball on the same city team. Emily was the ideal wife. She made chocolate-drop cookies for the neighbors. And the kids ... Jacob ... Sarah ... They were dead? "The Klassers?" he whispered.

"Jones, I'm Adam Horne, Federal Bureau of Investigation." The tall, balding man showed Omar his identification, then looked around for another agent. "Take him downtown."

The interrogation room was stark, just like the ones Omar had seen so many times on television. He'd been waiting alone for a half hour. His palms were sweating. He needed to call his boss.

The door opened and in walked Agent Horne, a thick manila file folder in his hand. The man sat down across the table from

Jones and opened the file. He rifled through a few sheets of paper until he came to a specific report.

"Jones, we have a witness who saw you come out of the Klasser home on the evening of September 10."

Omar had been gone a month. The tenth had been the night before he left on vacation. He'd arrived home late because he stopped to buy a few last-minute things for his trip to hike a section of the Appalachian Trail. A new sleeping bag and a rain poncho.

"I got home late," he said. He hadn't seen anyone. This was all a horrible mistake. But he had to keep his wits and think straight.

"What time did you get home?" Horne asked.

"I don't know. About eleven."

"Was anyone with you? Anyone see you?"

"No. I live alone. But I bought some stuff at the mall."

"Then you have receipts," Horne said.

Panic set in. Jones hadn't used a credit card or written a check; he had used cash. He'd thrown away the receipt that first night on the trail.

He had grabbed a bite at a Burger King, but had used the drive-through. It had been so long ago, no one would remember him.

He'd killed some time watching kids playing football in a park in Red Oak, but he'd never gotten out of his car. No one had seen him there either.

No one had called him on his cell phone and he hadn't made any calls. He couldn't prove where he'd been.

"No, I paid cash," Jones said. "I didn't get home until almost midnight. I left before five the next morning. This is all a mistake. I love the Klassers like family!"

The agent turned over a few more pages in the file. "Do you know Martin de la Cruz?"

"Yes, he lives down the street."

"Mr. de la Cruz told us that he spoke to you at eight on the night of the tenth. That you talked for about five minutes right in front of the Klasser home. He saw you come out the side door of that house. Do you remember he asked what you were doing?"

"No, it wasn't me."

Horne ignored Omar's denial. "And you told him you'd been arguing with Mr. Klasser over religion."

How could that be? He hadn't seen Martin when he got home that night. He hadn't seen anyone. Why was Martin lying? Why would he lie about anything?

The man waited for an answer, then said, "Where were you born?"

Suddenly everything became clear. Jones knew why he'd been arrested. On September 11 the whole world changed. When those planes flew into the towers, Omar Jones had been transformed from a naturalized citizen and college graduate with ten years in the workforce into an enemy of the state. It didn't matter that he'd come to the United States at the age of sixteen months. It didn't matter that he'd been adopted by Americans. It didn't matter that he'd been raised as a Christian or that he'd been an honors student and had a master's degree.

The only thing that mattered now was that he'd been born in Baghdad, in Iraq. On September 11 his Arab roots, his birthplace, had put a target squarely in the middle of his forehead.

"Where were you born?" Horne asked again.

Jones shook his head. "You know the answer."

"And you knew the Klassers were Jewish."

Jones nodded.

"And that Albert Klasser worked for the Federal Aviation Administration."

With that final link, Omar felt as though he'd fallen into a hole so deep there was no light. Truth no longer mattered. He had been born to a Muslim woman. Even though he'd been adopted by Christians, they saw him as a Muslim who lived next door to a Jewish man who worked for the agency that oversaw the aviation industry.

One final question from the imposing agent removed all hope.

"Jones, can you explain why your DNA and fingerprints were found at the crime scene?"

Omar Jones stared at the floor. Being late for work no longer mattered. Nothing did. His life as an American was over.

They believed he was a terrorist.

2

LIJE EVANS SAW THE HAND-HEWN BOARD OF THE doorframe crack a split second before he heard the thunk.

The shot, fired from a rarely used logging road that ran along the highest point of Swope's Ridge, barely missed Diana Curtis as she started out the door with Lije right behind her. They both plunged back into the safety of the old house and slammed the door.

"That was close," Curtis said.

"You okay?" he asked.

"Fine."

They waited a few moments in silence, ears straining for any noise. Nothing.

Lije moved back toward the door and opened it just a crack. The shot had splintered the rock-hard wood harvested generations before in the Bavarian Black Forest. The home had been built like a fortress in the late 1940s by a German soldier. To Lije it felt as if World War III had started here in Arkansas, on a hillside called Swope's Ridge.

"Think he's gone?" he asked.

Curtis, a former agent for the Arkansas Bureau of Investigation, crawled to the door and looked up toward the top of the ridge. Another blast put a second hole in the doorframe. Curtis dove back as the sound of the shot echoed through the hills.

"He's still there. That shot was no accident."

They knew the shooter hadn't meant it as a warning. Whoever had pulled the trigger had a clear target lined up in the gunsight. If her head had been raised just a little more ...

They waited and listened. Nothing. Then the sound of a car starting up and wheeling away.

"He just drove off, or he might be moving to a better spot. We're still pinned down."

"He could still be watching us," Lije said. "Still waiting to make his move."

She nodded.

"We're trapped," he said.

He finally took the time to check on his legal assistant, Janie Davies, who exhibited her normal calm, and his partner, Heather Jameson, who cowered in a far corner behind an overstuffed chair.

"We're trapped but safe," Janie said. "That door's the only way into this place, and if he tries to come through it, Diana's gun will no doubt provide a welcoming note. So we're safe — really safe. After what we've been through, that's a lot to be thankful for."

As always, Janie provided wisdom in a moment of chaos. The Ozark foothills were littered with boulders, but none were more solid than this diminutive blonde whose blindness had tightly honed her other senses. She had a vision he lacked and a logical steadiness in the midst of calamity. If she wasn't an angel, she would surely make a good prototype for one.

"Janie's right," Lije said. "We're safe as long as we stay in the house. Nothing's going to happen to any of us while we're inside."

Heather nodded but pushed deeper into her spot behind the chair, like a rabbit hiding from a wolf. She would've likely pushed into the thick wall if that had been possible.

Lije couldn't predict what would happen next. That was entirely up to whoever had fired the rifle. Knowing they couldn't dictate the person's actions, they all looked toward the door and listened intently for signs of an approaching gunman. All they heard was the symphony of the majestic rushing water of Spring River as it cut its way through the foothills, and the rustling of leaves on the tall trees surrounding the six-decades-old structure. These sounds framed the moment with an aura of peace.

Lije was ready for a showdown. He glanced over at Curtis, who fingered the grip of the nine millimeter she had pulled from her purse. It looked as though she was itching to charge out into the sunlight and take on the assassin who had nearly ended her life. But she waited, perhaps convinced Janie was right. The German's stuffy home offered sure protection against a foe carrying a lethal weapon.

The minutes dragged by as they each held their positions. No one spoke. Then, silently, Janie got up and walked toward the door. For a moment he considered pulling her back down to the floor. But in her uncanny way, she avoided any position where she could be seen from outside. Could she sense the sunlight pouring through the partly open doorway, or was it the slight breeze that led her?

He watched as she continued to move. When she drew near the front wall, she reached out and touched the door's thick frame. Her left hand lingered there for a few seconds, then she made a slow pirouette and rested her back against the wall. She stood unmoving, her toned body relaxed but her face showing obvious signs of concentration. What was she doing? What did she perceive that he could not?

She'd moved to the door to better hear the outside world. She'd know long before any of the rest of them if someone was approaching. In a strange way, the blind woman had become the lookout.

"A car's coming through the gate." Janie turned her head in Lije's direction.

"Are you sure?" He picked up a loose brick he'd pried out of the wall a few weeks ago.

"Yes, it's moving slowly, but it's heading this way."

Another minute passed before he heard it. He squeezed the

brick, then got down on his hands and knees and crawled over to the door. The home's native stone floor felt cool.

"What do you think, Diana?" he whispered. "Who is it?"

The former ABI agent shook her head. "I don't know."

Curtis was a solid CSI type. Lije knew that from watching her work. She had investigative skills he deeply respected.

"It's not the same car that's coming now," Janie whispered. "Not the one that drove off on the ridge."

"You sure?"

"The one we heard after the shots had a distinctive squeak, like a spring was broken. This one doesn't. And driving up here on that bumpy, rocky driveway would make that squeak even more pronounced. I guarantee it's not the same car."

Lije hadn't noticed any squeak, just the sound of a car driving off. Glancing over his shoulder, he looked at Diana. She shrugged. She'd missed it too.

So if this wasn't the guy who'd just shot at Diana, who was it? Who would be coming to this spot, so secluded that cell phones couldn't find a signal?

Still clutching the brick, Lije moved to the edge of the door and peered through the narrow opening. A postcard-like scene displayed the awesome majesty of the unspoiled Ozarks. Two robins flew overhead, and a squirrel raced up the trunk of a tree. A nervous turkey scurried between rows of blackberry bushes. Nothing in his field of vision was unusual. In fact, this was as close to peace on earth as he could imagine.

Though he still couldn't see the approaching vehicle, like Janie he now could hear the sound of a motor moving closer. Would there be a violent confrontation, a life-and-death struggle in this remote, idyllic setting?

"Get ready," Janie whispered. "He just parked the car and turned off the motor."

Curtis moved to Lije's left side, lifted her gun, and aimed at the point where an intruder was most likely to approach their sanctuary.

Lije felt a sense of extreme curiosity, as if this might be the most important moment in his life. Would he finally look the killer in the eye? Would he finally get answers to the nightmare that had started that fateful night on Farraday Road, the nightmare that had left his beloved Kaitlyn dead?

Mentally voicing a quick and sincere prayer, Lije hefted his brick and readied himself for the fight. Yes, it was time! It was long past time.

"He's walking this way," Janie whispered. "He's alone."

Lije nodded, then realized their alert sentry couldn't hear the motion.

"Here he comes," Curtis whispered. "I see his shadow."

Lije glanced out and saw a silhouette floating over the wind-blown grass. It appeared to be a man. He had stopped moving.

Time seemed to halt as surely as the intruder, now twenty feet outside their door. The clock wouldn't start ticking again until the mystery man took his next step.

3

LIJE WAITED, HIS BODY TENSED, READY FOR ACTION, ready to lunge through the door. Janie touched his shoulder and kept him glued to his post. Patience, she seemed to tell him. Patience is what you must have now.

Why didn't the visitor move? Why didn't he rush in and start shooting? As if in a bad dream, the shadow remained anchored. Lije couldn't see the flesh-and-blood form of the man creating that shadow.

Lije continued to stare at the dark, ill-defined figure, watching for any movement. His mind flashed back to a time when Kaitlyn had introduced him to MP3s of old radio dramas from the 1930s and 1940s. She'd had hundreds of them on her iPod and liked to listen to them as they traveled. She'd said classic radio programs made a long trip seem shorter.

While she had loved *Boston Blackie*, *Richard Diamond*, *The Lux Radio Theater*, and *The Whistler*, her favorite program had starred Orson Welles. She often mimicked the great actor's well-known line, "Who knows what evil lurks in the hearts of men? The Shadow knows!"

Kaitlyn would've seen the irony of this moment.

There it was! Barely perceptible at first, but movement. The shadow took a cautious step forward. Another short step. Then another. From where he knelt, Lije could now see half of a dark-brown hiking boot. Whoever this was, he was prepared for the rugged terrain that covered so much of Swope's Ridge. Did he know something they didn't?

Moving his attention from the boot to the shadow falling on the tall grass, Lije saw a hand move. It seemed to linger at the man's side for a moment before pulling something from the pocket of his pants. The man took that unknown object and aimed it. What was it? Lije tensed even more. Curtis slid her left hand to the screen door. She was ready to shove it open and fire. But she held back, perhaps waiting for one more step by the intruder.

Lije heard a faint sound. It stopped. Then another soft burst. The sound was familiar, but what? He glanced over at Curtis. Shaking her head, she looked up at the woman leaning against the wall. Maybe the blind woman's ears could somehow see what they could only hear. Maybe she could put a picture with the sound.

"He's spraying something," Janie said. Her nose wrinkled as the breeze carried the scent into the room. "It's Off."

"What?" Curtis said.

"Off. You know, the insect repellent."

Janie had just finished her explanation when a deep voice hollered, "Lije? You up here?"

The anxiety in the room evaporated. This wasn't a gunman; it was a friend.

"It's McGee," Curtis said, rolling from her belly onto her back and easing the gun to her side.

"Yep." Lije laughed. "The Shadow knows."

"What?" Janie asked.

Not bothering to explain, Lije jumped to his feet, pushed open the screen door, and strode out into the sunlight. As he did, the state's top defense attorney took a couple more steps forward, finally revealing himself to his host.

"Stopped by the house in Salem," McGee said. "When I discovered you weren't there and your assistant wasn't home either, figured you were up here trying to find something new."

Janie, Curtis, and Jameson emerged from the dungeon-like confines of the German's home. McGee laughed, "So you've got the whole Scooby Crew with you. What's with the building material?"

Lije shrugged, dropped his brick to the ground. "Somebody took two shots at this place a few minutes ago from higher up on the ridge. We thought you were the guy coming down to finish the job."

McGee glanced over his shoulder to the spot where his friend was pointing. "The old logging road?"

"That's right," Curtis said. "One shot missed my head by an inch."

McGee grimaced, suddenly serious. "It's anything but over, then."

4

KENT MCGEE LOOKED AT THE PHOTO OF THE BUS IN the old high school yearbook. "So you think your great-aunt's disappearance might be tied to something that happened on Swope's Ridge? Imagine! When you consider everything else that's supposedly tied to this place, this property could be the capital of Crime, U.S.A."

Lije shrugged. "Mabel Dean did claim it was cursed, and even though I don't believe in that sort of thing, I can now see why she does. As for Aunt Josephine being tied to this place, well, it's a long shot that I wouldn't even consider if not for the fact the annual's the only book in this house printed in the United States. I find that weird. Everything else came from Germany."

He thought it strange that a man who had had no friends, welcomed no guests, and lived as a hermit for five decades would have latched onto and kept a high school annual. That had to mean something. It was time to be logical and work clues like a puzzle, fit pieces into place.

"Let me rephrase that," Lije said. "If you're asking, 'Did what happened to JoJo have anything to do with Kaitlyn's death?' I'd say not likely. But the pages in the yearbook where the bus appears show signs of having been looked at more than the others. And Schleter bought a bus to live in while he built this house. That one out in the brush could be the same one.

"Consider this: we've been through this house with a fine-toothed comb and have nothing to show for it besides the annual. Others have gone through this place, too, but it's obvious nobody has looked inside the bus. Not us, not the ABI, and not the man who killed Kaitlyn. She was murdered right after she bought Swope's Ridge from Mabel. There has to be a connection. If you can think of a better place to search than that bus ..."

McGee grinned, turned, and strolled out the door of the old brick home. When Lije joined him, the criminal defense attorney was staring intently at the tangle of vines and underbrush all but hiding the transportation relic from a very different age.

"It's going to be a challenge just to hack our way in," Lije noted.

"Couldn't we just pay someone to do it?" McGee suggested. "I'm into sports, not yard work."

Lije slapped his friend on the back. "No, we can't and you know why. And don't worry, I've got a chain saw. Besides, you're dressed for the job. It won't be nearly as much work as you think. It'll be good for you. Looks to me like you've put on a few pounds, old friend."

"I should've stayed in Little Rock," McGee moaned. "I'm going to need a lot more Off before this day is finished. And ..." He patted his stomach. "I weigh the same as I did in college."

"Yeah," Lije said. "That statement proves some lawyers lie. Now come on, Kent, let's get the tools and get to work. That old relic might have the answer to Kaitlyn's murder. And knowing you, I'm sure you want to find it almost as much as I do."

"Probably snakes too. I don't like snakes. And you're an attorney, so no more lawyer jokes."

The two men turned toward Lije's SUV to get the tools just as Curtis came out of the house.

"Listen, guys," Curtis said with an air of authority. "Don't you think we need to let the law in on the fact that someone took a shot at me? This is the kind of thing the police like to investigate."

As Lije lifted the chain saw from the floor of the SUV, he

wondered why she would want to report it and have police crawling all over the place, especially her old boss. He didn't trust the ABI director. Barton Hillman had done nothing to help find Kaitlyn's killer. He'd even let an innocent man die on death row—a memory that still haunted Lije. Whose side was Diana on? She had quit the ABI, but now she wanted to drag back in the same people who had screwed them up just a few months ago?

Lije clenched his jaw. "Why? All the locals would do is look around, then bring in the ABI. That'd mean Hillman would be back up here. Do you want him here? Or do you want out? You know what I think."

"But there's a killer out there," she argued.

He knew he couldn't stop her from calling the authorities, but that wasn't the test he had just presented. He had to see where her loyalties lay. Was she with him or was she still part of the old ABI mentality that had crippled the investigation of Farraday Road? That had let Kaitlyn's killer escape. He waited for her response.

Her eyes avoided his. "I don't know," Curtis said. "It could be Smith."

"Could be," Lije shot back. "Maybe he's after you now, but don't forget he killed my wife."

Curtis hooked her thumbs in her jeans pockets and looked down at the ground. With the toe of her boot, she drew a small circle in the red dirt. "Okay, I'll play it your way, but we still need to check the spot where the shots were fired. So, if you don't mind ..." She offered a slight grin. "I'm going up to the logging road and see what I can find."

"Good idea. That's why you're needed. You've got skills we can't begin to touch. We'll be here when you finish."

Pulling her keys from her purse, she walked over to her Ford Focus and got in.

"Be careful," McGee yelled as she started the car.

Lije watched as she drove out of the gate and over the ridge.

He felt uneasy. Was the shooter still out there? Who had taken the shots? Should he have gone with her?

"Saw's going to make a lot of noise," McGee said.

"Nothing out of the ordinary. With the price of heating fuel so high, there are chain saws working up and down Spring River every day of the week. Besides, everyone around here knows I'm cleaning up this place. If anyone asks, I'll just tell them the bus and thicket are eyesores and we're getting rid of another blight that's spoiling this superb hunk of nature."

"Still think it'd be better to hire someone," McGee said. "There are a lot of folks looking for extra work."

"Give it up, Kent."

5

IT TOOK THE MEN A BIT OF WORK TO CUT AWAY enough tree growth and brush to get to the side door of the bus. In the process they scared a snake out of a good hiding place. McGee jumped, Lije laughed, and the reptile hissed, then slithered off toward the river.

Even with the chain saw, nothing about cutting a path to the bus was easy. It was the hardest work either had done in months. Finally, assuming the worst was behind them, they discovered the bus door was secured by one of the largest padlocks they had ever seen. They scanned the discolored windows. All were covered with bars. Even the front windshield wore thick security braces. The door was the only way to gain access to the rusting hulk.

"You really think his old bus is important?" McGee asked.

"It's worth a look," Lije replied. "Think about it. Folks have been searching for something valuable on Swope's Ridge for years. Yet they've found nothing. What's the one place they haven't looked? This bus."

"You got a hacksaw?"

"In the Explorer," came Lije's dog-tired reply.

While Janie had contented herself with keeping the workers supplied with cold water, Jameson had moved the brush the men had cut into a meadow just to the right of the home. She was more than ready for a new assignment. When neither man made a move toward the SUV, she said, "You all stay there. Rest up. I'll get the saw."

No one argued.

Lije had never ridden on a school bus route, but he had taken plenty of rides on the yellow carriages to ball games and field trips. He looked at the vintage vehicle and thought about all those who had once walked through that locked door. If the old bus had a voice, what stories could it tell? Years of daily runs on washed-out back roads, hundreds of students whose route to school began and ended in this vehicle. How many girls and boys had shared their first kiss inside this rig? How many found the loves of their lives? How many studied for tests as they rode in the early hours of the morning? And how many of those passengers were still alive today?

So many secrets. So many stories. Would anything here bring him closer to understanding why Kaitlyn had been murdered? Or was this a waste of time? Another dead end?

McGee sat down on a tree stump while Lije moved around the bus to study it in more detail. With his leather-gloved hand he rubbed at the decades of grime near the windshield. The bus had been painted green, not the usual yellow.

Ash Flat hadn't had a high school in four or five decades. What were the odds? Here was bus number 3, the same number as on the bus pictured in the annual they'd found. He worked his way around an old cedar tree to the front bumper. The unique *V*-shaped grill was identical to the one in the book. This was a 1936 flathead Ford.

He studied the bus. Amazingly, despite the assault by nature, the old people carrier was in solid shape. A series of small dents indicated the bus had been through several hailstorms. The roof looked a bit caved in, perhaps from heavy snow. The hood was rusty but intact. The sides had weathered the seventy years in the woods even better than the hood and top, and while the tires were cracked and flat and had settled a few inches into the ground, if a person wanted to clear a path through the brush and bring in a strong wrecker, old number 3 could be yanked off the ridge and restored. That would be cool. Few of these things ever showed up at car shows. Might be a project worth considering. He envisioned the possibility of bringing this long-dead chunk of iron back to life.

"Got it," Heather announced as she made her way through the freshly cleared path to the bus. "And look who's come home."

Lije worked his way around the bus to the door. Curtis was heading toward them.

"Did you find anything?" Lije asked.

The investigator shrugged. "Only one shell casing, no prints. And the tire impressions were from a tire so common that making a mold would do us no good. What about here?"

"What you see is what we have," McGee replied.

"Cutting through the brush," Lije said, "we've created enough firewood to last two winters. But we'll soon be inside what I hope is the hillbilly version of King Tut's tomb."

Janie, who was rounding the corner of the house, yelled, "Have you stacked any booby traps in my path?"

"No," Jameson yelled back. "Stay straight and you're clear."

"This'd be so much easier if I hadn't left Harlow at home," Janie said. "Too many ticks and fleas out here. Besides, I have Lije as my guide today." The blind woman slowly made her way along the newly cut path to join them.

Jameson whispered to Lije, "Who's Harlow?"

"Her new guide dog."

"Oh, makes sense."

Lije went to work. The padlock was thick and his saw blade was old and dull. Sweat poured down his forehead and soaked his cotton shirt. He was almost ready to give up and ask McGee to take a shift when the ancient security device surrendered.

Twisting it to the left to clear the clasp, Lije removed the lock and yanked on the door. It groaned, but didn't move. A few tugs finally opened the metal entrance just enough so he could slide his body into the opening and shove the door from the inside. The door squealed and moaned, but finally yielded. Energized, Lije climbed up the stairs and into the old cabin. Curtis quickly pushed her way ahead of the others to join him.

All signs of the bus's former duty had been erased. The old seats were gone, replaced by a cook stove that vented out a hole cut in the roof. Nearby stood a small wooden desk and a metal folding chair, along with a metal cabinet and a tiny iron-framed bed minus its mattress. A few empty cans lay beside the stove.

Lije opened the cabinet door. The shelves were bare. The desk beside the bed didn't contain so much as a pencil or scrap of paper.

Curtis wiped dust off the top of the cabinet. "Looks like Schleter simply cleaned out what he wanted after he finished the house."

"Not much of a home," McGee said from the doorway. The others crowded in behind him.

"It was temporary," Lije said. "Just lived here during the months he was building the house. Kind of like camping out in a Depression-era RV."

"Wonder what happened to the old bus seats," Heather said.

Curtis pointed toward the rear. "Over there. He took them apart and stacked them in the back."

Lije walked over for a look. The sections had not so much been stacked as vertically arranged like books on a shelf, set on their sides and slid into place. Grabbing the seat back in the middle, he tried easing it out of its storage spot. It moved about six inches, then hung on something. He tugged several more times, but it wouldn't budge. He couldn't see what was holding it in place.

"Anybody have a flashlight?"

Curtis pulled a small but powerful Maglite from her pocket and pitched it his way. Lije caught it, dropped to his knees, and shined the beam at the floor of the old bus. "How do you like that."

"Got something?" McGee asked.

"Yep, another big padlock."

Curtis leaned over Lije to see. "Looks like a trapdoor."

6

McGEE TOOK THE FIRST SHIFT CUTTING THROUGH THE huge padlock. “Can’t you shoot this thing?” he asked Curtis.

“I could, but having a bullet ricochet in here is a sure way to get someone killed. Besides, seeing the great Kent McGee do physical labor is much more fun. I know some judges who’d pay big money to watch this.”

McGee went back to work, but quickly gave out. Though Lije hated to admit it, he wasn’t used to this much physical exertion either. When he needed a break, Janie took over. The woman, who spent more time exercising each week than the two men combined worked out in a month, labored at a steady but unhurried pace. When she finished, she put the saw down. “It’s ready,” she announced as she pushed herself up off the metal floor.

After pulling the lock off the door, Lije looked back at the group. “Do you think it’s another dead end?”

“Everything else has been,” Curtis noted.

Lije grabbed the clasp and pulled up on the lid. Even using both hands he managed to lift the heavy metal rectangle only a couple of inches. “Need some help here,” he groaned.

The others moved in, positioning their hands on the metal slab.

“On three,” Lije announced as he repositioned his hands to push rather than lift.

"One ... two ... three!"

The old trapdoor began to move, its metallic groans mixing with the labored breaths of the quintet. Finally it swung free, hitting against the back wall of the bus with a deafening clang.

The hole beneath it gaped pitch black. Grabbing the Maglite, McGee gave everyone their first look at what their hard work had uncovered. Hidden beneath the bus was a crude rectangular wooden crate inside what appeared to be a concrete bunker. They could see no markings on the wood.

"What do you make of it?" Heather asked.

As if on cue, Curtis took the light from McGee, got down on her knees, and rapped on the crate. Moving her hand to a corner, she pushed it forward, causing a loud scraping sound as the crate slid about an inch. She leaned in closer and shined the light on a series of nails along the edges of the crate.

As he watched the investigator work, Lije wondered if he was looking at the reason his wife was killed. Would this rough box explain the mystery of Swope's Ridge? Was this the Arkansas version of King Tut's tomb?

"It's not that heavy," Curtis said as she tugged at the crate, shining the light down between the box and the concrete sides of the vault, "so we can forget about gold bars or other treasure the Nazis looted in Europe. It appears no one has pried it open since it was sealed. And we know by the brush and tree growth that this bus has been unmolested for decades, not something the old German used. So that makes me think it's not filled with paper money either. Yet it must've meant something special to him at one time, seeing the effort he made to secure it—building the vault and hiding the hatch underneath the old seats. Might contain what Smith is looking for."

"Let's get it out of here so we can open it up," Lije said. "Diana, move out of the way. Kent, on the far end. I'll get down here. If it isn't that heavy, maybe the two of us can lift it out of the hole and carry it into the house."

Curtis had a suggestion. "Let's leave it where it is and use a pry bar. Have you got one?"

"In the Explorer. We'll need a hammer too."

"Good," Curtis said. "Let's get a couple of lanterns from the house. I want a lot more light in this old bus."

Heather rushed out to get the tools and Curtis left to retrieve the lights. As they waited, Janie leaned against the old desk.

"So is this it?" she asked.

"Hope so," Lije replied. "What do you think?"

"Describe things to me. Tell me what you see."

Janie listened intently as Lije painted a word picture of what lay at his feet. He described the kind of construction, the type of wood, the size of the nails. He even took a tape measure from his pocket and gave the exact dimensions.

"Don't think I'd want to try to sell this at a garage sale," she said.

"What do you mean?" McGee asked.

"Just a hunch."

7

AFTER THE LIGHTS WERE SET UP IN THE BUS, LIJE grabbed the pry bar and went to work on the edges of the crate's top. The nails securing the top for so many decades had been pounded in every two inches along the edge of the lid.

"That old German wanted to make sure it was secure," Curtis said as Lije finished prying along one of the long sides.

With the additional leverage, the job became easier. Each push of the pry bar created a loud groan. In the close confines of the old bus, the noise was deafening.

"This is like fingernails on a chalkboard, only worse," Curtis yelled. "I've got to get away from this racket. I'll be outside."

Twenty minutes later, Lije had just fit the bar under the last side of the crate's top when a much different noise echoed through the chamber.

"Gunshot!" McGee yelled.

Seconds later, Curtis rolled back into the bus. "Someone's shooting at us … from up on the ridge. Somebody's really trying to kill us."

"Maybe just you," Jameson said.

"What do you mean?" Curtis said, never taking her eyes from the open door.

"We've all been out there for hours and you're the only one

anyone's shooting at. Maybe that enemy is your enemy, not ours. Maybe you're the target."

Curtis glanced back at the others. No one jumped to her defense.

It was Lije who finally broke the awkward silence. "Where's your gun?"

"In my car," Curtis said.

"That's not good," Janie said.

"If I stay low," Curtis said, "I can get to the car. Except for the twenty-foot dash to the edge of the house, I'll have cover."

"Sounds good," Lije whispered, "except for that twenty-foot part."

"You got a better idea? That high-powered rifle can easily pierce this bus. My gun is our only option and the mad dash is mine."

Lije was about to offer a second option when Curtis began her dash across the meadow. She got to the back of the house, then disappeared around a far corner. They all waited for the sound of rifle fire. Thirty seconds became a minute and then two minutes. The woods remained quiet. Even the birds had ceased singing. It was as if God had pushed the world's Mute button.

"Do you see anything?" McGee whispered.

Lije shook his head. Finally, just as he was about to make his own dash for the house, Curtis headed back to the bus.

"Got the gun," she said as she climbed up the steps of the bus.

"No more shots," Jameson noted.

"No. I'll keep a lookout up front here," Curtis said. "I think he took a shot and moved on. That seems to be his MO. You all go back to work and give me a holler when you get the lid off."

Curtis was cool under fire, no one could argue that, but was she making any sense? Why would someone take just one shot and move on? And if the shots really could go right through the bus walls, why not let loose with a series of volleys? None of this added up. But then, nothing on this ridge did.

His curiosity outweighing his fear of the sniper, Lije took a final look up at the place where the old logging road cut through the ridge, then walked back to the rear of the bus. Picking up his tools, he again climbed down in the hole. But instead of going back to work, he looked up into Janie's blue eyes and whispered, "Did a car leave the ridge?"

She nodded.

"Squeaky spring?"

She nodded again.

"So we're safe."

"For now."

Trusting Janie's ears more than his own instincts or Curtis's proficiency with a gun, Lije confidently stuck the pry bar back under the edge of the crate's lid. He soon was down to the final end. The lid was so loose he was able to easily pry up those last nails.

"Grab that end," he said to McGee, "and we'll shed some light on this."

Curtis joined the others at the hole in the bus floor. As the top was lifted off and yellowish lantern light finally found its way into the box, it was as if the air had been sucked from inside the bus.

8

CURTIS, MCGEE, AND LIJE FROZE WHERE THEY STOOD, their eyes locked on the horrifying sight. Jameson quickly looked away. Thoughts of the shooter on the ridge evaporated.

Janie listened to the eerie calm. "I'm guessing I was right. It is a coffin, but whose?"

The horror Curtis felt soon morphed into professional curiosity and the cool demeanor of a seasoned investigator. While having a body—especially one hidden for at least six decades—appear in the dim light of a lantern was a new experience, seeing a dead body was not. She dropped to her knees to more closely examine the corpse.

"He's dressed in a wool suit," she announced, the beam of her flashlight playing over the fabric. Her tone was as flat as the wheat fields of the Great Plains. "Looks like it was nicely made too. The label will tell us more. Might have even been a custom job. The hand-painted tie, the cut of the shirt collar, and the shoes make me think he died in the 1940s or maybe even earlier."

"What about the sniper?" Jameson asked, moving away from the body and walking toward the bus door.

Not bothering to look up, Curtis said, "I'm sure he's long gone by now."

"How can you be so sure?" Jameson stared toward the ridge.

The investigator didn't respond. This was her crime scene. "I'm guessing he was in his late thirties or forties. The vault must have been almost airtight. The level of preservation is amazing. He looks like he's been in here less than a year. And we know that can't be true." She continued to examine, but not touch, the body.

Lije asked, "Wonder why he's here. Could this have anything to do with why Swope's Ridge is so valuable?"

"Can't answer that," Curtis said. "Let's pick this box up and take it into the house. I need better light. Then maybe we can get a few more answers. But before we move him, I need to get my camera and take a few pictures just as he is. No one touch the body."

As she left the bus she saw Lije and McGee crouching down behind her to get a closer look. They were obviously curious, but she hoped neither got close enough to touch the dead man. She hurried back with her camera and crime kit. Good. They'd had enough sense to keep their hands to themselves.

"I was hoping for money or a treasure map," McGee said. "We've found way too many bodies on this place. The curse must be real."

"Wonder if we'll ever know who he was," Lije said. "And don't even think that there's a curse. That's just superstition."

After taking a number of photos, Curtis signaled everyone to surround the box. "Remember, don't touch the body. Lije and I'll take the head of the box. McGee, you and Heather take the foot. On three."

It was easy enough to lift the coffin out of the vault. The problem came when getting it out the bus door—the crate was narrow enough to go through the opening, but turning the corner required a maneuver that few professional movers could have managed. Backward, then forward, then backward again, and still they had only a few inches sticking out the door.

"Can't we just take the body and leave the box here?" McGee asked.

"No," Curtis said, "the body could break. We can manage this."

By moving inches at a time, they finally made the turn. Then it was just a matter of lugging the homemade coffin up the gradual slope to the home's front door. Once inside, they set the crate in the living room.

"Shouldn't we call the police?" Heather asked.

They all looked at Curtis, who ignored them as she walked around the coffin to view the body from every angle.

When at the ABI, Curtis had avoided autopsies, but that didn't mean she didn't know what to look for when she had to. It was now time to put that experience to use. The answer to why a finely dressed gentleman had been buried for sixty years beneath an Arkansas school bus intrigued her as much as any case she'd ever been given. And this case was all hers ... for now.

"Let's get as much information as we can. I'll record everything. We'll call it in later," Curtis said in answer to Heather's question. "Heather, I want you to find every light you can and bring them into this room. Remove the shades. We need to really brighten this place up.

"Lije, you and Kent drag the kitchen table in here. It's heavy and I think it's long enough. We can set the body on it for an examination platform. This guy looks to be only five ten, five eleven.

"Janie, try to find some kind of sheet or tablecloth or blanket to put on the table."

"How about a plastic drop cloth?" she suggested.

"That would be even better," Curtis said.

"There's one in the tool box. I'll bring it over."

Curtis pushed all the living room furniture against the walls, clearing a place for the table. She was transforming the German's living room into a crude post-mortem examination facility. Using extension cords and a few ropes, she even managed to arrange the available lamps to brighten up the area. It didn't look like much, but it would work.

"Anybody got a blanket or a sheet?" Curtis asked.

Lije left to retrieve one from his vehicle. When he returned, she handed him a pair of latex gloves. "Put these on. We're going to move the body to the table so I can get a good look. We'll support it with the blanket."

She rolled the blanket lengthwise and placed it next to the body in the casket. "Now roll the body over on its side toward you and I'll shove this edge under. Good. Now let's switch sides. Roll him the other way." She pulled the rolled edge of the blanket to the side until the blanket was spread out under the body.

"Okay, now we're going to lift him up and place him on the table. McGee, Heather, you take one side. Lije and I will take the other. Spread your hands a little so we're supporting the body. Don't want it to sag."

On her signal, they slowly lifted the man from the crate. With the body free of its coffin, they walked to the end of the table and, with two on one side of the table and two on the other, walked sideways, moving the body until it was in position.

"Good thing this is a narrow table," Curtis said. "Now gently lower him onto the table ... Good work."

She reached for her digital camera and, taking shots from every angle, slowly circled the corpse. Then, starting at the head, she began to carefully examine the body.

"What's he got in his left hand?" Lije asked.

She carefully pulled the leather-bound book free from the man's clutched fingers. Moving it to the kitchen counter, she and the others studied the cover and the first few pages. It was an English King James version of the Bible, published in the United States.

"Look," McGee said. "There's a name. Henrick Bleicher. Do you think that's our cadaver's name?"

"I'd say that's a good assumption," Lije said.

Curtis moved back to the body. The wool suit was riddled with small moth holes. No, wait. Two larger holes. She took closeup photos, then leaned in closer and shined her flashlight directly into them. Unbuttoned the suit coat and carefully moved the fabric to each side. The white shirt revealed a large dark-brown stain in the middle and three holes.

"It appears this man died from multiple gunshot wounds," Curtis said. As McGee and Lije leaned in to get a better look, she added, "Looks like he was executed by a firing squad."

"Kent, any idea what states were still using firing squads in the 1930s or 1940s?" Lije asked.

"Not something I ever looked into," McGee said, "but a quick search of the internet should tell us. When we return to civilization."

"Well, if there are any bullets still in the body," Curtis said, "we can probably figure out who ordered his death. The states that did use firing squads would have records that'll give us the make of gun and of the rounds. Should also check the various branches of the military. If we can trace the ammunition to a state or even the military, we can verify whether this is in fact Henrick Bleicher. And we would find out why he was shot."

She glanced at the man's neck. "No dog tags, so probably not military. The lack of a uniform agrees with that. I'm guessing our mystery man was an American."

After again photographing the body with closeups of the bloodstain and the bullet holes in the shirt, she unbuttoned the shirt, examined the wounds, and recorded it all with the camera.

"Let's see if there's some kind of ID in his clothing."

The man's coat pockets revealed a pipe, a small pouch of tobacco, a toothpick, and some lint. In his pants pockets Curtis found a partially used matchbook, six one-dollar bills, a five, a twenty, and seven coins, but no billfold or any type of identification.

"Lije, take a look at the money and see if it reveals anything about our guy," she said.

Lije picked up the pocket items and moved them over to the counter. McGee joined him. Heather had stationed herself by a window and was staring up toward the logging road.

"Heather, he's gone," Curtis said. "His MO is that he watches, shoots, and then moves away. He's missed twice today; he's not going to try it again."

"How do you know that?" a still frightened Heather said. "How can you be so sure?"

"Just like a fisherman knows when the fish have quit biting. I know the guy's finished for the day. It's all about experience. The only person who's been shot at today is me. If I'm not worried, you shouldn't be either. Lije, have you found anything in the money?"

"The bills are all silver certificates, and the newest one is dated 1944. Coins come from the same era, but two do stand out."

"Why?" McGee asked.

"One's from Mexico. The other's from Germany."

"The German coin could've been a war souvenir," Curtis said. "And he could have picked up the Mexican coin on a trip. No mystery there. It really gives us nothing, other than he wasn't robbed. All the clothing is from American manufacturers. There's an Arrow shirt, Brooks Brothers suit. I didn't see a laundry tag on the suit. The shoes came from Amarillo, from a men's store, according to the stamping on the heel. The other clothes could have been bought anywhere."

Curtis turned back to the body on the table. "He seems to have suffered some type of facial injuries not long before his death. My guess is that he was beaten. I believe he was tortured before he died. When the post mortem is done, the coroner will do an MRI and CT scan to find out the complete nature of his injuries. I think someone was trying to get information out of him."

"There was a lot of gang activity during the thirties and forties," McGee said. "Maybe he was a criminal and a gang worked him over."

"Not likely," Curtis replied. "The style of execution is all wrong for that. This was a formal shooting, carefully staged. A gang rubout is most often accomplished with a single shot to the head or a volley of machine-gun fire that fills the body with bullets. This was precise."

Across the room Janie sighed. "There are only a very few moments I could say this, but I think this is one time I'm glad I can't see."

"Don't ask me to describe anything," McGee replied. Then, as if startled, he walked to the table and the body. "Can we get a look at his arms? Maybe cut open the sleeves?"

"Why? What are you looking for?" Lije said.

"Tattoos. Marks on the arms. The Germans were big on marks."

Heather went into the kitchen and returned with a pair of scissors. She handed them to Curtis.

"I guess it won't hurt," Curtis said, carefully cutting the sleeves of the suit coat and the shirt, right side first, then over to the left. On the inside of the left arm, she saw what appeared to be a tattoo.

"Look at this," the investigator said, pointing at the stiff appendage. "Our friend here seems to have what must be his initials tattooed on his arm. The state of decomposition makes it hard to read, but it appears to be a pair of letters, a highly stylized *J* or *S* here on his arm."

"Let me see that," McGee said.

"You have to look close, but it's right here." Curtis pointed to a spot on the man's arm.

McGee inspected the arm, careful not to touch it, then moved to the other side of the table. Leaning forward and using his pen to push the fabric out of the way, he pointed at a mark on the other arm. "There are a series of numbers tattooed on this arm."

"It's like you expected those numbers to be there," Lije said.

"Even if the numbers hadn't been here, the other arm proves all I need to know. This guy probably deserved what he got."

Curtis looked up at McGee. "So this means something special to you?"

"Yeah, wrote a paper on it in grad school. Those aren't letters, they're lightning bolts. They mean this man was a member of the *Schutzstaffel* during World War II."

"*Schutzstaffel*?" Jameson asked.

"The SS," McGee explained. "We often call them 'secret police' or 'storm troopers,' but that was really another group altogether. *Schutzstaffel* was the real name for a military gang of sanctioned thugs. Himmler's henchmen. Almost all of them had the twin lightning bolts tattooed on their left arm. A few added their military serial number on their right. We should have no problem identifying this guy now. He was obviously proud of who he was. We can track him down in the German war archives."

"What does that say about Schleter, the guy who built this home?" Lije asked.

"If we had his body," McGee noted, "we could make certain of one thing—we'd know if these two were fraternity brothers."

Curtis looked down at the man on the table. She knew Lije wanted their discovery to contain the answer to the Swope's Ridge riddle. But she'd seen the body as something much simpler. She thought the German had murdered the man and hidden the body. But the evidence of an execution muddied that theory. Now the tattoos might well put the Swope's Ridge mystery back on the table.

"Diana," Lije said. He was looking down into the crate. "There appears to be a bullet in here."

Grabbing her flashlight, Curtis quickly moved across the room. She studied the object where it lay, took several photographs from different angles, then picked it up with her gloved fingers. "It must have been lodged in the body," she said. "Then when the body dried out, it fell out. Looks to be the proper vintage to go with the money. I'd guess it probably was fired by an FG42."

When no one said anything, she realized they didn't know the significance of the weapon she had just identified. "This bullet is from a Mauser. That's German. This was probably fired by an FG42, a weapon carried by the German infantry in World War II. Looks like our victim was shot by his own people. Might even prove he was a traitor. Working against Germany."

While working for the ABI, Curtis had once investigated the

accidental shooting of an elderly woman. The woman's husband had brought the weapon home from Europe at the end of World War II. The ammo was the same in that case as in this one. She was certain of it. It seemed, for the moment, that luck was on her side.

9

CURTIS REARRANGED THE FABRIC OF THE SLEEVES on the man's arms, then found a tablecloth to cover the body, again taking a careful photographic record.

Lije walked over to her, the open Bible in his hands. He pointed to a few underlined verses: Genesis 7:17–23.

"Kind of a strange choice," he said, "at least to my mind. If this man really was Henrick Bleicher, why would this be the only passage in the whole Bible that resonated with him?"

Curtis shrugged. "What's so special about that?"

"Have no idea."

"What's it say?"

Lije handed her the Bible.

> And the flood was forty days upon the earth; and the waters increased, and bare up the ark, and it was lift up above the earth. And the waters prevailed, and were increased greatly upon the earth; and the ark went upon the face of the waters. And the waters prevailed exceedingly upon the earth; and all the high hills, that were under the whole heaven, were covered. Fifteen cubits upward did the waters prevail; and the mountains were covered. And all flesh died that moved upon the earth, both of fowl, and of cattle, and of beast, and of every creeping thing that creepeth upon the earth, and every man:

All in whose nostrils was the breath of life, of all that was in the dry land, died. And every living substance was destroyed which was upon the face of the ground, both man, and cattle, and the creeping things, and the fowl of the heaven; and they were destroyed from the earth: and Noah only remained alive, and they that were with him in the ark.

"I don't get it. Why the flood story?"

"Maybe," Janie said, "this guy saw World War II as a second destruction of the world."

"As logical as anything, I guess," the investigator said.

"We also found four purple-satin page-marker ribbons, all identical, no writing other than that of the funeral home that gave them away. They look almost new, two inches wide by eight inches long. The Bible looks new. The pages don't show any wear."

"I have a question," McGee said.

"Shoot."

"Was he embalmed?"

"I don't know," Curtis said. "We'll have to wait for the autopsy. My guess is he was killed in Germany during the war, put in the crate, and shipped here. Then, for some reason, Schleter created a tomb for him. The money was probably Schleter's, and he put it in the pocket as some kind of superstition. It's not uncommon for people to place special tokens with the deceased. A lot of cultures do."

"I wouldn't be surprised if he wasn't embalmed," McGee said. "During wars, men were usually buried with no body preparation. If this man was considered an enemy of the state, he wouldn't have been given any kind of special treatment after death."

"I can buy that," Lije said, "but why didn't they just toss him into a mass grave or burn him? This man was evidently shipped to the United States. That doesn't make sense."

"That is strange," Curtis said. "We've found nothing that would've called for him to be preserved and hidden as he was, much less crated up for a sea voyage."

"Then maybe he was executed here," Lije said.

His observation amused Curtis. "This thing's bizarre, but now you're really talking fairy tales. Bleicher, or whatever his real name is, was killed by a weapon carried by the Germans during World War II. It was an execution. If the shots were fired here, those carrying out the sentence would've used an American-made weapon."

Lije walked over to the counter where they had laid out the contents of the man's pockets. He picked up the matchbook she'd found and tossed it her way. Catching it, she turned it over and noted the English words: BUY WAR BONDS TODAY!

"Open it," Lije suggested.

Flipping the cover, she saw a hand-scrawled word and a number written in pencil: Jupiter 4-7623.

"That's an old American method of writing phone numbers," Lije explained. "Jupiter was the easy way to remember the first part of the number. The J-U in Jupiter would have been translated into 5 and 8. This man wrote it on a matchbook. That number, 584-7623, would have caused a phone to ring somewhere in the U.S., not in Germany. I think this SS officer made his way to America, called this number, then was executed by other Germans who were already here. Maybe Schleter was in on it. Maybe Henrick Bleicher was gunned down right here on this ridge. What I want to know is who would've answered when he dialed that number?"

Curtis was stunned. That theory could explain why the corpse was holding an English-language Bible and had United States currency, but it didn't answer *why* the man was here. And it didn't explain how he met his end. After World War II, German immigrants didn't execute other German immigrants. In all her studies of crime, she had never read of that happening.

"We need to know a whole lot more about this man," she said. "And the place to start is Germany. Schleter and Bleicher both were there before coming here. If we can find what tied them together, we just might begin to understand why they both ended up on Swope's Ridge."

"I'll make our reservations," Lije said. "Been several years since I've been to Europe."

Then the words in the letter he'd received from Jonathon Jennings hit him. Jenning's pen pal, Omar Jones, needed help. The clock was ticking. Lije had a favor to fulfill for an innocent man who didn't get a reprieve. So no matter how much he wanted to, he couldn't go to Europe. He not only had to stay but needed Janie, Heather, and McGee too. Looking over at Curtis, he said, "I've something I really have to do. Can you handle going to Germany alone?"

"What?"

"A death row case in Texas."

Curtis seemed confused. "You're going to Huntsville?"

Lije shrugged. "I have to save an innocent man. Can't have another Jennings haunting me."

Curtis nodded. "Okay. No problem. I know German and I know the country. I have some contacts who can help me gain access to information. I'll catch the first available flight to Berlin. You do what you have to do."

Lije nodded. He would try. But was he up to the task?

10

BARTON HILLMAN PULLED UP TO THE EXXON-MOBIL station just inside Batesville and stepped out of the Crown Victoria issued by the state of Arkansas. Sporting a police package, the car used super-unleaded fuel. He yanked the nozzle out, shoved it into the gas-tank neck, and squeezed the pump's trigger. He ignored what it cost to fill the twenty-two-gallon tank. This was on the state's bill, not his, even though the outing was not state business.

He was a hero. A shootout with drug dealers in West Memphis a month ago had confirmed that. The series of speeches he was making at various small-town chamber dinners and civic clubs was great public relations for the state and would not go unnoticed by the legislature, which would probably be generous with funding in the next session. Essentially, Hillman was on top, his foot on the throat of anyone who would dare challenge him.

Still, he left nothing to chance. He controlled every action and person who came into his sphere of influence.

After finishing at the gas pump, he stretched, then got back into the car, pulled onto Highway 167, and headed north. He drove across the White River bridge and up the winding four-lane blacktop to the summit of a nameless but formidable Ozark hill. After stopping at a traffic light, he rolled through the small community of Southside. Ten minutes later he eased into a deserted rest stop, retrieved his mobile phone, and scanned the directory. Finding the number he needed, he hit Send and waited for a reply.

"This is Barton Hillman, head of the Arkansas Bureau of Investigation. I need to speak with James Ray, please."

During the early 1980s, James Ray Burgess and Hillman had been fraternity brothers at the University of Texas. Each was smart, straightforward, and ambitious. They had come from lower-middle-class blue-collar families. They shared a love for athletics. After graduation, Hillman had made his way back to his grandparents' home state, Arkansas, and landed at the ABI. Burgess had stayed close to home and gotten an administrative position in the Texas penal system. For the last few years he'd been the warden of a special unit called death row, located just outside of Livingston. The actual death chamber remained in Huntsville. Due to the state's very efficient assembly line of death, the warden had made more trips to the death chamber and had witnessed more executions than anyone else in the country.

"Barton," a voice broke onto the line, "it's been a long time."

"Too long, my friend."

The two caught up on each other's lives, engaging in the usual banter. But when Burgess asked if Barton had found a new love, Hillman went silent. A clear image of a beautiful young woman took the place of the scene outside his windshield. For a moment, time moved backward, and the warmth in his heart mixed with a chill on his spine. How long had it been? In one sense the time had flown by, but in another, each day was still an exercise in pain and anguish.

As a matter of self-preservation he shook loose the memory like a dog ridding itself of an unwanted flea. He had to avoid looking back. "No, still haven't found anyone. Too busy, I guess."

"Beth was quite a girl," Burgess said. "Such a waste. Did they ever catch the hit-and-run driver?"

"Nope," Hillman answered, attempting to force his voice to remain steady and strong. "And after twenty years, I doubt they ever will. It's just another cold case." He took a deep breath before adding, "We had ten wonderful years. That's more than a lot of folks have."

Not all the memories were cold. Not all were bitter. At least one he had never told anyone brought him great satisfaction. A decade later he still kept that one concealed. "You know, it might sound strange, but in my gut I'm sure that driver has paid for what he did. That's more than I can say about a lot of unsolved crimes."

An awkward silence was broken only when the warden changed the subject. "That shootout in Memphis was big news even in the Dallas and Austin papers. Your quote to the press was one that'll no doubt live forever. Even Leno used it."

"Leno, huh? So I made *The Tonight Show*. I didn't know. I missed it. But doing *Larry King* was a blast. He said my quote much better than I did."

Burgess chuckled. "I missed King's try at imitating you, but let me give it my best: 'They shot first and they shouldn't have missed.'"

The press had loved that line. They had run with it from the moment it had pushed from his lips. It had legs too. At this rate it would probably be chiseled on his tombstone.

"So, Barton," the warden continued, "I can't believe they got the drop on you. That's a first."

Hillman laughed. "All a matter of luck, good and bad. And their luck was bad." In truth, he had been in no real danger. He'd known the two dealers were there, and he'd gotten the drop on them. But the press would never know that. Dead men don't talk.

Burgess sighed. "You were always a lot smoother than I was."

Hillman noted a hint of envy in the response. "Not at all," the ABI director said. "I just always looked for the angle. You saw everything in black and white."

"Guess that's true. My job calls for me to see things that way. Barton, we may be friends, but I know you well enough to know you didn't call me just to gab. What can I do for you?"

"Yeah. You know me too well." The small talk was behind them. "James Ray, what can you tell me about Omar Saddam Jones?"

"Ah, the man the press tagged as the other 9/11 terrorist."

"That's the one."

"Nothing special. He goes to the chamber in little over a month. His lawyer's state-appointed. I doubt there'll be any delays. Besides, the FBI nailed him. Strong evidence. He's a model prisoner, always polite, doesn't talk to anyone outside the unit, avoids the other prisoners, and has no family. Seems to be a gentle soul. I can't picture him doing what he did, but sometimes folks just snap."

"True," Hillman said. "I've seen kind folks lose their minds and wake up to find they murdered someone. At least the evidence in the Jones case is solid. You won't be sending an innocent man to the gallows." Then he added what he knew was a lie. "I can honestly say that since I've been at the ABI, Arkansas has not executed anyone who didn't do the deed."

Burgess fired back with, "Why do you want to know about Jones?"

"Oh, I have no interest in the case, but a lawyer from Salem will probably be jumping on board to try to help the guy. His name is Elijah Evans. One of my former agents is working with him. A friend asked Evans to speak to Jones."

"So what do you want me to do?" Burgess asked.

"Give him whatever he wants. Bend the rules a little. Provide him with as much access to Jones as he asks for and any records he needs to see."

"That doesn't sound like the law-and-order man I know."

"You're right. But this is a sad case. Evans lost his wife earlier this year. Now he feels a need to help people. After what happened to my Beth, I identify with him. I think working with Jones might help him work through his grief."

"That's awfully kind of you, Barton."

"Well, you know what happened to me. Oh, and there's one other thing."

"Sure."

"Let me know when Evans contacts you. And whenever he comes down to the prison. Call me on my cell, not my office line. I want to keep this unofficial. And, whatever you do, don't mention my name. I don't want Evans to know I interceded. You take the credit for being the good guy."

"No problem," came the quick reply. "I understand. Hey, I've got a meeting so I need to wrap this up."

"Thanks for your help. Remember, call me when you hear from Evans."

As Hillman slipped his phone back into his pocket, he smiled.

11

DEATH ROW.

Lije had made a trip to death row before and had been unable to help an innocent man. Jonathon Jennings. The memory haunted him. So if he was going to make the trip to Texas to visit another death row, Lije wanted his most trusted friends with him. He needed their company as well as their insight to bolster his confidence.

On the day set for the initial meeting with Omar Saddam Jones, Lije shut down his office in Salem and had his partner and his legal assistant accompany him on the trip to Texas, adding McGee in Little Rock.

Once on the ground in Houston, they rented a car and headed into the Piney Woods of the southeastern part of the Lone Star state. Except for the intense humidity, it wasn't a bad day to travel. The temperature was in the lower nineties. But overcast skies provided relief from what would've been an unrelenting summer sun.

With Lije at the wheel, they were halfway to their destination when a confused Heather Jameson pointed out what to her seemed to be a problem. "We're going the wrong way."

"What do you mean?" Lije asked. "Avis logged the information when we rented the car. I gave them the address. I'm sure we're fine."

"But I distinctly remember Curtis mentioning Huntsville," Jameson explained.

"She did," McGee said, "but I saw no reason to correct her. Huntsville is where death row used to be. After a number of escapes from what is the nation's largest death row population, the prisoners were moved to a prison a few miles outside the small town of Livingston. They still perform the executions in Huntsville, but the state houses the men at the more secure Polunsky Unit."

"So Curtis doesn't know everything," Jameson said with a grin. "What's it like?"

"Pretty much like every other prison that houses those doomed to die," McGee said. "Depressing, confined, and not a place to visit if you have claustrophobia. I've been to a bunch of these units, and I always leave feeling as if I need a long, hot shower. The only way I can describe the experience is numbing. Numbs your mind, your body, your spirit. As I drive off, I never look back."

The image painted by McGee cast a pall that stifled conversation for the remainder of the trip. A gloomy environment permeated the place as they were processed and then, as a group, were escorted to the administrative wing. A gray-haired woman, whose nametag designated her as the warden's administrative assistant, ushered them into a large private office.

A balding man smiled as he stood up behind his modern walnut-veneer desk. "I'm James Ray Burgess. Please, come in. Would any of you like something to drink?"

They all shook their heads. "No, we're fine," Lije said.

Smiling, the warden extended his hand. "You must be Mr. Evans."

"That's right," Lije said as he shook hands with the shorter man. He wondered how a man could work in this place, be the warden to these men facing death. Did his mind constantly flash back to those he'd seen die? To the faces of those about to die?

"Let me introduce my partner Heather Jameson, my assistant, Janie Davies, and—"

"No need to tell me who this is," Burgess said. "Mr. McGee and I met here on another case—Alvin Vaughan. You were called in to help Jeff Brayton back when we were still at Huntsville. You and Jeff managed to get Vaughan's sentence reversed using DNA. Glad you came along when you did. Or we would have executed an innocent man."

McGee smiled.

"Mr. Evans, I hope the information we gathered and sent your way on Omar Jones was adequate."

"Very thorough," Lije replied. "Much more than I expected either you or the organizations to give us. I learned things about this case it would've taken us months to dig up on our own. And we don't have months."

"I'm sure you can see this is not a circumstantial-evidence case, like many others I see. The FBI and the Texas Rangers covered all the bases. They proved their case. My job is to provide these prisoners a bit of peace before the end. This may surprise you, but I like Mr. Jones. He is a model inmate. I'd like his exit to be as painless as possible. That's what I wish for all these men."

Lije nodded. Burgess was right on one count: the case file presented evidence that not even McGee, who knew more tricks than any other defense attorney in the nation, could contest. After reading everything on the case, it seemed clear that Jones was the one who had committed the murders. Yes, the man had been given poor legal representation, but even if he had hired the best, he was doomed from the start. Lije considered this a waste of time. And cruel. Giving Jones any hope of getting off was like tearing the wings off flies. Maybe it was better just to leave him alone.

Yet, because of a debt he felt he owed, for the innocent death he hadn't been able to stop, he couldn't walk away.

Jennings believed Jones had been framed. If this was a frame, it was the best one Lije had ever seen in all his years as a lawyer — the corners were square, the glue was strong, and the picture the frame held was detailed and clear.

After glancing at his watch, Lije said, "Mr. Burgess, could we see the prisoner?"

"Of course. As we've been visiting, I've had him taken to a large holding room. You'll have a table, chairs for each of you, glasses and a pitcher of ice water, and as much time as you need. He'll be chained, that's the law, but I don't view Jones as a threat of any kind, so there will be no guards in the room. And I guarantee there are no bugs. You can talk freely."

"We appreciate your efforts," Lije said as he got up. Slipping his arm around Janie's, he and the others followed Burgess out of the room, into a hallway, through two security doors, and down another hall. After going through a door that required both a code and a fingerprint scan, they were escorted into a room where a small, thin, dark-headed man sat in a chair behind an old oak table. He looked more like a beaten dog than a human being.

"Mr. Jones," the warden announced, "these are the people I told you were coming to see you. They can have as much time with you as they need." Burgess looked back to the legal quartet. "If you want anything, just pick up the phone on the table. My office extension is 942. Can I get you anything else?"

"No," Lije said, "we have what we need. Thank you for your cooperation."

"The guard outside the door will lead you back to the office. When you're finished, just knock."

The overhead fluorescent lighting was bright, but the dark furniture, windowless walls, and tile floor gave the room a cold, hard feel. The air conditioning made it feel like winter, not the middle of a hot Texas summer.

The door closed and Lije first led Janie to a chair. Jameson pulled out a chair at the far end of the table and sat down. She retrieved a legal pad from her briefcase and a pen from her purse. McGee grabbed a place beside Jones. Finally Lije slid a chair out directly across from the prisoner in order to carefully observe the man's expression as he answered their questions.

"Mr. Jones, my name is Lije Evans. I'm an attorney from Salem, Arkansas."

Lije stuck out his hand. Jones stared at him for a moment, then nodded and hesitantly brought his manacled hands out of his lap, extending a hand in an almost apologetic way to gently grasp Lije's. It was a strange shake, unsure and soft. The jingling of the metal restraints reminded the small-town lawyer of the ghost from the movie *The Christmas Carol.* Trying to quell the eerie feelings created by that association, Lije introduced the team.

"To your right is Kent McGee. McGee is one of the best defense attorneys in the nation."

This time Jones' hand extended even before McGee could lift his arm off the table. As the two shook hands, a sudden air of hope entered the room, and Lije thought he saw a tiny smile push its way onto the man's tightly drawn face. Maybe there was a hole in the wall of evidence. Maybe Jennings' belief in this man's innocence would be proven right.

"On the far end of the table," Lije continued, "is my law partner, Heather Jameson. She looks young, but she's sharp." He waited for Heather's eyes to connect with the prisoner's before he continued.

"Finally, the last but certainly not the least member of the group is Janie Davies. She's my legal assistant, has a lot of experience in working with lawyers on criminal cases, and has even been a part of a team that won acquittals for two people who had been accused of murder."

"Nice to meet you, Mr. Jones," Janie said, cocking her right ear in the man's direction.

Dressed in his orange jumpsuit, the inmate carefully observed Janie, then spent the same amount of time studying the other three. He was obviously confused.

"Why are you here?" His first words were delivered in a whispered tone.

Jones was direct. He wasted no words. He wanted answers.

"I can appreciate your question," Lije replied. "In fact, we all can. To put it simply, we're here as a legal team examining your case. We've studied the files, the transcripts from your trial, and all the records, from the moment the Rangers and FBI arrested you until the last appeal filed by your court-appointed attorney—the man you fired last week. We've tried to review every bit of the evidence. We came to Texas to speak to you and get your thoughts and see if perhaps you would like us to represent you in the appeal process."

"If you've done all that," Jones began, "you have to believe what everyone else does: that I'm guilty."

Lije glanced over to McGee. The experienced defense attorney understood what his friend wanted. It was his turn to pick up the questioning.

"Mr. Jones, Lije and I wouldn't be honest if we told you that the case the state laid out wasn't strong. But we wouldn't have gotten on a plane to Texas and driven up to see you here in prison if we were going to judge you strictly on the evidence. We came to hear your story. We came to see if you can present your case in a way that will enable us to believe in your innocence."

"I didn't do it." Jones was blunt.

"So you've said," McGee replied. "Then I need for you to begin our discussion by answering two questions. The first concerns the man who claims he spoke to you in front of the Klassers' home the night of the murders."

"Marty."

"Yes. Martin de la Cruz."

"I've thought about that a lot. Marty is not a liar. He was a good friend—as good a friend as I had in this world. I don't know why he said what he did. But I have a theory. The Klassers' bodies were discovered on the evening of September 11, the same day of the terrorist strike on the World Trade Center and the Pentagon. The men who hijacked those planes were Arabs. Look at me. I look like them. On that day, everyone who looks like they're from the Middle East suddenly became the enemy. Maybe what happened when the towers fell ended my friendship with Marty. Maybe I scared him."

"Are you saying he lied?" McGee asked.

"I wasn't there that night," Jones said. "He must have lied. In the years since that day it's about all I've thought about. Why did he say that? The other evidence could've been planted, but I still can't believe Marty would turn on me. He knew me better than that. Maybe Marty was bought off. Judas turned against Jesus for a pretty cheap price. I know Marty was having a lot of financial problems. He was in debt."

McGee had warned the others that death row was filled with the greatest con artists. Jones seemed sincere, but of course he'd had years to perfect his act. Behind those dark eyes and seemingly frustrated demeanor might be an actor capable of playing an audience. Maybe they were being played, but it sure didn't seem like it.

"Can I call you Omar?" Lije asked.

"Yes, sir."

"You knew Mr. de la Cruz very well, didn't you?"

"Yes, we were about the same age. We hung out together."

"Tell me about him."

"As I said, Marty was in over his head with credit card companies. He just had to have stuff. He bought big TVs and expensive cars and took vacations all over the place. He liked to gamble. Was so good at it casinos in Vegas and Shreveport banned him. In 1999, after he couldn't play poker at the tables, his luck gave out. He wasn't nearly as good at picking the horses. He worked at Softtech, mid-management level. Started to have problems paying for his lifestyle. He told me collection agencies were hounding him. He was close to losing his home. He sold his pride and joy, a 1957 Chevy convertible, and lost big on that deal. I think he was about to lose his Hummer. He never hit me up for a loan, but I offered a few times. He was a nice guy. I can't believe he would turn on me, but financial pressure can change people. It was a lesson my dad preached all the time."

Lije remembered something he had read in the prisoner's file. His parents had died in a car wreck during Jones' first year of college. He wondered how the man dealt with the loss. Could it have caused a mental breakdown? Perhaps he had killed the Klassers but didn't realize it. But the battery of tests Jones had been put through back in 2002 before the trial showed no hint of mental illness. Nothing there could save him.

McGee took over. "Omar, your DNA, hair samples, and fingerprints were found in the Klassers' home. Your blood was found on the box cutter used to slit the family's throats. You had a cut on your left index finger that matched the box cutter's blade perfectly. And a box cutter just like the one used in the crime and found at the Klasser home was missing from your tool kit. That's pretty solid evidence. I need you to explain how this could've happened if you were not in the house that night."

They waited for an answer. Above, the ceiling fan methodically sliced the air in the stark cubical. Jones was now as stiff and unmoving as a prison wall. It was as if the life had been sucked from his being. How could he answer this and prove his innocence?

Finally he whispered, "I don't know. I just don't know."

"You'd been in the house many times," McGee noted.

"Three or four times a week at least."

"That means your DNA and fingerprints would've been in the house. Had you ever injured yourself in their home? Been cut in any way while there?"

Jones paused, then shook his head. "No, not that I can remember."

"When was the last time you used your box cutter?"

"I told the police several times. It's probably in your report."

McGee leaned toward the convict. "I want you to tell me. I need to hear it from your lips. So do the other three people at this table."

"Sorry. I cut my finger September ninth, the day before the killings, when I was opening a box that contained my new laptop."

"What happened to the box?"

"Threw it away. It would've been picked up the next morning, on September tenth."

"How about the computer?"

"I don't know what happened to it. I set it up, but didn't take it on my hiking trip. They probably picked it up after they arrested me."

"Who picked it up?"

"The FBI."

McGee leaned back in his chair. As he did, Lije brought his fingers together in front of his chin. Looking over his hands, he asked, "And you didn't have any idea that the Klassers were killed until you were arrested in October?"

"No, I was away from home a month, hiking the Appalachian Trail. They said I was running away from what I had done."

"You knew one of the 9/11 terrorists," McGee said, sounding more like a prosecutor than a friend.

"I found that out a lot later. I met him once, but when the host told him I was a Christian, he just shook his head and walked away. We didn't speak beyond exchanging something like 'Nice to meet you.' That was years before the attacks. I didn't recognize his picture or name until the FBI reminded me of the meeting. Don't know how they would even have known that. So no, we weren't friends, though that's the way it's been portrayed in the media."

"Doesn't look good," McGee noted.

"Mr. McGee," Jones said, "where are your people from? What country did they live in before they came to the United States?"

"Ireland. My grandfather on my mother's side was born in Dublin."

"If a member of the IRA blew up a building in New York, would everyone stare at you as if you were guilty? Would your neighbors suddenly think you're a terrorist?"

Everyone at the table understood what Jones was trying to say.

It was a sobering thought. What if this was about race? Ethnicity? What if this was about where you were born and what you looked like, not what you believed?

McGee finally said, "You're right. Your skin color and ethnic look set you apart. I wouldn't have been subject to that. Still, no matter what I looked like, if the case against me was as airtight as what they have against you, I'd have been convicted. I know that."

"I didn't do it."

12

THE WORDS WERE SO SIMPLE, SO HAUNTING. "I DIDN'T do it."

Lije couldn't read the minds of the other three, or of Jones, but he was now experiencing a combination of doubt and fear. Could Jones be telling the truth? The evidence clearly proved him guilty. But what if he wasn't? What possible motive could there be to create an elaborate frame like this? Why pick on Omar Jones? Why set him up? And who set him up? The government? Lije didn't think Jones had the demeanor or personality to become the face of homeland terrorism. So maybe someone else was behind the frame. But who? De la Cruz? Doubtful. Who else would have something to gain?

"You're a Christian?" Janie asked, breaking the long silence.

"Yes. My parents were very active in the church. I grew up a Methodist. I was the president of the youth group as a teen. I went on mission trips to Mexico, sang solos, helped with vacation Bible school. I did it all. Church was my second home. After my folks died, I didn't go regularly, but I didn't secretly convert to radical Islam as the prosecution and newspapers claimed. I'm a Christian. My address may have changed, but not my faith."

"Anything else you need, Kent?" Lije asked.

McGee shook his head. "No."

"So that's it?" Jones demanded, his restraints clanging as his arms waved. "You just walk out and I go back and wait for the needle?"

"We'll walk out the same way we walked in," Lije replied, "but we're going to try to find out how you were framed and why."

"You ... you believe me?"

"Yes. A man on death row in Arkansas assured me you were innocent. You were in his final thoughts. Just before he was executed, he wrote a letter asking me to help you."

"Really?" Jones was stunned. He couldn't fathom anyone having any compassion for the other 9/11 terrorist.

"Yes, he believed in you," Lije explained. "From the letters you two exchanged, he evidently developed a lot of faith in you. He was convinced you are what he would have called a 'right guy.'"

The prisoner shook his head. "Did you read the letters?"

"No," Lije admitted. "I don't even know what happened to them. Do you still have the letters he wrote to you?"

Jones seemed confused. "What was the man's name?"

"Jonathon Jennings."

The prisoner shook his head. "Never heard of him. I've not written a single personal letter since I've been on death row."

"What did you say?" Lije stood up, shocked.

"Why would I lie about that? I have everything to gain by telling you I knew Jennings. I didn't. I don't even communicate with the men on death row here, much less in other states. The only mail I get is hate mail. I'm the poster boy for politicians who need to scare folks. Nobody wants to hear from me. Your friend never wrote to me and I never wrote to him. That's the truth."

Lije slumped back into his seat. What had just happened? Why had Jennings written this kind of lie?

"You still going to try to help me?" Jones asked.

Lije looked across the table. "I'll let you know."

13

KENT MCGEE HAD LEARNED A LONG TIME AGO NEVER to be surprised by anything that was said on death row. Yet even he was taken aback by what he had heard. Someone was lying, and if Jones wasn't lying, then who was?

What a break that information had given them. What an insight he now had into the case. He was ready for the hunt, absorbed in the chase, and fully devoted to the cause of getting what he was now sure was an innocent man off death row. Still, he wasn't surprised when no one shared his enthusiasm. The others acted as though they had just witnessed a tragic death—their own. When the time was right, he would clear that up, but McGee wanted to be well away from the warden and the prison before he dropped his bombshell. So, like the others, he put on a sad face as he said his goodbyes to Warden Burgess and was processed out of the unit. He kept frowning even after leaving the prison.

As the four rode in silence, it was all McGee could do to keep from using his phone. He had to make a call. Then he would change a few attitudes. Yet he continued to act downhearted until they neared a Dairy Queen. "Let's grab something here," he said. "The food's probably not bad and it's not crowded."

No one nixed the motion, so Lije pulled over. As he, Jameson, and Janie moved toward the entrance, McGee hung back. "You go ahead and order me one of those steak baskets. I've got a call to make."

Pulling an iPhone from his coat pocket, the attorney hit a familiar number. As he waited for his call to connect, he noted two robins sitting on a branch of a live oak tree. They were singing their hearts out. He saluted them and wished he had the talent to join them in song. Problem was he couldn't carry a tune.

"Hello?" A voice popped onto his phone, taking his attention away from the treetop tunesmiths.

"Ivy, it's Kent." McGee grinned as he considered the job he was about to give his favorite detective.

"You've got something."

Not bothering with small talk, McGee pushed forward. "Oh, yeah. I need you to find the address and phone number of a Martin de la Cruz. He worked for a Dallas-based company, name of Softtech, in 2001 and lived in Waxahachie. I want you to find him. Today."

If the seasoned detective was annoyed by the tight deadline, he didn't sound like it. "Want me to talk to him? What am I digging for?"

"No, that'll be my job. Just find him for me."

"Anything else?"

"Yeah, do you remember the story of the other terrorist from 9/11?"

"Sure, Omar Saddam Jones. The guy who murdered the Jewish family."

"I need to find out more about the man Jones supposedly killed. His last name was Klasser, and he worked for the FAA in Arlington, Texas."

"Why? It's old news."

"I need to know the whys behind his murder."

"It was an Arab killing a Jew, a story as old as the Bible," the detective said. "The conflict goes back to Ishmael and Isaac in Genesis. The huge split is based on who followed one brother and who followed the other. We're still fighting wars over that family feud."

"Ivy, on the surface that's the way this case reads—an ancient biblical feud gone wrong. But there may be something more to it. The story that convicted Jones is too neat, too convenient, and too easy to put together. I'm smelling a setup. So get me everything you can get on Klasser, right down to his family, his work records, and any contacts he had that might have given someone a reason to kill him. I want to know him as well as I know you. But I need de la Cruz' information first."

"Okay, boss. How long do I have on the Klasser thing? That's not just old, it's very sensitive. When I start poking around, it'll no doubt make some folks pretty hot."

"Can you handle the heat?"

"Don't even ask."

"Okay, call me as soon as you get the information on de la Cruz. And don't be afraid to run up a tab getting the dope on Klasser. This thing might be our biggest case yet."

"Or it might end our careers."

14

WARDEN JAMES RAY BURGESS SOUNDED LIKE A SCOLDING mother when his call was finally answered. "Barton, why didn't you answer the first time I called?"

"I was being interviewed by Fox News. Had the phone turned off. I take it Lije Evans came for a visit."

"Yes, he was here. I wasn't there during the interview, don't know the results, but he left about four hours ago."

A grin crossed the director's face. It certainly looked like the fish had taken the bait. "So, James Ray, did Evans leave interested?"

"I couldn't tell. All four were closemouthed when they left. No one said anything about needing more information or scheduling another meeting."

Four? Hillman had figured this would be a solo trip. His contacts had told him Curtis was on her way to Germany for a mysterious meeting, so who else had Evans taken with him? "Sounds like a gospel group. Who came along for the ride?"

"It's on the log, let me check. Mmm. Janie Davies."

"The blind woman. She helps in his office, so that makes sense. Was Heather Jameson there?"

"Yes, her name's here. She looks way too young to be an attorney. Good-looking gals, both of them."

"Well, James Ray, Jameson looks young because you and I are

getting old." Hillman was stumped. Who else would go along on the trip? Evans didn't work with anyone other than those two. Where would he pick up a fourth? "Who was the fourth?"

"Figured you'd know," Burgess said. "After all, you and I have both run into him in the past. If he was any more familiar to you, he'd come to your family reunions."

"I don't have time for riddles," Hillman shot back. "Just who the devil is the guy?"

"Fine, don't get your drawers wadded up. It was Kent McGee."

"McGee?"

"The one and only. I'm betting the suit he wore cost two grand. The women in the office are still talking about him. By now I figure every prisoner in this place knows he was here. Jones just became king of death row."

Barton straightened up in his chair. McGee? Why McGee? Lije and McGee were college roommates, but they hadn't traveled in the same circles in years. Except after Evans' wife died. That must've brought them back together. The rules of the game had just changed. The bait he'd used to hook Evans was now no good. McGee was smart enough to catch on to a ruse. He'd probably seen through the setup in ten minutes.

"Hang on a second," Hillman said. He rolled over to his ABI computer. Propping the phone between his shoulder and neck, he struck a few keys and watched as the American Airlines flight schedule rolled up. A bit more typing and a password got him into the reservations list for the late flight on American from Houston. Three names he was looking for popped up: Jameson, Davies, and Evans. It showed McGee had a booking, but hadn't checked in. For some reason he had remained in Texas.

"Barton, you there?"

"Yeah, James Ray, I'm here. You see a lot of these. Surely you've got a guess if Evans took the case."

"He didn't say," the warden replied. "But if the look on his face was any indication, he was pretty discouraged. I doubt I'll see him or the others again."

"Okay. Let me know if you hear from any of them."

"Why—"

Barton hung up and tossed his phone on the desk in disgust. If he had figured McGee for part of the team, he would've at least picked a death-row inmate who had a remote chance of being innocent, not one who was guilty when he wrote the letter. McGee had messed things up. He would've talked Evans out of taking the case.

Yet, if he had, why stay in Texas? Alone? It didn't make any sense.

Hillman was still kicking himself for his carelessness when he heard a soft knock on his office door.

"Yes, come in," he barked.

The door opened and his secretary, still standing in the doorway, said, "I'm leaving, boss. You need anything?"

"No, Betty, I'm fine."

"You look a bit disappointed. Something go wrong on the Fox interview?"

Hillman shook his head. "No, that was perfect. Just waiting for a couple calls. Impatient. See you tomorrow."

"Okay. There's no one at the switchboard, so I'll make sure the calls ring through to your office. Can you switch it back to the night operator when you leave?"

"No problem. No, wait, just switch it now. The calls are coming in on my cell."

"Okay. Good night."

As the door closed, Hillman walked over to the window and looked at the capitol building. One call could clear this thing up. He didn't like being in the dark. Not one bit.

He walked back to his desk, unlocked a private file cabinet, and pulled out a personal directory. On the fourth page, he found the phone number for the one source he trusted for information. He dialed the number. A few seconds later his hopes rose as he heard a familiar name.

15

INTERSTATE 35 HAD BEEN UNDERGOING EXTENSIVE repair for more than a decade. It seemed as if construction would never be completed. The highway was crowded and bumpy, with provisional lanes that moved a few feet to the left or right, seemingly put together just so they could take drivers through a series of corridors surrounded by temporary concrete walls three to four feet high. Accidents happened. Daily. In the ninety miles between Austin and Waco, Kent McGee had been forced to slow twice and stop once just to get by three different wrecks.

A trip that should have taken an hour and a half ended up costing him almost three—precious time robbed from a man on death row. For the next thirty days, McGee would have to move quickly, cover lots of ground, and dig through mounds of condemning evidence in the hope of giving Omar Jones the chance for a little more time to breathe.

Thanks to the extensive highway construction, the Waco city limits sneaked up on him. Waco, like a lot of communities dissected by the interstate highway system, could do that. Except for the Texas Ranger Museum and the back side of Baylor University, there wasn't much of Waco to see along the interstate except typical road-related businesses.

It hadn't always been this way. More than five decades earlier, downtown had been decimated by a massive tornado. More than a hundred people died that day, and in some ways so did the vitality of the community along the famed Brazos River. Shops rebuilt, but some never reopened. Most moved to the suburbs. The once thriving downtown, crowned by Alico Tower, never fully recovered.

Exiting the interstate, McGee guided his Impala down a maze of streets—a left and then a right and another left—until he found himself at the address Ivy Beals had given him that morning.

He pulled into the driveway at the side of the house and stepped out into the midday Texas sun. It was just over eighty-five but felt at least ten degrees warmer. Shedding his suit jacket, he studied the red-brick home. Like hundreds of others, the home was nondescript, its most outstanding feature a ten-foot-wide fully covered front porch that ran the length of the front of the house. A fashionable middle-class home when designed many decades before, it was now just another piece of rental property.

According to the information dug up by the investigator, Martin de la Cruz had moved to Waco from Red Oak, Texas, three months before. After he identified Omar Jones as the man he saw coming out of the Klassers' home the night of the quadruple murders, de la Cruz had moved four times and held five different jobs. Yet in spite of his moves and spotty work history, he had managed to repair his credit problems. Though he was technically unemployed, the three-year-old Corvette parked in front of the home's separate two-car garage and the chrome-laden Harley-Davidson peeking out the open garage door indicated the man must've been able to stash some cash away for the lean years.

The yard was freshly mowed, though the flowerbeds were devoid of anything but weeds. That would've signaled to even an amateur detective that the most likely resident was a man living alone, adding weight to the information Beals had given McGee. The biggest concern for McGee was whether the man was inside. He didn't want to lose any more time waiting for him to return home.

McGee took the six steps to the porch in three and rang the antique doorbell. No one responded, so he tried pounding on the door. Finally, after rapping several more times, a sleepy, unshaven man peered through the front door's glass pane. He studied his visitor, then unlocked the latch and opened the antique door.

"What can I do for you?" he grumbled.

"Are you Martin de la Cruz?"

The man yawned, stretched, then pulled the bottom of his thin white T-shirt over his considerable belly. "So? What if I am?"

"I'm Kent McGee and I need to speak with you."

"I don't know you. What's this about?"

"It's about Omar Jones. May I come in?"

De la Cruz shrugged. "Long time ago, ancient history. You a reporter? I don't talk to reporters."

"No, I'm a lawyer."

"I sure as heck don't talk to them either." He started to close the door, but was stopped by McGee's $250 black loafer.

"We can do this the easy way or the hard way. I don't care, but I'm not leaving without speaking with you."

De la Cruz picked at his shirt while he studied his uninvited guest's face. Finally, after yanking his faded jeans up under his bulging waist, he signaled for McGee to follow. "The living room's to the right. Just push those newspapers off the couch. I can't spare much time."

As McGee moved a week-old copy of the *Dallas Morning News* from the cushion to the floor, he said, "I'm sure you have several important appointments. You must be an extremely busy man."

"What do you mean by that?" de la Cruz shot back as he plopped down in a well-worn La-Z-Boy recliner.

"When's your next poker game?"

"What? You here to collect somebody's debt?"

McGee grinned, leaned back, and crossed his right foot over his left knee. As his host tried to get a make on him, the lawyer inventoried the contents of what, in the home's heyday, had been called a parlor.

De la Cruz was a textbook example of a man who was always sure he was just one game away from a big win. The man's college degree in computer programming had somehow been lost in this chase. Pride had walked out too. His desk was stacked with old lottery tickets and more than two dozen decks of cards. The computer screen displayed a site that handicapped dog races. On the coffee table were brochures from at least half a dozen horse-racing venues. He was a sad study of human nature, a smart man living a solitary life blanketed in bad luck created with his own hands.

"I don't care about your gambling," McGee said. "If you want to let your life ride on your instincts, that's fine with me. If you're dodging debts, so be it. I only care about what you saw on September 10, 2001. Give me that information and I'll leave you alone."

"I told the police over and over again. Then I told it during the trial. I never changed anything. I can't add any more now."

"Yes, I've read what you told the FBI and everyone else. In every case, it's always the same. Almost word for word. That's not normal. No witness ever remembers it all the first time. It takes a while for a mind to process all the information and recall the details. Those whose stories never change are usually spitting out a script someone else wrote for them. Is that what you've been doing? Did you even see Jones that night?"

The words that should have stung didn't. De la Cruz showed no sign of feeling the slightest bit insulted. Instead, like a gambler knowing he has the winning hand, he leaned back in his chair, smiled, and closed his eyes.

"Your name is Kent McGee," he began as if reciting lines from a stage play. "You first knocked on my door at 12:03. You probably rang the doorbell first, but it doesn't work. You knocked seven times. The first four you rapped your hand five times, the next eight, and finally the last two you beat on the wood eleven and nineteen times. You have a yellow-gold school ring on your right hand. The stone is purple; your initials are on one side. The year you graduated, 1991, is written on the other. Ouachita is the name of your school; the etchings on the ring indicate your major was in humanities and your mascot is a tiger."

He paused momentarily, licked his lips, but did not open his eyes. "Your watch is an analog type, silver expandable band, but there was not enough of the face showing from under your shirt sleeve for me to read the brand. The stitching in your shirt indicates it was custom made. Your initials, KBM, are on the cuff. Your belt has a simple gold buckle; the leather is triple stitched on both edges."

De la Cruz opened his eyes, smiled, and added, "And, if you want me to go on, I can tell you other things, including a description of the small scar on your forehead and the flecks of gold that are only in your right eye, not your left."

McGee smiled. "You have keen powers of observation. I'd expect no less of someone who's been banned in Vegas."

De la Cruz suddenly seemed proud. "You've done your homework. I'm impressed. But if you think this is just the power of observation, then you're mistaken. It's a lot more than that. I have a gift." He smiled while allowing the fact to soak in. "Have you ever heard of hyperthymestic syndrome?"

"No."

"Few people have. Give me a date, sometime in the last thirty years."

"June 12, 1982."

Without a moment's hesitation, de la Cruz began, "Three quarters of a million people gathered in New York's Central Park to protest the spread of nuclear weapons. Simon and Garfunkel played a concert to rave reviews in Rotherham. I got up at nine-thirty a.m. It was a beautiful morning in Ada, Oklahoma, where I lived. I dressed that day in a blue T-shirt and my jeans had a hole in the right knee. My Little League game was rained out by a thunderstorm that started at five-fifteen p.m. I took my bath at nine-thirty-five p.m., found a single chigger bite on the inside of my left calf, watched the weather and sports, then went to bed. My sheets were red and white stripes, and the rain, which had stopped at eight-fifteen, began again at eleven-o-two.

"I could go on, but I think you should be able to understand my unique abilities. If not, let me explain my gift this way. Most people remember things for a moment, then those images start to fade. At first their memories just move into soft focus, then they become somewhat transparent, the details disappearing into almost nothingness. I'm one of a handful of people who never forget anything. I can tell you what clothes I wore on March 15, 1992—a gray sweater, blue slacks, and black socks, the left one with a hole in the heel. I can tell you the details of every bet I've ever made."

De la Cruz tapped his forehead. "It's all here, day by day, moment by moment, and year by year. What I saw on September 10, 2001, is as clear now as it was at 8:03 that evening. My story will not change because it can't change. When I think back, I see it as if I'm watching it right now."

16

AS HIS HOST FELL SMUGLY BACK AGAINST THE recliner's cushion, McGee weighed his next move. De la Cruz was obviously the perfect witness for the prosecution—any prosecution. His abilities were shockingly accurate. No one could challenge those abilities in any way. What chance did a suspect have if he was fingered by de la Cruz?

But what if this man was using hyperthymestic syndrome to craft a false story? It would be the perfect cover. Because of his diagnosis and track record, his story would ring true even if he was telling a lie. His remembering every moment of his life didn't mean he was telling the truth. But how do you prove that a man who can't forget is a liar? Cracking a guy like this was going to take some outside-the-box thinking. How could he separate fact from fiction?

McGee decided to start with praise.

"I'm not going to question your ability," he began. "I'm very impressed. No doubt you could've used your gift to break the bank in Vegas if they'd just given you a chance. In fact, I'm surprised they didn't hire you. Looks to me like you'd have made a great employee."

"My skills got me the 'Vette by the garage," de la Cruz bragged. "Won it in a local game last week."

"I'm surprised you ever lose."

"Well, at cards I usually don't," he said, "but I've got to move around a lot to find folks who haven't heard about me. My reputation's my biggest enemy. My skill doesn't help me with the ponies or dogs. I just like to gamble. There's a rush like nothing else when I'm in that moment with everything riding on one race or one play."

"I guess it's kind of like waiting for a jury to come in."

"Maybe. I wouldn't know."

"Martin, let's be clear on something. Your skills don't mean you're always honest. I'll bet five dollars you're smart enough to bend the rules when you see the chance."

De la Cruz' eyes lit up. "I never get caught. That comes from watching the details and avoiding the traps that catch other cheaters. So if you can't catch me, I'm not cheating."

"Let me flip that a bit," the lawyer cut in. "The fact that you do bend the rules, using your reputation and your gift to work a game to your advantage, means that you could've invented the story about seeing Omar Jones. After all, who would question a man with a perfect memory? I'm thinking you invented the whole thing and used your well-known gift to legitimatize your lie."

This time de la Cruz was insulted. McGee could read the anger on his face and in his body language. Leaning forward, his cheeks a deep red, the gambler shouted, "I ought to—"

"You ought to what?" McGee said as he rose and glared at de la Cruz' contorted fleshy face. "Maybe it's time for you to use your powers of observation. I'm taller, stronger, and quicker than you. I could take you in a minute and still have time to adjust my tie."

Quickly lifting his hands in surrender, de la Cruz stumbled for words to get him out of a possible whipping. "I-I-I said that wrong. I mean, well, what I mean is that I said what I said in the wrong way. I'd never attack you or anyone else. But I didn't make anything up that night. You can strap me up to a lie detector. It'll prove I'm telling the truth."

De la Cruz paused, leaned back in his chair, and held out his hands. "I play the percentages. I had nothing to gain by lying. If I'd lied, it would've been to protect Omar. He was a friend. I liked him. I really liked him. It broke my heart to have to testify against him in court. I can't forget the look he gave me when I told that story. That look cut through me like a knife. But I wasn't going to perjure myself."

"Especially when the whole country would've come after you if you had stood up for him."

"Hey, they had DNA evidence. They'd have convicted him without my testimony. I'm not the person whose words put Omar on death row. He killed four people—that's what nailed him!"

Sweat now rolled off the fat man's face and his armpits were soaked. He was not enjoying the hand he held in McGee's game. The worst part was he couldn't fold.

"Not long after you fingered him," the lawyer continued, "you came into a lot of money. Enough to settle your debts."

"Yeah." De la Cruz nodded his head. "I can tell you the exact moment the gifts came in and amounts of each check. But I didn't know it was going to happen. It started after the story got out and the press made me out to be a hero. Big companies, some church groups, and even individuals heard about my financial woes and gave me gifts because I'd been such a super patriot. That's how I paid off $213,421.22 in debts. Then I moved and started gambling again. I've been up and down ever since. I'm a few bucks above even right now, so life is good. But I didn't lie for money. I don't care if you believe me or not; it's true."

De la Cruz was a master card player, but was he really able to run a bluff in real life when the pressure was on? McGee didn't think so, and it was time to make him show his hand. "Martin, your story was the same every time you told it. Was that just due to your gift?"

"Maybe," he admitted, "but the questions were always the same. Interview after interview they always asked the same things in just about the same order. It never changed. I tried to get them to let me bet on what the next question would be, figured I could take them for some money, but they wouldn't play. It was boring, and they kept doing it day after day, week after week, and month after month. It only stopped when they found Omar guilty."

Made sense. Why change the order or nature of the questions if the results the first time gave a perfect score? The only time questions changed was when investigators didn't get the results they wanted. So maybe there was a question or two the FBI felt they had no reason to ask. If this guy's memory was perfect, then the answers to those unasked questions might open a new direction, give a new perspective on the conversation between de la Cruz and Jones that night. It was worth a try.

"Martin, when you saw Omar that night, was there anything about him that was different from all the other times you had seen him?"

The response was immediate. "Sure. Omar was always upbeat and excited, kind of nervous. Nothing would be going on and he was still edgy, like he was expecting lightning to strike. But that night he was really, really calm. I'd never seen him so cool. He was kind of distant, and he was never like that. When I learned later what had happened, I wrote it off as his trying to act like everything was normal. An attempt at covering his tracks."

"Anything else that surprised you?"

"Omar loved to talk, but not that night. It was like he couldn't wait to get away from me. I remember I was trying to tell him about the Texas Rangers game. I had won five hundred dollars on it, and he said, 'Martin, I've got to go. No time to talk now.' He'd never brushed me off like that before. When I found out about the murders, it almost all made sense."

"Almost all?" McGee asked.

"Yeah, almost all. He had always called me Marty. That was the first time he'd ever called me Martin. That was weird. Maybe it was just his nerves, but it kind of sounded funny coming out of his lips. Like it was rehearsed."

Marty. Did that mean anything? Maybe, but not enough to go to a high court and ask for a delay in the execution. Buried in the gambler's willing mind had to be something else the original investigators missed. But what was it?

"Did the FBI ever ask you about his hands?"

De la Cruz shrugged. "What do you mean?"

"Just what I said. Did they ask you if he had a bleeding finger?"

"No, no one asked that. But I can tell you he didn't. His hands were clean. No cuts."

Praise the Lord for making a man who couldn't forget! This was a break—a huge break! Still, it wasn't enough for an appeal. He needed more.

"Martin," McGee continued, "what did he do after he left you?"

"Like I told the FBI, he got into his car and drove off."

"Sure it was his car?"

"I guess. It was a blue 1999 Mazda. That's what he drove."

"Anything different about the car that night?"

"It was cleaner than usual. Otherwise, nothing."

"You didn't see a tag number that night, did you?"

"No, only glanced at the car. It was a half block away and it was turned sideways. So couldn't see the plates."

McGee walked over to the still reclining de la Cruz. "Thanks. You've been a huge help."

His host struggled out of the chair and they shook hands. McGee took a business card out of his pocket and dropped it on the table. "I know once you look at it you'll remember the number. If you ever need anything, call me."

"Thanks."

McGee almost bounced out the door and onto the porch, then jumped from the front porch and sprinted toward the car. Once in the driver's seat, he pulled away from the curb and retraced his route while whistling an old jazz number. A few verses later, when he was nearly to I-35, he hit a number on his cell.

Ivy Beals didn't bother with any of the standard greetings. "How did it go?"

"You ever heard of hyperthymestic syndrome?" McGee said.

"Yeah, really rare. It causes a person to remember everything in great detail. And I do mean every minute detail. Don't ever ask one of those folks to tell you about a movie, because the story will take longer than the film itself. I worked with a man in the CIA who was hyperthymestic. You can imagine how important that was in the spy game. He was the MVP of our unit. No doubt about that."

"Well," McGee said, "Martin de la Cruz might well be the MVP of this case. And for the same reason."

"Glad you got a break. He really doesn't forget anything. That's just weird."

"I'll email the report later. Anything on your end?"

"Before I answer that," Beals said, "let me ask, you got a tail?"

"Like a tiger. Had one all day."

"Figured you might. The good news is that I've uncovered something pretty interesting."

"I'm all ears."

"Albert Klasser was the only one from his clan who lived in the United States. His other three brothers and their families reside in Israel. Klasser was born there but went to prep schools in New York, stayed in the States for college at Cal Tech, and never moved back home. His oldest brother, Seth, is a history professor at a university in Tel Aviv. A younger brother, Isaac, is a doctor and also lives in the capital. It's his third sibling, Joshua, who might be the key to explaining why Albert was murdered. Joshua is a high-ranking operative in the Mossad."

"Israeli intelligence. That's an interesting twist. Could offer us an alternative motive for the crime. The guys in that group play hardball and make a lot of enemies. Where is he now?"

"At this moment, Washington, D.C."

"Can you get to him?"

"Maybe. I still have some contacts from my time in the agency."

"Good. Get me what I need. Call me when you've got something concrete."

McGee felt like a new man as he dropped his secure phone in his pocket. Maybe he could take on the whole government, including the FBI and Department of Homeland Security. He had something they'd missed.

But there was still the troubling aspect of who'd been imitating Omar Jones that night and why de la Cruz didn't spot the difference. Maybe the light was so bad the man's face was shielded. But what about the blood, the DNA, the fingerprints? Could he create enough doubt on those vital elements to at least gain an opportunity to argue the case before an appellate court?

Glancing into his rearview mirror, he noted the now familiar gray Dodge Stratus. It was hanging five cars back, but it was still there. McGee laughed. Wonder where the guy wanted to stop for lunch? If he had his number, he would call and ask.

17

IT WAS WELL PAST MIDNIGHT WHEN DIANA CURTIS dragged herself out of the war archives building and onto Berlin's dark, empty streets. For eight hours she had turned pages on moldy books and papers and asked historians and librarians questions. They had tried to help, sending her on one wild goose chase after another, up and down stairs and into parts of the musty building devoid of human life. She had zipped through microfilm until her eyes crossed. Her fingers tingled from rifling through card catalogs.

And what did she have to show for it? Though her legal pad was filled with pages of notes and interesting doodles, she still had no answers. There was no record of a Henrick Bleicher ever having been in the German military, much less the elite and infamous Schutzstaffel. And not a single SS member's serial number matched the number tattooed on the body found at Swope's Ridge. So while her years of work at the ABI had given her contacts in Washington whose German cohorts threw open the door to seldom seen records, it appeared the trip had been a waste of her time and Lije Evans' money.

After thanking a housekeeper who had allowed her to stay three hours after closing, Curtis exited the six-story stone building and walked down the steps leading to the street. That's when she realized she was as alone as she had been when searching the miles of bookshelves. There were no taxis and she had no idea if city buses ran this time of night. Her hotel was a mile away.

Her briefcase at her side, she began the trek north. She had taken only a dozen steps when the rain started. Within a block, the skies let loose with a steady shower.

When she stopped at the first street corner to wait for a truck to pass, she thought she heard something. She turned around and looked back toward the library's entrance. Nothing. No, wait—there was something or someone, but who? Had it been a shadow or did a figure just slide into the darkness beside a gift shop? Sure her fatigue affected her vision and judgment, Curtis shrugged her aching shoulders, put the furtive image out of her mind, and crossed the thoroughfare.

She was three blocks from the library when on instinct she suddenly spun in her tracks. As she did, a figure about fifty feet behind her casually looked into the window of a lingerie store, then began walking south.

After studying files on Nazis all day, Curtis was almost ready to believe that she was being tailed. But why? She didn't know anything that would interest anyone on this side of the Atlantic, and she surely hadn't found anything worth noting in her research. Still, she would have felt much better if she'd been able to bring her gun.

The man was no longer paying any attention to her. He strolled the other way. She now realized the firearm wasn't as necessary as a raincoat.

Satisfied she was safe, Curtis turned and picked up her own journey. Yet as she walked, she couldn't shake an ominous feeling, one that was as persistent in her mind as the rain hitting her head. It was as if the ghosts of the evil men whose names she had read had been invited into her world and had manifested themselves in the form of a solitary figure.

Though it seemed a waste of time, she launched into investigative mode. Why had a person picked such an odd time for window shopping—especially a man who looked as if he had stepped out of an old black-and-white movie? Why was he on the street at this time of night? Then the thought of SS ghosts leaped back into her head. She shuddered.

Okay, she had to concentrate, keep her mind clear and embrace all that she'd learned as an investigator. That would be the key to her staying calm. It was time to ask the questions a cop always asks witnesses to a crime. She had seen him for only a moment, but how tall was he? When she compared him with the height of the window of the store, he was at least a foot shorter—about five feet nine or ten. He seemed thin. He was wearing a hat, a trench coat, and was carrying an umbrella she wished she had right now.

She giggled as she realized she had just identified Humphrey Bogart as her tail. Suddenly feeling silly, she stopped, turned, and in full voice toasted the night, "Here's looking at you, kid." And there he was, just forty feet behind her.

Curtis no longer questioned her fears. She picked up her pace, her two-inch heels clicking rhythmically against the concrete. Halfway to her hotel she again was forced to wait for the traffic light to allow her to cross the street. This time she didn't turn around. Instead she used a plate-glass window as a mirror. That reflection showed he was now only twenty feet behind her, and this time he hadn't stopped when she did. Suddenly, from out of nowhere, a string of cars appeared. Why was there suddenly a parade? Not wanting to wait for an opening, she turned right and hurried down an empty sidewalk. Glancing over her shoulder, she noted the man was matching her movements and her speed.

One block became two and two became three. The silent but relentless chase continued. Never had she felt more vulnerable. There was no one to call for backup. She was no longer headed for her hotel and safety. She was in a dark and seedy part of the city, away from the lights of the business district. When she realized her mistake, there were no cars on the street, no pedestrians, no policemen. The only sounds were of two sets of shoes hitting the sidewalk at a faster and faster pace.

Should she try to outrun her tail? Should she change direction? Maybe she should just face him. Maybe it was time to use her briefcase as a weapon. Yet if he had a gun, she'd never get the chance. She'd be dead before she could swing the briefcase in his direction. Then again, maybe this wasn't about who she was but what she was. After all, who knew Diana Curtis in Berlin? On these dark streets she was just another female. That realization made the situation seem so much worse.

With her heart attempting to pound its way through her chest, Curtis continued to walk. She could no longer tell the rain from her sweat. She was soaked, frightened, and frantic. Her problems were now many. She had no way of defending herself. Her cell phone had been broken at the airport. She had no idea where she was. And it appeared that each step was taking her farther from safety.

She was almost at the end of a row of warehouses. Intent on outpacing the person in the trench coat, she never saw the other man step out of an alley. She felt his hot breath and looked up. He was large, maybe two hundred and fifty pounds and well over six-six. He grabbed her by the arm, spun her around, and dragged her into the alley. A dim streetlight revealed his scarred face. She tried to scream, but nothing came out. He shoved her up against a brick wall and held a knife in front of her face. He smiled. She'd never seen such a smile. It was crazed.

And if he was working with Bogie, she was dead—or worse.

18

AS SHE WAITED FOR THE KNIFE TO DIG BETWEEN her ribs, a voice from the street shouted something in German. Forgetting about Curtis, the hulking figure whirled like a cat. Ten feet away, the stalker in the trench coat casually presented a large handgun as if for inspection. It was all the identification the attacker needed. The hulk collapsed his shiny blade, lifted his hands in surrender, and backed away from Curtis. She watched as he slunk farther into the darkness of the alley and disappeared.

Trembling, Curtis turned back toward her stalker. In the dim light she could see the man was well groomed, from his fedora to his shined shoes. She had been wrong. He didn't look much like Bogart. In fact he looked more like Mr. Edlebrook, her elementary school principal. Of the two threats, this one appeared to be the lesser. Yet the gun, which had quickly discouraged her other attacker, still put her at a distinct disadvantage.

"You're Miss Curtis?" His tenor voice reflected a distinct British clip.

"Who are you?" she demanded.

"That's only important if you are who I think you are."

"Okay. I'm Curtis."

"Then the description I was given was spot on. Of course, with the wet hair, it's a bit harder to tell." He grinned, a friendly grin.

He didn't look like a predator, at least none she had arrested in her days at the ABI.

"Looks to me like you have had a rather harrowing adventure," he noted. "He *was* a rather grotesque creature. So why don't you allow me to escort you back to your hotel. Maybe we could have a spot of brandy. The rain's made things a bit nippy."

Though he hardly sounded like a rapist, his good manners didn't soothe her nerves. Criminals took on the persona of gentlemen. "I don't normally drink with stalkers."

"Oh, that bit of rubbish." He laughed. "I wasn't going to bother introducing myself or even allow you to see my face until I was sure you were Diana Curtis. Of course, having to save you from that bloody creature did prompt me to change my plan. In fact, until that rather awkward moment, I was about to write you off as just another student of World War II history. You see, I know where you are staying. The Strousberg. If you had walked straight back and gone into the lobby, I would then have made your acquaintance in a much more appropriate fashion."

"Quite a story."

"Right-o! I'm sure it sounds that way, but if I wasn't looking for you, how did I know your name and where you are staying?"

Curtis nodded. At least that part made sense. Still, she didn't like the thought of being a prisoner, even to a polite jailer.

"Put the gun away and don't lay a glove on me. You lead the way. Once we get into the lobby of my hotel, we'll find a very public place to sit. Then we can discuss whatever it is you feel a need to discuss."

He grinned and let the impressive silver firearm fall to his side, then reversed it in his hand and shoved it in her direction. "I can do better than that. I'll let you hold the gun and I'll carry your briefcase. How does that sound?"

He extended the revolver and waited for her to take it. Once Curtis had her fingers around the grip, she put her case on the ground and pushed it toward the stranger. He again smiled—he did have a nice smile—picked up the attaché case, and turned toward the east. As he started walking away, he announced, "By the way, I'm Peter Wilshire."

"Mr. Wilshire, just keep walking and don't look back. If you really do know where I'm staying, then lead the way. In the meantime, just keep your mouth shut and your feet moving."

"As you say, my lady."

19

It was past one when Diana Curtis and Peter Wilshire slipped out of the rain and through the Strousberg Hotel's circular doors. The century-old building, one of the few that had survived Allied bombing during the war, had a small, quaint lobby featuring dark wood and red carpet. The room was devoid of life except for a sleepy desk clerk leaning over the counter reading a magazine, his head supported by his arms. Curtis pointed to a table and two chairs in a far corner. Wilshire blazed the trail. After he'd taken a seat, she followed, lowering the gun to her lap but keeping her index finger securely locked on the trigger.

"How do you know who I am and why am I so important to you?"

"Miss Curtis, you're nothing if not direct. I like that in a woman. As humans we often spend so much time on small talk. It's a bloody waste. We English are the worst of the lot in that department. Nice to meet someone who gets right to the point. Oh, it is Miss, isn't it?"

Curtis didn't answer. Instead she leaned back against the padded green-velvet cushion and observed the man who'd saved her from a fate too gruesome to consider. He was dapper, with a slender but solid build. As if harkening back to another time, he sported a pencil-thin mustache. Under the trench coat, he wore a tweed jacket. His eyes were lively, his nose narrow and long, his lips full. He could have been anywhere from fifty to seventy. And overriding everything else, he was confident. She was sure he thought of himself as a player, and she was just as sure the game was something she was not interested in pursuing on this night or any other.

"Mr. Wilshire—"

"Please call me Peter."

"Okay. Peter. My marital status should be of no interest to you. I see the ring on your left hand. So let's begin there."

"Oh, that. Yes, I'm married; have been for more than forty years. Martha is a delightful gal. We have three kiddos and seven grandchildren. I have snaps if you'd like to see them."

Why did the British call pictures *snaps*? Why didn't they call them pictures or photos like everyone else? "No, that won't be necessary."

He grinned. "Now I get your line of reasoning. I guess my words were a bit ill chosen. Please allow me to apologize. I wasn't trying to find out if you were married in order to—what do you Americans say—hit on you. I have a daughter who is surely much older than you. I just wanted to know how to address you. You know, Mrs. or Miss. Or maybe, as you Yanks say, Ms."

"Diana will do."

"Thank you. That does make things a bit easier."

"And," she added, "thank you for rescuing me from the goon. But that fact does not mean I'm going to forgive you for stalking me."

He shrugged. "I made a miscalculation on that strategy. I say, I could've saved us both a lot of trouble by simply introducing myself as you came out of the archives. But I feared it would give you a terrible fright."

She couldn't help it. She loved the way he talked. Still, that fact didn't melt her anger at his methods. Even if he was being straight with her, it was time to put him squarely in his place. "As if trailing me didn't give me a fright?"

"Sorry."

He had kind eyes and a soothing voice. Maybe he was a gentleman. Yet he also carried a big gun and might have another in his coat. No reason to trust him yet.

"Why were you looking for me?"

Wilshire smiled, lifting his bushy eyebrows and creating at least a half dozen deep furrows in his forehead. "Do you remember Helga Schoal?"

Curtis nodded. "I met her when I checked into the archives. I'm guessing she's close to retirement. A bit stocky, brown eyes, a deeply lined face, a square jaw."

"I've known her for years. In fact, three decades ago she tried to help me in my search for answers about a member of the SS. Back then I never got out of the fog. Did you do any better?"

"No," she admitted, "my quest was unsatisfactory. Yet the fact that we both struck out at the archives doesn't answer the question about your interest in me."

"No, it doesn't. But perhaps a little background will build a bridge between us."

He paused, the seemingly perpetual smile now giving way to the stern, pensive expression doctors wear right before they tell a patient he has only a few months to live. "I met Helga," he began, "because I was looking for information on my father."

"But your accent …"

"Oh, yes, I grew up in Britain, but I was born in Germany in 1945, during the last days of the war. I don't remember ever seeing my father. He disappeared on a mission and never resurfaced. My mother moved to England in 1946. She was sure he had died; she told me so many times. But I believe she loved him so much she really never gave up hope that he had somehow survived the war. Whenever she saw someone who looked like him, she stopped. It was almost like she was being haunted. That continued even after she had remarried. Yet he never came back. On her deathbed she gave me a couple of snaps I'd never seen and told me a story I'd never heard. That's when I found out that my father had been in the SS."

Relaxing her grip on the gun, Curtis raised her eyebrows. "Must've been a shock."

"You have no idea. That's why I first came to Berlin and began digging. Helga helped me all she could, but my father's name was not in the files."

Curtis nodded, "I ran into the same thing."

"I know. Helga called me soon after you signed in. She told me the name of the man you were looking for. Her call was a favor that went back almost three decades."

Curtis had no idea what he meant. "So you live in Berlin?"

"No, London. As soon as I received the call, I caught a plane in an attempt to get to the archives before they closed. I didn't make it. But Helga had already informed me where you were staying. If you recall, she asked you for that information. The sleepy clerk over there informed me you hadn't come in. I called Helga at home and discovered you were working late. So, after running my own errand, I decided to wait outside the building for you to come out. I know I should've simply asked you your name and introduced myself then, rather than following you to see if you were headed to the Strousberg."

What she'd heard smelled distinctly of fish. There could be no reason for anyone to fly from London to Berlin just to meet her. This had to have something to do with the archives. Helga had probably mistaken her for someone else.

"Other than my name, what else do you know about me?"

"Nothing, just that you were trying to find information on an SS officer named Henrick Bleicher."

"And that prompted a trip from England? You're either very wealthy or have too much time on your hands. Maybe both."

He tilted his head and pushed a strand of gray hair off his forehead. "My mother remarried not long after we arrived in England.

Her husband was a commodities trader named Henry Wilshire. He adopted me. But my real father was Henrick Bleicher."

The news took her breath away. She pushed back into the thickly padded chair. So Bleicher was in the SS. But where were the records? And was he the man they'd found under the bus?

"Do you have any pictures of your father?"

Wilshire reached inside his coat pocket, retrieved an envelope, and tossed it on the table. Leaving the gun in her lap, with her left hand Curtis slid out a single photograph. She studied it as it lay on the table. There were four men in the black-and-white image. One was Adolf Hitler. Two she didn't recognize. One man looked like the mummified body they'd found under the bus at Swope's Ridge. She was sure it was Bleicher.

20

CURTIS STUDIED THE IMAGE THAT SOMEHOW PUT breath into the corpse they had found.

Wilshire said, "The picture was taken at Berchtesgaden."

"The Eagle's Nest."

"You are a student of history. That was what many called Hitler's retreat in the Bavarian Alps. I've tried to find the exact spot where the snap was taken, but never could. Time changes things, especially when nature is allowed a free hand."

"What's it feel like ..." Curtis allowed the rest of the question to stick in her throat. She quickly regretted saying anything.

Wilshire's eyes grew sad. "You were going to ask, what does it feel like to find out your father was a member of the most monstrous group in the history of the world?"

She nodded.

"If you actually dwell on it, then you can't sleep. Remember the old line, 'the sins of the father'—well they have visited me often, at least in my nightmares. But no matter what he might have done, even though I don't remember him, he was still my pop. So I just keep digging, trying to find at least one good thing he did. And I wonder, of all the thousands of SS men, why is his name missing? I still hope one day to run into someone who can give me a bit of insight into him. I have long prayed that before I die I could learn a wee bit about his personality and his goals. And on that day, if it ever comes, I just might be closer to understanding his motives and his relationship with this fiend who ordered the death of millions in concentration camps. When I consider that fact, the haunting begins all over."

Curtis studied the pained expression etched into his face. For the first time, he looked his age. She suddenly felt sorry for Wilshire. "Most people would run from the facts," she pointed out, "or ignore them. Maybe even try to bury them so deep that no one could ever dig them up. Your father has been erased from the history books. Except for your pictures, he never did exist. They can't trace his sins to you. At least he's not one of the names that shows up on the History Channel once a month. At least no one is knocking on your door asking about him. That has to be some comfort."

"He's been erased, all right. And it's not just his war records. There are no birth records either. Isn't that amazing? You can find birth records on Eichmann, Barbie, and Mengele, but not my dad. Why do you think that is?"

Curtis shrugged.

"My mum, on her deathbed, told me that not long before the end of the war, several members of the *Gestapo* forced their way into our home and took everything that was his. That included all his papers, his clothing, his books, his jewelry, even their wedding certificate. They missed a couple of photographs hidden in my mother's sewing basket. It was as if he never lived."

"Why? Do you have any idea?"

"Mum never told me. Guess it caused her too much pain. Looking through a few old letters, I found out my father was a member of the SS and was Hitler's associate, but that's all. I've no idea why every sign of his existence was removed by the very people he once called his friends.

"Diana, I've told you a great deal. What I want to know is why are you, only the second person in more than thirty years, trying to find information on Henrick Bleicher?"

It was a fair question. She was researching his father, so he had a right to know. He also had a right to know that Bleicher hadn't just disappeared, that he'd somehow made it to America. But how much should she reveal? "Can I see some form of identification?"

He reached into a pocket of the tweed jacket. Retrieving a bill-fold, he tossed it on the table. Curtis picked it up and as it opened she noted a name as legendary as the FBI.

"Interpol. That explains how you were able to fly with a gun."

"You'll find papers inside the right pocket that will also prove I work with Scotland Yard. In truth, if I hadn't been looking for answers about my father, I'd have retired years ago. Working on what you Americans call 'cold cases' is all about contacts. As long as I'm active in these two law enforcement agencies, I can tap into sources."

She glanced through the rest of his identification, noted the photos of his children and grandchildren, and slid the billfold back his way. She then pulled the gun from her lap and set it on the table.

He took both, carefully tucking them under his coat. "Why are you looking for information on my father? I think you realize that I can't leave here without finding out."

What should she admit to knowing? What were the limits? The prudent course seemed to call for wrapping a bit of the truth in a white lie and waiting for his reaction.

"On a piece of property in Arkansas, at the home of an old German immigrant, a friend of mine found a book with your father's name and SS serial number written in the pages. I'm an investigator, and the man who now owns that property paid me to find out who owned this book. There's not much more than that."

Her twist of the details caused a brief twinge of guilt. Yet there was enough truth in the tale for her to judge if Wilshire's story would hold together. If he proved to be honest and offered to share other elements of what he knew, then maybe she'd come clean as well.

"What was the German immigrant's name?" he asked.

She smiled. "Do you have a guess?"

The reply was direct, the tone flat. "Schleter."

She nodded. "How did you know?"

"It was a name Mum once mentioned when she spoke of my real father. It was unusual, so it stuck with me. But until this moment I never understood the connection. In my research, the only Schleter I uncovered was a simple truck driver. Without a first name, I didn't have much to go on. I just guessed he'd died in the war and been buried in an unmarked grave. America ... Arkansas, you say? He made it that far from his home?"

"Yes, he lived there for almost fifty years. Kept to himself. Kind of a hermit." She waited for a few minutes to allow him to digest what had to be surprising news. "Peter, you said there was another person who also searched the archives looking for information on Henrick Bleicher."

He nodded. "About ten years ago. Helga called me then too. But I didn't get here in time to visit with Mr. Helmut Spiel. Even using my connections, I couldn't track him down. The name and the identification he used were evidently fakes. When he walked out the door, he simply vanished. All I have known for the past decade is that he was an older German who acted very nervous whenever Helga spoke to him. I assumed it was Schleter. Then, today—and I don't know why it hadn't dawned on me before—I realized I had his identity within my grasp. I was stupid to never understand how close I was to it. Diana, tell me how Helga made you sign in to do your research."

She was tired, suffering from jetlag and long hours of fruitless research. In the last two days she had barely eaten. What Wilshire had told her was interesting, but worth little. Now the man was posing a question that seemed to have no significance. But he had saved her life, so she said, "I had to sign a note card, which she dropped in a box."

"Exactly. You not only left your name, you left your fingerprints. When Helga told me she was holding your card when she called me, I realized I had missed the most important clue in my own investigation. Sherlock Holmes I am not. Sadly, I seem to be much more like Dr. Watson."

"Fingerprints." Diana smiled. "So all we have to do is go back to the archive tomorrow, retrieve the card, and check for prints. The only two that should be there are Helga's and the disappearing man."

"You're half right," he said. "The card does contain two sets of prints. Helga was kind enough to drop that card into an envelope and leave it for me at the Interpol office here in Berlin. The prints were being run as I left to meet you. My associates sent me a text two hours ago giving me the real man's name and address."

"So he has a record."

"In a way. He's been treated several times for mental disorders."

"Well," she replied, her energy level rising with her curiosity, "let's get moving."

"Otto Mueller lives about sixty kilometers from here in a nursing facility for the elderly and mentally disturbed. It will do us little good to go there now. Let's get some sleep, let the skies clear, and drive up there tomorrow. I've access to an automobile."

Wilshire was nice, he seemed sincere, he appeared to be what he said he was, but … "Peter, could I see your billfold again?"

The man reached into his pocket and pulled out the stuffed leather wallet. He watched as she picked it up but didn't bother opening it.

"Where are you staying?" she asked.

"I have a room here. That's the irony I mentioned earlier. I always stay here when I'm in Berlin. What are the odds of you and me ending up looking for the same man and staying in the same place?"

"Long." She smiled. "What time do you want to leave?"

"The café across the street serves a good German breakfast.

The sausage is excellent. Why don't we meet there, around nine? That'll give us both an opportunity to grab some sleep."

"Sounds good. I'll see you then."

"Ah, Diana, you have my wallet."

As she rose, she unzipped a pouch on the side of her briefcase and dropped the billfold into the compartment. "You'll get it back when you pay the bill for breakfast."

He smiled. "You don't trust me."

"A wise woman trusts no one, not even a man who saved her life. Thank you again and good night."

"Before you leave, would you tell me what book you found in Arkansas? If I knew what he was reading, it might help me understand him a bit better."

She nodded. "The King James Bible."

"Really?"

"Yes."

She felt his eyes on her as she crossed the room to the stairs, but she never looked back.

21

THE NURSING-CARE FACILITY THAT WAS NOW HOME TO Otto Mueller was anything but first class. Located on the outskirts of Beeskow, the facility was sterile and uninviting, as was the staff. It was one of the coldest places Curtis had ever visited, and that included several maximum-security prisons. No one smiled. Few of those in the lobby even spoke. Hopeless. That word covered the look of the patients, both young and old, being guided down the hallway by the staff. Most appeared almost catatonic, as if they were floating in a plane of existence not of this earth. It was an incredibly sad and gloomy place.

As Curtis waited, Wilshire went to the desk to ask to see Mueller. A desk nurse bluntly rejected his request. She explained firmly that the man was mentally unstable and was kept in an isolated room. Only relatives and staff allowed. When Wilshire inquired as to when the last family member had visited, the woman shrugged, as if no one had ever come to see the resident. It was as if he had been removed from the world, had died, and no one told him.

Wilshire flashed his Interpol credentials. That bought their escape from the desk nurse and entry into the office of the home's supervisor, a short, fat man with thick glasses and dyed black hair. He eyed them suspiciously for several minutes, questioning again and again their motives for the visit. Finally, convinced they weren't government health inspectors, he said they'd have to obtain orders from a doctor in Berlin. He pointed to the door.

Curtis was about to protest, but before she could open her mouth, Wilshire grabbed her arm and yanked her back into the hallway.

"What are you doing?" she demanded. "I didn't come this far to give up."

"We're not giving up, young lady." He smiled. "We'll get what we need. We just have to go about it in a different fashion."

"You mean get permission from the doctor. Who knows how long that will take. I need to get back to the States. I can't hang around here! I'm not waiting around for a written statement from the doctor."

"Not *the* doctor," Wilshire corrected her, "but rather *a* doctor."

The Brit dragged her down the hall, stopping only when they'd reached the front desk. In German, Wilshire thanked the grumpy matron for her time and inquired if he could use the restroom. She waved toward a far hall.

"Diana, you stay right here. Don't move a muscle. I'll be back in just a moment."

True to his word, a minute later the Englishman strolled back to Curtis and quickly escorted her out of the building and to their rented Mercedes. "Get in," he said. When she had fastened her seat belt, he started the white sedan, put it in gear, and drove over the rise and into the parking lot of a small grocery. "Now get out."

"What?"

"Lassie, we're going back, but we'll be taking a different route and using a much more discreet entrance."

"Which one?"

"Through the staff's locker room. It's by the men's restroom. I stole in there and unlocked the outside window, which we will soon be climbing through. Come on, we need to make the short hike through the city park and then stroll across the employee parking lot."

Five minutes later, the pair arrived unnoticed at the designated window. Wilshire slid it up, grabbed onto the sill, and swung up. He was not only strong but very agile for a man his age. He reached back through the opening, offering Curtis his hand for a boost. After he'd pulled her shoulders through, he went over and locked the door. After a few seconds hanging halfway in and half-way out, she shimmied through the window.

"Go through the lockers until you find a uniform you can wear," he said. "I'll check the left side for something for me."

Now she understood what Wilshire had meant when he told her the doctor would allow them to visit Mueller. "You really do look like a distinguished physician," she noted a few minutes later.

"And you give all the appearances of a sympathetic nurse."

"I've still got a concern. How long can we walk around before someone realizes we don't belong? I'm more than a bit uneasy."

"I take it you haven't done much cloak-and-dagger stuff."

She shook her head.

"Lassie, I've pretended to be other people so many times I could go on stage as a character actor. You ought to hear my accents. Might even try to get some roles on the telly when I finally retire."

"I like the personality and accent you have when you're just being you. They're charming."

"I don't have an accent, you do."

She smiled.

"We don't need much time. Mueller's on the second floor. I checked a patient list when I took my washroom trip. Security is pretty lax. As big as this place is, I doubt anyone will finger us very quickly. Are you ready, nurse?"

22

PETER WILSHIRE DIDN'T WAIT FOR AN ANSWER. HE unlocked the door of the locker room, glanced up and down the hall, and confidently marched out. Diana quickly followed, trying her hardest to appear as if she knew what she was doing. When they came to the elevator, he pushed a button and waited. Before the doors opened, three staff members came toward them, discussing a reality show on TV and laughing as they walked past. The elevator doors opened. They had cleared their first obstacle.

A short ride took them to the second floor. A nurse stepped on as they got off, but she was reading a chart and didn't bother looking up. Curtis glanced both ways and kept her head down as she stepped into the hall. Behind her a smiling Wilshire, his head held high, waved at two members of the staff and, acting as if he knew what he was doing, quickly walked to room 271. When he pushed on the door, it didn't budge. A major roadblock. But if the locked door perturbed him, it didn't show.

"Stay here and look busy," he said. Before she could reply, he was strolling back toward the floor's central command center. He stopped at a housekeeping cart and said something to an Asian woman. She laughed, reached into her pocket, and handed him her keys. Wilshire then walked back to 271 and unlocked the door.

"Be right back," he said. After handing the keys to the housekeeper, he returned and the two slipped into Mueller's tiny cubicle.

The Interpol agent's smile was gone. He walked over to the window and opened the blinds to allow daylight to enter the gloomy room. He walked to the bed and took a long look at the man they had come to see.

"He doesn't even know we're here," Curtis said.

"He's probably heavily sedated. It's easier to manage a large caseload if you keep the ones who have no family in a daze. Look, he's restrained. Must be a handful when he's awake."

Acting very much the doctor he wasn't, Wilshire pulled the chart from the plastic file holder mounted on the door. He studied it for a moment, then said, "I'll be right back," and left Curtis alone with the feeble patient.

Cautiously, she moved to the side of the bed. Mueller's skin was almost transparent and so tightly drawn she could make out the distinct shape of his skull. He was bald, with only wisps of gray hair clinging to a few places above his ears. No one had shaved him in days. His fingernails needed clipping. It was as though he'd been pushed into a corner and forgotten. No dignity. No respect for this man who was helpless.

Looking at his emaciated body, she wondered how Mueller had the strength to lift his chest to breathe. Was he starved? Were they simply waiting for him to die? Why wasn't this man being given better care? And why was he restrained? She didn't figure he could lift his head, much less a fist.

Hearing steps, she nervously looked over her shoulder at the door. She tensed as it opened, then relaxed. In walked Wilshire.

"Just what we need," he announced, holding up a vial. "Smelling salts."

"Are you sure that'll work? Could it cause some medical issues?" she asked.

"No, I'm not sure, and I doubt if he has any medical issues left."

Maybe Mueller could help them understand why people were being killed on the other side of the Atlantic. Maybe this man knew Bleicher and would solve that mystery. But were they risking his life? Did the good of the many outweigh the needs of the one? It was an age-old question. Hillman would be on the side of the many, regardless of the cost. And that was probably the belief of this Interpol agent. But did she believe it?

While Wilshire snapped the vial in two and attempted to get the man to breathe in the vapors, Curtis walked over to a table to look at the one book the old man at one time had been reading. It was a Bible and, like Bleicher's, it was in English, not German. How strange.

She opened the cover and saw Otto Mueller's name written on the title page. Yet there was one major difference in the two books. Unlike the apparently new one they had found buried with Wilshire's father, this one was well worn. Many of the pages were dog eared. Yet, as she thumbed through the chapters, she saw no verses underlined. Most people who read Scripture enough to show wear on the pages also marked passages and wrote notes in the margins. These pages were clean.

Then she remembered the passage marked in Bleicher's Bible. Rapidly flipping the pages from the back to the front, she landed in Genesis. And like a forty-foot neon sign, there it was. Mueller had underlined the same passage: Genesis 7:17–23.

There was a link between Mueller and Bleicher and with Schleter, with Swope's Ridge. Those underlined words proved it. If she had actually thought to pray, she would have considered her discovery an answer to that prayer.

All doubt vanished. She was suddenly sure of her motives and had the faith to believe they were correct. Why else would that Bible have been there for her to find?

23

"HE'S COMING TO," THE ENGLISHMAN ANNOUNCED. "Diana, keep watch outside the door. This conversation has to be quick. Give a light knock as a warning."

Curtis was not going to depend on a man she barely knew, so she ignored Wilshire's order. She could not walk away from an interview this important. She believed this was an opportunity destined to happen and not just of their making.

"We're fine," she assured Wilshire.

Mueller's arms began pulling at the restraints; his eyelids fluttered, and his breathing became a bit deeper, more intentional. The smelling salts were working, but how much of the man would come back to them and what was the state of his mind?

"Otto," Wilshire whispered. He followed by asking in German, "Can you hear me?"

The old man slowly nodded.

"How did you know Henrick Bleicher?"

"Bleicher?" Mueller whispered.

"Yes, Bleicher."

The old man smiled but said nothing. Wilshire glanced at Curtis. "You really need to be watching outside."

She nodded, walked over to the door, opened it a crack, and looked down the hall. She eased the door shut. "We're clear."

In German, Wilshire said, "Otto, tell me about Bleicher."

"English," the old man said.

"No, he was German," Wilshire said. "He was in the SS."

Instantly agitated, Mueller formed his hands into fists. His eyes glaring, he growled, "English. English."

Curtis moved toward the bed. Wilshire said, "I'm guessing he knows I'm English and doesn't trust me."

"No!" Mueller said.

"Calm him down," Curtis said, "or we're going to have company."

"English!" Mueller almost yelled again.

"Peter, tell him your father was Henrick Bleicher."

"English!" the old man said again.

Curtis looked at the Bible on the table. "I know what he wants. Talk to him in English." Leaning close to Mueller's ear, she asked, "Do you know John Schleter?"

"Yes," the old man said. "You know Schleter? Where is he?"

"In America. He moved there after the war," she said.

"Who was he?" Wilshire asked.

"The driver," Mueller said. "And Henrick, did he get out of the country too?"

Wilshire said, "What do you mean, did Henrick get out of the country?"

"How do you know Henrick?" Mueller's voice was much softer.

"He was my father."

The old man cocked his head and studied his guest. "You are Peter?" Tears welled up in his eyes. "My child, I held you when you were so tiny. So long ago. So long ago."

"Yes, I am Peter. Tell me about my father."

"We thought Henrick was dead," the old man whispered. "Now I know. He accomplished the mission. I worried for nothing. That's why no one died in America. All these years, I kept waiting for news of the deaths. And your father … how many millions he saved. Did he destroy all of it?"

Curtis looked to Wilshire. What was he talking about? What had Bleicher destroyed? Or was it still on Swope's Ridge?

"Mr. Mueller," she said, "why were you so worried about the people in America?"

"The Ark of Death," Mueller said. "It must have been sunk. It must all be on the ocean floor. Our prayers were answered."

"Ark of Death?" Wilshire asked.

A smile crossed Mueller's face. "Your father must have stopped it. The last time I saw him, he was trying to get away from the storm troopers. He told me to pray for him. So many bombs that night. So many bombs. I prayed in the church all night long, but when I didn't hear, I was sure he didn't make it. But he must have stopped the Ark. My prayers *were* answered."

Mueller looking up at Wilshire and whispered, "Your father was a good man. So brave! He gave up everything to fight Hitler."

"To fight Hitler?" Wilshire asked. "He was an SS officer."

"So they thought." Mueller smiled. "Like me he was a double agent. He had to get to America before the Ark did. If he hadn't, Hitler's plan ..."

The look in the old man's eyes grew distant. He blinked and took a very deep breath. Curtis and Wilshire leaned closer. Finally Mueller whispered, "He stopped the planes. Schleter helped. He couldn't have done it alone."

Otto Mueller's eyes locked on Peter. "You have his smile. He had a wonderful smile. He ... was ..."

The room was strangely silent.

"He's drifted off again," Wilshire said.

"Did you know about the Ark?"

"Not really. But now I know my father was erased from history because they found out he was a working for the Allies. That must be why it was so easy for Mum, a German, to gain admittance to England after the war. That's why she never quit looking for him. Because some disaster didn't happen, she expected him to find her."

Curtis picked up the Bible and walked over to the door. She looked out. "The hallway's clear. Let's get out of here."

Wilshire nodded. He looked down at the old man and touched his head. "You didn't need to worry. My pop took care of it."

24

DIANA CURTIS HAD NEVER SEEN AN EXPRESSION LIKE the one now on Peter Wilshire's face. It had been plastered there ever since they sneaked away from the nursing facility. As soon as they were back in the car, his whole body relaxed. It was as if a great weight had been removed. Until that moment, he had been calm and formal, like a true Brit, but now he acted like a kid. One visit with a feeble old man had transformed him.

As soon as they were certain they weren't being followed, they stopped at a small cafe about ten miles north of Berlin. Curtis ate in silence, unsure what to say that could put the day's events into perspective. Instead she waited for Wilshire's reaction. But his eyes looked right through her. It was as if he was in a trance and didn't want to wake up. Yet the silence wasn't awkward. There was something beautiful about it. The lack of words came from joy and happiness ... and peace.

They left the cafe and Wilshire headed toward a small flower-filled city park instead of the car. They strolled down a brick path and sat on a bench. It was twilight. A light breeze surrounded them with the fragrance of new blooms. On the other side of a stand of trees, a group of children laughed.

Stretching his legs, he put his hands behind his head and looked skyward. "See it? The first star."

She nodded.

His eyes fixed on the darkening sky, Wilshire said, "Schleter. He must have been my father's driver in those last days in Germany. That's what Mum meant. She knew they were together. She knew if I found Schleter, I'd find out the truth about my father. I was afraid I'd never know, that I'd die before I found out the truth. But I've always been afraid of the truth, afraid of what I'd find. Now I know I had nothing to fear. You found Schleter, and you found the Bible with my father's name, and that led you here. In a way, this afternoon, Schleter drove my father home one more time so I could know him as he really was."

"Yes," Curtis said, "in a way he did. But there's more."

And she launched into the story of the tragic night on Faraday Road, Schleter's fortress-like house on Swope's Ridge, the rumors of a curse, the deaths somehow tied to that land. She then told about the old, abandoned school bus and finding the trapdoor under the bus, the vault that had so protected the coffin for decades.

And before she could say more, Wilshire said, "My father was buried there."

"Yes." She had thought the Brit would be angry at her previous deception. But hearing the truth seemed to fill him with pride.

"Hard to believe my father died in America. The mission led him there. But how did he die? And why was his body hidden so securely?"

"He was shot by a German rifle. To pull off something as big as Mueller made this mission of death sound, the SS would have had men on the ground in the U.S. Even after the war ended, they probably kept looking for those who had deceived them, and that included your father. Somehow he stopped the mission. He must have found the Germans. Or they found him and got the drop on him."

"In our business," Wilshire said, "most of us die because someone gets the drop on us. I've been lucky." He studied the sky and in a wishful tone added, "I'd like to find out how he died, what this mission was all about. Now that I'm sure he was working for the right side, it makes me want to know more about him. He must have had a lot of courage. He must have been a jolly good gent."

Curtis nodded. "A lot more courage than I can imagine. Going undercover as part of Hitler's inner circle would've been invaluable to the Allies and would have taken nerves of steel."

"You know, Diana, I'm no longer a young man. I was born in 1945, so you can do the math. For several years now I've seen my life winding down and wondered what you do when you retire. I've long tried to run from that thought. Yet maybe I've been so restless, so dogged in my pursuit of criminals, so devoted to my life as a law officer because I was trying to make up for the great harm and pain that I believed my father had helped foster in the world. I blamed the SS for his not being in my life. I blamed it for my mum's heartache. Believing he was so bad made me yearn to be a better person. It gave me purpose. It drove me. Looking back on it now, maybe that was good. Maybe he was teaching me all along."

Glancing back up into the night sky, he said, "Now what will drive me will be knowing what he sacrificed in order to save millions of lives. I no longer have to keep myself busy trying to prove my family's worth to mankind. It's already been proven. Anything I do is just a bonus."

"I'm sure you're right, Peter. A shame you had to wait so long to understand that."

He nodded. "Back at the nursing home, when Mueller kept saying that his prayers were answered, I realized so were mine."

"I guess they were," Curtis agreed.

"No, don't write off what I just said as another cheap 'thank God' whisper in the night." He turned to face her, his tone serious. "Wrap your brain around it. Understand that I've been sincerely praying an impossible prayer for more than three decades. That prayer asked God to rewrite history. I kept begging and begging for a way I could embrace who I am, who my father was. Your finding his body in Arkansas, your visit to the archives, our trip to see Mueller—all those unrelated events led me to know who my father really was.

"God did answer my prayers. History was rewritten. That is impossible ... and yet it happened!

"I have to believe that for Pop to do what he did, to sacrifice all that he did, meant he believed, he had faith. Suddenly faith is alive in my life too." He thumbed his chest. "I feel it inside here. I've never felt so alive!"

25

CURTIS WAITED, ALLOWING HER COMPANION TO SAVOR the moment a bit longer. Night had cloaked the park in a darkness broken only by circles of light under the lampposts. A few people walked the paths, some with dogs, others alone, maybe cutting through the park on their way home. Finally she decided to find out if he knew the story of the Ark of Death that Mueller had mentioned. "Because of what you've been looking for all these years, I assume you know a great deal about World War II history."

"I know some."

"The Ark of Death. Did that mean anything to you?"

Wilshire shook his head. "When he said it, no. But there's a story I once heard about how Hitler planned to use a specially built *Sterbenden Schiff,* which means 'dying ship.' I heard it when I was young in England. It scared me to death. I thought the ship was out at sea, hiding in a fog bank, waiting for an order to launch an attack and wipe out all life on earth. As an adult I figured the story's sole purpose was to frighten children at bedtime. What you Yanks call a bogeyman tale."

"That's all there is to it?"

"Maybe not. I once overheard my mother speaking to a relative in the kitchen. They were talking in German, and it sounded serious, so I hung back by the door. I heard Mum whisper, '*Bogen des*

Todes.' My Sunday school teacher the week before had told us about Noah's Ark and described it as a boat of life. So *Bogen des Todes,* which means 'Ark of Death' in German, caught my attention."

"Anything else?"

"Consider this: Nazi scientists used concentration camps as testing grounds for poisons. They were looking for more efficient ways of killing large groups of people. Maybe they discovered something, some weapon of mass destruction, perhaps a kind of poison gas. Think of the hysteria if such a bomb were dropped from a plane or fired from a ship. A whole city could be destroyed. It would've turned the war around. Maybe a ship was sent and my father intercepted it and somehow sank it. Maybe the Ark of Death was real."

Curtis nodded. That made sense. But if the war ended with no one dying, why was Mueller still so frightened even now? She had seen his face and heard his voice. He was terrified. "Why is it that we spend so much time finding new ways to create death and so little looking for ways to enhance life?"

Peter, probably still caught up in the truth about his father, didn't respond.

"We need to be heading back. I want to get to the States tomorrow and figure out how this ties in with the mystery I'm trying to solve."

"Do you think it does?"

"I don't know," she admitted.

As they strolled back through the park gate, Wilshire asked, "When you have this thing figured out, could you send my father's body back to me?"

"Of course. I'm guessing your family's going to be very excited to know the real story."

He shook his head. "They don't even know he was in the SS. I've hidden that from everyone. Now I can talk. You can't imagine how it feels. Thank you, Diana." He leaned over and kissed her on the forehead.

They walked back to the white Mercedes in silence. Unlocking her door, he waited until she was safely inside, shut her in, and walked around to the other side. He had just closed his door and was reaching for his seat belt when something caught his eye.

"Diana, I've a favor to ask of you."

"Sure."

He reached into the back seat and picked up Mueller's Bible. His fingers lightly traced the embossed words on the cover. "Could this old Brit have this?"

She nodded.

He smiled, then his expression changed. With no word of explanation he grabbed her hair and forcefully pushed her head toward the floor. Caught off guard, she screamed as pain shot through her neck and down her spine. The glass on the passenger side of the rental car shattered in a volley of shots. Peter's tight grip relaxed. She heard squealing tires and a roaring engine, then nothing but stark, foreboding silence.

Stunned, Curtis sat up and studied the man who less than twenty-four hours before had saved her life. Now he had done it again, but this time he'd paid the ultimate price. Like his father, he had been executed. But this hit had been delivered mob style.

She fought the urge to run. She fought the urge to scream. She even fought the urge to cry. Instead she forced herself to study his bullet-riddled form, trying to memorize every detail of the senseless death illuminated by tranquil moonlight. Blood seeped from a dozen different wounds. His back was pressed against the driver-side door panel. His head had flopped over on his shoulder. And just like his father, who had died more than sixty years before, Peter clutched a Bible in his left hand.

She turned her head away, pulled her purse from the floorboard, and reached for the door handle. She was about forty feet from the car, hidden by the midnight shadows, when the first person exited a nearby building to see what had created all the commotion. The curious observer was quickly joined by a few others.

From her hiding place, Curtis tearfully watched them move slowly toward the car. Then she heard the first wails of police sirens. She wiped her eyes with her sleeve, turned, and walked away.

Thirty minutes later she was on a train to Berlin. Two hours later she was packed and in a taxi heading for the airport. By dawn she was flying over England. But no matter where her body was or what window she peered from, her eyes saw a horror she couldn't fathom — Peter Wilshire's lifeless eyes staring straight into her soul.

26

LIJE EVANS PULLED HIS 1936 CORD WESTCHESTER into the barn behind his house. He had taken the car out for a cruise as much to relieve boredom as to allow the classic's juices to flow. Yet even being behind the wheel of this motoring icon didn't hold his interest for long. The evening air felt stale and the concrete ribbon of Arkansas 9 bored him. So he'd driven only a few miles from his home on Shell Hill before he made a U-turn and headed back home to his log-and-native-stone house overlooking Salem, a town of twelve hundred that his family had called home for three generations.

What a house it was. More than eighty years old, a small forest must have been cleared just to build it. From the massive native-stone fireplace to the huge great room, the home was impressive. Its game room looked like a 1950s malt shop. A gourmet kitchen was the workshop for a dining room that seated twenty. The master suite was as large as most New York apartments. When his wife, Kaitlyn, was alive, it had been a place of great warmth and comfort. But that time had passed.

The life-and-death crises of the last few months and his determination to solve the mystery that had left him a widower had, in a strange way, been a gift. They'd helped him avoid the reality of his loss. Yet, at night, when he had nowhere to go and no one to talk to, the feeling of being completely alone dogged him like a recurring nightmare.

Walking back into their house on the hill always made it worse. In their home, Kaitlyn was everywhere. Several times he had considered burning the home to the ground as the best way to bury her spirit. And yet he couldn't do that; she had loved the place too much. Instead he found himself looking for busywork to occupy his mind.

That first month he had spent hours each day in research, looking for motives for his wife's death. He researched the history of Swope's Ridge. He googled every keyword that might provide a lead. There had to be a reason, but he could find none.

In desperation he detailed his 1936 Cord, his Explorer, and the Prius so many times he was sure he'd soon rub through the paint and find himself polishing primer.

He turned to television, watching everything from home-improvement fare to reality shows. He had searched for programming so often he'd memorized the location of dozens of channels on his satellite guide. He could even repeat verbatim dialog from episodes of *Gilligan's Island.*

The computer became another gobbler of time. He read the front pages and the major stories of a handful of different newspapers and TV news sites. He joined a host of message boards that embraced online chats on cars, classic films, food, basketball, and even collecting baseball cards, but discovered that waiting for someone to answer one of his posts was torture.

He eventually found eBay, the world-famous auction site that soon offered hours of diversion each evening. What kept him on eBay was the hunt. He sought out scores of items he could bid on. The quest helped him fight off the ghosts that surrounded him.

As he walked back to the house, Lije called McGee to find out what he had learned about the Jones case. McGee said he was waiting for a private detective to uncover something; he'd call when he knew something.

He started to dial Curtis after he got in the house, but realized she was still in Germany. She hadn't called him, which was odd, and he wondered if she'd had any luck tracking down the two Germans.

He logged on to eBay and considered his options. What did he need? Glancing around his home office reminded him that in the last month he'd bought most everything a person could use with a computer. He had external hard drives stacked four high and six printers to apply ink to everything from DVDs to photo paper. There were different mouse types he had bought and tried, only to go back to the mouse that came with his computer. No reason to search the tech auctions. He also had no need of new shoes, DVDs, or used books.

He finally clicked on car parts. That was a comfort zone. Backup parts for the Cord. And if finding them should prove a challenge, so much the better. It would take time.

What was the best way to search? If he typed in "Cord," then hundreds of thousands of items would come up. Though he wanted to kill a lot of time, even he didn't want to wade through that many choices. But if he got specific and typed in "1936 Cord Westchester 810," results might yield little, and use little time. Besides, a lot of the sellers might not even know model number designations for a car that rare and he would miss items that might not be made for a Cord but that would fit one. He typed in "1936 Cord." A few seconds later a list of 209 items popped up. The list was shorter than he had hoped, but it was a start to killing the hours that stretched out before him.

None of the first ten items had anything to do with cars, but a "new in box" Canon camera caught his eye. He didn't make an offer.

The next auction selection that grabbed his attention was a 1936 Philco radio with an original cord. Starting bid was fifty dollars, so he jumped on it. If he managed to win the antique, he figured it would look good in his office.

After making a bid, he went back to the main list. The first car-part auction he discovered was for a box of six-volt light bulbs. The seller guaranteed the dozen bulbs were "new old stock" and if they didn't work he would refund the winner's bid. Lije already had two boxes out in the barn, so he passed.

At the top of the second page something that seemed out of place popped up. What did a cord have to do with a 1936 high school class ring? On eBay being curious separated the average buyer from the pro. It was a fact that many a bargain had been found by typing in a wrong spelling. Lije himself had once won a valuable Jean Harlow autograph at minimum bid because the seller had accidentally added an "e" to the end of the movie star's last name.

So what had triggered the ring to pop up? He clicked on the listing. Clicking on the photo led him to a page that contained four more photos and a description that began with: "Strike a cord with the past." The seller had left out the "h" when penning the witty opening and the spell checker hadn't flagged it. Mystery solved.

Lije started to hit the Back icon. His cursor was hovering over it when two words caught his eye: "Ash Flat." That was where his Aunt JoJo had gone to school.

> Strike a cord with the past. Up for bid is a 1936 high school class ring from a school named Ash Flat. I bought this item at an estate sale, and as there is no record of a high school by that name in my state, I don't know where this ring is from. As you can see from my photo, it is a simple gold ring with the name of the school, a green stone, an engraving of some kind of bird, and the year 1936. It is a small size, so it probably belonged to a woman. This would be a great accessory for a costume or theme party. With such a low starting bid and no reserve, you could have it for practically a "school" song.

Wow! What were the odds? A missing "h" had landed him here. Maybe this ring belonged to his aunt. Only one way to find out—ask. Learning where the seller had purchased the ring might provide some answers on the fate of a woman once known as JoJo.

Calling up the link for questions, he typed, "Could you please tell me where you are located and whose estate you obtained the ring from?" He clicked Send.

He watched the screen for a quick reply, but none came. He got up and crossed through the living room to the kitchen. From the refrigerator he retrieved a few slices of smoked turkey and a jar of mayo. He hit the pantry next, grabbing a half loaf of bread and a can of Pringles. He added a knife and a plate to the mix and, after a shake of salt, his supper was prepared.

He poured a tall glass of iced tea. Turning out the lights, he sat down at the bar and gazed out the floor-to-ceiling windows toward his small lake, all the while listening for the glassy sound that indicated he had email. An hour later, his meal long finished, he was still sitting on the stool, looking out but not seeing the water below.

The problem with being alone, the problem with having nothing to do, and the problem with waiting for something to do were all the same. When his mind quit working, Kaitlyn came to visit. Was the pain of remembering so great because he had loved her so much, or was it because there had been no closure? If he knew the reason why she'd been killed, would that allow him to think of her without his heart breaking? And if he never found out why she had to die, if he never faced the person who'd pulled the trigger, would he ever really be able to move forward with his personal life? Dr. Phil might yell at him to move on, but if the TV answer man ever did that, Lije was sure he would deck him. Moving on was possible only when you had a place to store your baggage.

Over the past few months he had read several books on grief. In the case of violent deaths, some writers spoke of their need for vengeance. For them, dealing with the pain could happen only if the Old Testament rule of "an eye for an eye and a tooth for tooth" was allowed to play out. Maybe due to the kind of life Kaitlyn had lived and the person she had been, Lije didn't yearn to put a bullet between the eyes of the mysterious Mr. Smith. He just wanted to know why. He was somehow sure that knowing why would make all the difference even though it wouldn't stop the loneliness or the pain.

Pling.

The sound had come from his office. Pushing memories to the side, Lije hurried across the living room, all the while praying this wasn't another one of those emails from Nigeria telling him some person was dying and had chosen him to receive their millions. Clicking on his mailbox, he waited as the email opened.

> *Thanks for asking about the ring. I'm an antique dealer in Liberal, Kansas. I bought this item and many others from the brother of a farmer in Sublette, Kansas. The man died, left no living relatives other than a brother who opted to sell items he didn't want.*
>
> *You can see the other things I picked up from this estate by clicking on the "view seller's other auctions." I think you'll find some of these things I obtained more interesting than the old ring.*
>
> *If I can be of any help or you have more questions, just email me at my private email address listed below.*
>
> *Ralph*

Lije went back to the ring's auction page and clicked on the "other auctions" link. A few seconds later, more than a hundred items popped up, everything from coins to dishes. Except for the ring, nothing seemed to have a direct link to a woman.

Near the end of the list was one item that intrigued him—an old military medal. Lije clicked on the link to see a larger photograph and the description. He didn't recognize it.

Ralph evidently had no idea where the medal came from either, or how old it was, only that it had been found in the bottom of a jar filled with foreign coins. Picking up the phone, Lije tapped in the number of one of the best-informed historians he knew.

"Hello."

"Professor Cathcart, it's Lije Evans. I want you to check something for me."

"Lije, of course. What is it?"

"I'm going to send you an eBay link to an auction for what I believe is an old war medal. I'm hoping you might tell me its origin. Let me warn you, the picture is not clear, so you might not have enough detail for an ID."

"Ah, military medals." Cathcart laughed. "I collect them, you know. Have some from every one of the major modern wars."

"I know," Lije said, "which is why I thought of you. I'm sending the link now. Call me back when you've had a look."

Lije walked into the game room and pushed two buttons on his 1959 Wurlitzer jukebox. Though he loved his iPod, there was something magical about the pops and hisses of a vinyl platter. He listened to a series of clicks and watched as a mechanical arm lifted a vintage forty-five record into place. As the needle hit the record, a country single from the 1980s named "Save Me" began to play. Leaning over the curved glass top of one of the music industry's first stereophonic jukeboxes, he sang along with Louise Mandrell. It was a good song, with a solid beat and message that really hit home for the lonely.

Just as his duet finished and his partner in song was being returned to her slot, the phone rang. Crossing quickly back to his office, he picked up the receiver just as it began its third ring.

"Hello, Evans here."

"Lije, it's Cathcart. The medal is from World War II. It is called a Narvick and was given to German flyers who served during actual aerial combat. From a collector's standpoint, it's not worth much. They're pretty common. If I might ask, why are you interested?"

"Wild goose chase, I think," he admitted. "There was another item the seller was offering that has some local connection, so I was just seeing if there was any way I could tie this medal to it."

"By your reaction I'm thinking you didn't."

Lije forced a laugh. "Probably not. The wild goose appears to still be loose."

"If I can be of any more help," the professor said, "just let me know."

"Will do. Thanks."

Hitting the Reply button in his email program, Lije typed in a couple of short questions for the eBay seller he knew only as Ralph. He didn't have to wait long: "The late man's name was William Schneider. He died on May 14. The initials inside the class ring from his estate are J. W."

Josephine "JoJo" Worle. Maybe his long-lost great-aunt. Lije began an online search for William Schneider of Sublette, Kansas. He found a one-line death notice in the *Liberal* newspaper and a short obituary posted by a Kansas funeral home: "William Schneider died May 14 at his farm outside of Sublette. He is survived by his brother, James. There will be no services and his remains are to be cremated and buried at a later date at the community cemetery."

Lije was surprised there was no listing of the man's birth year and no mention of a wife. He apparently didn't belong to a church or club either. The man's historical footprint was indeed small.

Jumping back to Ralph's eBay listings, Lije studied each one as carefully as a chef examining fresh produce. Every item fit into what one would expect to find in a bachelor-farmer's estate—except for the foreign coins, the medal, and the ring. The medal and ring had received no bids. Jumping headfirst into the game, Lije topped the one-dollar minimum bid on each item by a hundred dollars. In twelve hours, when the auctions ended, they would surely be his.

The 1936 Ash Flat Eagle yearbook they had discovered in Schleter's home lay on a table in his office next to the small love seat that had once been owned by his great-grandmother. That woman had been Josephine Worle's mother. He sat down and quickly moved through the pages until he found the senior class photos. He counted twenty-nine graduates. Flipping through the next few pages assured him that only one had the initials J. W.

Before she disappeared less than a year after the end of World War II, JoJo had been a pilot. His mother had shown him pictures of her standing beside combat aircraft. She had joined the WASP, earned her wings, and ferried bombers all over the United States. A dynamic force she surely was.

How had JoJo's class ring ended up in an apparently unmarried farmer's home in Sublette, Kansas?

As Lije played with a host of theories on the fate of his great-aunt, he suddenly realized his loneliness was gone. He could focus on something other than his own loss.

An answer to prayer that had happened only because someone hadn't typed in one letter in an eBay description.

27

Ivy Beals arrived at the office of the FAA in Arlington, Texas, just after four on a Friday afternoon. As he pulled into the half-empty staff parking lot, he decided more than a few employees must've gotten an early start on the weekend. The last time he'd visited the place, just three weeks before, every spot had been taken.

He pulled the keys from his black Mustang's ignition, donned a red Texas Tech baseball cap, and casually walked through the government agency's front door. He introduced himself to the male receptionist, who made a call. Beals was soon being led down a hall to the office of the assistant director.

"Mr. Beals," came the greeting from a redheaded, freckle-faced executive whose fair skin looked as though it had never seen the Texas sun. "I'm Brian Speers. Please, call me Brian. I'm so happy to make your acquaintance."

"Thanks for making time to see me on such short notice, Brian."

"No problem at all. Things are usually pretty slow on Friday afternoons in the summer anyway. We've got a lot of folks on vacation and a lot more who wish they were. So not much work is getting done today. Let me see, on the phone you told me you wanted to talk about my former boss. Know this: there were two men who made a really deep impact on my life. The first was my father, the second was Albert Klasser. A much-too-short life."

"That's a wonderful tribute," Beals said.

"I know you're a private investigator, but in this matter I have no idea what you could be looking into. Al's life was an open book and his death's a closed case."

"You're probably right," Beals admitted. "But I have to cover everything. Here's the gist of it. Omar Jones is going to be executed very soon. When he dies, we lose all chance of ever understanding why a man like Mr. Klasser and his wonderful family were killed. I'm trying to gather everything I can find out about motivation for the crime so that I can then go to Jones to see if he'll finally admit the real reason for his actions. I'm sure you're aware he has always claimed his innocence and therefore has never given us a chance to find out the truth. So I'm looking for anything the FBI and Texas Rangers might've overlooked back during their investigation."

With the admission of Jones' guilt seemingly established, Speers relaxed and nodded. The man was ready to talk freely.

"It was my understanding," he began, "that it was probably an ethnic dispute timed to coincide with 9/11. At least that's what the investigators told me when I was interviewed."

Beals nodded. "The state did feel that Jones killed a Jewish family with ties to the FAA because Jones knew about the impending attack and wanted to create a sense of horror and fear in the heartland. Don't forget, Jones had met one of the hijackers. But I've been wondering if there was more to it. In crimes like this, things are seldom that clear cut."

"Really?" Speers was obviously interested. "What could it be if not that? Seems pretty clear to me. In fact, one of those investigators working the case told me there were probably a dozen others like Jones around the country who were supposed to murder either FAA executives or prominent Jewish leaders. Supposedly all of them but Jones got cold feet. I even heard a couple of them were rounded up and taken to Gitmo."

"There are all kinds of stories out there," Beals said, "some wilder than others. But before Jones is killed by the state, I need to know which of those wild tales is true. So, if you don't mind, let me start by stating the obvious: I know that Klasser was a model employee, husband, father, and community leader."

"He was all that and more," Speers said.

"He seemed to have had no enemies. And no debts. Is that correct?"

"Yes."

"Then that leads me to wonder if there was something going on here at the FAA that might've sparked a motive for the murders. It seems that would be the only area left to explore."

"Hardly a path worth traveling." Speers sounded a bit defensive. "Let me assure you that everyone here loved him. He was a motivator, not a tyrant. He was the kind of person you looked forward to seeing, rather than tried to avoid. As I told you, he was my hero and mentor, and the same could be said by a dozen other men and women who worked with him."

"Brian, you misunderstand me. I know all that about him. He was a man we should all hold up as an example and role model. My question centers on a matter of simple observation. You were the one who was closest to him, his right-hand man. Did Mr. Klasser act any differently the last few weeks or days of his life than he had before?"

Speers leaned back in his desk chair, lost in thought, as if rolling through a Rolodex of filed memories. "That's kind of a strange question. As I think about it, I'm surprised no one asked me that back then. In fact, I guess because they had Jones dead to rights, they barely asked us anything."

"So does that mean you noticed nothing out of the ordinary?"

"Just the opposite. The day before he died, Al came in as high as a kite. He and I talked about the Disney World trip the family had just taken. He even showed me photos. I remember laughing later that morning when I saw him drinking coffee from a cup that sported mouse ears. He gave me a salute, a grin, and started singing the old *Mickey Mouse Club* song. He was on top of the world.

"Later that afternoon I saw him walking down the hall as if he were in a daze. I said something to him and he didn't even hear me."

"Any guesses on what might've upset him?"

"I asked him later that day if something was wrong. He just shrugged and told me not to worry. He then went into his office and closed the door. He never closed his door except when he was having a meeting. But that day he closed and locked the door. Every time I went by, it was closed. Very strange."

Speers paused as a pained expression crept up from his chin and seemed to paralyze his mouth. He picked up a cup and took a long swig of coffee, but even as he picked up his story, his eyes seemed to see things not in the room.

"The next morning he was even more withdrawn. He kept his office door closed and locked. I asked Betty Roman, his administrative assistant, what was happening, but the only thing she knew was that he was making phone calls."

"Did you ever find out what so changed his mood?"

"No. Betty said something about a telephone call that had really set him off. That seemed so strange, because he always took everything in stride. Even when we had to investigate a plane crash, he was the one who stayed calm and focused. So this was highly unusual. It was like he'd become someone else. Like he'd been suddenly possessed." He paused, shook his head, and added, "That must sound pretty strange to you."

"No, in my line of work I've seen violent and severe unexplained mood swings many times. Go ahead and finish your story and don't worry about how it sounds."

"At the time I was worried that maybe there were going to be some government-mandated cutbacks and he was concerned about having to let some people go. I found out that wasn't it. Later, after his death, I wrote it off as a sign of the trouble that was brewing between him and Jones."

Beals nodded. Both of the man's guesses seemed logical, but he figured both were wrong. He picked up with the next obvious query. "And Ms. Roman, does she still work here?"

"Yes, I can call and ask her to come in if you like."

"That would be wonderful."

As Speers dialed an extension, Beals studied the man's office. It was large, neat, well organized, and filled with memorabilia connected with the air industry. There were at least a dozen models of various commercial planes as well as countless books on the history of aviation. Yet the only thing besides family photos that seemed to reflect the real man rather than his position was a large color photo of Speers dressed in full World War II flight gear standing by a vintage B-17 Liberator bomber.

"Betty will be down here in a few moments," Speers said.

"I see you have an affection for B-17s." Beals pointed to the framed photo.

"My father flew one, *The Spirit of the South*, when he was in the service. Made a lot of runs over Germany and somehow survived. I helped restore that one in the photo and I'm one of the men who flies her to air shows all over the country. One of my big thrills was getting to take my father up a few years before he died. That flight, with him serving as copilot, opened the door to my hearing a lot of stories he'd never told me."

"So I guess you have a vast knowledge of B-17s."

He nodded. "They were incredible planes, but I love all the aircraft of that vintage. I've flown ships from all the major nations that fought in World War II, including some of the planes that ran missions attempting to stop my father and his group. Some folks love baseball, others gardening or classic cars. My passion is planes that participated in World War II."

Speers got up from his chair and walked over to the photo. "You know the B–17 was one of the few planes that could be literally blown apart and still stay in the air. There was one that—"

A knock on the door halted his impromptu lecture. Beals was

as disappointed as his host at the interruption. Both wanted to continue their flight to another time and another place. Yet events from World War II could not affect the Omar Jones case. It was time to return to the present.

"Come in," Speers said.

"Someone needs to see me?" a slim gray-haired woman said. She was attractive and at one time might well have been a beauty. Her dark-green eyes glowed like emeralds.

"Ivy Beals, this is Betty Roman."

The introductions done, Speers explained Beals' link to the Klasser case. "Mr. Beals is exploring the possibility that Albert's murder was motivated by something greater than simple ethnic problems connected with 9/11. I informed him that Al had been behaving a bit differently during his final days with us."

She said, "He acted very strange toward the end. It was like he knew something bad was about to happen."

"A premonition?" Beals asked.

"Don't think so. I believe it was a phone call that set him off."

"Do you know who called him?"

"Yes, it was his brother Joshua. I answered and spoke with Josh for a few moments as I waited for Al to get back to his desk. Josh was a great guy and visited us about once a year here at the office."

"Any idea what the call was about?"

"No, but the two were close; they spoke often. I just assumed it was a family matter, maybe an illness or something. What else could cause that kind of dramatic swing in emotions?"

Beals rose from his chair and walked over to a window. In the distance he saw three planes approaching the Dallas–Fort Worth airport. He turned back to the woman. "Brian told me that Mr. Klasser was still very distant the next morning."

"Not just the morning, but all day. He simply wasn't himself. He stayed on the phone. You know, in all the years he worked, he never left the office early, but that final day he did. He was out of here by three."

"Did he tell you why he was changing his routine?" Beals asked.

"Not in so many words, but he did tell me he had a meeting later that night and might be late coming in the next morning."

"And that was it?"

"Well, almost. Just before five he called and asked me to go into his office and retrieve a number from his files. He said he needed to change his appointment with Eric Johnson."

"And who is Mr. Johnson?"

"Actually, he was an FBI agent out of Dallas. The two of them had worked together a couple of times on matters where the FAA and FBI both had interests." Roman's voice trailed off. "I can't think of anything else that was unusual."

"I want to thank both of you," Beals said as he walked over to shake hands with Speers.

"Were we any help?" the man asked.

"Yes, I think so. You led me to someone else who might be able to give me some insights."

"You mean Mr. Johnson?" Roman asked.

"Yes. Wouldn't have a number on him would you?"

"No one does," she said. "He died in a car wreck a couple of hours after the Klassers were murdered."

28

BARTON HILLMAN LOOKED EVERY BIT THE SPORTSMAN as he stood in the flat-bottom bass boat. The fourteen-foot rig was driven by a sixty-horsepower Mercury motor. The ABI director had on canvas pants, a short-sleeved Hawaiian shirt, and an Arkansas Travelers baseball cap. In his hand was a Shakespeare "ugly stick" rod that sported a Bass Pro Johnny Morris reel. He appeared more than ready to fill his string with fish, but this Friday afternoon trip to the lake was all for show.

Usually Hillman was very particular about the type of bait he used. On this occasion he had chosen his lure by simply reaching into the box and picking up the first thing he saw. For the last hour he had tossed a mostly green Weber Champ toward a clump of brush along a place the old-timers called School Crossing. The yellow-tailed lure had accomplished just what he wanted—he hadn't had a single nibble. And rather than move on to a new spot, he kept tossing the Champ out and pulling it back in. To all who passed him that day, he looked very much like the focused fisherman, intent on hauling in a large mouth bass before the lake swallowed up the sun.

As the setting sun reflected a path on Lake Catherine, he scanned the water for other boats. All around him were fishermen anchored in their favorite spots. He could hear some of their conversations. A few discussed politics, others what lures worked in what seasons. One guy harped on a problem at the office. Voices traveled across the still water; he wished others realized this fact so a trip to the lake could be a more peaceful experience.

Today he ignored the talk and stared out at the place where the Champ had impacted the placid lake. He didn't look up when he heard the barely audible whisper of an electric trolling motor pushing a ten-foot aluminum boat past the edge of the cove to his right. Instead of checking out the new arrival, he pulled in his line, took off the Weber lure, put on a new hook, and reached into a small container by his foot. Retrieving a live cricket, he carefully slid it onto his hook before looking into his tackle box. On the bottom he found a large red-and-white bobber that was almost the size of a golf ball. He attached it to the line about eight feet above the bait. Then, while still sitting, he effortlessly cast the now hapless insect near a shallow pool about twenty feet from the tree line. Setting the reel's brake, he leaned back, his eyes glued to the bobber.

"What you fishing for?" a voice called out from the approaching boat.

Glancing over his shoulder, Hillman answered, "Right now, a nice fat bream. What about you?"

"Came out to do some night crappie fishing. I heard they'd been running about ten this week."

"I can't stay that late, but it sounds like fun."

"Hope so."

As the man drew within ten feet of Hillman's boat, the fisherman asked, "Do you have anything to drink? I forgot my cooler in my truck."

"Yeah, I've got some Cokes here. Would you like one?" A few minutes ago he'd listened in on a dozen different conversations while wanting to hear none of them. Now he was the one whose voice carried over the water.

"You don't mind, do you?" the stranger asked. "Don't want to take your last one."

"Naw. I'm about to head to the dock anyway."

"I'd feel better if you let me pay for it."

"No need to do that."

"Well, I won't take one if you don't let me give you something for it. I pay my way. Something my daddy taught me. And I'm mighty thirsty, so I'll pay."

Hillman laughed. "Okay, slip over here and I'll hand it to you, but you really don't have to give me anything."

The ABI director reached down and grabbed a canned drink from his cooler. As he did, the other fisherman cut his electric motor and extended his hand toward the director's boat.

"Here you go," Hillman said, carefully handing the soft drink to the stranger.

As he took the can, the man reached into his pocket and retrieved a dollar. "Hope this covers it."

"More than covers it. You need anything else?"

"No, I'm fine. Good luck with the bream."

Hillman nodded as the man restarted his motor and slipped quietly off toward the sunset. The director turned back toward the bank, his eyes again glued to the bobber. He remained a stoic study in patience for another fifteen minutes. Then, with no fanfare, he pulled in his line, started the motor, and turned his boat back toward the marina.

After guiding the fourteen-foot rig into his rented slip, he picked up his gear and walked across the dock to his truck. Noting that no one was around, he leaned against the bed, reached into his pocket, and pulled out the dollar. He studied it for a second, a smile crossing his face. The brief note, written in pencil on the bill, said: "It has been taken care of."

He slipped the dollar into his pocket. He set his tackle box and rod in the back of the truck, then opened the driver's door and got in. A blue canvas duffle was in the seat. Putting the truck in gear, he drove up to the private marina's checkpoint and waited for a guard to step from the small wooden building.

"Mr. Hillman," a young uniformed woman said. "I hope you had a good afternoon at the lake."

"It was perfect. You're looking beautiful today, Ashley. Is that a new hairstyle?"

"No, you normally see me with my baseball cap on. Too hot today."

"You got anything special planned for the weekend?" He reached into his pants pocket and retrieved the dollar bill. As he handed it to her, she glanced at the money and nodded.

"Mr. Hillman, something big's happening tomorrow night. I know that for sure." She smiled.

"That's good. You youngsters kick up your heels. I want my weekend to be calm and steady."

"You have a good one, sir."

"I will."

Slipping the Dodge into drive, he reached into the seat, grabbed the duffle bag, and tossed it out the window into Ashley's waiting arms. As he drove off he watched her in the rearview mirror. She pulled open the zipper and looked in, waved, and returned to her post.

Ten thousand dollars was a lot of money. Sometimes it was just the bait needed to make a big catch.

29

DIANA CURTIS LIMPED INTO LIJE EVANS' OFFICE. He was leaning against the corner of his desk. Behind him Heather Jameson sat almost catlike on the room's window seat.

"You didn't call," Jameson said, sounding like a mother scolding a child. "It's after five."

Curtis nodded. "Dropped my cell at the airport. Just got a replacement this morning. Was so busy cramming things into that short span of time, I had very little time to talk anyway. Looking back on the trip, I think I spent more time in planes and airports than I did working, eating, or sleeping. I lost five pounds. Picked up these incredibly dark circles under my eyes, so you can see how little of the eating and sleeping part I managed."

She dropped her briefcase on the floor and collapsed into one of the overstuffed leather chairs positioned in front of Lije's antique desk. As he watched, she folded up like a damp towel. For some reason, the fact that she was so completely done in amused him. He tried to hide the grin, but couldn't.

"What's so funny?" she demanded.

"You just don't look much like the always-in-control Diana Curtis I've come to know and appreciate. You appear a lot more like a woman who just survived the dollar-day basement-bargain sale at Macy's."

Jameson added, "Using the old cowboy vernacular, you look like you've been rode hard and put up wet."

"You have no idea." Curtis turned and shot a glare in the direction of the other woman.

Lije decided the horse comment had not been good. "Care to catch us up?" he asked.

The former ABI agent took a deep breath, allowing air to fill her lungs, then slowly expelled it. Pulling one leg up into the chair, she rested her chin on a knee. "It was anything but easy, but I've got some information. And you won't believe what I had to do to get it."

"That sounds interesting," he said. "Need something to drink?"

"A Dr. Pepper would be nice."

Lije retrieved a can from a small refrigerator behind his desk.

Curtis now had both legs up. She looked like a little kid—her hair in a ponytail, her face bare of any makeup, and dressed in jeans, a red T-shirt, and a pair of Nike cross-trainers. Yet when Lije looked into her eyes, he saw a different person. She appeared to have aged about a decade. Evidently the trip had taken a toll.

She remained quiet for a few moments, savoring the taste of the soft drink, then began her story.

"The archives had nothing on our man, but my time there wasn't a complete waste. A woman who worked there gave me a lead to another man who'd been looking for information on Henrick Bleicher. By the way, not only were all records of Henrick Bleicher being in the SS missing, but so were all the records concerning his life. From a legal standpoint, he was never born."

"You're kidding," Lije said.

Curtis took another swig. "The information I received led me to a nursing home just north of Berlin. I was able to question a former friend of Bleicher's there."

"Well," Jameson noted, "at least you found some kind of connection. Doesn't sound like this part of the job was too hard."

Curtis glared at the other woman for a moment. "Otto Mueller was old, very sick, and very hard to get to. In fact I was turned away at the front desk. I had a bit of help and I literally had to adopt a disguise to pull off my visit." She smiled. "In his room I found an English Bible with the same verses marked in Genesis as the one we found in Bleicher's hand when we opened the crate. Mueller informed me that Bleicher was a double agent. The best I could tell was that he'd infiltrated the SS and was feeding information to the Allies.

"A couple of months before the end of the war, Bleicher disappeared from Germany. Mueller told me he was trying to get to America with the intent of stopping the Nazis from using some kind of super weapon on us. As the weapon was never unleashed, Mueller seemed sure that Bleicher's final mission was a success."

Curtis paused and took another long draw of her soda. "Schleter was, at one time, Bleicher's driver. I have no idea which side he was playing for, but he and Bleicher were at least friends. For them to end up together is not that big a stretch."

Lije rose from his desk and walked over to the window. There were several rose bushes blooming across the alley, so many vibrant colors in such a limited space. The problem with having so many different kinds of flowers in one small spot was that sometimes the colors all blended together. It was hard to see the beauty of each new rose. That was also the problem with all the information they had uncovered. Everything just kind of blended together without anything jumping out. Lots of stuff, but nothing important. Nothing that stood out.

Diana's trip to Germany had cleared up one puzzling element. At least they knew why two Germans finding each other in the middle of the Arkansas Ozarks was not as far-fetched as it had once sounded. And, if Curtis was right, the man in the crate might well have been a hero.

But here was where the colors all ran together again. If Bleicher had succeeded, then why was he shot? And did that make Schleter a member of the firing squad? If so, then how was Schleter involved, and what had he hidden on Swope's Ridge that was so important?

He walked back over to the chair beside Curtis and sat down. "Did you find out anything about this super weapon?"

"There's a legend that was used to scare children," she explained. "It was about a boat called the Ark of Death. Mueller seemed to think that our man was involved in sinking it before it could unleash its terror on the United States."

"Ark of Death?" Jameson asked.

"Yes, that's it. I know it sounds funny, but to Mueller just the thought of it surviving was scary. You should've seen his face when he spoke of it. It was as if he had seen the devil himself."

"So," Lije cut in, "anything else? Anyone else? Do you have any more information on this Ark of Death? Where we can go to find out more about the legend?"

"No. It seems we're the only ones who care about Bleicher, the Ark of Death, and how all of this ties to something hidden on Swope's Ridge."

"No one else?" Lije asked.

"I met an Englishman." Her voice drifted off. "He gave me a few clues, but he can't tell us any more than he already has."

"You sure?" Jameson asked.

"Positive."

Lije had hoped for much more. He wanted documents to review and photos to examine. Instead he'd been told about a legend that was probably nothing more than myth. The fact that Curtis had found no thread to anyone else interested in Bleicher was disappointing. This meant the body they'd found probably had nothing to do with Kaitlyn. They were no closer to finding answers to her death. And now, where else could they look? Curtis hadn't come back with any leads that pointed them in a new direction.

He sighed and stood up. Without a word, he left the room, walked through the reception area, and stepped out into the late afternoon air. After unceremoniously plopping down on one of the city's wooden benches, he watched the last of the farmers who'd been selling produce near the courthouse pack up and head home. In three hours the city square would again come to life as musicians from all over the county brought their instruments to town for the weekly Saturday-night singing. Until then, the squirrels would hunt through the grass for anything the farmers had left behind.

This was small-town life. Normally he loved just soaking it in, but now it offered no solace. What he needed were answers.

30

THE LAST OF THE FARMERS HAD JUST DRIVEN OFF when Lije's law partner joined him on the park bench. Jameson allowed her eyes to follow Lije's to the courthouse lawn.

"The white one's still there," he pointed out.

"The albino squirrel?" She seemed genuinely shocked. "You mean he's being accepted by the others?"

"More than accepted. This guy now appears to be in charge. I guess sometimes it's good to be different." He turned to face her. "What do you think?"

"The information's solid, but where does it get us? Knowing who the body is, that's good. Knowing that he was not really a member of the SS takes a bit of the 'ick' factor out. But I can't see that it helps us uncover why the Ridge is so important to the people who tried to kill you. Something's missing."

"I know, but we deal with what we have. Right now we have no more."

"Lije, I think Curtis is holding out on us."

He was shocked. What did Heather mean? Curtis was the one who had come the closest to getting hurt or killed. She seemed to be the member of the team who had the most to fear. She had voluntarily gone to Germany and obviously worked hard looking for answers. She'd even found a few. So why did his partner think the former ABI agent was withholding information? "You have reasons behind your hunch?"

Jameson shrugged. "I don't trust her. I don't think she's on our side. I just feel she's hiding something."

He had sensed a growing animosity between the two. They also appeared to be in competition to be top dog in the investigation. If things were going to work, these two needed to lay aside their differences and quit worrying about pecking order.

"Cut her some slack and give her some room. She'll prove herself." He looked at her, but her eyes were on the squirrels frolicking across the street. Sensing she wasn't going to answer, he rose from the bench and reentered the office. "Diana, you want to get something to eat?"

"Sure." It seemed the mere mention of food had revved her motor. She wandered into the reception area, looking as if she was raring to go. "I need to get my purse out of my car."

Jameson, who was standing at the front door, said, "I'll get it."

"Naw," Curtis replied. "The car's locked. Why don't you two close things up here. Maybe over dinner you can tell me how the Jones case is going. I heard McGee is hard at work on it. Can't believe he tracked that guy down in Waco."

Her words had barely cleared her mouth when Lije's cell rang. He pulled the phone from his pocket, glanced at the screen, and said, "Speaking of the devil. Hey, Kent."

Lije listened, then nodded. "I understand. Sounds like a good lead. Let us know if it pans out."

He paused, holding his left hand in the air to signal the women to wait for a moment. "Listen, Diana's here. Bleicher was a double agent, but I guess she already told you that."

Lije glanced back toward the investigator. "Really. Well, nothing that has to be discussed tonight. I'll catch you up when you get back to the hills. Keep me informed."

He closed his phone. "I'm ready if you all are. Want to go to Fred's Fish House?"

"That'd be great," Curtis said. "Let me get my purse."

She walked outside, and Lije and Heather began to flip off the lights in the century-old stone building. Lije had just checked the back door and walked into his office when an explosion shook the building. He was knocked into a wall and slid to the floor. He was sure the ceiling, which now had jagged cracks in it, would fall down on him at any moment.

31

DUST FILTERED DOWN FROM THE CEILING AS LIJE screamed, "Heather, you okay?"

An old light fixture was swinging and a pen rolled off his desk. He pulled himself to his feet. Then the smell of smoke hit him and he rushed out toward the front of his office.

Heather was in the hallway. The two raced through the reception area and stopped just a few feet from the room's plate-glass windows. Curtis's Ford Focus was engulfed in flames. Whatever had ripped through the car had done so with such great force that no one in or near the vehicle could have survived. The doors and hood had been blown off and the glass in every window was shattered.

"My Lord," Jameson whispered.

"Don't think this was his work," Lije muttered.

He heard a siren. Someone had already called 911.

"Diana!" he said. She'd been lucky two other times; the bullets had missed. But this time, whoever wanted her dead had succeeded. What did she know that had cost the woman her life?

Lije stepped out of his office just as the first fire truck rounded the corner of the square. Two more followed. A unit from the local police force was next. But the lawyer's eyes were drawn to the flames. The vehicle had all but melted. Metal, vinyl, glass, and leather had been transformed into an almost indistinguishable mass.

As the first blast of water hit what had once been a car, black smoke pushed toward the office. Covering his face with his arm, Lije struggled to stay on the raised sidewalk. Still, the combination of heat and smoke was about to drive him inside when he heard someone coughing to his right. He glanced over, expecting to see Jameson. Instead, he saw Diana Curtis leaning against the front wall of his office.

She was alive? How?

A bit of overspray from a fireman's hose hit him. He raced over to Curtis, grabbed her arm, and yanked her through his front door. Slamming the door shut to keep out the smoke and smell, he stared at her. "I thought you were in the car."

She didn't answer.

"Heather, get me some water," he barked as he led Curtis to a chair. "Okay, kid, how did you get out of this with your life?"

She looked up into his gray eyes and shook her head.

"Here you go," Jameson announced as she handed Diana a cold bottle of Ozarka Spring Water.

Curtis nodded, took the plastic container, and lifted it to her mouth. As she drank, she peeked up at Lije.

"How did you get out?" Jameson demanded.

"I wasn't in the car," Diana whispered, her eyes never leaving Lije's. "I unlocked the door, grabbed my purse, and the wind caught a newspaper that was on the front seat and blew it out into the street. I ran to get it. A few seconds later it sounded as if the whole town had exploded. The force knocked me to the ground and I crawled over to the sidewalk."

"You're lucky," Lije noted.

He walked back toward the front window. The firemen had knocked out the flames. But no amount of water could wash away the questions now burning in his mind. Why? Why did someone need her dead? Did this tie in to the body on the ridge? Was this the reason the Bible verses were underlined? How could there be so many clues and so few answers? He was so consumed in thought he didn't notice Jameson walk up beside him.

"They always just barely miss," she whispered.

"What?"

"They always just barely miss her."

"Yeah. She's a lucky one, all right. If it hadn't been for the wind ..." Glancing back over at Curtis, he smiled. She had more lives than any cat he'd ever known.

"Lije," Jameson said.

He turned to face Heather. "What is it?"

His partner leaned closer and whispered, "What did Kent tell you that shocked you a little?"

"What do you mean? I don't recall anything."

"You answered something he said with the word 'Really.'"

Had he said that? What had set it off? McGee hadn't given him anything new on the case. In fact he was at a dead end. Oh, yeah, now he remembered. Bending, he whispered to Jameson, "McGee wanted to know what Curtis had found out about Bleicher. Said he hadn't talked to her since her return to the States."

Jameson nodded. "Then how did she know about Kent working so hard on the Jones case? And finding the guy in Waco."

Lije turned back toward Curtis. No one knew ... except ...

He glanced down at her jeans. There was no dirt on the knees. If she had been knocked down by the blast and crawled ...

32

JANIE DAVIES WAS UP BY SIX-THIRTY ON SUNDAY. After feeding Harlow, the smooth-coat collie she'd named after her favorite classic film star, the woman drained a glass of orange juice and slipped into her workout gear. She warmed up by stretching and doing some light weight-lifting, then hit the treadmill for an hour.

She'd set a goal of running in a marathon before Christmas. She'd convinced Heather Jameson to team up for the roadwork. The duo was doing at least two ten-mile runs a week up and down the hills surrounding Salem. Just breathing in the fresh air, feeling her strength growing with each step, challenging her body, made the runs one of the most exhilarating experiences she'd ever known. Yet even as Janie reveled in them, she knew her partner dreaded each day.

Their first real test would be a half marathon in Little Rock a month away. Janie was ready, but Jameson still needed to push herself. Because the blind woman could run only as fast as the sighted person leading her down the course, she prayed the lawyer was ready to kick her training up a notch.

After her indoor workout, Janie showered and got ready for church. She usually caught a ride with her neighbor Marge, a widowed teacher who lived down the block, but she was out of town, so Lije was picking her up. She tapped the top of the clock that sat beside her bed and heard "Nine-thirty-five a.m." She still had time for a bowl of cereal and a banana.

She was just finishing her Special K when she heard the doorbell. Putting the bowl in the sink, she navigated through her two-bedroom home to the front door.

"You're early," she said, then added, "At least for you you're early."

"And how did you know it was me?" Lije asked.

She could hear the curiosity dripping from his voice. "Do we have to play this game again?" She laughed.

"Yes. I want to know. I really want to develop your skill."

She ignored his need to fully understand her. After all, a magician didn't give away secrets. She enjoyed that the team thought there was a mysterious power only she had harnessed. It gave her a leg up and it meant each of them listened when she spoke.

"You be good while we're gone, Harlow." Janie picked up her Braille Bible and stepped out of the house. "Not many clouds." She walked down the sidewalk toward the driveway. Stopping, she turned and asked, "Did you park where you were supposed to or are you playing with me again today? Marge is must nicer than you are. I never walk into the front fender of a car when she picks me up."

"I hit my mark."

Smiling, Janie confidently marched to the driveway, took a side step to the left, six more steps, then a right and four more strides before reaching down and grabbing the passenger door handle. She grinned. "Lije Evans, I've got you pretty well trained."

They both buckled up and Lije backed the car down the driveway. Again he prodded, "How did you know it was me?"

Janie offered her quirky smile. "This is really getting old now, but here it goes. For starters, it's the car. You drove the Prius. When you drive it, there's no sound other than the tires rolling on the driveway. Anyone else who picks me up would still have a car whose gas engine was running, but since yours is a hybrid, it's almost completely silent.

"Next, you carefully closed your door, trying so hard not to make any noise. Who else who visits me does that? You really are predictable. It's the same way at the office. You always try to sneak up on me, but I can hear you a mile away. All of your shoes have telltale nuances. The squeak one pair makes drives me up a wall, and you've probably never even noticed it.

"Then there's Harlow. If it'd been a stranger, she'd have let me know. So you passed the dog test. Only a few people do that. So I was sure it was you.

"But the final sign was evident when I went to the door. I could smell your Old Spice aftershave. You're probably the last person in Fulton County who still wears that. What's wrong with one of the newer brands like Gray Flannel?"

"I've got to fine tune my senses more," he said. "That's amazing. Oh, and I like Old Spice—my dad wore it and my grandfather wore it."

"And if they'd drive the '36 Cord off a cliff, would you do that too? I don't think so." Janie smiled. "It might be months away, but I know what I'm getting you for Christmas, and you'd better wear it. Now, what's wrong with your sense of direction? We should've turned right at the last stop and we turned left."

"I've got to stop by the office. In the confusion after Curtis's car being bombed, I left something I need."

"Have you talked with her this morning?"

"Actually, no. She told us last night she was going to sleep in this morning. Wouldn't doubt she sleeps the day through. She was pretty wrung out." He pulled in and parked. "We're here, but I guess I didn't need to tell you that. You want to come in?"

"No, I'll wait in the car. Just don't be too long. I hate to be late for Sunday school."

As Lije opened the car door, Janie smelled the stench of burned rubber that still lingered in the morning air. She had heard the explosion at home, but it had been more than two hours before Lije called and she found out what had happened. He'd told her Curtis had been lucky, but Janie didn't believe in luck. There was a reason the woman hadn't been blown to bits. In fact, when you slice away all the camouflage that most people see, there were always obvious reasons why things happened.

"Got it," Lije announced as he got back in the car.

"Got what?"

"My old Bible. I haven't looked at it in years because I use a more modern translation now, but this one has a whole section that goes into great detail concerning the history of the King James edition. That's what we're discussing in my class today."

"Are you teaching?"

"No," he admitted as he made the left turn onto 62.

"Then you grabbed it to appear smart. You're trying to show off your biblical knowledge, when all you'll be doing is pulling facts from the pages in front of you. That's cheating, you know."

His silence told her she was right. That was good. She'd been told Lije had once had a fun side to him. In the days she'd known him, that side had rarely appeared. The fact that it was now presenting itself in little ways, like the need to win the classroom battle of knowledge or his trying to sneak by her, meant he was healing. Still, until they found all the answers to what had happened on Farraday Road, the wounds would continue to bleed into everything he did. They could be covered from time to time, but underneath they were still there and seeping.

"You singing in the choir today?" he asked.

"Actually, no," Janie replied. "They're doing a special and I missed practice when we went to Texas. So I'll be out front today in row three. You're welcome to join me. Or you can be stuck up and sit in your normal spot in the last row."

He didn't answer until they arrived at church. "I'll be there."

Her class, filled with young men and women her age, went pretty much like it always did. They laughed some, talked of the explosion on the square, and even took a few minutes to go through the material provided for class. As they were about to dismiss, a young mother asked for prayer, so Janie was a bit late getting to her pew. She smelled the Old Spice before she took her seat.

Leaning his way she asked, "Did you wow them with your vast knowledge of King James and the history of his translation of the Bible?"

"No," Lije admitted. "I picked up the wrong Bible."

"How'd you do that?"

"I pulled mine off the shelf, put it on my desk to look for a pen, picked it back up, and came out to the car. But what I picked up off my desk was not my Bible; it was Bleicher's. I sat there like a bump on a log as others expounded on history. I looked ignorant."

"That's rich," she whispered as the organ began to play.

Four songs and two prayers later, the Reverend John Hodges began his message. Janie leaned back in the padded pew, letting her right hand fall to the cushion. It landed on the Bible that Lije had mistakenly brought to the service. Her fingers traced the old leather cover, feeling the still stiff edges and noting the embossed words that declared this book to be the "Holy Bible." Even she could read that.

Picking it up, she took in its musty odor. Then as she listened to the preacher's voice, she carefully turned the pages until she found the seventh chapter of Genesis. She knew it had to be the seventh chapter because of the way the underlined section had created slight indentations in the thin paper. She'd thought a lot about these verses, even reading them again and again in her Braille edition, and yet, for a change, she saw nothing that others didn't see. Why was this passage so important that two men had each chosen to highlight it? The passage didn't point out a location or a person. It didn't appear to be a code. What did it mean?

Now on a mission, she carefully and quickly worked her way through the remainder of the German's Bible, feeling each page for anything unusual that the others might have missed. Each time she came to one of the large satin ribbons once used as bookmarks, she laid it in her lap. She found four page markers.

She could tell the pastor was getting into the last five minutes of his message; his words always came out more quickly, as if he was pushing down on the gas pedal, gunning for home. All around her folks rustled in their bulletins to find the number of the closing hymn. She still had more time to kill.

Janie placed the Bible back on the pew and picked up a ribbon. Since childhood, she had never been good at sitting perfectly still. She always fidgeted. When she lost her sight and her fingers took on an even greater importance, they were hardly ever at rest. She began to carefully examine the ribbon, occupying her time as she counted down the last few minutes of the service.

One side was nothing but satin. The other had words pressed into it. She ran her finger over the letters. She'd found out what they said at the German's house when Jameson read them aloud: "Koffman Funeral Home" and "We're here to serve you." They hadn't yet figured out where the funeral home had been located. It might just be a location Bleicher had once visited. Still, she couldn't leave the ribbons alone. She had to "look" at them for herself.

The first three ribbons all felt the same. There was nothing to differentiate one from the next. After she had explored each one, she put it back in the Bible. She'd just picked up the fourth vintage page marker when the pastor surprised everyone by wrapping things up and asking everyone to stand. After a short prayer and three verses of "Softly and Tenderly," the service ended.

Lije and Janie walked down the center aisle, chatting with church members, some of whom asked about the blast outside the office, until they finally worked their way to the car. Then it was on to lunch at Sonny Burns' Barbeque. During their meal, Lije changed the subject from food to something of a much different nature. "Give me your impression of Diana."

The former ABI agent was a part of the team, a woman who had uncovered valuable information in Germany. Janie wondered why Lije now asked that question. "Bright, focused, and driven would be how I'd start. She must be really attractive too. I can hear that."

"You can hear attractiveness?" Lije asked. This time she heard confusion in his voice.

"In a way, yeah. When she's in a room, any man who comes in always takes a deep breath before talking. I don't imagine he's doing that because he thinks she's brilliant. So that pause tells me he's checking her out. She gets checked out a lot."

"When did you notice that?"

"Remember a couple of months ago when she dropped by the office?"

"She brought me some papers concerning our case."

"Well, we suddenly had a huge influx of visitors that morning, and all of them were male. It was so bad I could actually feel their leering eyes."

She could hear Lije's smile in his answer. "Sure they weren't looking at you?"

She grinned. Blind or not, she knew she was cute and she drew attention. But Curtis took men's breath away. That put her on a completely different level. "Lije, what are you really asking? Tell me what you're looking for."

"Do you trust Diana?"

"What triggered this? Did something happen?"

"Sometimes I sense Diana's not giving me the whole story," Lije said.

"She's not. We all hold back things. That's part of being human. We're scared to really reveal the things that make us seem weak. How often do you talk about Kaitlyn anymore?"

He didn't reply.

"Rarely," she continued. "And you don't because it tears you and exposes the hole in your heart and your life. Suddenly you're not this macho guy; you're a man who breaks. No one likes to break. I know you well enough to know you don't want us to see that part of you, so you avoid talking about the one thing that you feel most strongly about."

She paused, looked up, her sightless blue eyes trying to find and lock onto his. After she was sure she had his full attention, she asked, "Did you ever have a hero who really disappointed you?"

"Yeah, Pete Rose."

"For me it was my cousin. He's an incredible person—great businessman, super father, wonderful friend. He's involved in so many different charities. He'd always been so good to his wife. Then I found out he was having an affair with an old flame from his college days. It cut me to the bone."

She let her head drop, as if looking at the last part of her sandwich, and added, "But I still want to believe in him. I still know that he'd do anything for me. So because he was my hero, there's a lot of room for forgiveness and an instinct to still trust him. Just like, deep inside, you want to believe that Pete Rose can somehow come clean and be redeemed."

Lifting her head, she again directed what would've been her gaze at the man on the other side of the table. "The ABI was Diana's life. She doesn't want to reveal the flaws she now knows are a part of the organization. She still wants to believe in Hillman, even after everything he's done. Hey, Heather wants to believe her alcoholic dad will quit drinking and get his life together. So Diana and Heather are both dealing with the pain of broken trust. They're a lot alike. Because what they're trying to cover up is similar, they know each other's weaknesses. They look at each other and see themselves. You're not blind, Lije, surely you can see that."

"There's more to this than you know."

"There's more to most things than I know. If you really want my honest observations, then give me the rest of the story."

"Diana told us something last night that she shouldn't have known. It was something only those of us who went to Texas know. She knows McGee is hard at work on the Jones case, but she hadn't talked to any of us or to McGee during the time she was gone."

"Did you ask her how she knew about it?"

"No."

"Might start there. She still has contacts beyond the ones we know. One of those might've told her. Don't believe the worst until you have real proof."

Lije was silent.

"Are you nodding yes or shaking your head no?"

"What's the sign for conflicted?"

"If you're blind, there isn't one unless you talk."

"Okay, I'm conflicted and confused," he admitted.

"Diana's valuable. She brought back key information. You told me that last night on the phone."

"So we trust her. I understand."

"Maybe. What do you know about taming a mountain lion?"

"Nothing."

"It can't be done," Janie said. "They often seem like they're gentle, but you can never fully trust them. At heart, they're still wild and at any moment they might turn on you."

"What are you saying?"

"Only this, that animals, even wild ones, are much more predictable than people."

"I think I get your point."

He got up and let his hand linger on her cheek for a moment.

In that moment she felt him smile. He was innocent in a lot of ways. There was a charm in that.

33

Only after Lije dropped Janie off at her home did she realize she had something that belonged to him. She'd stuffed the fourth ribbon into her suit pocket during the invitation hymn and never returned it to Bleicher's Bible. No one thought the ribbons were important, so she didn't bother calling her boss. Instead she placed the page marker on her dresser, changed clothes, fed Harlow, and switched on the radio.

A couple of hours later, she searched the top of the dresser for a brush and again touched the ribbon's edge. Her fingers paused. Something was different. Something didn't feel right. As she lightly ran her index finger along the edge of the antique bookmarker, she noted tiny stitching. The others didn't have this. Picking it up, she thought back to the ones she'd examined in church. Though none of them weighed hardly anything, this one seemed heavier. Her perceptive fingers also told her it was thicker. She wished she had one of the others for comparison.

Moving to a chair, she examined it closely. The writing was the same as the others in every way but one. This ribbon had words on both sides. That, combined with the stitching, told her that she was actually holding two ribbons that had been stitched together. Why would anyone go to this much work? There had to be a reason, but what was it?

Placing the bookmarker on an end table, she allowed her hand to brush across the satin. About an inch from the top she detected a subtle rise. Her fingers stayed at the level until about a half an inch from the bottom of the ribbon. Her bright unseeing eyes lit up. The ribbon was a hiding place. Why not? Who would look inside an innocuous page marker?

Excited, she grabbed her sewing kit and took out a thread ripper, then carried everything to the dining room table. Once seated, she found an edge and slipped the blade into the almost invisible seam. Working with great precision, making sure she didn't harm the two ribbons or whatever was hidden between them, she moved from the top to the bottom of the marker. After she had removed all the side stitching, she slipped her finger between the two pieces of satin. There it was, a thin piece of paper she judged was about two inches by four inches.

She carefully pulled out the paper and placed it on the table, then ran her fingers over both sides of it. It was onionskin. Someone had written something on just one side. They must've been in a hurry because they'd pushed hard with what she thought was a lead pencil. The marks seemed too wide for a pen. The impressions she could feel weren't deep enough for her to read with her fingers. What did it say? She couldn't see and Harlow, who was resting her head in Janie's lap, couldn't read.

Having done as much as she could, she slipped the paper into her Braille copy of *To Kill a Mockingbird* and placed the book on a shelf.

"Harlow, this is going to make someone we know very happy." She headed for the phone, but her dialing was interrupted by the sound of a car pulling into her driveway. She touched the top of a table clock. "Three fifty-five p.m."

It had to be Heather. They were supposed to go for a long run. "Harlow, I'm literally running late."

Janie moved over to the door and opened it just as her visitor knocked. "I got caught up in a project," Janie said. "Give me a second and I'll get changed."

"Sure," Jameson said as she walked in. "What were you working on?"

Janie opened her mouth, but remembering her advice to Lije, the words caught in her throat. "Kind of hard to explain to someone who's not blind."

"Okay, I'll just sit down and wait for you. I'm not looking forward to the hills today. Hope you have lots of cold water."

"Got some yesterday at the store," Janie said as she left the room.

"Tell me again," Jameson moaned, "why our doing a marathon will make us better people."

"Trust me, it'll change your life."

"Yeah, if I live through it."

As Janie slipped off her blouse, the obvious hit her. Jameson could read the note and she'd know what she'd found. Why not let her see it? It wasn't that she didn't trust the woman. So what was holding her back? She wanted to find out what was on the paper, so why not ask for help?

Maybe she was afraid to reveal her weakness. No, surely it wasn't that. She might be blind, but she wasn't weak and she definitely wasn't scared.

No, this was Lije's mystery. It had to be Lije who saw it first. She'd call him later this evening or just wait until tomorrow and give it to him at the office. The paper had been hidden for more than six decades. A few more hours or even a day wouldn't matter.

Now it was time to run, to really run.

34

IVY BEALS WATCHED AS JOSHUA KLASSER GOT OFF THE elevator in the lobby of the North American Bank Tower. Wearing a Brooks Brothers suit, white shirt, and conservative gray-striped tie, Klasser looked every bit his title—investment counselor for the European Limited Money Group in Washington, D.C. His corner office on the fourteenth floor cemented his status as a financial wizard. He even had his name spelled out in huge gold letters on the door. Yet thanks to his experience in the CIA, Beals knew the office and title were a cover. The few deals Klasser pulled off were just for show. He had much more important investments to oversee, and banking had nothing to do with it.

For more than two decades, this man had been an operative in Israel's premier intelligence agency. This was a fact Beals would've never known if, many years before, he had not viewed classified intelligence information on industrial spying in the petroleum industry. The report, given to him by his superior, contained some prime information, including one tidbit that could've undermined much of the intelligence gathering in the entire region. The CIA supervising agent had failed to remove the name of the Israeli contact for the operation. Beals had immediately corrected the oversight so no one else in his unit learned that name, and saved the value of the covert operator. Yet even though he had blocked it out on the paper, he hadn't wiped the information from his mind. Like money in a cookie jar, he'd simply squirreled it away for a rainy day. Now it was time to put that old card into play.

"Joshua Klasser," Beals announced as he approached the man who hurried through the ornate granite-filled three-story lobby.

Klasser stopped just short of the front doors, adjusted his glasses, and studied the powerfully built bald man. "You have me at a disadvantage. You seem to know me, but I am afraid I do not know you."

Klasser looked nothing like an officer in the feared Mossad. If anything, he resembled a jeweler. His accent was slight but apparent enough to give away his roots and heritage. The fact that he refrained from employing contractions revealed that English wasn't his primary language. Yet, this, along with the glint in his brown eyes, the slight hook in his nose, and his small stature, truly made his cover believable.

"My name is Ivy Beals."

"Well, Mr. Beals, if you will call my secretary in the morning and make an appointment, perhaps I can squeeze you in later this week. Today would be impossible. I am leaving for an appointment, and I am not coming back to the office until tomorrow." He smiled. "And, as I am being transferred back to our Middle East office in Tel Aviv in a week, it might be best if you spoke with one of our other advisers. Might I suggest Marie Felts. She is bright, well read, has great instincts."

"No, it's you I need to speak with."

Klasser took a step to his left and waved. "Then call my office and set something up for later in the week."

Beals followed the man out the door and into the bright morning sun. Klasser headed toward a parking garage. Just before entering, he stopped and slowly turned back to face his stalker.

"I am not used to having a shadow. If you persist, I will call security."

"Actually," Beals said, "you are much more used to being the shadow."

Klasser shrugged. "You seem to be a strange man who has equally strange ideas. I am a wealth manager. You must have me mistaken for someone else. Now leave me be." After waving his hand and rolling his eyes, he turned and continued his trek into the garage. Beals allowed him five steps.

"The Sykes report. You wrote it when assigned to Aman. The detailed information you and your agents gathered revealed the identities of five Saudis who were actually in the United States working for the big oil companies but were also spying for the Chinese. Thanks to your investigation, false information was fed to those operatives and they were disgraced. It was a clean job that required no blood."

Klasser glanced over his shoulder but kept walking. "I have no idea what you are talking about."

"By this afternoon, you will have requested and received a complete file on me. You'll know what I did while I was in the agency and you'll find out how I found out about you. You should also know that I was the one who covered the mistake that would've outed you to the entire world. If I hadn't done so, you would have become nothing more than a desk jockey. Or maybe, if the wrong people had found out first, not be breathing today. We will talk. The question becomes, will it be now or later?"

Satisfied with his performance, Beals turned and casually strolled out of the garage. He was halfway across a quiet city park, two full blocks away from the garage, when he felt a hand on his shoulder. It was much larger than Klasser's. Experience told him not to turn around.

"You're either very bold or very stupid," a deep voice informed him.

Still looking straight ahead, the detective nodded. "I'm neither."

"If what you said is true, why do you think I won't kill you?"

"NHS."

"NHS?"

"Not his style," Beals explained.

"You want to talk to Klasser. Is this about the old report?"

"No. Something potentially much better than that."

"Do you see that bench about fifty feet to your right?"

"Yes."

"Go to it and sit on the far end. He'll join you in a few minutes. Don't look at him when he speaks. Do you understand?"

Beals nodded and, when he felt the hand slip from his shoulder, made his way toward the bench. Spotting a *Washington Post* on top of a trashcan, he picked it up and, after shaking off a few peanut hulls, took a seat. He'd completed three stories on the front page when Klasser joined him. Neither spoke for five more minutes. Beals continued reading while the other man tossed peanuts to a very interested squirrel.

"You said your name is Beals," Klasser began, pulling a file folder from his briefcase and pretending to read.

"Your memory has long served you very well."

"You are not with the CIA?"

"Left ten years ago." Noting a woman walking her large white poodle, he turned back to his newspaper. Neither man spoke until she'd passed.

"Then if you are not with the CIA, why seek me out now?"

"It's about your brother. I work for an Arkansas-based attorney who's looking into the matter of his death. I just want to know why your brother was killed."

Setting the file in his lap, Klasser flipped a page. "Everyone has read the story. It was a hate crime, pure and simple. We Jews have been targets for centuries. You know that. Even your former agency has been guilty from time to time of going after us simply because of our ethnic background. Let us not go into what Richard Nixon said about us."

Beals turned to page three of the paper, casually glancing in both directions before continuing. "Do you believe it was only a hate crime?"

"Why not? Have you read the case files?"

"Yes."

"Then you know why I would not question the verdict."

The detective pressed on. "You called your brother the day before he was murdered."

Klasser nodded.

"That was not in the files. I found it strange that the FBI and others wouldn't have dug deeper. I know the folks who worked with your brother would have loved to talk. How do you think I knew of the call, yet the investigating agencies missed it?"

"Knowing of my call would only have put another noose around Jones' neck. One noose was sufficient."

"Meaning you weren't going to blow your cover if the case was airtight."

"I would not have blown my cover even if it had allowed Jones to walk out of prison. Some things are more important than family. You see, for me my country is my family too. Serving my country is my life."

Beals shifted slightly to his right and folded the newspaper to the next page. Then, after he was sure no one was watching, said, "Your call upset your brother. Your calls had never upset him before."

Still pretending to read the report, Klasser said, "Brothers often have disputes. It is as old as time itself. Have you heard of Cain and Abel?"

Beals didn't need a history lesson. "Disputes that require one of the brothers to leave work early, breaking a routine that he never broke before? Disputes that required making a late-night appointment with an FBI agent? An agent who died later that very night?"

"What is your point?" Klasser's tone became terse.

Beals put down the front section and picked up the sports section. "You told your brother something that was very important. What you told him led to his death. This was no simple hate crime. There was no conspiracy to kill Jewish American families of FAA employees to stir up fear in this country. That was a myth spun by my government to help push an agenda to consolidate power in the hands of the executive branch.

"Even if the FBI doesn't care, I care. I want to know what you told Albert on September 10 that cost him his life."

35

KLASSER'S TONE REMAINED STEADY AND ASSERTIVE. "You are fishing and I do not understand why. Jones killed four members of my family. He was caught. Why he did it is no longer important as he will soon die. The score will be settled."

"Then what does it hurt to tell me what you told Albert that sent him to Eric Johnson?"

Klasser was blunt. "You know the answer."

"Ah, yes, national security." Beals laughed. "I saved your skin once. You're still undercover and breathing, thanks to me."

"Who screwed up?" Klasser asked. "How did you know my name?"

"Vanderberg gave me the report. He failed to black out your name in one place. I got rid of it."

"Vanderberg is a fool."

"No argument there."

"Still, your protecting me is no reason for me to give you the information you seek. You know that as well as I do. You were doing your job, covering the rather large aft section of an idiot."

"Joshua, I wouldn't care a thing about what you told Albert except the man I work for is convinced Omar Jones was framed."

Klasser didn't answer. Instead he pulled out a Blackberry and looked at the screen. "So your boss, Kent McGee, has no problem ignoring DNA, fingerprints, and the story of a witness who cannot forget."

Beals was amused. How much more did Klasser already know about him? "I'm betting you could plant evidence like that in less than a minute."

Klasser smiled. "It might take a bit longer."

Seeing the first dent in the man's armor, Beals pushed on. "Did you go to the trial?"

"No, my brothers did, but I did not."

"What kept you away? Guilt?"

Klasser went mute and looked more intently at the report he held in his hands. When he finally answered, he turned his head and stared at his adversary. "Yes, I did not want to face that my information led to his death. Are you satisfied?"

"No." Beals looked down and acted as if he was reading a story on the Washington Redskins dropping another game. "I'm not here to drag you through old memories for the purpose of opening wounds. I need information in case Jones is innocent. I don't want to see another innocent man die like your brother, his wife, and their children did. They were all innocent. In fact, I'm guessing that your brother's actions on the day he died, if he had gotten to finish them, would've been considered heroic—not just by your country but by mine too."

Beals hoped his words had stunned Klasser, penetrated his heart, but he knew he dealt with a man who was used to death as part of his work. Yet as seconds became minutes and Klasser remained silent, Beals began to hope.

"You are close, Mr. Beals. In fact I think you have figured it out. Let me spread some light on what you now suspect. In the weeks before 9/11, there was a lot of chatter on our channels. We actually overheard talk of flying the airliners into specific U.S. buildings. I called my four most trusted contacts who had connections to Al-Qaeda. Three of the four felt the information was correct. The one who did not was an Iraqi who had worked with us for five years. His name was Abdul Arif. He had gone underground and had met Osama bin Laden. Arif had bin Laden's trust. His information was usually accurate. So I sat on the story for a day."

Klasser paused as a group of children ran by with their mother trailing five paces behind. The exasperated woman was begging her brood to slow down, but they ignored her. Only when they were well out of hearing range did he continue.

"On September fifth, I took the story to my contact at the CIA."

"Let me guess. Vanderberg."

"Yes, that jackass laughed it off. I doubt if he even took a second look at what we had."

"So you told your brother, hoping his connections with the FAA would put their folks on alert."

"I did. And his calls to the FAA were disregarded. He did have a man he trusted at the FBI. I had done some research on Johnson. He was dependable and had the guts to push information to higher sources. Albert made the call and set up a meeting. By that time I was sure the plot was set for either the eleventh or the twelfth. You know the rest. The meeting never took place. My brother and his family were slaughtered and Johnson died in a car crash. I have no doubt his car was sabotaged."

"Your team, the group that gave you the information. Why did Mossad set it up?"

"It was a practical matter. We were to protect Israeli business interests in the United States by preventing attacks on them. We knew that it was just a matter of time before terrorists began hitting big targets in the United States. Bin Laden was outraged over the U.S. building bases in an area of Saudi Arabia he viewed as holy ground."

"The man who told you the 9/11 intelligence was faulty. What happened to him?"

"Arif drifted away. One day he was easy to contact, the next he was gone. The final time we used him was 2003. Last time I spoke with him via phone was a year or two later."

"What does he look like?"

The Mossad agent shook his head. "We have no photos and I saw him only once. In a dark alley outside of Paris. He was perhaps three inches short of six feet, wiry build, a full but well-trimmed beard, hair to the bottom of his ears, dark eyes. Because of the bad light, I could not make out any more details. If I saw him on the street today, I would not know him from a hundred other of his people. The only real identifying factor that set him apart was that his English was perfect. He spoke as well as you and with no hint of an accent."

"Could you get me his file?"

"Some parts of it, but others are still classified."

"I'm more interested in personal information."

"I can get that to you."

Beals reached into his pocket and retrieved a card. He started to hand it to Klasser but the man had already put his report in his briefcase and gotten up to leave. Looking over his shoulder he smiled. "Ivy Beals, we are now fully aware of your home address, cell number, and all seven of your email addresses. We do not need your card to provide you with information. You will have it before a day has passed. Now just sit there for five more minutes. And remember, we spoke only of investments, if we spoke at all."

Klasser headed back toward the parking garage, acting as if his morning schedule had not been interrupted. Turning to the arts section, Beals went back to reading the *Post.* Ten minutes later, after completing a story that contained an interview with Brad Pitt, he got up, tossed the newspaper back in the trash, and headed toward the lot where he had left his rental. He was almost to the park's edge when he saw the woman with the poodle approaching him.

"Excuse me," she announced as her dog barged into the investigator's path.

Forced to stop, Beals replied, "No problem. Nice looking dog."

"Thank you." She smiled. "I noticed that you dropped this

envelope as you left your seat. It must have fallen out of your pocket as you read your newspaper."

Not questioning the woman's obvious mistake, he took the plain white envelope and dropped it into his coat pocket. "Thank you."

She nodded, yanked the poodle back to her side, and walked off. He now knew why the woman and the dog had moved up and down the sidewalk. He smiled and continued to his car. Once inside, he pulled the envelope out of his pocket. There was no writing on the outside. Slipping his finger under the flap, he carefully tore it open. Inside were a piece of paper and a key. He slid them out. The key was small, generic. He opened the folded paper and read the one handwritten line: "Central bus station, green lockers, #148, 5:00 p.m."

Klasser worked quickly. Beals wondered how many of his operatives, other than the poodle walker, had been watching them. How many were watching him now. A chill gripped him as he buckled his seat belt and started the car.

36

FOR THE FIRST TIME IN WEEKS, LIJE WAS RUNNING late. He'd overslept. Then, just as he was about to leave, McGee had called to update him on the Jones case. On his way to the car, he'd gotten too close to a ladder stored in the garage. A metal corner tore his shirt, forcing him to switch to a backup. And on this day of all days. He fumed as he drove.

The lawyer charged through his office door. Janie Davies immediately stood and said, "Lije, if you have a minute, I've got something to show you."

He ignored her. "Do you know where the extra key to our post office box is? I left mine in my other pants pocket."

Janie opened the middle drawer of her desk and ran her fingers over the compartments in the well-organized space until she felt the key ring. "Here you go." She tossed it his way. "Before you leave—"

"Good throw, Janie," he said as he caught her keys. "Be back in a second."

"But Lije," he heard her call after him as he closed the front door and headed across the square.

It was cool for this time of the year, with temperatures in the high sixties. The slight breeze made it feel invigorating. Lije didn't notice. He was on a mission and, for the moment, that mission was his sole focus.

He opened the door to the 1960s brick building that housed Salem's post office and walked directly to his post office box. He inserted the key and opened the door. There, sitting on top of a half dozen envelopes, sat a small box. He pulled it out and checked the return address—Liberal, Kansas. This was it!

Like a kid hurrying home to try out a new bike, Lije rushed back across the square. He was so lost in thought he almost didn't notice Diana Curtis studying the burn marks on the pavement in front of the office.

"Can't believe how much it scarred the concrete," she said as he rushed by and jumped the steps leading up to the raised sidewalk.

"Uh-huh." He opened the door to the office.

He stopped just inside the door. Heather Jameson blocked his path.

"Lije, did Kent call you?" she asked.

"He did." Lije walked around his partner and headed to his office. "Check your email later this morning. He told me he was sending an assignment your way."

Janie, with Harlow leading the way, tried again to talk to Lije, but he closed the door to his office before she could get there.

Lije hurriedly unwrapped his treasures. The class ring had been polished recently and, except for a bit of wear around the edges, was in remarkable shape. The old Nazi medal was damaged. The years in the bottom of the coin jar had taken a toll. And yet here they were. He was holding them in his hands.

The Ash Flat ring, with the initials J. W., had to have been worn by his great-aunt JoJo. How had it gotten to Kansas? Would he finally answer the mystery of JoJo's disappearance?

And how had the German medal gotten to the middle of America? Was it just a war souvenir, carried home by some GI? Why had it been the only medal in the estate sale?

His thoughts were interrupted by a knock on the door.

"Come in."

"Lije, my friend." Dr. Robert Cathcart had a grin on his face as he walked in and closed the door behind him. "I've found something very interesting. You're going to love this."

Lije stood up to shake the older man's hand. "I have something for you too, professor. Have a chair."

"I know I should've called first," the gray-haired professor said.

"No, I'm glad you're here. Let's sit at the table. I have to show you these. Came in the mail this morning."

Cathcart picked a chair by the bookcase. Lije moved another chair so he could sit next to his guest. "Look at these," he said as he placed the ring and the medal on the table. "I bought them on eBay. Remember, I called you to look at the medal?"

"Yes," the professor replied, his tone showing he was unimpressed. "The medal's not worth much, but it's an interesting piece. If you're into that sort of thing."

"But look at the ring." Lije all but begged his guest.

"Mmm. It's in really good shape," Cathcart noted, turning the ring over with his fingers. "But again, except for sentimental reasons, it has little value. No offense."

Taking the ring from the professor, Lije held it up as if to emphasize its importance. "This belonged to my great-aunt who disappeared in 1946. Recently it was sold out of the Kansas estate of a bachelor farmer, as was that medal. How would a farmer in the Midwest end up with JoJo Worle's ring? Makes the mind spin."

"I've got no explanation," Cathcart said, "but it does spell out a somewhat tantalizing mystery. Still, I'd think it can wait—"

Ignoring the fact that his long-time friend was trying to tell him something, Lije said, "Professor, I need to tell you about something we found on Swope's Ridge."

Cathcart seemed to forget his original mission as, over the next half hour, the lawyer told him about the body they had discovered under the bus and what Curtis had learned in Germany. As Lije spoke, the professor picked up the ring and took another look at what he had thought was nothing more than an insignificant family heirloom.

"You're telling me that you believe this all ties in to something that happened more than five decades ago in Kansas? That the body under the bus, the ring, and the medal are all connected?"

"I don't know, but wouldn't it be worth three days of your time to find out? You love mysteries."

Cathcart glanced down at the old Nazi medal. "It is interesting, but I don't relish a long drive right now. It's not like we're going to Little Rock."

"We don't have to drive. Great Lakes Airlines serves Jonesboro. It's a ninety-minute drive there, then we catch a plane that will do a bit of puddle jumping. We might have a couple of layovers, but that's all it will take to get us to Liberal, Kansas. We rent a car and thirty minutes later we're at the Schneider farm. We can leave tomorrow and have this whole thing cleared up by Friday."

"Okay," Cathcart said, his tone reluctant. "Call me when you find out when we leave."

Lije grinned at his old friend. "I'll let you know by this afternoon."

Cathcart took a final look at the ring and headed for the door. "See you tomorrow."

37

LIJE HAD ALREADY PICKED UP THE PHONE WHEN JANIE walked into his office.

"Just a second," he whispered to her.

"I really need to show you something," she insisted.

"Let me make these reservations." He held up his hand as if she could see the gesture. "Yes, sir, I need two tickets for tomorrow on Great Lakes that will take me from Jonesboro to Garden City, Kansas. The names on the tickets will be Elijah Evans and Robert Cathcart ... Yes, that's right ... American Express ... If you're ready, I can give you the number."

While the reservations were being made, Janie stood patiently waiting to be acknowledged. Finally Lije hung up, smiled, and said, "I'm sorry I've been so busy. You've been trying to catch me all morning. What can I do for you?"

Janie never got the chance to speak. Jameson stormed in. "What about the stuff McGee's going to send me? Checked my email. Nothing there. And I'm leaving for Little Rock in a few minutes."

"Call his office and pick it up there," Lije said. "By the way, Heather, I'm going to Kansas for a couple of days, so hold down the fort. If you need me, I'm just a phone call away."

"What's in Kansas? You looking for Oz?"

"Believe it or not, maybe some answers about Swope's Ridge."

"Really. What could … No, tell me later. I'm late." Jameson hurried out of the office.

Janie cleared her throat. "I need you to look at something."

"Sure, what is it?"

"It's—"

Curtis barged in, moving past Janie and Harlow, waving a piece of paper. "I just got a report from the sheriff's office on the bomb in my car."

"Good. Anything useful?"

"The ATF said the bomb used to transform my car into a twisted metal hulk was a professional job."

"No doubt," Janie said.

"The ATF said the device was set on a timer to go off within a few seconds of the car being entered. Opening the door triggered the countdown. It was supposed to take me out as I was driving away from the office. Oh, and they think it was hidden inside a Coke can."

"No way of knowing who did it?" Lije asked.

"No. They were careful. And there are no surveillance cameras in this block. Are there even any in this whole town?"

"So we still have nothing," Lije noted. "We still have no idea who's been trying to pick you off."

"No. I need to go to Batesville and pick up a new car. Okay if I leave now? There's an insurance guy waiting out front for me."

"Fine. I'll probably be gone all day tomorrow."

38

THEY HEARD THE FRONT DOOR OF THE OFFICE CLOSE. Lije looked back toward Janie, but as he did, the phone rang.

"Let it go," she said. She reached into her pocket and pulled out an envelope. Inside was the piece of onionskin paper. "I found this yesterday."

Taking the thin paper from his assistant, Lije looked back to the phone that was now hitting its third ring.

"Don't even think about it," Janie warned.

How did she know he was considering answering the phone? While the phone continued to beg for his attention, Lije moved to his desk and sat down. Janie found a chair in front of the desk and took a seat. Harlow plopped down beside her.

Lije held up the small piece of paper to get a better look, with his desk lamp illuminating the writing from the back. This note had to mean something, though no words leaped from the page. The person who had written the note had excellent penmanship. The writing was careful and precise; there was a complete break each time the writer had picked up the pencil at the end of one letter and started the next. These weren't words, at least none he knew. It looked more like a chemical formula. He had no idea what the series of letters and numbers and symbols meant. "What is this?"

"I was hoping you'd know."

"Where did you get it?"

"When we were in church yesterday, I noticed one of the satin ribbons used as a page marker in Bleicher's Bible was different from the others."

"No, I examined them when we found the body." His tone was defensive but not harsh. "All four were the same. They were from some funeral home, purple and in pristine condition."

"One was actually two ribbons. They'd been sewn together to look like one. When I pulled out the stitches, I found that paper hidden inside."

Lije got up, rushed over to the office door, and closed and locked it. He returned to his desk and sat down to carefully examine the note.

What was recorded? Why was it hidden in the Bible that they'd found with the body? What made it so important? Did it have anything to do with the Ark and the legend that brought Bleicher to the U.S.?

He turned to click on his computer, waited for the screen to refresh. He hesitated, his hands over the keyboard. If this paper was the key to unlocking the mystery that had cost so many lives, he couldn't risk sending out an electronic transmission. Email could easily be intercepted. Using the phone was not an option either. He needed to have the writing, which looked like a formula, analyzed. He needed someone he could trust.

"What is it?" Janie asked.

"Some kind of formula."

He picked up the phone and pushed redial.

"Reservations, please." He waited a few seconds. "This is Elijah Evans. I made two reservations for Garden City, Kansas, a few minutes ago. I need to cancel them ... That's right ... Thank you."

He pulled out his cell, scanned his directory, and hit Send. A familiar voice answered.

"Dr. Cathcart, this is Lije. Something just came up. Would you go with me to OBU tomorrow? I'll explain when I see you ... Good, I'll pick you up at seven."

"Why are you going to Ouachita? And with Professor Cathcart?" Janie asked as he snapped the cell phone shut.

"Only you and I know about the formula. Don't tell anyone else in the office. I need to have someone I trust look at the formula. He's at OBU. And I need a cover for why I'm going to the university. If anybody asks why my plans changed, tell them Cathcart needed a ride to Arkadelphia and I felt I owed him."

Harlow turned her head and yipped. It almost sounded as if the dog was issuing a greeting. Strange, Janie thought.

"What's up with Harlow?"

"I don't know. She usually doesn't make a sound. Do you think this piece of paper holds the answer?"

"I don't know, but it was hidden for a reason. Someone was very careful to preserve it. Without your special touch, Janie, it might never have been found."

39

UNTIL HE ACTUALLY STEPPED ONTO THE GREEN LAWNS of OBU, Robert Cathcart had forgotten just how much he missed teaching. It felt incredible to be back at a college—the students walking across the campus, the instructors standing under trees sharing stories, and the unmistakable feeling of learning in progress. He had found the fountain of youth. The energy that was a part of higher education seemed to wipe twenty years off Cathcart's age.

The four-hour drive had been wonderful. Lije Evans was an interesting fellow. He was driven to find the truth. Yet he had a unique way of looking at life in multiple hues. The lawyer saw things not in black and white but in shades of gray. His clear sense of right and wrong did not inhibit his ability to forgive those who blended that distinctive line. That was a good quality needed in more classrooms, pulpits, industries, and in government.

Lije had asked him to see if he could dig up more information on the Ark of Death legend in the World War II archives kept in the history department's library. He figured that would give him time to take care of other business in a different building.

Lije parked the Prius and led the way to the heart of the campus. "The history department is in the building just to your right, Lyle Hall," Lije said. "The person you need to meet with is Dr.

Edith Lehning. She's expecting you. She can get you into the right section of the archives."

Edith Lehning! How many years had it been? Until Lije said her name, Cathcart had had no idea what happened to her. They'd each been working on a master's at Brown. They'd shared notes and conversations. A few years later, he discovered she was teaching at the University of Iowa. Then he lost track of her. How many times had he promised he would find her? Yet he never had. Why not? Now, all these years later, the tall, willowy brunette with the startling aqua eyes had landed in Arkansas.

"Dr. Cathcart," Lije said. His words snapped the professor's chain of memories, the late-night study sessions, the concerts, a kiss under an archway at a long-forgotten boarding house.

"Yes," Cathcart answered, trying to refocus.

"You go ahead. I want to visit a friend in the Jones Science Building. We went to school together and it's been years since I've seen him. I'll wait for your call and meet you wherever you are."

"I might be a while." It was as much a wish as anything.

"Take as long as you like. I'm sure Nate and I can kill a couple hours."

Cathcart watched his friend walk into a newer brick building before turning to the steps that led to the history department. He suddenly felt like a kid on a first date. Lehning's office was just inside the front door on the right side of the hall. He stood just outside her office and wished he had more time to get himself ready for the reunion. Wished he had worn a suit—the gray tweed one would have been perfect.

He stuck his head in and saw no secretary or assistant, so he walked through the outer office toward an open door on the far wall. She was there, sitting at her desk, her head down, reading what appeared to be a student's paper.

Had it been forty years? Maybe for him but not for her. Yes, there were a few gray streaks in her shoulder-length hair, but her skin still glowed with the freshness of youth. Why had it taken him so long to get back to this place in his life?

He knew he needed to speak. He had to announce his presence, but something held him back. Like a gangly teen, he searched for both courage and words.

"Edie?" Did he just say it or did he only think it?

She raised her head and their eyes met. "Bobby?"

Like one of those plaster dogs with the spring-mounted neck, his head bobbed. His throat was suddenly dry.

"Bobby." She smiled. "It's you. It's really you. Are you still chasing trains?"

40

"ACTUALLY," CATHCART SAID WITH A GRIN, "I CAUGHT one, Edie."

She stood up, swept around her desk like a ballerina, opened her arms, and together they erased the empty years. He had no idea what she was feeling, but the tumble of emotions falling on him was like a strong summer rain. As her heart beat with his, he suddenly knew how much he had missed.

"Would you like to sit down?" she asked as she stepped back.

Was that a tear in her eye? Surely not! Nodding, he took the chair to his right. She studied him for a moment, then chose a matching chair, dragging it to a spot right in front of his, so close that as she sat down their knees almost touched.

"That train you finally caught," she said, "I saw the stories on the news. That was something you talked to me about when we were in grad school."

"I talked your ear off."

"I think it's why you never married."

Was there a hint of sadness in her tone? "Time sometimes rewards us, but it also shines a harsh light on the many things we should have done. I have regrets."

"We all do, but we also have so many blessings. My students. They are the children I never had."

"You never married?"

She shook her head and smiled. "Too busy trying to become too smart ... Now ... why are you here?"

He wished he didn't have a reason. He wished he could just spend one more day with her. It seemed a sin to break the spell that had magically wiped away so many years. Yet he was on yet another mission, one that would again take him away from where he wanted to be. And if Lije was right, lives were in danger. "I need your help to track down a World War II legend. Ever hear of the Nazi's Ark of Death?"

"Heard of it! That legend is my old train." She chuckled. "You'd know that if you had ever given me a chance to tell you. It's not a legend. It's real!"

"Oh ... we need to work together on this." He hoped she would agree. "But it might be a dead end. I can't guarantee this will lead anywhere."

"Maybe not, but it's more about what you learn from the search than it is what you find."

Those words! He had said them exactly that way so long ago. They'd been standing in front of a boarding house. Evidently she remembered that night too. Except then he had been talking about the risk of looking for love.

He looked into her eyes and realized that the impossible had happened—time had somehow backed up to a cool fall evening and the worn steps of a boarding house.

41

"NATHANIEL."

The man looked up from a microscope and grinned. "Lije Evans! Liji-Boy, you're looking pretty good."

Lije walked over and shook the hand of a man who'd once lived down the hall from him during his college dorm days. While Lije was not as close with him as he was with McGee, Nathaniel Brooks had been a good friend. They'd played on the same intramural basketball team and often double-dated. Lije couldn't begin to count their road trips to football and basketball games and the monthly hops over to Hot Springs to watch a movie or to bowl. Smart, athletic, driven, Nate had been at the top of the class.

Getting up off his stool and pushing it under the laboratory table, Brooks said, "Good to see you. Remember when folks used to call us Salt and Pepper?"

"Still haven't figured that out," Lije said, jabbing at his friend's shoulder.

"Don't suppose it had anything to do with the fact I'm black and you are … how can I say this … pale?"

"Naw. Must've been something else."

Joshing each other had long been at the center of their friendship. A part of it had been simple personality—they were both cutups. Jokes had also masked their rather obvious economic and cultural differences. Lije had come to school in a new car, sporting an expensive wardrobe and a hefty bank account he could tap. Brooks had ridden in from West Memphis on a Trailways bus with everything he owned packed in his grandfather's old Navy footlocker. Yet for reasons neither fully grasped, they had discovered a special bond that began when they sat next to each other in Dr. Root's Introduction to Writing their freshman year.

Brooks wrote a short note on a paper beside the microscope, then removed his white coat and draped it over a chair. With a roll of his head he signaled for Lije to come with him into his office.

"We're looking for a cure for MS," Brooks said.

"You hitting me up for a donation?" Lije asked.

"Not directly, but it never hurts to make folks aware. My junior and senior students are researching new ways to treat multiple sclerosis. There's some good work going on here; we just need more funding. These kids might just uncover something that would end a lot of pain and suffering."

The smile melted from Brooks' face. "I'm sure it's been hard for you," he said.

Brooks didn't have to say more for Lije to know what he was thinking. "I've tried to keep busy. I miss Kaitlyn."

"Not knowing who did it, that would be the toughest part."

"Nate, there are no easy parts."

"Your message was kind of cryptic, Lije. I don't understand what you're doing here today."

"Good. That's what I wanted." Lije's expression was now grim. "I wanted anyone who knew I was at OBU to be confused. As far as the world is concerned, I'm a taxi driver delivering Robert Cathcart to a meeting with the head of your history department."

Brooks nodded. "But the real reason for making the trip is ..."

What had seemed like a good idea when Lije left home now felt wrong. Should he involve this friend in something that had the potential for deadly fallout? This was not some college project. This might well be life or death. He ought to leave.

"Lije, I asked why you're here."

"It's not important. Just stopped by to check on you, relive some old memories."

"You never were any good at lying to me. You need something."

"I can get it somewhere else. No reason to waste your time."

"Lije, if this has something to do with Kaitlyn, I want in. Now what is it?"

Lije shook his head. "It's too dangerous."

"So's playing with test tubes. A friend of mine at Ole Miss was killed the other day when one of his research projects blew up in his face. So what's you got? If it has something to do with Kaitlyn's murder ..."

"I should never have come. Yeah, I do need someone with your skills. But just my talking to you might be aiming a gun at your head."

Brooks looked at his friend without saying a word, his dark brown eyes slitted. "I'll duck."

"You have to promise that this isn't talked about anywhere but here and now. My visit is just two friends killing time while I wait for Cathcart. If you don't agree, I won't tell you a thing."

Brooks was obviously intrigued. "I kind of like you having to come to me. How did you put it? Oh, yes, I have 'skills.'"

Lije leaned closer and whispered, "This is dangerous. This concerns finding a motive for Kaitlyn's murder. You need to know that someone is still after something that is hidden on some property I bought. And that someone is willing to kill to get it."

"So we aren't taking a walk in the park."

"No. Consider the risk carefully. In the last week, three attempts have been made on the life of an investigator who works for me, including a bomb rigged by a professional. We don't know who's behind this. I've tried to keep a blanket over the purpose of this trip. Only one other person knows, and she can be trusted. Even the man who rode with me thinks this trip is all about finding answers to an old legend. I can't guarantee that we can keep the lid on. I'm asking you to pass on this. I shouldn't have come. I suggest you tell me to leave."

Brooks grinned. "I'm all ears."

"This is no game, Nate. You can tell no one."

"I won't."

Just then a large yellow cat walked out of an inner office, slowly crossed the tile floor, and jumped up on the teacher's desk. The teacher, momentarily distracted, gently stroked the animal's head.

"What's its name?" Lije was glad for the diversion.

"What else? Tiger. I found him in a dumpster two years ago. He's become our department mascot."

"I thought there were rules against having pets on campus."

"There are, but everyone just pretends Tiger isn't a cat. The president was in here the other day, and when he left, he accidentally dropped a treat. That's the way this works."

"The real world needs to be more like college."

"Enough stalling, Lije. What do you need?"

Still wondering if his trip had been a mistake, Lije finally leveled with his friend. "I have a chemical formula. I need to know what it's for."

Brooks moved the cat to one side. "Let's see it."

Lije handed him a copy of the paper Janie had found between the two page markers. He watched as his friend studied it.

"Never seen anything like it. Kind of old school, the way it's written. The symbols, and therefore the chemicals, are common enough. But it's as complex as all crud. Off the top of my head, no clue. Let me run this through my computer and see if it triggers anything."

Brooks set the paper to one side and entered the information into a special chemical analysis program on his laptop. He hit Return and waited as his machine went to work.

"You're worried I might get killed over this?"

"There is that risk," Lije said.

The computer beeped. "My program informs me it's a harmless powder. I can't figure out what it would be used for. Is this the whole formula?"

"As far as I know."

"It seems incomplete. Could be a step in a process. Tell you what. I can order the chemicals, make some up, and run a few experiments. Maybe I can figure out what's missing. What do you think it is?"

"A weapon of death."

"Don't think so, but give me a few days and I'll see if I can spot something that would trigger an effect. I think it's harmless."

Lije nodded. "Even if you find it is, you must show no one the formula or your work. Promise?"

"You made that pretty clear."

"I'm serious, Nate."

"You've got my word. But if folks are killing people over this, then—"

"I think people have been murdered over this. And even if you find it's worthless, there are a few folks who won't believe that until they can test it for themselves. This is for your eyes only. Now, my breakfast was small and a long time ago. Want to grab lunch at Burger Barn?"

Brooks smiled. "You know my answer. Let me erase my entries on this formula and I'll lock this copy in my safe. Then we can go."

Lije was disappointed. Janie's find appeared to be just another dead end.

42

KENT MCGEE SAT ON THE DECK OF HIS VACATION HOME and looked out over Greers Ferry Lake, a manmade sportsman's paradise. The lake had been dedicated and officially opened by President John F. Kennedy in 1963. The president's action led to millions enjoying the pristine beauty of the Ozark foothills. But it became the political icon's last public appearance until the day of his death. An end and a beginning.

The attorney sipped a Dr. Pepper as he watched the setting sun. No words could properly describe the scene playing out before him. Three deer—two does and a fawn—had wandered out of the woods to drink at the shoreline. A raccoon was washing a crawfish a few feet farther up the sandy bank. A hoot owl somewhere on a timber-filled hill signaled that it was almost dusk, when his time of the day began.

Most of the recreational boaters had made their way to the docks. The true fishermen had the placid summer waters to themselves. Many were now anchored, setting out lights and waiting to drop lines into the clear water. For them, the day was just beginning.

In the distance a small boat driven by an outboard cut steadily across the still waters. When the boat veered to the left and away from McGee's private dock, the lawyer returned to his living room.

He switched on a table lamp between two large leather chairs and plopped down, laying his head back against a cushion. It was time to wait, time to reflect, and time to chart a course.

Earlier in the day, he had phoned Warden James Ray Burgess and asked to speak to Jones. After the conversation, Burgess had called back asking if McGee was officially on the case. Feeling no need to hide the fact that he was working to free the condemned man, or at least buy him some time, he had said he was. Burgess seemed pleased, a reaction that puzzled McGee. Most wardens did not welcome McGee's involvement with a death-penalty case. Maybe Burgess wasn't lying when he said he liked Jones. Or maybe there was a more sinister reason. No matter, the defense attorney was geared up to maintain his perfect record in death-row appeals.

He closed his eyes and listened for the lake sounds in this, the best time of the day. The first stars would be reflecting off the water. The only sounds were those created by nature—the croak of a frog, the splash from a jumping fish, the call of a bird, the symphony of insects. McGee listened to the rhapsody of nature for a while, then drifted off into a deep sleep.

Three hours later, a man's voice said, "Hey, boss."

McGee didn't move. He didn't even open his eyes. "You're late, Ivy."

"My flight was delayed in Atlanta."

"Figured as much. How was the meeting with Klasser?"

"He gave me some interesting things to chew on," the investigator replied, "and he also got us a file we may need."

"What did you tell Hillman?"

"That I was checking out Schleter. Made him real nervous. He still thinks I'm worth the grand a month he's paying me to keep an eye on you. Anything else you want me to feed him?"

"No. Just break down for me what Klasser told you." McGee still hadn't raised his head or opened his eyes.

It took just five minutes for the muscular bald man to tell what he had learned. It was far less than McGee needed.

"What about the file? Anything good there?"

"It concerns the Iraqi who was once part of Klasser's team. During his early days with the Mossad, the information he passed along was mostly generic stuff, but Abdul Arif became a star in 1999 and early 2000 when he gave his superiors letter-perfect reports helping to prevent at least three Al-Qaeda-linked small bombing operations in Europe. This led to several lower-level operatives being apprehended. So, when he was the one member of Klasser's organization who was sure the chatter before 9/11 was false, it carried a lot of weight."

"What else did you find on him?"

"He's single, no living family members, and was in the U.S. most of 2001. He pretty much dropped off the radar in 2004. Klasser doesn't believe he's dead, just thinks he opted to take his money and fade into seclusion somewhere in the Middle East."

"In other words, he retired."

"Looks like it."

McGee, his eyes still closed, said, "That doesn't give us anything for an appeal. Unless you've got something else, we still don't have evidence of a frame."

"The only other thing I have is personal information. Arif was born in Baghdad, raised in an orphanage until the age of two, when he was adopted by a professor of English at Baghdad University. He was educated there and is fluent in several languages. He has no outstanding physical features. Klasser said he speaks English like an American."

Arif was perfect for spy work, McGee thought. Smart, well informed, and generic. He knew the region, the people, but could still be just another nonspecific face in the crowd. Hollywood was the only place where spies stood out. In the real world they blended in. The file meant nothing ... Or did it?

McGee opened his eyes and for the first time looked at Beals. "Does the file have the date of his birth?"

Beals glanced down at the pages. "January 14, 1976."

That was it! Cause to celebrate! For the first time, they had real traction!

McGee hurried to his desk and flipped on a lamp. He opened a file, scanned several pages, stopped, and tapped his finger on what he had uncovered. He smiled. "Ivy, how are your contacts in Baghdad?"

"Never been asked that before."

McGee rubbed his hands together. "Do you know anyone who can get us birth records from Iraq?"

"If the records weren't destroyed in the war or the looting, I might have the means of coming up with something."

"We need everything we can get on Arif. Start with a copy of his birth certificate, and then get me school photos. Anything and everything. I need it all! And we need it fast. If you need to, fly over there. As Sherlock Holmes would say, the game's afoot."

Beals shook his head. "It'll cost ... a lot. Bribes in that part of the world are an accepted and expected business practice. For documents like this, the price is steep."

"Money I have, time I don't."

By now the exhausted Beals had been absorbed by his chair. It was hard to tell where his body began and the cushion ended. "Can I get some sleep before I leave?"

"As long as we can get the information, you don't even have to leave Arkansas. But hold off on sleep until you've run down your contacts in the Middle East and pushed them into action."

Beals shook his head. "Kent, I'm a bit lost here. Why is this so important? How does it tie to Omar Jones?"

"Ivy, go with me on this. I'm building a wild scenario that just might be crazy enough to be the truth." McGee was pacing as he did when addressing a jury during closing arguments. "It would appear the Israelis were being played. I think Arif was planted by someone in the Middle East—maybe even Osama bin Laden. After all, bin Laden needed to know what the West was thinking and what they knew. He allowed Arif to build a bridge of trust by revealing a few small operations before September 2001. This gave Arif credibility and cost Al-Qaeda nothing but a few bodies.

"Arif was on the inside when the Mossad overheard the chatter before 9/11. So he knew the CIA and the White House weren't buying into the talk of hijacked planes and had dismissed the chatter as meaningless. He reinforced that dismissal. But then he found out that Joshua Klasser was convinced the chatter was real and credible. With me on this?"

"Like duct tape."

"Good. If Arif was a double agent planted by Al-Qaeda, he knew that Joshua's brother Albert worked for the FAA. He might even have known about his link to Johnson, a known bulldog in the FBI. Let's assume he learned that Joshua Klasser was trying to get someone to take the chatter on the hijackings seriously. Arif's job then morphed into keeping an eye on Albert. And the best place to keep an eye on him was in Texas."

"Okay, I follow," Beals said, a second burst of energy now injecting life into his tired body. "Arif probably had a tap on Albert's phones—at least his cell and home phones. He could've even used his contacts to get a tap at the FAA office.

"He had probably been watching the Klasser home for a few days. Saw Jones, an Arab, living next door. Figured he had the perfect fall guy. He could've easily bought a car like Jones' car. That make and model is everywhere. He could've dressed like Jones.

"He learns about Albert's meeting with the FBI agent and gets rid of both. And the family. It all sounds good, but we still have a wall we can't get around."

McGee leaned back in his desk chair. "What have I forgotten?"

"It's simple," Beals said. "If de la Cruz is telling the truth, and you think he is, then how did Arif fool the man with the eye for detail? Every judge you face will never buy into the idea that the man with the perfect memory was fooled."

McGee tapped his desk. "That's why we need to get the information from Iraq on Arif. Ivy, what is the only case in which fingerprints, blood evidence, and DNA can't point to the killer?"

"If the guy's an ex-football player who won the Heisman Trophy?"

McGee shook his head. "No. All that perfect DNA evidence doesn't work if you're dealing with identical twins. Arif and Jones were born on the same day and the same year in Baghdad. They were both adopted. Arif got lucky. Somehow he found out that Jones was his twin brother. This made the murders practically foolproof."

The lawyer walked back over to the window. Two men from the same womb, split apart by fate, had each played into splitting the world asunder. It almost seemed biblical.

43

BARTON HILLMAN SNAPPED HIS CELL SHUT WITH A grim smile that defined his mood. The bait had been taken. In spite of a couple of hitches he hadn't anticipated, he now had what he needed. Evans would be focused on the Jones case for the next month. If McGee could wrangle a stay or an appeal, maybe longer. Yet, to really ensure he had the time he needed without any interference, there was one more thing he had to do.

He punched in a number on his phone.

"Harlan, Barton here. I've got something interesting for you. Why don't we meet? Discreetly. I'm headed over to the governor's office. I'll park in the south parking lot. Just be walking in that area when I arrive. See you in ten."

The director put on his gray suit coat, picked up his briefcase, and headed out the door. "Be back in about an hour," he announced as he strolled by the receptionist's desk.

"I'll hold the calls," came the disinterested response.

The short drive was uneventful. Stepping out of his car, Hillman took a moment to study the building that housed the seat of state government. It was almost an exact duplicate of the original capitol building in Washington. Several movies and television shows had used it for background in historical dramas that needed to show the Washington of the 1800s. He'd even been an extra in one, *The Blue and the Gray.* He'd played a Union captain, a rank he still felt was too low.

Today, little was going on. Most of the elected representatives were on vacation. With little news, the media would be hungry, and it was that hunger he had come to feed.

Harlan Brisco was the lead reporter for United Press Service in Little Rock. With more than three decades of experience, much of it overseas, he was seasoned and tough. He was used to filing reports from war zones and disaster areas. He had moved back to Arkansas because of his wife's cancer. Emily had fought the disease for three years, been told it was in remission, and decided she enjoyed having roots. She found her dream home and they moved in. She was happy, he was not. Harlan was starved for excitement and feared that if nothing changed, his batteries would discharge.

"Barton, what are you doing here?" The dark-eyed, well-built middle-aged man dressed in brown slacks and a cream dress shirt looked like something out of a 1930s MGM newspaper drama. Brisco was the perfect choice to stir up the director's recipe for chaos. And no one would suspect. To anyone watching, this would seem like a chance meeting.

"Harlan." Hillman stopped and waved. "It's been much too long. If you're going to the capitol, walk with me, catch me up on Emily and the family."

The reporter quickly matched the director's leisurely pace. "Emily's fine. She's beaten the cancer. The kids are in college." Brisco glanced over his shoulder. "I don't see anyone close."

Hillman nodded. "What I've got is a blockbuster that will run nationally. No one will have any advance on this but you."

"Sounds great. Tell me more."

Hillman pointed to a spot just to their right. "Let's sit over on that bench under the tree."

When both men were comfortable, Hillman said, "Do you remember Omar Saddam Jones?"

"Sure, the other 9/11 terrorist. I tagged him the '9/10 Terrorist,' but it didn't stick. He'll be executed in a few weeks. But that story has run its course. Except for his last day on earth, the yarn has no legs. I hope you didn't run me up here to talk about that."

"In a way I did. Jones has new representation. Trying for an appeal."

"Still not much of a story," Brisco countered. "Young suits are always jumping on a doomed train's last stop to gain publicity. No reason to give them what they crave."

"This one's different. The new legal guru is Kent McGee. I think that's a horse you can ride."

"Wow!" Brisco was obviously surprised. "McGee's taking a huge risk with that one. That's taking on all those who consider themselves patriots."

"It gets better. Remember Lije Evans? His wife was murdered and he was shot. He's on the team."

"Why? Evans is a legal lightweight. Why would he do something this stupid? Everyone feels sorry for him now. When this comes to light, he'll be the most hated man in the Ozarks."

Hillman maintained his mask. To make this work, he had to appear sympathetic. "I think his wife's unsolved murder has pushed Evans over the edge. Maybe he and McGee have become pawns of the ACLU or some other far-left group."

"They'll both get hung for this. This is a career killer."

Hillman looked down and shook his head. This was going very well indeed. The reporter's shock was now ready to be remolded into a crusade. With his flair for language, Brisco's words should form a noose that would easily slip around the necks of both McGee and Evans. And they wouldn't see it coming. "Are you in?" the head of the ABI asked.

"Who's my source? I assume it's not you."

"No, call death row in Livingston, Texas, the Polunsky Unit, and ask to speak with the warden. James Ray Burgess will give you confirmation and the dates the legal team visited Jones. Don't mention my name. I'm not to be connected in any way."

"Understood." There was an edge to Brisco's tone as he added, "I'll make the call today, get the story out this evening." His eyes locked on the director. "So why do you hate these two guys?"

He'd overplayed his hand. Now he had to regain some footing to make sure Brisco didn't dig into his motives. It was time to trot out the flag. "Harlan, I've got nothing against either man. But I'm an American. I can't stand to see anyone going against our system of government, our ideals, and abuse our laws just to coddle the guilty. What these two are trying to do is get a convicted terrorist set free. We all know he's guilty. In my view, that's an act of treason."

The reporter nodded as the director rose from his seat.

"Just do your job," Hillman said. "I'll bet you'll get back in the spotlight. Might even land a consulting gig with one of those cable news outlets. I've got a meeting with the governor. I'll read your story in tomorrow's paper."

He smiled as he walked toward the capitol. He'd played it perfectly. The reporter had bought it all. The outrage created by the story would keep McGee and Evans busy for a long time. And with them occupied elsewhere, he'd finally get what he needed.

44

LIJE EVANS REALIZED SOMETHING WAS WRONG SOON after he parked his car in front of his office. He waved to Julie Rosco, the manager of the Dollar Store, but she frowned and turned her back on him. Stepping up on the walk outside his office, he said good morning to Frank Stratton as he was unlocking the door to his feed store. Stratton glanced up, shook his head, and said nothing. Stratton had once coached Lije in Little League. He'd been like an uncle to him. Where was the smile, the always present "How's it goin'?"

Lije walked into his law office and was greeted by the cacophony of two phone lines ringing. Janie was already on the third line. Curtis and Jameson scrambled to catch the others.

"Kind of cool outside," Lije said. If anyone noted his sarcastic tone, they didn't show it. They seemed not even to notice him. He watched the whirlwind of activity that made the room appear more like a 1-800 call center than his quiet office. Was this about the bombing?

"Bit frosty in here too," Janie said, putting a phone down.

"You see the paper?" Curtis asked while placing her line on hold.

"No," Lije admitted. "Didn't open mine this morning."

"Then look at the one on the counter," the investigator suggested. "We've got a real problem."

Lije picked up the *Gazette* and was hit by a headline proclaiming he and McGee were representing the nation's best-known terrorist. The story was by Harlan Brisco, who portrayed them as unpatriotic and anti-American. The United Press Service writer was putting them in bed with Osama bin Laden.

"Didn't see this coming," Lije said, sinking into a chair. "Guess I should've. Any idea how Brisco found out we were involved in the Jones case?"

"Not from McGee," Janie said. "He was just as blindsided as we were. By the way, we've gotten requests for interviews from two dozen reporters. Some are big-time national names. Four TV news shows want you as a guest. *The View*'s called twice and a host of tabloid shows are on their way to ambush you."

Lije grinned. In a perverse way this was kind of funny. "After I ignore those folks, anything else on my plate?"

His assistant checked her Braille notes. "A couple of other things. McGee needs to talk to you. And so far we have gotten twenty-seven death threats."

"Twenty-eight," Jameson called from across the room.

"I stand corrected," Janie replied.

"Any of them serious?"

"The guy who identified himself as the Grand Wizard of the KKK sounded sincere," Janie noted. "One man called in ranting, but when I finished with him he asked me out. I turned him down. Sounded too old."

"Great," Lije said. "I'll call Kent. Shut down the phone system and forward all calls to our answering service. Otherwise we'll never get any work done."

Just then a loud thud rattled the front window.

"What was that?" Jameson asked.

Curtis walked to the front of the reception area. "An egg. I haven't been egged since my sophomore year in college. Take my word, eggs are far better than bombs."

"Might be best to stay away from the windows," Lije observed. "Wouldn't hurt to lock the door too."

Back in his office, he pulled out his cell and dialed McGee's private line. "How crazy is it at your office?"

"It's not crazy," McGee said, "it's bizarre. We've even had rocks tossed through windows."

"Just eggs here. Did you see this coming?"

"Should have. But I didn't think anyone would know we were on the case. Not until after I got the evidence to prove Jones was framed. We have nothing I can give the press now — that is, without alerting the one person I need to find — so I'm going to have to take some abuse for a while."

"Beals found something?"

"Sure did. I now know how and why this thing was done. What I don't have is proof, so I can't start pushing the case through the courts. Ivy's working on it, but finding the man who actually pulled the trigger in time to save Jones is a long shot. And this carnival outside my door is getting in the way." McGee took a deep breath. "I'm about to hold a press conference and announce you and your office aren't in on this. No reason to drag you down with me."

"But I got you into this. I asked for this fight. I can deal with it. Saving an innocent man is a lot more important than having folks slam me as some kind of traitor."

"I knew you'd say that," McGee said. "And I really do need your help in pulling off the magic this case needs. Beals and I can't do it alone. But if you let me announce you're not in on this, that Brisco's information was wrong, then you'll be of more use to me."

"How's that?"

"Simple. The media won't be hounding you because you're not on the case. All you did was go with me to Livingston. As soon as I pull the plug, the press will drop you."

"Are you sure you want to do it this way?" Lije asked. "I want to fight this war with you. I've played it safe too long. Time for me to take a stand. Nobody questions my patriotism and gets away with it."

"Yeah, and if it was just you, then maybe that'd be fine. But you've got three others in that office whose lives might be in danger. Some crazy just might take a shot at them. Kill one of them. Diana's in enough trouble with that stalker without adding more shooters. And how's Janie going to see someone taking aim at her?"

"But—"

"No, Lije, play it my way. I'll have things for you to do. I'll use you, but behind the scenes. When the time is right, you'll be there to help me free the innocent man. Are you with me on this?"

"I guess."

"Okay, I'm going out in ten minutes and transforming myself into an egomaniac who has been deeply injured by even the suggestion that I'd need the help of a small-town, hick lawyer. When I finish, you'll look like the Gomer Pyle of the legal profession. Know that I won't mean any of it." He paused and laughed. "Okay, not all of it."

"It'll be just like you used to treat me in college."

"Seriously, once you're officially off the case, you won't have any rights to see Omar Jones. Do you understand?"

"I guess so," Lije said. "But—"

"Unofficially, you're still with me, working on the case. We need to get the whole team together. On Saturday bring them down to my lake house at noon. Make sure you're not followed. That place is still in my aunt's name, and no one in the media knows I have it. We'll work out our plan."

45

LIJE WALKED BACK DOWN THE HALL TO THE RECEPTION area. He studied his grim-faced colleagues. They still looked shell-shocked.

"Did you talk to McGee?" Curtis asked.

"He fired us. We're not on the case. Have there been any more eggs?"

"No," Janie replied. "Diana said the last thing that hit the window was a tomato. I'm not sure I want off the case."

"Don't worry—if Kent needs anything, we'll be working with him. Right now he's waiting for information. Come on back to my office. Let's watch McGee grandstand for the press."

The press conference was deemed so important that even the networks broke in to their regular schedule to carry it live. McGee first lashed out at the media and all those calling him anti-American. Dressed in a tailored blue suit, white shirt, and red tie, McGee paraded out the Bill of Rights and the Constitution and assured those watching that Jones had not received a fair trial. He hammered again and again that he was in this fight not to trample on America but to show the world we are a nation of values and rights even in situations that concern the worst of crimes. He assured everyone that death threats, rock throwing, and editorials would not dissuade him from doing what he saw as his sacred duty to provide equal protection under the law. He pointed out that the attorneys representing Jones had been inexperienced or inept as well under funded and unprepared, and the man deserved better than that.

McGee then went after Warden James Ray Burgess for giving out the false information that Lije Evans was involved in this case. "Lije is my friend, he was my college roommate, but he is a small-town lawyer who would be overwhelmed by a case of this magnitude. In fact, my friend would surely not take a case involving a convicted terrorist."

Then McGee delivered the real blow. "The truth is Evans simply doesn't have the stomach for this kind of work. He's well suited for handling the foundation he set up to carry on his late wife's charitable work. That's what he does, along with the typical small-town legal work. But think about it: would anyone trust him with a death-penalty case?"

Smiling, McGee added, "I don't have time for questions. I have a case to prepare."

Lije hit the power button on the remote as the CNN field reporter began to sum up what McGee had said. The screen went dark. Everyone but Lije was stunned.

Janie finally broke the silence. "That was a bit harsh, even for a lawyer."

"He's always been about ego," Curtis added. "To him it's not about saving Jones; it's about getting the press. He lives for the flashbulbs and sound bites."

Jameson was silent. The color had drained from her face and her mouth drooped like a flower caught in the midst of a summer heat wave. "I thought he respected you. I thought we were going to be on the same team. I really liked that idea. I can't believe I liked him. He seems different around here. What a con! I can't believe I bought it."

Lije smiled and let his disillusioned team in on the secret. "We are officially cut from the case, and, let's face it, I am a small-town lawyer. Here's what not being officially on the case means." He paused. "None of us can visit Jones on death row."

"That's pretty obvious," Jameson cracked.

"But," Lije continued, "we'll still be working with Kent in an unofficial capacity to prove Mr. Jones is innocent. That news conference was all about getting the eyes of the press off this office and off each of you. It was also about Kent wanting to make sure no one here gets hurt."

"So—" Janie began.

"So we have a secret meeting with Kent on Saturday where we'll get our assignments. Until then we simply go about our business working on the legal items we have scheduled. Let's turn the phones back on and get to work."

Lije got up, walked back to the front door, and stepped out on the sidewalk. He was greeted by three television news crews, but no eggs or fruit.

"Is it true what McGee said?" a young man in a blue suit asked. "You're not on the Jones case?"

"You heard him," Lije said.

A woman held up a microphone and hollered, "He said you didn't have the stomach for that kind of work."

"He said that? The fact is this office has never officially been on the case. Two members of my staff and I did go to Texas with McGee, but that was our only contact. I guess you could call it an educational experience for us. We'd never been in that situation and wanted to know what McGee's practice was like. Today we are doing what we usually do, helping folks right here in Salem with routine legal challenges."

He then added a humorous note that he hoped would separate him from his friend's agenda. "So, as you can see, this hick lawyer needs to get back to his rather mundane job. No story for you here. I suggest you chase down Mr. McGee."

Seemingly satisfied, the news crews packed their gear in their vehicles and left. Frank Stratton walked up to Lije and said, "Knew you wouldn't do something like that."

"Really?" Lije asked.

"Yep, you'd never go to court for someone like that dirty Arab. You stick with your own kind."

So that's what Frank thought. That explains the cool reception that morning. And now that Frank believed he was off the Jones case, he was okay, back "with his own kind."

Lije thought of the teachings of Jesus and how they were to do for "one of the least of these." If he could help McGee reveal the truth about Jones, that he was innocent, then maybe a few folks would go back and reread Matthew 25:35–40.

46

KENT MCGEE'S WORLD WAS ROCKY. THE MEDIA HAD spent two full days hounding him at his Little Rock office. Police had been called three times to escort angry visitors off the property. One group set up a round-the-clock protest and recruited volunteers with its new HateKentMcGee.com website. Editorials were running nine to one against him for being involved in the case. Some clients were dropping him too, but because he was wealthy, that didn't bother him in the least.

Then there were the death threats. There had been so many in the first two days the staff no longer kept track. An eight-foot cross had been burned in front of his home Thursday night. That image quickly spread to the front pages of news sites all around the globe. Five different groups took credit for it.

Today was different. No one could touch him here. His lake house was off the radar and so was the team that would soon help him in what was surely a case to make or break his career. He needed the skills of those coming to join him, but he hated to bring them into this. He did not want any of them to be branded un-American or put at risk. Everything they did had to be undercover.

A buzzer sounded and the lawyer glanced at a small TV monitor. Lije Evans was tapping a number into the security box. A few seconds later the gate swung open. Right on time. Taking a last sip of coffee, McGee wandered out the front door and onto the covered porch just as the SUV drove through the gate and down his long lane. He snickered when he noted that his friend's ruse included pulling a ski boat for a day of fun on Greers Ferry Lake. He laughed out loud when they got out of the Explorer. Each had on a bathing suit.

"Good work, Lije." McGee said as he threw open the front door. "You all look like the real deal."

"What else do hick lawyers do on the weekend but play golf or ski?"

"Did I come off a bit strong at that press conference?" McGee asked.

His friend smiled. "Let's just say you're no longer on my Christmas-card list."

The troop came across the porch and headed for the living room, their noisy flip-flops sounding as if more than a dozen were in the group. With faces lathered in sunscreen, loud T-shirts, and sunglasses and rain hats, they would've been at home on any beach in the world. Even Harlow was dressed for the occasion, sporting a baseball cap and a Hawaiian scarf tied around her neck.

"Janie," McGee teased, "the shades are a nice touch."

"Thanks. Some trucker tried to pick me up when we stopped for breakfast. So I guess they're working. The guy backed off when Harlow snarled. Diana told me he was good looking." She turned her head his way, arched her left eyebrow, and smiled.

McGee had no idea if she was pulling his leg. "Well, I'm glad you ate," he said. "I don't have much in the way of food here."

"That's okay," Curtis chimed in. "We have all kinds of things in the cooler. The way Lije packed, we could live on the lake for a week ... if you like Vienna sausage."

Heather tossed a newspaper onto the dining room table. "Your new landscape art in this morning's *Gazette*."

McGee glanced at the photo of the burning cross. "Yeah, I thought about going out and toasting some marshmallows, but was afraid the crowd might pelt me with rocks. Amazing when the KKK is now considered more mainstream and admirable that I am. Online there are all kinds of folks praising the Klan for this move. I've learned that hate can sweep the country far faster than any known illness, and it doesn't take much to stir up the mob mentality. When it comes to race or religion, push the right button and normal folks become lunatics."

He pointed to the living room of the two-bedroom structure. "You probably don't need to be here long, so have a seat in the living room and I'll lay things out for you."

He remained standing as his guests found their places. When everyone was comfortable, he quickly went through his plan. "Heather, I understand you've been working with several law students setting up the Kaitlyn Foundation."

"Yes, they've been doing research and helping fill out the mountain of forms."

"That's perfect," McGee said. "Starting Monday, you'll need to be there every day, but instead of doing research on the foundation, you and three students will be studying every facet of the Jones case. I need you to find any mistakes, no matter how small, that were a part of the original case. Go right back to the arrest and processing. We're looking for anything that might have slipped through."

"What if the students tell the press what we're doing?"

"They won't. One of my best friends is the dean of the law school. He's already picked out three kids. They've been told that if they tell anyone what they're doing, including their families, it will essentially end their careers before they have a chance to start. The four students who have been working on the foundation, keep them going on the same work they've been doing. Make sure they believe that the three new kids are working for the foundation too."

"Okay. Sounds tedious, but that's the way law seems to be."

"Heather, I need anything I can get to delay the execution." McGee's voice conveyed a sense of urgency. "I want to bombard the court with filings. I've got to find something to push back the clock for Jones. So if there's a question about anything, let's use it."

"But that ultimately won't do much," she argued. "All it would buy at most is a few days or weeks."

"I know," he said, "but that might give us enough time to find the man who really killed the Klasser family."

The room became quiet. Even Harlow seemed to hold her breath.

"You know who it is?" Lije asked.

"I do," McGee acknowledged, "but can't prove it yet. In fact the only way I can do that is by tracking the guy down. If I can toss him out in front of a judge and prosecutor in a courtroom, Jones will walk. I guarantee that."

"Who is he?" Janie asked.

"The only person he could be," McGee explained. "The DNA evidence and the eye witness nailed Jones. There would seem to be no way around it unless you think about the fact that Jones was adopted. That's one thing we all know. I'm now ninety-nine percent sure that he was a twin. If my theory is right, that twin was in the U.S. during the week before 9/11. Maybe even earlier. He supposedly was working for Mossad."

"Israeli intelligence," Curtis chimed in.

"That's right," McGee said, "but there's much more. I think he was a double agent for Osama bin Laden. Albert Klasser's brother is in the Mossad. He told Albert about the chatter on the attacks, and Albert was about to tell the FBI. Could he have convinced anyone the plan was real in time to stop the attacks? Who knows. But Abdul Arif, the agent, couldn't take the chance."

"You say you're almost sure?" Curtis noted.

"Yeah, I'm waiting for a birth certificate and photos. I hope to have those in the next couple of days."

"Any idea where Arif is now?" Curtis asked.

"No, which is why I need you." McGee turned toward the former ABI agent. "While my guy is digging up the documents I need in Iraq, I need you to see what you can find on Arif. Use your contacts and see if he's in the States. He uses several different aliases. I have them listed in this file."

McGee picked up a folder from his desk and tossed it to Curtis. "You can start with these and see if they lead you anywhere. I'm pretty sure he's alive. He might still be working for Al-Qaeda, we just don't know. We have under a month to track him down and catch him in our net. You'll be the point guard on this end of the case. You find him, we come out smelling sweet."

Curtis nodded.

"What about me?" Lije asked.

"You're going on goose chases," McGee said. "I can't hunt down leads when we come up with them. When I'm not working on things in my office, I'll be a decoy leading the media and anyone else who's interested away from what I really need to see. You'll be my eyes and my legs. There'll be times Ivy Beals will join you, times you will work on your own. Once we find something, you'll be on the road."

"So," Lije replied, "what do I do now?"

"That depends on how fast Diana finds a lead. Until then, I suggest you work on the mystery on Swope's Ridge. That should convince anyone who's keeping an eye on you that we really have gone in different directions."

Lije nodded.

"Janie," McGee continued, "I need you to be the ultimate cover. You're going to get calls. Make sure no one picks up even a hint that we're working together. Crank out some meaningless correspondence to make the office look as if it has no focus on this case."

"Sounds boring," Janie replied, "but if that's what you need."

"I need something else too."

"Sure."

"Find out all you can on the three court-appointed lawyers who have represented Jones in the past eight years. I want to know them as well as I know myself. I want to know their moral weaknesses. I want to know how seriously they took their duties. I want to know what kind of toothpaste they used. I might be able to use something in their backgrounds to get an appeal or a delay. At your old firm you used to do a lot of this kind of work preparing for cases. Back then it was a scouting report on an opponent. This time it's just helping me find a place to drive a wedge."

"I've still got my sources from the other firm I worked for," Janie said. "I can get you want you need."

"Any questions?" McGee asked.

The room was silent. He hoped that meant they were ready and not overwhelmed. "Then have a good weekend and be ready to go to work on Monday."

"Okay, gang," Lije said, "let's get to the water."

"You mean you're really going skiing?" McGee asked.

"A good cover is carried through," Curtis explained. "We'll be out there all day."

"Nothing like a sunburn," Janie added, "to convince folks we're not interested in working on your case or any other case."

"Wish I could join you," McGee said. He looked directly at Curtis. She smiled. He continued to look at the former ABI agent as he added, "One more thing. We are the only ones who know of this plan. Not one of my office staff is on board with this facet of the operation. If the word gets out, it means one of you is a mole."

Heather looked shocked. "Are you accusing—"

"No, just being cautious. Someone's out to ruin us. They've already gotten some information before I was ready to make it public. Brisco was tipped off to call Warden Burgess; it wasn't the other way around. I'm just as sure none of you had anything to do with that.

"I have to play the rest of this life-or-death game very carefully. A man's life is at stake. We have to find Arif now, and we can't have any more slipups. If the press gets wind of what you're doing, the circus will return to Salem, and none of you will be of any use to me. If that happens, an innocent man will die."

47

DIANA CURTIS HAD BEEN GLUED TO THE COMPUTER screen for seven hours. After a quick start filled with unexpectedly detailed information — so detailed it appeared Abdul Arif had been intentionally putting down a trail — things had gone cold. The last record of Arif using his passport was in 2005. He had presented it to customs at Heathrow Airport, entered England, and vanished. He never left the UK, was not arrested, did not use his charge cards, set up no bank accounts, bought no property, and never registered for a driver's license. He hadn't died, at least not under his own name nor any of his aliases.

Curtis stretched her lean frame, took a sip of lukewarm coffee, and picked up a legal pad filled with worthless notes, much like her notes from the war archives in Berlin. Until Peter Wilshire found her there, she'd had nothing. He couldn't help her today. So who could? How was she going to find Arif without a Peter Wilshire?

She went back to the computer and typed a short email: "Need a contact in London with government intelligence. Who do you know?"

She knew her source could help, but would she get a response? She studied the screen as if her stare would trigger a quick response. It did. Less than a minute later an answer popped into her inbox. "Don't know anyone in intelligence. Contact Terry Best at Scotland Yard. Might be able to help. The private number is 1-020-555-1212."

Grabbing her cell phone, Curtis typed in the number and waited. On the third ring, a woman answered with "Yes."

"I need to speak to Terry Best."

"You are."

Curtis had expected the Yard officer to be a man. Hearing a bright soprano voice surprised her. "Miss Best," she began, "I'm Diana Curtis with the Arkansas Bureau of Investigation. My badge number is 7134." She paused, hoping that the outdated information might buy her the confidence she needed to request information.

"Nice to hear from you," came the matter-of-fact reply. "By the way, are you aware of the time here in London?"

"I'm sorry about that," Curtis replied. "I'm trying to dig up information that might halt an execution in Texas."

"Ah, yes," Best said, "barbarianism is still alive and well on your side of the pond. If I can do anything to help you get rid of that inhumane practice, even in just one case, I'm in the game."

So far so good. She'd hit a nerve. Now it was time to drop the bombshell. If Best couldn't help, maybe she would connect her with someone who could.

"I need information on a man who disappeared in the UK a few years back. He entered Britain under the name of Abdul Arif."

There was a pause. "Arif, you said? Was he Iraqi?"

This was better than she could have expected. It seemed Best either knew the man or at least knew of him.

"That would be him," Curtis assured the Yard officer. "By your tone I'm guessing that name means something to you."

"Bloody well," she replied. "Arif was actually sent to me by one of our top men, Peter Wilshire. If Peter were here he could give you a bank vault of information."

Incredible! Could the world get any smaller? Wilshire, the same man who'd save her life while giving his own, knew Arif.

"Miss Curtis," Best said, "where's this going? I'm afraid I'm treading on some pretty thin ice here. I probably shouldn't have told you what I just did. The shock of Peter's recent murder and your dropping that particular name in my ear caught me a bit off guard. As you Americans say, I let the cat out of the bag and now I might need to put it back in."

Curtis knew it had been too easy. The roadblock was going up. How much would she have to admit to get Best to take another step? If possible, she needed to leave Jones' name out of it. If that got out, then the circus, as McGee had put it, would visit Salem. So how did she move forward? As the Yard officer was obviously anticapital punishment, might she be able to use that as a wedge? Curtis plunged ahead.

"I'm working with a team that believes Arif was responsible for a murder that a man on Death Row in Texas was convicted of. It was a brutal, multiple homicide with political implications."

"Are you positive?"

Curtis took a deep breath. "Yes."

Best was still there, she could hear her breathing, but the Brit was not speaking. Was she going to shut down or open up? What could she do to push her into talking? "Officer Best?"

"Inspector," she corrected Curtis.

"Inspector Best, I knew Peter Wilshire. Can you tell me why he was working with Arif?"

"You knew Peter?"

"Yes, we met in Berlin once." At least that wasn't a lie.

"Peter did holiday in Germany a great deal," came the reply.

That comment seemed to keep the door open a little, but still there was no sign of any more information coming forth. Time to push the next button. "I also know that Peter worked with both the Yard and Interpol."

Those magic words broke the dam. Best seemed much more relaxed as she continued. "Peter actually knew Arif through Interpol. Had something to do with a terrorist attack that was prevented in 2000 because of information provided by Arif. It seems that Arif came to Peter claiming he needed to go undercover. He said there was a hit of some kind on him by Al-Qaeda. At Peter's request, I arranged a new identity for the man."

"Can I ask what was the name he was given and if he's still in England?"

Best took a deep breath. "I think I've already told you more than I should have. If Peter were still alive ... It's kind of a sticky wicket. We cannot ethically out someone we are sworn to protect. I think you understand."

"But Inspector," Curtis argued, "this man's a murderer. If I don't find him, an innocent man will die."

If that didn't cause her to break loose, then the gate would be forever closed. Curtis waited. She could have read a great deal of *War and Peace* while the Brit considered the situation.

"I don't know what I can or should tell you," Best finally whispered. Still obviously conflicted, she added, "Would it help you to know he's no longer in the UK?"

"It's a big world," Curtis shot back, "and the UK is only a small part of it."

"We got him a job in Germany."

"Where?"

"The War Archives in Berlin. Peter had a contact there."

"Name?"

"You know I shouldn't do this."

"I also know you don't want an innocent man to go to the death chamber. If you don't want innocent blood on your hands, I need the name he's now using. The clock's ticking even as we speak."

"Joseph Gonzales. He spoke fluent Spanish, so we built an identity around that. We gave his birthplace as Mexico City."

"He's still at the archives?"

"No, he only worked there a few months. He left and took a job in a nursing facility north of Berlin. We are alerted when the people we help move."

"Beeskow?" Curtis asked.

"Yes," a shocked Best replied. "How did you know?"

"Just a guess. Is he still there?"

"No. Let me check my files."

As she waited, Curtis considered the odds against Arif ending up at the same place she and Peter had visited. There had to be a connection.

"Here's what I've got," the inspector explained. "And I don't want my name involved in this. I've never broken the rules, but executions should've gone the way of steam trains. I have no stomach for them. They're bloody inhumane."

"Thank you," Curtis replied, "I won't betray you."

"Arif flew to Mexico earlier this week. Our contacts in MI6 have since lost track of him. He may very well be using a different name now."

So British Intelligence was in on this too. This thing was getting bigger by the minute.

"Why," Curtis asked, "did you keep such close track of him?"

"Peter trusted him," Best answered. "I didn't. So I alerted a contact I had in MI6 and asked him to keep an eye on Arif for me. Normally he probably would've tossed me off. They often make fun of Scotland Yard—they have kind of a haughty attitude and all—but they had a request from a high-level member of the Mossad to alert them to Arif's movements. My stock went up when I provided them with his new identity. It seems everyone had lost track of him until last week."

"Interesting," Diana said.

"I've got to go," Best replied. "Keep me out of this unless you find him. If you do, then let me know."

"Understood."

The line went dead.

48

CURTIS BEGAN THE SEARCH FOR THE ELUSIVE JOSEPH Gonzales, aka Abdul Arif. Using hacking methods she had learned at the ABI, she tried to locate the man through flights and purchases. While there were thousands of Joseph Gonzaleses, only one had recently used a passport to leave Germany. His destination was Mexico. He had arrived in Mexico City three days before and had not used his passport to leave the country. Hundreds of flight and credit card entries for that name popped up. Which one was the right Joseph? There was no way of knowing. Trying a different tactic, she began a search of the other identities Arif had used in the past.

Typing in a dozen other known aliases spit out mainly blanks. The one exception was Hassam al-Bakr. A man with that rather uncommon name had spent the last two days in a Gulf Coast resort hotel in Ciudad Madero.

Jumping up, she hurried down the hall to Lije's office. A quick look through the open door showed he wasn't there. Reversing her course took her to the reception area. She found the lawyer studying a printout.

"Lije."

"Yeah," he replied without looking up.

"I'm pretty sure that Arif is in Mexico. I think he knows the

Brits are interested in him. He's reverted to an earlier alias, Hassam al-Bakr. A man with that name is now staying in the city of Ciudad Madero."

"That's strange," Janie said. "The guest speaker at church yesterday—And where were you, Lije, and what was your excuse for playing hooky?"

"I was—"

"Didn't think you had a good one," Janie said. "Anyway, the guest speaker was a pastor from that same city in Mexico. Fascinating man. Told of his father, who'd been a poor fisherman, being killed by some strangers in 1946. He would've died too except another stranger led him to safety."

"Quite an adventure," Curtis noted. She had little patience for Janie's preacher story. It was time to move. "We need to get to Mexico as quickly as possible. Maybe Arif is hanging out there or we can at least get a line on where he went. I need to call Kent."

"There was a boat," Janie added, her tone begging for attention. "Reverend Pedro Hernandez spoke of a large white boat that blew up that night his life was saved. It seems the old-timers in the village still tell of the fire on the water."

"In 1946?" Lije asked.

"That's what he said."

"You all thinking what I'm thinking?" he asked.

If Lije was on the right track, Curtis thought, this might actually tie in. Wilshire knew Arif. Arif went to work at the archives because of his connection with Wilshire. If Wilshire trusted him and knew he had Mossad ties, he might have told Arif about his father. While working at the archives, Arif found out about Mueller and went to work in the nursing facility. He used Bleicher's name to gain Mueller's confidence. Then found out everything he could about the Ark of Death.

"I need to check something on the web," Curtis said.

Jumping on Google, she began a search for Pedro Hernandez of Ciudad Madero. As expected, she found a website. What pastor or evangelist didn't have one? Copyright information placed its launch date as 2004. Fortunately, Hernandez had thoughtfully mirrored each Spanish-language page with an English counterpart. She raced through the menu until she came to his testimony. Reading through it, she found the parts dealing with that February night in 1946. The area where Hernandez and his father had run into danger was remote, unpopulated. The men they'd run from had been in uniforms. Hernandez had first seen the men working on five unmarked airplanes parked on the beach. A large ship was anchored just off shore, but after the planes took off, the ship had blown up.

If she hadn't met Wilshire, this would have meant nothing. But now ...

Curtis next typed in a search for a Mexican legend based on fire on the water. Several entries came up, most dating back to Mayan and Aztec times. One from right after World War II was about a huge ship blowing up and covering the Gulf of Mexico in flames.

So what did she know? Arif not only killed the Klassers, he'd probably shot Peter Wilshire and tried to kill her. Now he was in Mexico looking for the secret behind Hitler's legendary killing machine. If that kind of power really existed and Bleicher hadn't destroyed it, then it would be the ultimate weapon for Al-Qaeda or anyone else who wanted to bring the world to its knees.

Did Smith and his boss now have company or were they all working together?

She now knew Omar Jones had simply been in the wrong place at the wrong time.

49

LIJE EVANS SAT IN HIS LIVING ROOM WATCHING HIS guest munch on Janie's homemade peanut-butter cookies. Normally Lije would've been digging in, but he and Diana Curtis were focused on pulling ancient information from the Reverend Pedro Hernandez' memory. And all he seemed interested in was setting the record for cookie consumption in a single setting. Time was running out. They had a flight to catch.

"Reverend Hernandez," Janie said as the man reached for another warm treat, "could you tell us about the night your father was killed? As I explained, Lije and Diana were not at church last night and missed your talk."

The short, dark-headed man paused, savoring the taste delivered with each slow thrust of his jaw. With his childlike enthusiasm, he seemed ageless. He had few wrinkles and no gray hair. His dark eyes sparkled. Only the age spots on the backs of his hands gave any indication this man had been alive over seven decades.

He finished the last bite of cookie, picked up his glass, and washed the final crumbs down with a swig of milk. Finally he leaned back, ready to tell his story.

"Papa was a fine man, a very fine man. He was just a poor fisherman. In that way he was like Jesus, and in other ways too. Never had anything, but how he loved us. Our home was always filled with love and laughter."

"Reverend Hernandez," Lije said, "he must have been wonderful. Which must have made what happened to him on that night all the more shocking. Would you tell us about that night?"

The visitor pushed back into the large leather couch, folded his arms, and cleared his throat. "On that cool winter evening he ran into our home after a day spent on the gulf fishing. He was so excited. He told my mother, my little sister, and me about this huge ship that was anchored just off the beach. It was almost dark. He wanted us to come look at it. Mama told him she was too busy cooking and Maria was too young."

The Mexican pastor smiled and looked over to Lije. "I'd never seen him so excited. I wanted to go. He usually walked very slowly, but that night he ran toward the beach. As if he was a child again. We came over a hill and there it was, a large ship, white, and it had a red cross painted on the side. I knew it was a long way from shore, but it was so big it seemed that if I reached out my arm, I could touch it."

"Sounds like a hospital or relief ship," Curtis noted. "I remember reading that a lot of the vessels used during the war for military purposes and troop transport were converted for use by charity groups who were feeding and caring for refugees."

"Perhaps it was one of those." Hernandez nodded. "But we didn't know of such things. We barely knew of the war. Our village was small, we were poor. Most people didn't read and we had no electricity. The war was just something that was far away. We were sure it would never touch us."

Lije nodded. He understood.

"That night," Hernandez continued, "my father was convinced that the red cross on the ship stood for the saving blood of Christ. He was sure these were Christian people who had come to our village to help us because of how poor we were. We had prayed for help, and this seemed like an answer to prayer.

"We walked along the shore, our eyes too filled by the ship to notice anything else, and then we heard voices. We ran about a hundred yards and saw five silver airplanes on the beach. You cannot imagine how I felt. Only a few times I had seen planes in the sky, but never on the ground. I was almost breathless as I stared at these shiny wonders."

The wonder of that moment long ago seemed to transport the man back to his youth. He was not just seeing it, he was feeling it.

"Reverend Hernandez," Lije said, "were there any markings on the planes?"

"No, not even numbers. They were just plain silver. A barge loaded with large tractor-like equipment was headed back to the white ship. When we got there, just the planes and five men were left on the beach."

"How were they dressed?" Curtis asked.

"In dark-gray suits, like uniforms, and tall black boots. They had stuffed their pantlegs into the boots. My papa told me they were Christians and we needed to welcome them to our village. So we started walking toward the planes. Papa yelled out, '*Buenas noches! Bienvendio!*' "

Suddenly Hernandez' childlike expression was replaced with one of terror. He appeared old and tired. Tears pooled in his eyes, then slowly slid down his face.

They all waited. Impatience had given way to respect as an uncomfortable stillness filled the room, marked only by the solitary ticks from an antique mantel clock.

"They looked up at us," he said. "The one closest, a large blond man with a scar over his right eye, yanked a rifle from beside one of the planes and took aim. Just before he pulled the trigger, Papa screamed, 'Run, Pedro!' I was running toward the hill when I heard the shot.

"The man screamed something in a language I did not know. A second shot dug into the sand beside my left foot. He fired a third time, but I was over the hill. It was almost dark. I ran toward some small trees, but I fell. That's when I saw him."

"Saw who?" his audience asked in unison.

"A man. He ran past me and tackled the man with the gun just as he came over the hill. They wrestled. He hit the man who had killed Papa and he took his gun."

"Was the man who saved you one of your people?" Janie asked.

"No, no, he was a gringo or Anglo," Hernandez said. "He had fair skin. He picked me up and carried me to the woods. I led him to my house. Then we heard the planes start up. We looked up as they flew over real low. They were heading north. Mama told the men in the village about Papa. They grabbed the few guns they had and all of us went back to the shore. Papa was lying face down in the sand. He was dead.

"The big white ship was heading out to sea. It must've been about two miles out, maybe more, and it blew up. The sky and water were full of flames. Some started running away. We were all scared. Except the stranger. He stood there staring out into the Gulf. It was as if he had expected the explosion."

"Reverend Hernandez," Lije said, "who did the villagers say the strangers were?"

"Smugglers. Who else could they have been?"

"What happened to the man who saved you?" Curtis asked.

"He left. He got a ride with the only man who had a car. Before he left, he gave my mother a hundred dollars. That was more money than we had ever seen."

"What was his name?" Janie asked.

"Ricardo," Hernandez said. "We later found out he bought a ticket on a bus headed to America."

Lije got up and walked over to the windows overlooking the pond. "Ricardo" might be what a small Mexican boy would remember about a name with "Rick" in it. Was it Henrick Bleicher who had saved Hernandez' life? Was it that act that allowed five pilots and their planes to take off? Where had they gone when they headed north? What were they carrying? Was Arif looking for the planes and their cargo or was what he wanted still on the ship?

Curtis joined Lije at the window. "Mexico!"

"We're leaving tonight," he whispered. "McGee arranged it—a private plane that can spirit us down there so no one will find out where we've gone."

Lije walked back over to the couch and took a seat beside his guest. As he did, the Mexican took a silver chain from around his neck and handed it to his host. "You see them?"

Lije and Curtis both stared at two seemingly unrelated pieces of metal. "I see them," Lije answered. "One is a cross, the other's a bullet."

"The cross was Papa's. He lived each day for what that cross stood for. He was a good man. That bullet killed him. I wear these two things to remind me of how he lived and how he died."

"Lije," Curtis whispered, "this bullet looks like the right vintage. It was likely fired from the same type of gun that was used to kill Bleicher."

"Reverend Hernandez, please wait here for just a moment." Lije went to his office and wrote out a check for one thousand dollars, then returned to the living room and handed the check to his guest. "We greatly appreciate your time and have been deeply moved by your story. Please use this for your ministry."

The man's eyes lit up. "*Gracias!*" He quickly stood up and shook Lije's hand.

Guiding the man toward the front door, Lije said, "You must be tired. Diana will take you back to your host family. We wouldn't want to keep the Perrymans up too late. I know they're early-to-bed and early-to-rise folks. And thank you so much for giving us your time."

"You're welcome," the man answered, looking down at the check. "God bless you."

As Curtis walked Hernandez to her car, Lije mumbled, "What are the odds this guy would be here, in the Ozarks, now?"

He should have known the woman with the super ears would

pick up on it. "God puts people where you need them," Janie called out from across the room.

Two different threads, two different stories, had now merged into one. Saving the life of Omar Jones might well mean finding the answer to the mystery on Swope's Ridge. Were they getting close? Or was he reading too much into a legend?

50

KENT MCGEE HAD AMAZING CONTACTS. EVEN NOW, despite being the most hated man in America because of his defense of a convicted terrorist, the attorney could work miracles. A private jet had taken Lije Evans and Diana Curtis from the Ozarks to Tampico, Mexico. McGee had put the deal together in minutes with just two phone calls.

The flight was uneventful. Lije and Curtis slept for most of the trip. The sun was just rising when they landed at a private field outside of Tampico and were greeted by a well-dressed local who led them to his Mercedes. Within half an hour, Lije and Curtis found themselves at a dock where a Donzi excursion boat awaited them. On the rig was the very latest in underwater sonar and imaging equipment as well as scuba gear. As they motored away from the dock, it truly seemed nothing had been forgotten.

They headed north along the coast for thirty minutes until a text message gave them directions to a beach southeast of the city of Aldama. There, waiting on the sandy shore, was Ivy Beals. The detective waved as Curtis guided the boat to shallow water.

"Good to have you all in Mexico," Beals said as he stepped into the Donzi. "I'll give you an update as we head out to the wreck."

Pointing over his shoulder, the detective said, "Best that I can figure, this is where the ship dropped the planes. It matches elements of Hernandez' story. This morning a few old-timers from a village just up the way confirmed this is where they found Manuel Hernandez' body."

Lije glanced over to the treeless spot. If the preacher was right, that meant the white ship would've gone down a mile or two to the east. The water was clear, the sun was bright. If Beals knew how to use the equipment, they just might get lucky.

"Let's get rolling," the detective suggested. "By the way, Miss Curtis, we've never formally been introduced. It's nice to meet you."

"And you, sir."

"Take this thing due east, right into the morning sun," Beals said, "and I'll watch the imaging on the screen. If I see anything, I'll let you know."

With Curtis at the helm and Beals parked in front of the screens, studying the images produced by the ocean floor, Lije relaxed. He leaned back in the seat and took in the unspoiled beauty of this overlooked section of the Gulf of Mexico.

"What did you find out on Arif?" Curtis asked Beals.

"We were a day late. He checked out of the resort yesterday. He left no forwarding address and the name he used is on no flight reservations list. And, before you ask, he didn't use any of his other aliases either. So where he's going and how he's getting there is an unknown."

"So your getting here twelve hours before us didn't get us anything of value?" Lije said.

"He did hire someone to drive him up the coast to where we are now. He also spent two days out here on the water. I talked to the boat crew. They said he found a wreck, dropped a camera down, took some photographs, and had them head back to the dock. Then took off."

"Anything else?" Lije asked.

Beals grinned. "Something real interesting. I showed a photo to everyone who came in contact with him. The people at the hotel, the men on the boat, and those at the dock all identified him from that picture."

"Didn't think Mossad had any photos of Arif," Curtis said. "Thought you came up dry. Did you find a passport or something?"

"Nope, I was showing them a picture of Omar Jones."

That seemed to confirm what they believed, that Arif and Jones were twins. But with Arif gone, they were still working just a theory. They had to have the man in order to spring Jones. And the world offered a lot of hiding places.

"Shouldn't we hold off on looking for the Ark of Death," Lije shouted into the wind, "and go after Arif?"

"Don't think so," Beals replied. "He was here to view this wreck. That's the only clue we have. To get an idea of where he went, we need to know what he learned, if anything."

"Any idea where the spot is?" Curtis yelled, her long hair blowing in the wind. "There's a lot of wide open sea out here."

"I had the captain Arif hired come out this morning and mark it for me. If you look about a mile ahead, you'll see a red buoy."

Beals had done his homework, greased the right wheels. Arif's head start was not as big as Lije had feared.

"Get your gear on, Lije," the detective shouted. "We're almost at the dive site."

It had been a few years since Lije had donned a wetsuit, but he was well trained. He'd made several salt-water dives in the Caribbean and had spent time under the surface in North Fork and several other American lakes. Opening each of the large canvas bags, he made a quick inspection of the almost new Aeris equipment. The tanks were charged and the regulators appeared to be in good order. The fins and suits looked factory fresh. He was adjusting his mask when Curtis slowed the boat and coasted to the floating marker.

"Look at the sonar image," Beals said. "We're right on top of something big. I'll get my stuff on and let's go see what it is. Diana, keep an eye on the horizon and make sure no one knows why we're here."

"Sightseeing," she replied with a grin. "If anyone asks, we're sightseeing."

"Sounds good," Beals said, "but we don't want anyone checking our identification. After all, I'm to McGee what Paul Drake is to Perry Mason. Everyone knows McGee and I work together. Having me caught with you two would drag you back into the media circus."

As Beals changed into his gear, Lije looked over the side at the water, a brilliant aquamarine. He wondered about the ship on the bottom and what they might find.

"You ready?" Beals yelled from the back of the boat.

"Yeah."

"Got the camera?"

Lije nodded.

"Let's get wet."

51

Lije and Beals dove down through the warm water. With the detective leading the way, his bright light shining down into the depths, they slowly worked toward their objective. Ten feet became twenty, then forty, eighty, and finally there was the ship at one hundred and fifty feet.

Six decades in the water had turned the vessel into a rusting hulk. The torn edges of metal looked as if the charge had been set in the lower middle section of the ship. That initial blast probably had led to others, creating the very real image of fire on the water. The cargo had been tossed out of the hold and was now spread across the sea floor like giant toys across a playroom at Christmas.

The ship had settled on its port side. They swam slowly while Lije shot a video of everything Beals' light touched. Colorful species of marine life observed them, some coming close enough that Lije had to shoo them away. Most seemed interested in the bubbles coming from the regulators.

Swimming from stern to bow, they saw occasional curls of white paint stubbornly holding onto their aging iron canvas. About halfway along the football-field-length hull, Beals' light caught what Hernandez had seen as a child. A huge red cross, probably twenty feet from top to bottom and side to side, each arm three feet wide. A close examination revealed the symbol had been applied with little care. It would have looked fine from a distance, but up close it was easy to spot the crooked edges and drips and runs of red paint.

The light picked out a tank inside the ship, a swastika on the side. The hatch was open. No longer a killing machine, the gray German Panzer was now a hiding place for fish.

In front of the tank were several earthmovers piled up like discarded toys in an area where the massive blast had ruptured the hull. One hung halfway out of a huge gash in the starboard bow. Beals swam closer to the vessel and, using his gloved right hand, rubbed dirt away from the ship's name, *Die Bundeslade.*

Pointing toward the surface, Beals headed up. Lije shut off the camera, slipped it into his belt, and followed the detective. For a hundred feet it was a normal ascent, then, at the forty-foot depth, he realized something was amiss. Looking over his head, he saw nothing. And that was the problem—there was nothing there. The Donzi was gone!

Beals surfaced first. By the time Lije found the morning air, the detective's mask was propped up on his forehead and he was treading water, turning a full three-sixty. "She's gone!"

Curtis was gone, but they weren't alone. Two sharks, one about eight feet long, the other at least ten, were circling some twenty feet away.

As he treaded water, Beals yanked a knife from his belt and cautiously watched the two uninvited guests. If they approached, he would make sure they paid for any meal.

"You ever been in this situation?" Lije whispered.

"Abandoned or shark bait?"

"Either."

"I've been left twice, though not in the water, and never had to deal with sharks. Don't guess you have a knife, do you?"

"Ah, no."

"Don't panic. Keep your eye on the fins. If they move in for an attack—"

"Yeah, I know," Lije said. "Grab his gills, poke him in the eye. I'll do whatever is open."

"You've got the drill."

As if on cue, the sharks began to cut the distance between them. What had been twenty feet became fifteen and then ten. It was now just a matter of time before the fish made their move. The small one reacted first, making a sudden left and taking direct aim at Beals. Holding his knife up over his head, the detective waited until the shark bumped his leg and then drove the weapon downward. It found its target in the tough hide right behind the creature's head.

Lije had no time to see if the strike discouraged the intruder. Just as Beals' knife struck flesh, Big Daddy bore down on Lije. With no knife, he pulled down his mask, closed his fist, and slipped under the water. Sensing the move, the shark rolled toward his victim and, as he did, he exposed his snout to the man's right flipper. A swift kick found its mark just above the creature's tooth-lined mouth. Yanking himself to the left, Lije drove his fist into the shark's head. Temporarily discouraged, the shark cut to the right, swimming directly through a cloud of blood that had oozed from his teammate. Round one to the humans, but there would be no break before round two.

Spinning, Lije spotted Beals about ten feet above him. The detective was doing his fighting at the surface. He landed another blow, but his wounded adversary was closing fast for another hit.

Lije had lost his shark, but Big Daddy had not lost Lije. With a blow that felt like a bulldozer, the shark plowed into his back, then swam off. Lije had no strength left. When the shark turned back, it was too close. There was no time to fight ...

He heard the gunshot the same moment he felt a bump. But he felt no pain. The shark floated motionless beside him, a cloud of blood forming around its head.

Back-pedaling away from the creature, Lije heard another gunshot. He saw Beals and the other shark in another red cloud.

And then Lije saw the underside of the Donzi a dozen feet away. It appeared Diana's aim had been right on both times.

Surfacing, he spit out his mouthpiece and sucked in a deep breath of fresh air. He worked his way over to the boat's ladder, pulled himself up, and rolled over the side onto the vessel's floor. Moments later the rock-solid detective landed beside him.

52

"YOU GUYS OKAY?"

"I think so," Lije said.

Curtis took another look at the now bloody water, then moved over to the men. "Sorry I had to leave. There were some Mexican lawmen who seemed to be a bit too interested in what we were doing. I figured it'd be wise to take a short cruise until they cleared the area. I cut the buoy loose."

"Getting back a bit sooner," Beals gasped, "would've suited me a lot better. But I thank you for what we got. Especially your target practice."

Lije rolled onto his knees and steadied himself, then tried to stand. He fought to find his sea legs. Not only were his legs weak, his back was screaming in pain.

"Look at your tank!" Curtis yelled.

"That's a big dent," Beals said, struggling to his feet.

Lije unclipped his equipment and lowered the gear to the deck. They were right—his air tank did need some bodywork.

"So what did you find?" Curtis asked.

"The ship's down there," Beals replied, still trying to catch his breath. "It's the one Hernandez described to you two last night. Still some white paint, and the red cross was visible."

"So was some Nazi war machinery," Lije added as he collapsed on a cushioned bench. "We even found the name, but it's in German."

"I know some German," Curtis volunteered. "Do you remember how it was spelled?"

"Let me think. Die ..."

"The first three letters in the second word were B-U-N," Beals added.

"Yeah, that's right," Lije said. "Bun ... D-E, I can almost see it. I have it on video, but let's see if I can picture it. I remember thinking it reminded me of death ... Yeah, S-L-A-D-Y-E-D."

Curtis grabbed a marker and a writing board and scribbled what she had heard. She held it up for the men. "Is this it?"

Lije studied it for a moment. "No, I remember now." Grabbing the board and marker, he slashed through the second word and rewrote it. "It sounded like 'slayed,' but was spelled this way."

"*Die Bundeslade*?" she asked.

"Yeah," Beals agreed, "that's it. Any idea what that means?"

"'Ark of the Covenant,'" she replied, confusion reflected in both her face and her voice.

That made a weird sort of sense. The best way to hide an instrument of death would be to call it an instrument of life. With its name, its red cross, and its camouflage as a cargo ship turned relief vessel, *Die Bundeslade* would have been ignored in the days after World War II. Anyone who saw it would have automatically believed it was a hospital or relief ship. Those who saw it in the Gulf would've assumed it was on its way to Houston to get a load of food for starving refugees.

"Launched in the final days of the war," Lije said, "it was the perfect cover for carrying deadly cargo to the United States. I'm guessing what we saw was the Ark of Death."

"Makes sense to me," Curtis said. "Still, I'm confused. We know it went down in February of 1946. So why keep pushing the mission? The war had been over for six months."

Beals was pulling off his swim fins. "For some people the war is never over. They continue to follow orders long after their leaders are dead. That's how strongly they buy into ideas and how hard it is to give up on those same ideas."

"Two Japanese soldiers," Lije said, "remained in hiding in the Philippines until 1974. When told that Japan had lost, they refused to believe it. They had remained ready for battle for decades. Who knows how many other loyal troops died over the years in the jungle while following orders to never surrender?"

After unzipping and peeling off his suit, Lije sat back down and studied the calm Gulf waters. "There were probably men just as loyal to the Nazi cause. Even after the war ended, true extremists would still try to follow Hitler's order. Especially if that plan meant causing great harm to the nation that defeated Germany. There were Nazis who hid out in South America for years planning for ways to regain power in Germany."

"Arif," Beals noted, "probably believes that whatever super weapon was carried by that ship was flown toward America in those five planes the Mexican boy saw."

"What do you believe?" Curtis asked.

Beals' expression was grim. "We know the weapon you learned about in Germany was never used. We know people have been killed over it. Hope I'm wrong, but I think it's still out there and Arif has been assigned to find it for Al-Qaeda."

In spite of the balmy weather, Lije felt a chill. What they were looking for had kept the men on that ship fighting for an already defeated cause. What if Arif now knew what it was and where it was?

"Drop me off at the beach," Beals said as Curtis fired up the motor. "We don't need to be seen together. I want to check a couple of things before I go back to the States."

53

JANIE DAVIES HAD RISEN EARLY, FINISHED HER workout, eaten her breakfast, and gotten ready for work before she noticed it. What she discovered brought her to her knees. Her guide dog was sick. As she was snapping Harlow's harness into place, the dog had staggered and fallen. Now the animal couldn't get up. Panic seized her. No! Not Harlow!

"Don't worry, baby," she whispered as she stroked the smooth-coat collie's head. "I'll call Dr. Young."

She grabbed her purse, fished for her cell, and called the vet. Frantically, she explained that Harlow had fallen and was now having problems breathing. She was told to continue to hold her dog and keep talking.

The five minutes it took for Dr. Young's assistant to get to Janie's door seemed like years. Beth Meyer quickly scooped the distressed animal into her arms and raced out to the car. Janie grabbed her purse and followed as quickly as she could.

In the small clinic's examining room, the vet and two assistants flew through the initial exam. Janie gently petted Harlow as they worked. Her hands told her that Harlow was growing weaker. Had she gotten her here in time? Janie prayed that she had. She begged God to give her another chance.

"Janie," Dr. Young asked, "has Harlow been outside today?"

"Just in the backyard for a few minutes when I worked out."

"She's gotten into something," he explained. "We'll probably know what in a few minutes. We'll pump her stomach and see what we find. Beth will take you back to the waiting room. I'll be out as soon as I know something."

The bond between a guide dog and master is strong. Harlow was Janie's right arm, her eyes, and more. The collie gave her a degree of independence she wouldn't otherwise have. Without the dog, she couldn't freely walk around town, do her shopping, or even get to work without help. In Janie's solitary world, Harlow was her companion.

The next thirty minutes seemed endless. Tears filled Janie's eyes and spilled down her cheeks. It had been years since she had felt this alone. Bombarded by thoughts of life without Harlow, Janie felt her dark world become much darker. Yes, she could get another dog, and someday she knew she would have to, but she couldn't face that now. Not now.

God, please don't let this happen. Please don't let me lose my eyes again. I need Harlow. I'll do anything you ask; just give her back to me.

What had she failed to do? Was it something she could've prevented? Why had this happened when everyone she worked with was gone?

Then it hit her. Without Harlow, when she was alone, she was vulnerable.

The darkness that had been her world for twenty years now smothered her. It was as if her usually sharp senses had been switched off. Pulling her knees up with her arms, she began to rock, unaware of her surroundings.

"Janie," Dr. Young's voice startled her. Why hadn't she heard him walk up?

"Yes. Is she . . . ?"

"She'll be fine," the doctor said, his voice as soothing as a cup of cocoa on a cold night. "She was poisoned, but you caught it in time. She'll have no lasting problems. But I want to keep her a day or two, just until I'm sure she's okay."

Poisoned? Who would do something like that? Everyone loved Harlow. Could this have something to do with the Omar Jones case? "You said she was poisoned?"

"Rat poison," the vet explained. "My guess is that someone must've accidentally dropped it from a truck going down the alley and it got washed into your yard during that heavy rain we had early this morning. Beth's going over to your house to make sure that none of it's left. Don't worry, we'll take care of that so it can't happen again."

Wiping her eyes with a tissue, Janie nodded. "Can I see her?"

"Sure, let me guide you. Then Beth can take you back home."

"No," Janie said, "she needs to take me to work. Everyone's out of town, and I'm holding down the office today."

The dog was already feeling better. As Janie stroked her fur, Harlow licked her face. It was reassurance Janie needed. She left the clinic feeling far less helpless than she had a few moments before.

Still, the rest of the morning held a sense of solitude that all but choked her.

At work, with no one to talk to, Janie turned the radio on and prayed the phones would ring, but they didn't. After lunch at Fannie's Cafe, she continued the research McGee needed on Omar Jones' previous lawyers. It wasn't easy. She had to make call after call to run down judges and other officers of the court who could provide her with honest evaluations of the trio of court-appointed lawyers. Yet the tedious busywork actually thrilled her. As she built her profiles, conducting one interview after another, the time passed quickly.

She had just put the office phone down after speaking with a district judge in Texas when it rang.

"Evans and Jameson," she announced.

"Janie, it's Dr. Young."

"Is everything okay?"

"Better than we expected. Harlow's up and around and crying for you."

A smile crossed her face. "Should I come down? I can close up now."

"No," Dr. Young assured her, "she needs to keep food down to satisfy me she's ready. I could bring her to the house around seven-thirty tonight."

"That'd be super," she gushed, "but could you bring her to the office? I'll be working late on a project."

"No problem," Dr. Young replied.

"Thanks, doc."

54

HARLOW WAS COMING HOME! ALL WAS RIGHT WITH THE world. The black cloud had lifted, and Janie again felt she could do anything. There were no barriers.

At seven, information in hand, she called Kent McGee's private line. He answered after the first ring. "What did you find out?"

"I'm fine," she countered. "Thanks for asking."

"I'm sorry," McGee said.

She laughed. Satisfied she had fully regained her assertive nature, Janie let her fingers fly over the notes that had spit from her Braille printer. "Jordan, the first attorney, has barely hung on for years. He's lost a lot more cases than he's won. He just slips by on wills and divorces and doesn't do a very good job on those either. He's been married three times and all of his ex-wives hate him. I couldn't find one person who had a single good thing to say about his work."

"Well, that figures," McGee replied.

"McClowsky, lawyer number two, was young, green, and eager. His heart was in the right place, but he was in way over his head. He believed Jones' story at first, but the prosecution whipped that out of him over time. When his mother developed cancer, he used that as an excuse to bolt."

"Again," McGee noted, "that's about the type of representation

I'd expect to be provided for a man like Jones. What about the last guy?"

"Richter was once a solid defense attorney, but that was three decades ago. He had a son killed in the Gulf War and, when that happened, he fell into a bottle. He took a nightly bar exam that had nothing to do with the courts. He's been swimming in booze for almost two decades."

"So he's a drunk?"

"A very good one, but no longer a good lawyer."

"Thanks, Janie, I'll pass this on to Heather. In circumstantial-evidence cases, this would probably be enough to get us a good chance at an appeal."

"Yes, but when the evidence is stacked as well as it is in this case, I don't think what I've found will make a dent. You need the man who really did it to give Jones a chance."

"I know that."

"And," Janie added, "he wasn't in Mexico. At least not where our guys went."

"So you've heard from Lije."

"They landed two hours ago. He called. Told me Curtis was doing something in Batesville tonight and he was coming straight home. Did you know the office phone rang only once all day? I'm starting to miss the death threats."

When McGee failed to laugh, she said, "Lije would've been here an hour ago, but I ordered him to visit his Aunt Mildred at the nursing home in Ash Flat. She's been begging for him to come for weeks. So I put him on a guilt trip. And if you're fishing for information, he didn't tell me any more than I just gave you."

"Beals will be back in Little Rock tomorrow," McGee added. "I'll get what I need from him. Thanks for your work, Janie, and have a good evening."

"I think I will."

She placed the phone back in the cradle and rolled her neck. What a day!

As she stretched her arms, her chair creaked. If Lije were here, that would drive him crazy, but as he was still not home, no use in getting out the WD-40 and fixing it. She hit a button on her watch and a mechanical voice announced, "Seven-fifteen." Almost time. She got up from her chair, moved to the front door, and reached down to twist the lock to allow Dr. Young to walk right in.

That's strange. The door was already unlocked. She was sure she had locked it at five. Standing very still, she listened. The old wind-up clock was marking each second, her computer was humming, one printer was still turned on, and the icemaker in the small break room was dropping a fresh batch of cubes. But there was something else. The fluorescent lights were on. She could hear the hum. She hadn't switched them on when she came in. No one else had been here.

Her hand found the light switch. She gently moved it down and walked back to her desk. If only Harlow were here. The dog would know what she was missing.

With no one to guide her, her survival skills came into play. Act as if nothing is wrong. Concentrate. She had to concentrate so her ears could see.

There it was—a squeak. She could barely hear it, but it was there. She heard it again. A floorboard. That was it! There was a section of wood in Lije's office that gave under any kind of weight. There it was again.

This time there was something else too. It was a kind of squishing noise. It was faint, but it was there. It seemed to be getting closer. It sounded like a new athletic shoe.

Should she act as though she didn't know anything was wrong? If she did, would they leave her alone? And why were they here? What were they after? Had they already found it or were they still looking?

Janie reached down and hit the button on her watch, "Seven twenty-one." If ever Dr. Young needed to be early, this was the day. But were doctors ever on time for anything?

Nine minutes ... Got to stay safe for just nine more minutes.

She reached for the phone and yanked it from the cradle. Holding the receiver in her left hand, she began to tap in a nine, but there was no dial tone. She punched the second line and the third. They were all dead. They'd been working earlier.

She knew the lights in the reception room were off, but what about the hallway? She clicked the power button on the computer. That was one light she was now sure was out.

Where was her purse? She reached down beside her chair, but it was gone. She'd picked it up and carried it with her when she had gone to the front door. She had set it on the small bench. She had to get it.

Rising slowly, she tried to look casual as she moved around her desk and to the door. She found her purse, picked it up, and felt for her cell. It wasn't in its pocket. Her nimble fingers pushed by her billfold and checkbook. It wasn't in the main section of her purse either. Where was it? Had she left it on the desk? No, she'd dropped it back in her purse when she spoke with McGee. She would've heard it if it had fallen out. That meant the intruder had taken it.

Squish. There it was again. It was behind her and to the left. She yanked on the doorknob, but the door wouldn't budge. Someone was holding it! She could hear breathing right next to her.

She again hit the button on her watch. "Seven twenty-eight."

Two minutes! Got to do something. The back door was at the end of the hall. There was nothing in her way, she knew that, so she could run with no fear of tripping over something. It was now or never!

Janie made her break. She was out of the reception area in three quick strides. The hall was thirty feet long, so she could cover it in ten steps.

Squish! Squish!

"I know you're here," Janie yelled as she flew down the hall. "Help's on its way! You'd better get out of here before it's too late!"

Was that the seventh step or the eighth? The next one slammed her into the door, her face striking the antique oak just before her knee met the barrier. She should've crumpled to the floor, but fear managed to hold her upright.

Squish!

Ignoring the pain, she grabbed the knob with her left hand and worked the tricky latch with the other. It was stuck. It was always stuck. Leaning against the door freed it. A second later the latch moved. Yanking the knob, she stepped back and threw the seldom-used door open. She'd won! She could smell the night air, the flowers, and hear a cat meowing.

Squish! Squish! Squish!

"Ooof."

Janie's legs wobbled. Her hand dropped from the door. She felt a warm liquid run down her head and neck.

Then nothing.

55

LIJE EVANS HAD JUST LEFT HIS AUNT'S NURSING home when his cell rang. He waited until he'd made the left turn onto Highway 62 before he hit a button on the steering wheel that opened his phone in Bluetooth mode.

"Evans here."

"Lije, it's George Herring."

Herring was a good family man, a fine doctor, and his bass voice added something special to the church choir. He had moved from Dallas several years before in search of a quiet place to raise his family. He'd thought he'd found it until earlier in the year when the events of Farraday Road had spilled over into his emergency room. Then the horrors of working so many years at an intense and insanely busy Dallas trauma unit revisited him in a way that was far too personal. Lije considered George a friend, but not one who called.

"I'm guessing there's a problem," Lije said.

"Janie was attacked in your office tonight."

The response was so straightforward that it almost didn't resonate. Had he heard the doctor right? "My Janie?"

"Janie Davies," the doctor confirmed. "It happened sometime tonight while she was working in your office. Dr. Young found her about 7:45 when he was returning her dog to her."

Lije accelerated. "What happened?"

"The police are working on that now. Janie has contusions on her forehead and right knee and a very bad concussion. Someone hit her with a blunt object on the back of the head. It should have split her skull open. If Dr. Young hadn't found her when he did, it's doubtful she'd have made it. She hasn't come to."

"That's serious."

"Yes, though I don't know yet how serious," came the honest reply. "I know she'll live, but I can't say if there will be any lasting brain issues. When she regains consciousness, we'll run some tests, ask some questions, do some observations. Whoever hit her meant business."

This had to be tied to the case. No one would hurt Janie. Why had he left her alone? After the shootings and the car bombing, he should have hired a bodyguard for her. If she suffered from any long-term disabilities due to this, it was his fault.

"I'll be there in less than twenty minutes."

"Take your time, Lije," Herring suggested. "She's not going to wake up anytime soon. You can't do anything for her right now. None of us can."

"George, I've got a favor to ask."

"Sure, anything."

"Let Harlow stay in ICU with her."

"That's not the way things work in hospitals."

"Janie will know she's there. She needs that dog."

"Okay. Dr. Young has the dog now and he's in the waiting room. I'll go talk to him."

Lije pushed the Prius hard around the curves that led from the Sharp County seat to its counterpart in Fulton County. He alerted McGee. Ignoring speed limits, he slowed down only when he saw the squad cars parked outside his office. Lije pulled into a vacant parking spot, jumped out of the car, and raced up to where crime-scene tape had been stretched across the walk.

"Lije," a deputy called out.

He rushed up to her. "Just got back into town. I know Janie's in the hospital. I'm on my way there. Do they have any idea who did this?"

"No, they're dusting for prints, but it wasn't something random. It was too clean. It appears that nothing was taken. Either Janie stopped them or she was the target."

Lije ducked under the yellow plastic ribbon and walked into his office. "What's going on, Sheriff?"

Sheriff Calvin Wood pulled the lawyer to one side and whispered, "Has anyone told you what happened?"

"Someone mugged Janie."

"Yes, but we don't know why. Can you look around and see if anything was taken? I mean, her purse had all the stuff in it except her cell phone. We found that on the floor in the corner of the reception area. Nothing in the rooms looks out of place. She wasn't raped or anything. Maybe it was some idiot who didn't get the word you aren't involved in that terror thing. Or maybe it's tied to the car bombing."

"Let me take a look around."

"Put on some gloves," Woods said.

Lije took a pair out of an open crime-scene box. "But my fingerprints are all over here."

Woods nodded. "Hadn't thought of that."

The reception area appeared no different than when he'd last seen it on Saturday. There was the lingering smell of burned rubber from the car bombing. He checked Heather's office, the break area, and the conference room. Nothing seemed out of place.

As he walked down to his office, he noted blood on the floor by the back door. It was obvious Janie had been hit hard. Why would anyone do this? A person who couldn't see wouldn't have frightened most people.

Or maybe that was it. The person who broke in didn't know she was blind.

"No signs of forced entry," an investigator told Woods.

"She must have let the assailant in. Might have even known him," Woods said.

If the sheriff was right on that point, then there was reason to kill Janie. Still, what was the motive? Everything seemed fine.

Lije stepped into his office. Nothing looked different. He circled his desk, studied the bookshelves. The German's Bible was still on the right side of the desk. Wait! It shouldn't be there. That's where he had put it last week, but Monday morning he'd left it on the table. He hadn't touched it since.

Opening the top drawer on the right, Lije saw the ring and the German medal. The eBay purchases had not been of interest. Sliding open the right top drawer revealed three one hundred dollar bills. Robbery was not the motive. It appeared only the Bible had been moved.

He opened it and flipped through the pages. Three ribbons were still there, and the other two that had been sewn together were at Janie's house. Moving to the seventh chapter of Genesis revealed the marked page had not been taken. So why, out of all the books in the office, had this one been moved? What were they looking for?

He put the Bible back on the desk and walked out to the hall. "Sheriff, I can't see that anything is missing."

"Well, then I guess Miss Davies is the only one who can give us any answers. We'll just have to wait."

He looked over at his officers. "All right, let's go. We're done for the night."

56

LIJE LEANED AGAINST THE WALL BY THE FRONT DOOR. What were they after? What had he overlooked? It was time to backtrack through the office.

A walk-through of the reception area revealed nothing. The other rooms also appeared just as they had the first time he viewed them. That left his office. Only the Bible was out of place. Why?

Sitting down in his desk chair, he brought the fingers of both hands together in front of his face and thought back over the past few days. Was this tied to Omar Jones? Was it tied to Swope's Ridge? Was it tied to their trip to Mexico? Or had Janie found out something today? She hadn't earlier when he checked in.

He glanced over at the framed photo of Kaitlyn on the corner of the desk. Every facet of his life had spun out of control since that night when she'd been killed. Until then, everything had been so simple.

Picking up the photo, he stared into those deep brown eyes. When he did, he felt it.

Turning the photo around, he saw that one of the clasps on the back was out of position. It wasn't holding down the back of the frame. When he'd hidden the formula behind the photo, he had turned each of the six clasps back into the exact position they had been in for years. The shape of each clasp had made a mark in the green felt. Now each was a bit out of position.

His heart in his throat, he quickly moved the clasps and pulled the back off. The small piece of onionskin paper fell out and landed on his desk. It was here! So why would someone have moved the back clasps on Kaitlyn's photo? Janie wouldn't have. Curtis had been with him. Heather was in Little Rock.

He turned in his chair to face his computer. No one knew about the formula but Janie and Nate. And neither one of them knew where it was. He'd been alone in his office on the morning when he'd hidden it. All he'd done was make a copy to take to OBU.

He walked over to the HP combination printer/copier. He'd placed the formula on the glass, pushed the button, folded the copy, and put it in his pocket. Then he had turned off the printer and taken the original back to his desk, where he had hidden it behind the photo. His door had been open, but no one had seen him. He was sure of that.

Noting the green power light on the printer, he pushed the off switch. How long had that been on? He hadn't used it since making the copy of the formula. He was certain he'd turned it off. Only Janie was working today, and she wouldn't have used it. Then it hit him. They didn't take the formula because they'd made a copy of it. But who? And how did they know about it? How did they know where he'd put it? Had someone hidden a camera? Had the office been bugged?

What they didn't know was that it was evidently worthless. Nate's initial tests had proven that if Hitler was going to kill the world with that stuff, he was going to have to pack it in an atomic bomb.

He considered putting the formula in a new place. Perhaps even taking it home. But why? If they had already seen it, they wouldn't be coming back.

Lije put the photo frame back together, first placing the formula behind the photo. He carefully adjusted each of the clasps and set Kaitlyn's photo back on his desk.

Janie needed him. It was time to be at her side.

57

WAKING FROM A FITFUL SLEEP, LIJE GLANCED UP AT the large clock on the waiting room wall. It was almost six. He had fallen asleep in a sitting position two hours earlier. Church members had stayed all night too. A half dozen were still asleep. Others whispered to each other. Like him, they were all there for Janie.

Lije stole out of the waiting area and headed for the cafeteria. After paying a buck for a ten-ounce soda, he walked through another deserted hallway, past a nurse's station, and straight to ICU. Dr. Herring was just coming out of Janie's room.

"Lije, glad you're here," the doctor said. "The signs are encouraging. The pressure's down and she's no longer restless. All we can do now is wait. I'll let you know if there's any change."

Lije opened the door slightly and looked into the room. Janie's bruised forehead was darker than it had been the last time he checked three hours before, but her color looked better. She wasn't nearly as pale. Harlow, her guide dog, was sitting beside the bed, her nose pressed onto the mattress near the woman's hand. Janie was going to be all right; she had to be, for both Harlow and himself.

He headed to the garden area for some fresh air. The garden, located behind the hospital, was the ongoing project of a local women's group. It had started on an acre of land ten years ago.

The trees planted that first season were almost twenty feet high. Curving beds added colors with a broad range of flowers. Shrubs added variety to the landscaping. Swings and benches had been placed along the concrete walks, providing a welcome retreat for staff, patients, and visitors—a haven in which to just be alone, to think, to try to find answers. It was answers Lije needed, but he was also hoping to find some perspective on the turmoil in his life.

It was just light enough to see where he was walking, but not bright enough to make out the garden's rich colors. The semidarkness set the perfect tone. He prayed for solitude, but even at this early hour, the little garden of Eden quietly buzzed with activity. He politely nodded and smiled as he passed a couple sitting on a bench nearest the building. A stone's throw away, four people sat at a table. Farther down the walkway he passed a solitary figure sitting in one of the swings.

"Evans," a hoarse female voice called out. "Lije Evans."

He stopped and turned back toward the swing. The woman was heavyset, dressed in a robe. He didn't recognize her in the dim light. But like a distant echo on a lonely night, the voice sounded familiar.

"Good morning," he said.

"Thought it was you." She waved her hand. "I don't guess you remember me, do you?"

He remembered the voice. The name was on the tip of his tongue, but it just wouldn't slide off.

"Mabel Dean," she volunteered. "You visited my farm outside of Mountain View not long ago."

"Yes, of course I remember. I sat out on your porch and you told me about Jesse James' gold and Swope's Ridge."

Mabel coughed, forced a deep breath, and cleared her throat. Her voice a bit raspier, she said, "Didn't find Jesse's loot, did you?"

Mabel had sold the Ridge to Kaitlyn. Buying that property that Mabel's husband believed held Jesse James' loot had probably cost Kaitlyn her life. Yet it had also given Mabel the wealth the chain-smoking farm woman had dreamed of for her whole life. It had taken a death to bring Lije and Mabel together the first time and a near death to bring them back together now.

"No, not Jesse's loot. Did find some other stuff though."

"Just a legend." Mabel laughed feebly. "That's what I tried to tell Micah—just a legend." Her voice drifted off as the cough came back. She hacked a few seconds before once more gaining control.

"You visiting someone?" Lije asked.

"Naw." She again waved her hand. "I'm here for treatment. Lot a good it'll do."

"I'm sorry," he replied. "What's got you?"

"Four-pack-a-day habit caught up with me." She tried to muffle another cough. "The lungs filled with cancer. It's funny too. I mean really laugh-out-loud funny."

Lije expected her to continue, to explain what she meant, but instead she turned her face to the rising sun while futilely trying to grab a series of shallow breaths. Each attempt appeared to hurt more than the last.

Moving a step closer, Lije asked, "What's funny, Mabel? You lost me on that."

"Life." She sighed. "Just when I finally get my hands on all that money your wife paid for the place, I receive a death sentence. Just never get a break." A spate of deep hacking coughs took control. Eventually the spell passed. "I keep wondering what death is like. It's got to be better than this. You want to know something else funny?"

He could now see her face in the early-dawn light. She had aged twenty years in the few months since their only visit. "What's that?" he asked.

"I've got no insurance, so all that money is going to be used up fighting the Big C. It'll run out about the same time I do. I figured that out last night. I spent most of my adult life waiting to get my hands on money. And now I'll spend the last few months of my life spending that money to buy a few more days and make my death less painful. Life's a joke—a big, cruel joke."

Lije wanted to respond, to give her some kind of hope, but fatigue and his own personal loss and now the shock of Janie's attack had robbed him of any wisdom he might have been able to share. So he opted for a reply he was sure would ring hollow. "I'll pray for you." It was simple, direct, and he meant it, but it still seemed like a lightweight throwaway pledge.

The woman was quiet as she looked up into his gray eyes as if searching for something. Finally she smiled. "Would you? Would you do that for me?"

"Sure," he replied. "Been doing that a lot in the past few hours for a close friend who's here."

She paused, then posed a question. "Your wife was murdered, but you still believe God cares? I don't understand that. I lost hope when Micah was killed. Then, when I sold the place to your wife, I just figured the money would make all the difference. And now this ..."

He understood. He really did. If money provided all you needed, then he'd be the happiest person on the globe. It was companionship that mattered. Finding a way to make a difference counted. Kaitlyn understood that. Janie did too. He'd taken it for granted until he'd lost it. "I don't know why," Lije said, "but deep inside I do believe. If I didn't, I wouldn't still pray."

"Is it too late for me to start praying?" she asked.

"I'm not a preacher, but I don't think it's ever too late. Maybe if you start praying, you won't feel so alone."

"I might try that," she replied. "Not expecting miracles though."

"I'll check back in on you," Lije assured her.

"Please do," she said, her voice begging him to follow through on his promise. "I need to get back in my room before they discover I've flown the coop. Goodbye, Mr. Evans."

"Take care, Mabel."

Lije watched the woman slowly make her way back into the

hospital. It was a shame. She was one of those who'd been looking so hard for the pot of gold that she had missed all of life's rainbows.

Mabel Dean had banked her life on winning some kind of lottery when all along she probably already had what she really needed. She just couldn't see it.

58

THERE WAS NOW ENOUGH LIGHT TO MAKE OUT THE various colors and shades of the thousands of flowers in the garden. As he continued his slow walk, Lije saw them but didn't absorb this tribute to natural beauty. His mind was too flooded with guilt. He was sure Janie was in the hospital because of something he had done. He was the cause. How many more people were going to be hurt? Was finding out why Kaitlyn had been killed worth all he was putting others through?

Maybe it was time to admit defeat, sell Swope's Ridge, and walk away. Trying to make an impact required too much effort, caused too much pain, incurred too much risk. If he needed any proof, it was in ICU.

Maybe Swope's Ridge was having the same effect on him as it had on Micah and Mabel Dean. Maybe it was causing him to miss the most important stuff in life.

"Lije."

The male voice startled him. To his right, sitting casually on a wooden bench that faced away from the walk, was a sunburned face hiding beneath a blue baseball cap.

"Ivy, what are you doing here?"

"McGee told me to talk to you," he said. "Saw you walk out the door, figured this would be the safest place for a private meeting. How's Miss Davies?"

"Don't know yet. She got hit pretty hard."

"Tough break, but that's why I'm here. I might have some information for you."

Lije moved closer. "When did you get back?"

"Four hours ago. Met with McGee at the lake house and then hurried up here."

Lije was puzzled. "Ivy, what could you possibly know that you didn't know when we were together yesterday?"

"Maybe a lot, maybe nothing. Sit down. I need to talk here so no one sees us together."

Lije moved quickly to the bench. "Did you spot something on the videotape?"

"No, haven't been over the tape yet, but I'm sure the ship offers us no real information. What I've got happened after you all dropped me off at the beach. Once you were out of sight, I took a second look at the place where the planes must have taken off, then went back to the village where Pedro Hernandez grew up. Do you remember in the story he told you about the man who drove Ricardo to the bus station?"

"Yeah, sure."

"I gambled that someone might have known him, so I asked around. You're never going to believe this. I found out that guy's still alive. He's in his nineties, but sharp as a tack. When I fished ten one-hundred-dollar bills out of my pocket, his memories of that day became even clearer than Hernandez'. One part of it's really interesting."

Lije leaned closer so he could hear better.

"The morning before the elder Hernandez was murdered, a different man walked into the village looking for someone who spoke English. The person he found was the man who drove Ricardo. His name is José Sanchez. The stranger asked if there was a store where he could purchase some supplies. Sanchez told him the closest place was about ten miles, but he could drive him there in his Model T, for a price. A deal was made and Sanchez and a friend, Ramón Tristan, drove the stranger to the store. The man purchased some food and booze and had Sanchez take him back to the beach."

"So Sanchez saw the planes on the ground?"

"No," Beals replied, "but he saw the earthmovers making what we know was a runway. At the beach, the stranger gave Sanchez the money and offered the men a drink. He mixed up something in two of the drinks and handed those glasses to the Mexicans. Told them it would add a real kick. The stranger made a toast and the three men lifted the glasses. Tristan drank it down, but just as Sanchez was going to join them, one of the earthmovers fired up its motor and startled him, causing him to spill his drink. He told me he was too shy to ask for another, so he just pretended he had enjoyed it. A few minutes later the stranger paid them an extra ten dollars each if they would promise to keep quiet about what they saw. True to their word, they both did."

This added a bit to Hernandez' original story, but didn't seem worth a special trip to Salem. They still had nothing. "Did he get a name from the stranger?" Lije asked.

"You're going to love this. Johnson. And one more thing. Sanchez was the one who took Hernandez' hero, the man he called Rick, to the bus station. As he dropped him off, he asked where he was going."

Beals waited for a person to walk past them. Only when the man was thirty feet away did the detective whisper, "Oz."

"What?" Lije was sure he had misunderstood.

Beals said, "Rick told Sanchez he was going to Oz. I'm guessing Sanchez either misunderstood the man or Rick was trying to lead him up a blind alley. I've done map searches and can't find any place by that name."

"Anything else?" Lije asked.

"A couple of things. Don't know if this first one means anything, but about a week later, Tristan started to get sick. At first it was just a bellyache, then he was short of breath. The village had no doctor, so his family treated his condition with some native herbs. Each day he continued to get worse. Sores broke out on his skin, his heart began to beat faster, and his breathing became more labored. By the third week, he was nothing more than skin and bones and smelled like he was rotting. Sanchez said it was like some biblical plague; it was as if his skin was being eaten away from the inside. His teeth fell out, he lost his sight, and he died screaming. That was eighteen days after they had been to the beach. The villagers thought he was possessed."

"Interesting," Lije replied, "but where does it get us?"

"I don't know," Beals replied, "but here's the real kicker. After he finished his story and took my money, Sanchez informed me that another man had paid him two thousand the day before for the same information. When I showed him a picture of Omar Jones, he confirmed he was the person who had traded cash for information."

So Arif knew the story Hernandez had told them. 'Course, most of it was posted on the preacher's website. The rest the locals could probably recite verbatim. What had Arif seen in that story that they hadn't?

"Listen, Lije, I've got to go. I need to touch base with Klasser's brother. He might have a lead on Arif. He promised me he'd work on it. I'll contact you later today. If you come up with anything, let me know.

"Oh, and one more thing. I paid another grand for a rifle that was left on the beach that day. Obviously it's not the same gun used for Bleicher's execution, but I figured Curtis could tell if it's the same type. It's in the back seat of your car. You need to learn to lock up."

And then the big man was gone, almost as if he had evaporated into the morning air.

Lije walked back into the hospital, back to ICU and the plate-glass window that separated him from Janie. As he stood there looking at his assistant, it hit him. Arif was in Salem. Arif had almost killed Janie.

He backtracked to put logic with his belief. Arif must have watched them dive in the Gulf and followed them back to their plane. He found out who they were and where they were going.

Arif would have noticed the Bible on the table because of the one just like it in Mueller's room. He was trained in espionage. He would have known an amateur would hide the formula behind a photograph.

Finally, it was all beginning to make sense.

59

"How's Janie doing?"

Lije saw Reverend Hodges' reflection in the ICU window. The minister was new to the church and Lije had met him only a few times. "They tell me she's coming out of it. The next few hours will tell."

"That's something to hold on to. Let's pray that she's going to be just fine."

"That's what I've been asking for all night," Lije replied, his gaze intent on the events in the room.

Dr. Herring spoke to Janie. She answered. The doctor held up his hand, as if Janie could see the fingers. Then he obviously remembered, dropped his hand, and asked another question. From his smile, it seemed the answers were at least entertaining. Without taking his eyes off the two in the room, Lije said to the preacher, "Do you know Mabel Dean?"

"I've seen her name on the patients list, but never met her."

"Mabel's a bit coarse," Lije said, "but she's all alone and going through a tough time. Terminal cancer. I'd appreciate it if you could get some folks at the church to start coming by to visit with her. She needs something and someone to hang on to. Her whole life has been unhappy. It'd be nice if she could find some joy in her final days."

"I'll go down there now," Hodges said. "I'll be back."

"Thanks."

Dr. Herring, beaming a wall-to-wall smile, walked out of Janie's room. "It's amazing. Having half a church here praying for her must have done some good. Her mental capacities are fine. In fact, her biting humor's back. She wants to see you, but wear your bulletproof vest. Everything she shot my way was right on target."

"I appreciate the warning."

Thank God for big favors. Janie was going to be okay even though she was in that bed because he had involved her in his mess. He had put her at risk. That was a bitter taste he couldn't spit out.

"Hey, boss," she said as he opened the door.

"Hey, girl." He leaned over and kissed her forehead. "Let me guess: Old Spice."

"Gives you away every time." She laughed. "And if that kiss is supposed to make it feel better, it's not going to work. While I was asleep someone built a bowling alley behind my eyes. The strikes are easier than the spares. And let's not even talk about the gutter balls."

"I hear you're going to be fine," he said, relief in his voice.

"You were worried?"

"I should've been there. You shouldn't have been at the office alone. You should not be in this mess. It's far too dangerous. I've been thinking, to have a person—"

"To have a blind person? To have someone with a handicap? Is that what you were going to say?"

"Yeah … that's it. I never should have brought you into this. You were better off in Little Rock. You were safe."

"You hired me because you felt sorry for me," she countered. "You wanted to give the poor blind girl a break. All I ever was to you was a charity case. Nothing more. 'Poor little Janie.'"

"No," Lije shot back, "I hired you because you're good. I hired you because I saw things in you that proved to me you had great insight and wisdom. I hired you because the last firm you worked for thought your skills were tops."

"Don't you still need those things? That insight, wisdom, and skills stuff? Or has that changed overnight?... I guess it must have. You've obviously changed. I can read it in your tone. Sounds to me like you were the one who got hit on the head."

Like she'd done on so many occasions, Janie was painting him into a corner. "Yes, I need all those things. But working for me right now, the violence with Swope's Ridge, what we're doing with McGee, we're a target. I can see it coming. You can't."

"I can hear it before you can see it," she argued. "It's not your fault I got hurt. The reason it happened? Harlow was at the vet's. If she'd been with me, I'd have been much safer than you would've been if you'd been by yourself. I'm not going to walk away from my job. I don't scare that easily."

"But—"

"What do you want, Lije? Do you want to lock me in my house? For my own safety? Isn't that what they did to people like me a hundred years ago? My walking across a highway is a bigger risk than my working at your office. I like pushing my limits. I like trying to figure out this mystery. Don't trap me in a dark world. I want to live. I want to be involved with life, not hiding from it."

She paused. "Oh, and one more thing: if you fire me, I'll sue. I know my work has exceeded your expectations and the only reason you'd have for showing me the door is my handicap. You want to take me on in court?"

She was feisty. "Janie, how did anyone get the jump on you?"

"I fell asleep," she said. "I was too busy worrying about Harlow. If I'd been more focused, then I'd have picked up on it in time to do something."

"Any idea who it was?"

"Yeah. A man, six-foot-two, brown eyes, light sandy hair, three freckles over his right eye, walked with a slight limp. Wore a gray warmup suit."

That sounded a lot like—

"You're not actually buying that, are you?"

Her words caught him in mid-thought.

"I can hear things, but I can't hear freckles, brown eyes, and light hair." She giggled, then quickly changed her tone. "I have no idea. Could've been anybody."

Lije couldn't believe she had so easily reeled him in. "Whoever it was is still out there. How about if we hire a couple of off-duty deputies to provide office security for a while?"

"Might be good. Someone's after Diana. Don't want to see her hurt."

He laughed. "Yeah, this is all about Curtis."

"What did you find out in Mexico?"

"We saw the Ark of Death, a hundred fifty feet down, blown to shreds. It was disguised as a Red Cross ship. Confirms Hernandez' story. Arif was there before us, we're sure of that, but we don't know where he went after he left Mexico. Or if he's still there."

Lije looked at Janie and wondered again if he knew where Arif was—or at least where he'd been last night. But he saw no reason to mention it … yet. "Beals talked to the man who drove Ricardo to the bus station. In his nineties, but still sharp. Arif talked to him too."

"Well, at least you and Diana got a vacation at an exotic location. I can't begin to tell you the headaches I ran into at the office yesterday." She waited for his laugh, but it didn't come. "Okay, next time I'll go diving and you stay in the office."

"Deal."

Lije leaned over and again kissed her bruised forehead. He was almost to the door when she announced, "That kiss didn't work any better than the first."

LIJE PULLED OUT OF THE LOT AT THE FULTON COUNTY Medical Center and headed down Highway 9. A light shower had become a hard rain by the time he parked at his office and raced inside. He was surprised to find Diana Curtis in the conference room looking at the video of the shipwreck that Beals had forwarded via email.

"When did you get in?" Lije asked.

She paused the images. "About an hour ago. I actually got to my apartment about midnight."

"Thought you were going to spend the night in Batesville."

"No vacancies, so I drove back here. Slept like a baby. I was tired."

"Going to grab some sack time pretty soon myself. Janie's out of the coma. She's going to be okay."

Curtis quickly looked up, alarmed. "Coma? What happened?"

"She was assaulted here in the office last night. If the guy had hit her any harder, she probably would've died. Could've happened anyway, but Dr. Young came by a few minutes later. Got her to the hospital."

"Who did it?"

"Don't know, maybe Arif. At least he's at the top of my list. He might've followed us back and been looking for something in the office. No fingerprints. Just the ones that should have been here."

"What would Arif want here?"

Lije almost told her. He almost gave away the secret only he, Nate Brooks, and Janie knew, but caught himself. "Don't know. Nothing appears to be missing. Bleicher's Bible had been moved. I'm guessing he was looking through it to see if it was marked like Mueller's."

"Nothing else?"

"No, everything else is where it should be." And that was true too. The formula had been put back behind Kaitlyn's picture.

Why didn't he level with her? Why was he holding out on Janie finding the formula?

"Then it must have been Arif... Think he's still in the area?"

"Have no idea, but let's act like he is. Be careful."

Lije walked across the hall to his office. Opening the top right drawer, he retrieved the ring and medal and dropped them into his pocket. As he walked back down the hall, he yelled, "I'm going to Fannie's to get some breakfast."

The rain had stopped. He walked across the wet courthouse square and slid into his usual booth.

Fannie grilled customers with the same enthusiasm as she did burgers. Always seemed to know what was going on. "Hear Janie's going to be fine," the big woman announced as she slapped a menu on the table.

Good news traveled fast in a small town. "She still needs a few days, but she'll be back to work soon. No lasting damage."

"Who did it?"

Some things never changed. Fannie's latest query didn't surprise him. "That's Sheriff Wood's job, not mine."

"Then we'll never know. What's ya need?"

"Pancakes and sausage."

"Coke to drink?"

"You know me well."

As Fannie walked back to the kitchen, Lije pulled out the ring and the medal and turned them over in his hands. He stared at them. How had JoJo's ring and a Nazi combat medal ended up in an old farmer's estate sale? Why was JoJo's annual in the house at Swope's Ridge?

And Mexico. The shipwreck proved the Ark of Death was more than a legend. Was the formula worthless or a recipe for a catastrophe? And who had Sanchez taken to the bus stop? And why would the mystery man go to a place that wasn't on any map?

Lije knew he had the right pieces. Yet none of them fit together. What he needed was to find the key piece, then everything else would drop into place.

"What's on your mind?" Fannie asked as she set the food and Coke on the table.

"Oz."

"Yeah, a rainbow does make you think of that old movie. Look outside."

Lije looked out the window at the multicolored arch over the town and suddenly heard the words Judy Garland had said to her dog: "We're not in Kansas anymore, Toto."

Of course! Kansas! He looked at the ring and medal. It was time to go to the wonderful world of Oz.

61

IT WAS TEN ON FRIDAY MORNING WHEN LIJE FINALLY convinced Curtis to take off for the weekend. Her old college friends were having a mini reunion in Little Rock. Janie was healing much faster than expected, but had to spend the weekend in the hospital. Heather was still working with the students in Little Rock. So Lije was on his own.

He closed the office and drove to Hardy, where he picked up Robert Cathcart and the guest the professor had insisted was an expert on World War II history. Lije was sure Dr. Edith Lehning was on the trip more for personal reasons. After his chance reunion with Lehning at OBU, Cathcart had changed. At times he was almost giddy.

Two hours after leaving Cathcart's hilltop home, the trio boarded a Great Lakes Airways flight that took them to Kansas City. They changed planes at Kansas City International and finally deplaned in Liberal, Kansas. The mural on the small airport's wall proudly declared that they had landed in Oz.

After renting a Ford Focus, they drove north on U.S. Highway 83 until they reached the quaint prairie community of Sublette. The trip had taken eight hours, five hours of it in the air, but it seemed like so much more to the weary travelers. Still, as they pulled into the small community, their spirits rose. Parking the car on the main drag, Lije found that stepping out into the fresh Midwestern air was rejuvenating.

Western Kansas was a lot different from the hills of Arkansas. It was almost a culture shock. There were few trees and no hills. Glancing toward the west, the sky appeared huge and the horizon endless. There was a charm about the place, though. It was homey, friendly, and sturdy. It probably had to be sturdy just to stand up to the wind.

"Not much to stop the wind," Lije noted, pushing the hair off his forehead.

"I'd call this wide-open spaces," Cathcart said. "I'm famished."

Lije pointed to the Hamburger Palace across the street. The sign claimed the best food in the world. "We should be able to get some grain-fed beef in there."

The Palace's dozen or so patrons all glanced their way as the trio entered. The restaurant was small and quaint, with a 1960s feel. The booths had metallic red-and-white seats, the tables sported Formica tops, and the only menu was painted on the wall. Judging from the aroma, Lije figured he'd made a great choice.

"How you doing?" an elderly man asked. He wore jeans and a work shirt, topped with a John Deere cap. "Welcome to the flattest spot in the United States. You can see forever here."

"We've seen a lot of wheat," Cathcart said.

"And corn and wind turbines," Lehning added. "Looks like you all are on the cutting edge of green energy. But right now I want a slice of one of those cows I spotted on the ride up from Liberal."

"Then you've come to the right place. Shalee'll be right with you."

"Thanks," Lije said, sliding into a booth about halfway along the far wall.

An energetic high school girl waltzed over; her lively brown eyes and sun-streaked brunette hair framed a face that smiled as easily as the sun shined in the desert. She had to be both the head cheerleader and the homecoming queen because surely in a community this small there couldn't be two kids with this kind of beauty and charm.

"Haven't seen you before," she said, pulling a pad and pen from the apron she'd tied over her jeans. "You just passing through?"

"Kind of looking around," Lije explained. "What do you suggest we order?'

Shalee leaned closer. "I don't eat anything here. Too fattening. But you could go with the steakburger basket. The meat's real lean and I'll make sure they drain the fat off the fries before I bring 'em out. That way it won't be too bad for your system."

"Sounds good." Lije grinned. "I'll take a basket and a Coke."

Cathcart looked at Lehning, then ordered for both. "We'll take the same, with two glasses of water."

"Can you give me directions to the funeral home?" Lije asked.

"You have somebody pass away?" she whispered, the bright smile suddenly evaporating into a look of genuine concern. "If that's the reason for your visit, I'm so sorry." She was sincere.

"No," Lije explained, "but I need to ask a few questions."

"Then you must know someone who's about to die. Who is it? I've heard Ruth Willis is fading fast. You're not related to her are you? She was my babysitter a long time ago."

Lije shook his head. "No. No one I know is dying."

"Then why do you want to visit with our undertaker?" She seemed confused. "Healthy folks usually avoid him. Especially *him*!"

Lije considered how to answer that. Finally he opted for no explanation. "I just need to see him."

"Well," she replied, her disappointment obvious, "his name is Fred Murphy. He's sitting in that back booth all by himself. If all you need to do is visit, then just head on back there while I get your food."

Lije walked over to the back booth, where the funeral director was just finishing a sandwich. When he noticed the stranger approaching, he wiped his mouth. "Can I help you?"

"You're Fred Murphy?" Lije asked.

"Yes, I am." His voice was soft, his manner polite.

"Could I take a bit of your time?"

"I have all the insurance I need. And my pest-control contract runs for three more years."

Sliding into the booth, Lije smiled and said, "Nothing like that. I'm just trying to solve an old family mystery."

"A mystery?"

"My name's Lije Evans. I'm from northern Arkansas."

"Nice to meet you," Murphy replied, his voice again welcoming. "Why do you call it 'Ar-kan-*saw*' when it's spelled like Kansas?"

Lije ignored the barb. "A few days ago I bought a class ring and a World War II medal from an internet auction site. They both came from an estate sale here in Sublette. The dead man's name was Schneider."

"Oh, Schneider. William died a few weeks back. We handled the body, but there were no services. Used to be five of those brothers, but now there's only one left and he must be close to ninety."

"My great-aunt disappeared from Ash Flat, Arkansas, in the forties. Her class ring was in Schneider's estate. I thought maybe I could come up here and find out how her ring got here."

Murphy took another sip of milk. "There were never any women up at the Schneiders' place. Not a one. Afraid I can't help you. I wasn't born until 1958."

"What about Schneider's living brother?"

"James doesn't talk to anybody. None of those brothers ever did. They were loners. Never married. Worked their farms together, ate together, and never went anywhere except to sell their grain or buy stuff at the grocery or the feed store."

"You think James would see us?"

"If you took one step on his place, he'd shoot you. Only ones who get on that farm are the people he hires to help him with his crops, and there are certain buildings they aren't even allowed to look in. Strange people."

"No funeral."

"Nope, just sent the body off to be cremated, took the ashes out to the cemetery, laid him to rest beside the other three."

"Anything unusual about the body? Any tattoos?"

"Yeah, probably the family symbol or something. Two fancy *S*'s. All four brothers had it on the same place on their arms."

"Did they look like this?" Lije asked. Pulling a napkin from a dispenser, he drew the double lightning rods signifying Hitler's most feared men.

"Yeah, that's it. And there was one more thing. Really strange. They all had these really fancy boots. Never saw them wear them, but they had to have them on when they were cremated."

His hunch had been right. But how did JoJo tie in? He thanked the funeral director and walked back to the booth.

"Get what you need?" Shalee asked as she set the red plastic baskets on the table.

"Yes, thank you," Lije replied. "Just one more thing. Do you know any old-timers who have a grasp of history in this area?"

"Sure, but how much is real and how much is remembering big is hard for me to figure out. The way my grandfather tells it, the snows were a lot deeper and the farm a lot farther from school than it is now. The snow might have been deeper, but the farm and school haven't moved."

"I'm looking for someone who might remember events that happened right after World War II."

"That's a long time ago," Shalee said. "I'll do some thinking on it."

"One other thing: what are the first three digits of your phone numbers here? The three numbers that come right after the area code."

"Oh, 584." She was a bit confused why he would ask.

"Can I use the phone? It's a local call."

"Sure."

Lije pulled out Bleicher's "Buy War Bonds" matchbook. Opening the lid, he read again the Jupiter 4-7623, then tapped in the seven digits that went with the old letter-and-number system. Three rings later a man answered, "Yello."

"Who is this?" Lije asked.

"Schneider," the man replied. "And you?"

Lije smiled and dropped the phone back into the cradle. The number hadn't changed.

62

LIJE SAID NOTHING TO CATHCART OR LEHNING, BUT they should've been able to read the wonder now etched on his face. He'd found the needle in the haystack and he had eBay to thank. What luck! Or was it? Was there a hand guiding each move, pushing them in the right direction to uncover the answers to solve Kaitlyn's death and save Omar Jones? Whatever it was, he knew he'd soon be speaking face to face with the man at the other end of Jupiter 4-7623.

A few minutes later, just as they were finishing their sandwiches, the man who had greeted them when they first entered the Palace ambled over and pulled a chair up to their table. His expression was no longer open and inviting. It was now deadly serious.

"I'm Glen Osterbur," he said. "I'm old, my sight's not what it once was, I move pretty slow, but my hearing's still keen. I heard what you asked Murphy, and then Shalee put a bug in my ear that you were looking for some, what she called, ancient history."

Lije looked at the man. "Hope that's not a problem."

"No, sir. I just might be able to help you. My dad used to be the law in this part of the world. He was pretty good too. Not much got by him. You said you had a relative you traced to Sublette? When do you think she was here?"

"I don't know that she was," Lije said. "Josephine Worle was in her late twenties when she disappeared from Ash Flat, Arkansas, in 1946. One day she was at work and the next it was like she was simply caught up in a wind and blown away. She took nothing with her. My family never heard from her again. Then last week I found her class ring on eBay being sold by a man in Liberal. He'd bought it from William Schneider's estate."

"Was she raven headed, about five-foot-three, and had a creamy complexion?"

"Sounds like the pictures I've seen."

The man nodded. "As soon as you finish up here, take a drive out to the cemetery. Five miles north on the highway. Can't miss it. I've got to get something from my house and I'll meet you there. Don't take too long or it'll be dark."

Osterbur pushed the chair back under the neighboring table and shuffled out the door. He was getting into a fifteen-year-old Ranger truck when Cathcart asked, "What do you think that's all about?"

"He knows something," Lije said. "We're in the right place."

After leaving money on the table, Lije headed toward the door with Cathcart and Lehning right on his heels.

63

THE RIDE TO SUBLETTE CEMETERY WAS A STRAIGHT shot through farmland. The old burial ground was well cared for. Graves had simple markers. This far away from town, surrounded by nothing but farmland, it seemed a lonely place to Lije—although ever since Lije had buried Kaitlyn, every cemetery felt that way.

Lije parked his rental beside Osterbur's Ford Ranger. The man was standing in front of a grave marked by a small headstone.

Lije, Cathcart, and Lehning said nothing as they walked toward Osterbur. With no ceremony, he handed Lije a folder. The lawyer opened it and noted an eight-by-ten black-and-white photograph on top of probably a hundred pages of forms and notes. Though the picture had obviously been taken post mortem, he still recognized the woman. She'd been in many family photographs.

"Is that her?" Osterbur asked.

Lije nodded. Looking down at the gravestone, he realized why the man had brought them out to this place.

Unknown woman
Died 1946
May God Have Mercy on Her Soul

"My father spent most of his life trying to find out who shot her and why. She was dumped on a farm road a few miles from town. There was no ID and no area reports of anyone missing. He put out notices, but never got a response. He had her buried here.

"I was a kid back then, just a teenager. But even I sensed how this got to him. We had a big service for her. The case was so sad. The folks around Sublette kind of adopted her as our own. Even the Schneider brothers turned out for the funeral. My dad gave the money for the stone."

Lije felt a strange kind of sadness. Why should someone he'd never known, who hadn't even lived during his lifetime, evoke such feelings? Why did such an ancient death seem so fresh?

"You said she was shot?" Cathcart asked.

"Yes. Shot four times in the heart. The report's in the file. I figured you'd want it. They found some other blood that tests proved didn't belong to her. But never found another body. Who'd do a thing like that?"

Looking back at the photograph, Lije asked, "Did your father suspect one of the Schneider brothers?"

"Everybody suspected them of everything. They had moved here earlier in 1946. They were strangers, outsiders, so it was natural to be suspicious."

"How'd they buy their farm?" Lije inquired.

"Bought it a few months before they came to Sublette. Their agent was a man named Powers. When he signed the papers, he said he was purchasing it for some men who were fighting in the war. Heroes, he called them. He lived out there until they got here in 1946, then he just disappeared. The only thing he did while he killed time waiting was build a huge barn out behind the home where James Schneider lives now."

"What's in the building?" Cathcart asked.

"Nobody knows," Osterbur explained. "Nobody's ever seen the inside of that barn. I'm figuring no one will until James finally joins his brothers out here in the cemetery."

"Thanks."

"I've got something else for you," Osterbur said as he reached into his pocket. "They found these in the woman's pocket."

He handed Lije the wings JoJo had earned during World War II as a member of the Women's Airforce Service Pilots.

Maybe now she had a harp to go with them.

64

"LISTEN, HILLMAN, MEN ARE DYING. YOU REALIZE that? Every day you don't deliver, men die! It's that simple. We're tired of you telling us to wait just a little longer. I'm getting a lot of pressure. You shouldn't have breathed a word about this until you had it in your possession. Do you understand me?"

Barton Hillman's eyes narrowed to slits as he leaned forward in his desk chair. "I'm the one taking the risk. My career's on the line, not yours. I'm very close to getting my hands on what we need. And believe me, I don't like this midnight-meeting stuff in my home any better than you do."

The visitor adjusted his tie and walked to the door. As he reached for the knob, he turned and shot a look of disdain at his host. "You jumped that gun. You're not ready for the big leagues. Just tell me when you'll have what you promised. And it better be right this time."

"Things happen, but we'll get it. It's safe and no one knows what we're doing. I've made sure of that. I'll contact you ... soon. Just stay patient. After all, this is worth waiting for. Just imagine the power you're going to have."

The visitor took a final cold look at Hillman and walked out.

Hillman watched as the man got into his car and headed out the driveway. For years Hillman had looked for this kind of break.

He'd dreamed about delivering on a big job. And this topped even his wildest dreams. He was so close …

The ABI director had almost had it. Then McGee came along. Why was he there? Had he guessed what was going on? Hillman had been careful. He was sure he hadn't been double crossed.

He punched in a number on his cell and waited. When the call rang through to voice mail, he ended the call and hit Send again. He repeated it four more times. Finally a voice said, "Do you know what time it is?"

"Yes, and because of you I was hung out to dry. Do you know what that's like? We can't afford to make these people angry. You know what they can do!"

"Not my fault. You jumped the gun."

Hillman's face was red and the veins in his neck pulsed. "You should've contacted me."

"I tried," came the reply, "but things got in the way. We can't afford to be caught together. In fact, those were your orders. The press is everywhere. That's your fault. You set McGee up."

"But you destroyed it!" he shouted.

"I had to. Having it on me was a risk. I can get another."

"When?"

"Soon. Wait for my call. Now I'm going back to sleep. I'm turning off my phone."

The mantel clock chimed twice. Hillman threw his cell into a chair and stomped across the room. He'd seen it. He almost had it in his hand. And then he'd watched it be destroyed.

The secret of Swope's Ridge. Would that day ever come?

65

IT WAS TEN THE NEXT MORNING, UNDER CLOUDY foreboding skies, when Lije Evans pulled the rented Focus off to the side of the rural road leading to James Schneider's farm.

"Doesn't appear he grows much anymore," Robert Cathcart noted as he and Lije and Edith Lehning stepped out onto the gravel.

"It sure is humid today," Lehning said. "Kind of feels like southern Arkansas."

The professors were correct on both counts, but it was the first point that most interested Lije. The latter he'd just have to endure.

Schneider was growing wild prairie grass. It was strange that, during a time when grain was used for so many different things, including fueling cars and the world had millions starving, Schneider had turned his back on those profits. There were few farmers, even old ones, who'd walk away from a sure market. Even if they couldn't do the work, they'd hire it done or rent out their land. Yet hundreds of acres around the Schneider farm were unused. And that wasn't all that was suffering.

The man's two-story farmhouse was badly in need of paint. Compared with the other neat, well-maintained homes they'd driven by, this one hadn't seen a paintbrush in years. White strips peeled off every board.

But what most interested the visitors was behind the house.

The farm had six outbuildings. Five were typical corncribs, cattle barns, and utility buildings. One was unique. It stood out as surely as a dairy cow on a goat ranch.

The structure was more than sixteen feet to the top of its A-frame roof, at least sixty feet wide, and two hundred feet long. The front doors of the old wooden building were each at least twenty feet across. Though the doors were open about four feet, the agricultural cathedral remained so dark they were left to guess what was inside. On the one long wall they could see, the foreboding wooden mass had only one small door and no windows. What was its possible use out here in the middle of the Kansas prairie?

The sound of a John Deere tractor caught Lije's attention. As it slowed to a stop, the driver hollered, "You have car trouble?"

Lije shook his head. "Just wondering about that big building. Never seen anything like it."

"It's one of a kind," the farmer replied. "Been farming here for thirty years and never seen the doors open before. Never seen that truck there before either. If I didn't know Schneider would shoot me, I'd just drive up and satisfy my curiosity. Always wanted to know what the brothers kept in there. I'm moving on. Want to get this rig into the shed before the storm hits." Pulling down the throttle, the farmer eased down the road.

As Lije studied the fortress-like building, a man came out of the barn, jumped into the truck, and headed down the long lane toward the road. The truck had HighTop Dairy Products painted on the side. The driver smiled, his dark eyes shining, as he slowed to ease around their car. He waved as he passed, then hit the gas. At the next stop sign, the truck turned right. Soon it was just a blip on the horizon.

"Have you seen any dairy cows around here?" Lije asked.

Cathcart shook his head.

"Neither have I. Get in, gang, we're going to visit James Schneider."

"The morning's forecast on the motel lobby's TV did mention that conditions were right for severe storms today," Cathcart noted as he looked toward some ominous, green-tinted clouds. "And look how fast the front is moving!"

As he started the Taurus, a drop of rain hit the windshield. By the time he pulled up to the barn, the wind was gusting and rain was falling in buckets.

"Stay here," Lije said as he got out of the car and raced through the open barn doors. Stopping just inside the massive building, he took inventory. An old car was parked to his right, three International-Case tractors were to his left, and, just at the edge of the dark shadows, a man lay on the ground. The remainder of the interior was a black curtain of mystery.

Moving swiftly to his right, Lije reached blindly for a light switch. He found six. Flipping them simultaneously transformed night into day. And then he saw them: five silver tri-motor bombers. They looked like they had just come off the assembly line and could be fired up and flown at a moment's notice. The sight was breathtaking.

Heavy rain pelted the roof. Lije heard two car doors slam as he kneeled down next to what he assumed was Schneider's body. The dripping professors joined him.

"Amazing!" Cathcart exclaimed. "They look brand new!"

"They're Junkers," Lehning said. "Great planes. I've never seen one up close. The Ju-52s were so dependable, Hitler even used one as his private air transport."

"He's alive," Lije said as he carefully turned Schneider onto his back. The man groaned, then opened his eyes. For a few seconds he unblinkingly stared at the lawyer.

"Schneider?" Lije asked.

"*Ja.*" The voice was weak.

"What happened?"

"He took it," he whispered. "He took it all!"

"Calm down," Lije said. "We'll get you some help."

Schneider shook his head. "*Zu spat.*"

"That means 'too late,'" Lehning explained as she approached the man.

"Call 911, professor," Lije called out.

"I've tried," Cathcart said. "No signal."

Lije pulled out his own cell. He also had no bars. Storm must have knocked out a cell tower, killing service. They'd have to get Schneider into the car and drive him to a doctor.

The wind shook the big doors. They looked out just as one of the farm's few trees was yanked from the ground and spun before falling into the rental car.

"Don't think we'll be getting our deposit back on that one," Cathcart noted.

"Look!" Lije shouted. "Look at the twister on the other side of the house! That was a tornado that tore through here. It could've taken this whole place down."

He pulled a cushion from a tractor seat and slipped it under Schneider's head. "Who did this?"

Schneider didn't answer. His eyes were closed.

"Bleicher!" Lije said.

Hearing that name, the old man opened his eyes.

Lije leaned so close he could feel the man's breath. "Schneider, did you kill Bleicher?"

The old man didn't answer, but his eyes shot to a large square wooden post just to his right. The floor-to-ceiling post was solid except for a number of holes about four feet from the floor. Bullet holes.

So this is where Bleicher had been killed. Executed.

Lije got up and investigated. Beyond the post, in a cabinet nearby, were four rifles. The fifth one was surely at his home on Shell's Hill. Ballistics tests could match one to the bullet in the crate.

"Lije," Cathcart said, "he's trying to say something."

"Schleter?" the old man whispered as Lije fell to his knees next to him.

"Did he work with you?" Lije demanded.

"No," the old man gasped, he face twisted in anger. "He was *verräter*."

"That means 'traitor,'" Lehning explained.

"He ... the woman ... he stole ... formula."

"Did you shoot the woman?"

He nodded. "She saw us ... shoot Bleicher. She ... tried to run. She would have talked. They'd have killed us ... Bogen des Todes.... She was *nett und mutig* ..." His voice drifted off. He looked up, as if to a different place and time.

"'Nice and courageous,'" Lehning explained. "I don't think he wanted to see your aunt killed."

Lije nodded as he whispered, "You left her body by the road?"

"Bleicher too." He took a deep breath. "They didn't find him. Only her. We thought he'd lived. We went to the woman's funeral to see if he was there."

"Maybe he was alive," Cathcart said. "Maybe Schleter found him and took him back to Arkansas."

"If the shots missed the heart," Lehning explained, "he might have lived for a few days."

"But why hide his body?" Cathcart asked.

"Schleter was a foreigner, a German," Lije said. "If someone had found the body, he figured he'd probably be arrested." Looking back at Schneider he asked, "Why did you keep her ring?"

"My brother ... collected things. Always kept stuff."

"Lije," Cathcart called from the door, "the sky's getting darker. Major storm's coming."

Lije leaned back over the farmer. "What was the mission? Why did you need the bombers? Why did you come to America?"

He smiled. "To deliver death."

"Death?"

"We waited for orders. Never came ... All this time we wait

… General Renfelt … tell us our targets … never did. Now death gone. That man!"

"Lije," Cathcart shouted, "looking pretty mean! The sky's kind of sick green. Looks to me like hail's coming in."

The lawyer ignored the professor's warnings. What did Schneider mean by "death"? And why was it gone? Lije walked over to one of the Ju-52s. On a cart beside the plane were six small cylinders. "Are these bombs?"

Lehning nodded. "Probably small ones, but they wouldn't do much damage."

The front of the tubes looked as though they could house a detonation device, but more than three feet of the one-foot-wide tubes was hollow. A large caplike screw was on the floor. He noticed small bits of powder in several spots on the concrete beneath the tubes.

He hurried back to the injured man. "Schneider! Was the powder the death?"

"Ja."

"Where is it now?"

The old German flyer lifted his arm and pointed toward the door. "He … took it."

"Who?"

Schneider's arm dropped to his side. His eyes closed.

Lije leaned in closer and realized the man was no longer breathing.

66

"LIJE! TORNADO! IT'S GOT TO BE A MILE ACROSS!" Cathcart yelled over the howling wind. "It'll tear this place to shreds. Level everything!"

Lije looked back toward the planes and realized they were in a death trap. The odds of surviving here were minimal. If the collapsing barn didn't kill them, the flying projectiles would.

"You two!" Lije screamed over the clatter of hail hitting the roof. "Push that door all the way open!"

Schneider had maintained the planes. Lije had no doubt they would crank up even now. The tractors, even though one was fifty years old, were in perfect shape. He figured the old car, a 1934 Auburn 652Y Sedan, was also ready to run.

He opened the driver's door of the black-and-red sedan and glanced under the steering wheel. The keys were in the ignition. Sliding into the car, he spun the key, pushed in on the clutch, and flipped the old Startix switch down. The engine began to crank. Looking at the knobs, Lije pulled back on the one stamped C and pushed the gas pedal three times. The motor caught and stalled, but just like it had been built to do, the Startix box automatically restarted the car. By the time Cathcart and Lehning reached the vehicle, the six-cylinder Lycoming engine was purring.

"How fast does a tornado travel?" Lije asked.

"About thirty miles an hour," Lehning shouted, "but some have been known to reach seventy. This one looks like it's on steroids. It's probably moving like a freight train."

"I think we can outrun it. Get in and hang on!"

Lehning got into the back seat and Cathcart got into the front. Lije hit the gas and the old sixteen-inch, bias-ply tires squealed on the barn's concrete floor. The trio shot out of the building, the dark cloud looming in front of them. Hail and rain peppered the old hood and fabric roof as Lije twisted the wiper switch. The old six-inch blades went to work pushing moisture and ice off the glass.

Winding through the Auburn's three forward speeds, Lije drove directly toward the charging, swirling mass. Like two knights racing to meet on a jousting field, the storm and car moved recklessly toward a collision point.

Pushing back into the Bedford cord-covered bench seat, Cathcart screamed, "This is your escape route?"

Behind him, Lehning, her face amazingly placid, studied the storm that seemed to be reaching out to them.

"You a pray-er?" Lije yelled back to her.

"Of course!" she screamed over the noise of the car and the wind. "Been praying for years for Bobby to find his way back to me. Don't think God brought us back together to die here."

"Well, pray now!" Lije hollered. "We need angel's wings to get out of this mess."

One field remained between them and the twister. The strong forward winds were already lifting the car's nose off the ground. As he approached the road, Lije slammed the vehicle into second gear, mashed on both the clutch and brake, spun the steering wheel to the right, and fishtailed onto the road. He hit the gas.

"Now we can see what this baby will do!"

"Needs to do better than this!" Cathcart yelled while watching the storm through the driver's side window.

Lije hit fifty and was feeling like a miracle worker when a strong dose of reality hit. The road ended! They had come this close! A wall of tall cornstalks stood in the way. Then, about an eighth of a mile ahead, he saw a narrow strip of worn grass, heading like a path through the corn.

Jamming the car into second, he spun the steering wheel while ignoring the brakes. The car lifted up on two wheels but somehow made the turn onto the narrow trail that must have been used by farm equipment. With the tornado all but licking their rear-mounted spare, Lije hit the gas and pushed the ancient sedan into third gear. Even though the car was bumping along the path at fifty, the tornado still seemed to be gaining on them.

"You gotta get more speed," Cathcart urged, his body bouncing up and down in the seat.

Lije reached down to the center hub of the steering wheel and flipped a switch. If the Germans had done their maintenance, the vacuum-engaged dual-ratio rear end would still work and he could get another thirty miles an hour ... if he could keep it from sliding into a field or hitting a pothole and fracturing one of the car's wire wheels. He hit the switch, pushed down the clutch, and felt the car make the shift. He stomped on the gas and they began to gain speed. Looking in the rearview mirror, he saw that the storm was fading. If the car kept running, they could drive to safety.

"Look at that!" Lehning yelled.

The tornado hit the Schneider farm. The barn was dismantled before their eyes. Planes and tractors were tossed hundreds of feet into the air.

They finally got back to U.S. 83 and Lije turned south. The massive tornado was gone, pulled back up into the dark sky. A strange calm remained. When they reentered Sublette, it was as if nothing had happened.

"We made it," Cathcart said as the car stopped at the curb.

"We can thank E. L. Cord," Lije said. "Without this Auburn we'd be dead. Always admired the styling on these '34s, but now I'm a big fan of the engineering."

The trio swung open the suicide doors and stepped out.

A vaguely familiar figure stood on the sidewalk. He smiled at the trio and the vintage auto. "Guess I'm too late."

Lije glanced to the curb. He remembered this guy from classic car shows. "Collins, isn't it?"

"Yeah," he replied. "I drove five hundred miles because I heard about a 1934 Auburn. Wanted to see if I could buy it. But I guess you beat me to it."

"No," Lije answered, "just doing a test drive. Runs good too." He tossed the keys to Collins and added, "You might be able to get this in an estate sale that I figure will be happening pretty soon."

"Thanks," the man replied as he leaned over to check out the interior.

Lije studied Collins for a second only to have his attention suddenly diverted by the ringing of his cell phone. He looked over at Cathcart and said, "We have service again."

He put the phone to his ear. "Evans here."

"Lije, it's Nate Brooks."

"Nate, you're not going to believe what just happened."

"Lije, I was wrong." The chemistry teacher's tone was serious.

"About what?"

"The formula. Mixed some up, thought it was nothing until I stirred less than a gram into water. Tiger's dead. The cat. He drank just a bit before I could shoo him away. It ate him from the inside out in just three days."

Like the man in Mexico Beals had been told about.

"Nate, what would this do to a human?"

"It'd take longer, but it would be a horrible death. Lije, this is scary stuff. When mixed with water, it's lethal. A few pounds in a major city's water system could kill millions."

Lije was stunned. "Make sure no one sees it."

"Don't worry, no one will. You have the original, and I'm destroying all records I have and cleaning the computer trail. One more thing: in its raw powder form, it's highly combustible. It can easily be destroyed. I've already destroyed all I made."

"Good to know," the lawyer said. "I'll touch base with you as soon as I get back to Arkansas."

Lije snapped his phone shut. The German had said someone had taken the death. It had to have been the man in the milk truck.

"Did either of you get a look at the guy driving that tanker truck leaving the Schneider farm?"

"No, why?"

"I think I've seen him before. I just can't remember where."

"Let's get something to eat," Cathcart suggested. "I need a place to calm down this old heart of mine."

Lije followed them into the cafe and found his way to a booth, but mentally he was miles away. The others ordered and he barely heard them. He'd caught only a glimpse of the driver, but he looked familiar.

"Hello," Shalee said, moving her hand in front of Lije's face. The waitress grinned. "Looks like a dead man walking."

That was it! Suddenly Kaitlyn's death on Farraday Road made horrific sense. No longer were they just trying to save Jones. Now they were trying to save millions.

67

JOSHUA KLASSER LEFT HIS OFFICE, EXITED THE bank building, and walked to the parking lot. It was just past ten in the morning. He took a deep breath, casually looked both ways, then walked to his Mercedes. Slipping the keys into the ignition, he punched an address into his navigation system, started the powerful V-8, and backed out.

He drove in silence, ignoring three calls, carefully keeping just under the speed limit. He took I-66 across the Potomac River, cruised past Falls Church, Fairfax, and Centreville. At Catharpin, he exited and drove to the Manassas National Battlefield Park. Passing a campground, he eased into a picnic area, parked, and walked to a wooden table marked with a sign that said Butcher Family Reunion. It appeared, at least for the moment, he was the only participant in the big event.

A few minutes later a voice behind him said, "You follow directions well."

Klasser didn't flinch, nor did he turn around. "Beals, I saw you in my mirror the whole way. A waste of your time. You did not have to follow me. When I told you I would meet you, I meant it." The Mossad agent reached into his pocket. "And I removed the bug when I parked. Now what is so important that I had to book a later flight to London?"

"Arif."

Klasser continued to look directly ahead. "You have found him."

"No, we spotted him and we know what he's up to."

Allowing the Mossad agent to consider the words, the American investigator moved around the table and sat on the bench beside the other man. Beals rubbed his smooth head as he studied a face that gave away nothing. The man had to have Vulcan blood running through his veins.

"Arif. What is this to me? I see nothing here that was worth the drive."

The game was on. If Klasser meant what he'd just said, he'd already be back in his car. Yet he didn't move. He remained on the bench, his stoic face staring at the historic Civil War battleground.

"Strange," Beals noted, "how a place this beautiful can hold such horrific memories."

"Death is a relative stranger to Americans," Klasser replied. "Your culture has seen very little of it compared to most nations. We Jews have known so much death that at times it fails to sting us. In our world, death and life walk hand in hand. In yours, death is a foreign invader you do not have the courage to look in the eye."

"And so you don't care to look Abdul Arif in the eye?"

"It is the past. I live in the present."

"He killed your brother and his family," Beals said. "Surely you want to see him pay for those crimes."

"What is the value? That is what you do not understand. If a man has no value, then death is the option. Alive, Arif has knowledge that can be extracted. What could be learned from him would serve both our nations. Dead he is worthless. Ancient history is not worth reliving. You do not know where he is or you would not be here. Get to your point or I am leaving ... now."

Beals liked Klasser. He was direct, logical, and honest. But somewhere under that hard shell there had to be a heart. He had to care much more than he would admit. Given the opportunity, he sensed the Israeli would eagerly jump back into this game.

"Arif has obtained a huge amount of an old secret Nazi formula that, if placed in water systems, could wipe out millions. I doubt if he would've gone to all the trouble to track it down if he didn't plan on using it. We are talking millions who would die deaths unimaginable. The victims would suffer in agony for weeks."

If his words made an impact, it didn't show. Klasser's expression remained placid, his body relaxed. "Call in your own government; you do not need me."

Beals did need this man. He needed his contacts and his wisdom. Without him he had little chance of finding the target. "What would happen if you told that story to your organization?"

Klasser paused, then turned to face Beals for the first time. "They would think I was crazy. Arif's record with us makes him look like a loyal agent. I would have to launch an investigation and prove that he had turned. As I would have no evidence, the expenses allotted for this investigation would be small. Do you have any real evidence?"

"No," Beals admitted. "Only my word. And I can relate to what you just said. Last night when I told my contacts in the CIA and FBI, they reacted the same way. I have to bring proof before they'll get involved. They've been embarrassed by too many past instances where they've grabbed suspected terrorists, gotten huge publicity for the arrests, then had to let them go for lack of evidence. The news media ridiculed them for making the move and some lost jobs because of that exposure. They are much more careful now. Tip lines rarely ring anymore, and when they do, they are often ignored."

"Such is the way of life, my friend," Klasser replied. "You have just retold the story of the boy who cried wolf."

He was right. Too many innocent men and women had been targeted because of hoaxes. Now it seemed that every new lead was treated as a hoax.

"Joshua, I have one FBI agent who will work with me, off the books. No one else. He agreed because he's intrigued by the scenario

I've put together and he was the lead investigator in your brother's murder."

Was Klasser finally ready to crack? The man was so stoic, Beals couldn't tell.

Klasser's eyes looked straight ahead, his hands were folded. "What can I do?"

"A week ago Arif was in Germany. That was when he left for Mexico to obtain information on a long-forgotten Nazi plan called the Ark of Death."

"Arche des Todes." Klasser smiled.

"You've heard of it?"

"The stories scared me to death as a child, but I grew past those fears along with my beliefs in Dracula and the Mummy. It is a myth born of propaganda used to prop up Hitler in his final days."

"What if I told you I took a dive in the Gulf of Mexico and found the ship on the ocean floor? Arif saw it the day before I did. He also found out what happened to its cargo and beat us to it."

"You are telling me it really existed? Then why was it not used? Hitler would have gladly killed millions if he could have."

"The war ended before it could be deployed," Beals explained. "A group of extremely devoted SS men kept guard over the poison and the distribution equipment until two days ago. That's when Arif discovered it and killed the last remaining Nazi who knew of the Ark's existence. It seems he also broke into an office in Arkansas and stole the written formula. He has the poison and he can now make more."

"He will not use it," Klasser said as he waved his left hand. "That is not his way. He will pass it on to someone else to deploy. He will take the payoff. Arif is not a terrorist; he is a businessman. I wish my organization, the CIA, and Interpol understood that. Then we could push him out with the rest of the trash."

Beals grinned. He was sure the Mossad agent was hooked. Now it was time to reel him in.

"What do we do next?"

"We?" Klasser asked.

"Yeah, we."

"What you have told me is interesting," the agent said, "so I will delay my trip to Israel. I will go back to my office and put out feelers for chatter on potential targets and a timetable. I will have something by tomorrow."

"What if the deal is done and there is no chatter?"

"Then we have to figure out where the attack or attacks will be made. That requires guesswork and I do not like guessing on anything. If we are dealing with poison, then it is unlikely it could go very far before it is discovered. The collateral damage should be limited."

"This poison does not show up immediately," Beals explained. "It'll take days to begin to affect the body and then weeks to kill. The death is painful in ways that none of us can understand, though the eyewitness report I heard scared me to death."

"Antidote?"

"None that I know of. And likely no time to find one. If you had your hands on something like that and wanted to shake the world to the core, what target would you pick?"

The Mossad agent rubbed his chin and gazed off into the clear sky. It was likely a discussion he had had in one form or another several times before.

"If you wanted to cripple the world financially, you hit New York. That was the object of 9/11. That would also cause the most deaths."

"So that's what you think they'll do?"

"No, they realized their mistakes in the first attack. If they had it to do over again, they would have used all the planes to hit Washington, D.C. Chaos reigns when government leaders are brought to their knees. Imagine a scenario in which every employee in Washington suddenly died. The chain of command gone—not just one or two people, but six or seven steps below the top person. With no representatives, no senators, no Supreme Court, no cabinet, no FBI or CIA, no president or vice president, and no staff who work for all those groups, you have effectively ended the union. The only government you have left would be state and local. Who gives the orders? Who enforces the laws? Who stops the panic? No one would know. Anarchy would reign."

In theory the United States government couldn't be destroyed by any military, but one man could pull it off using old Nazi science.

Klasser stood. "I will let you know what I find. If what you say is true, Arif might well be the broker for the world's future."

The little man casually walked to his car, got in, and drove out of the park, leaving Ivy Beals alone at the aptly named Butcher Reunion.

The investigator walked over to a fountain and twisted the handle. He watched the water rise up and then fall into the basin. He released his grip, deciding he wasn't thirsty. He might never be thirsty again.

68

HARLAN BRISCO RUSHED ACROSS TOWN TO KENT McGee's office. He was running late. The attorney had been out of sight since Friday, but had now called a press conference on his defense of the other 9/11 terrorist, Omar Jones. A public-address system had been set up outside his office, and news media from all over the country had gathered.

Because he was late, Brisco couldn't get any closer than some thirty feet back from the mike. He wouldn't get to ask McGee any questions.

News was all about hooks and angles. Since he couldn't throw up any gotcha questions, maybe he could focus on the crowd that had been camping out around the office for days, ever since his story. Protest groups had each staked out their territory with their hand-held signs. Brisco saw a dozen robed members of the KKK, three large veterans organizations, a group representing the airlines, and several high-profile church leaders. They all had one thing in common—their hatred of McGee.

As he waited for McGee to arrive, Brisco began to feel uneasy. He'd written that first story revealing McGee's involvement in the Jones case with the idea of making one more big splash. It was a game to him. He had once won the Pulitzer. He had exposed wrongdoing. But as he scanned the crowd and realized its explosive anger, what he had done felt dirty. Wrong. Worse than the wrongs he had exposed before.

The common voice of the crowd grew louder as McGee walked out of his office and up to the podium. The lawyer smiled. The crowd booed and shouted. This was the Romans and the Christians, and one voice could never stand up to the mob's rage-driven racket. Yet for some reason, the lawyer seemed unflustered. McGee even laughed and ducked when a middle-aged woman tossed a tomato. He seemed content to simply wait them out.

Finally, curiosity calmed the crowd and McGee said, "In three weeks the state of Texas will execute Omar Jones."

"Let's do it now!" a man shouted.

"Hang him!" a teenager yelled.

Holding his hands up, McGee said, "I now have proof that casts considerable doubt on the conviction of Mr. Jones. The courts—"

Screams blotted out his words. McGee stepped back from the microphone, again content to wait. Finally, when the shouts had thinned to only a few random voices, he moved back to the podium. "Justice—"

Seven loud pops stopped his words. Amid the screams and chaos that followed, Brisco looked to the right. On a small rise just behind the parking lot stood a man with an automatic rifle still aimed toward the podium. He saw a police officer racing toward the shooter, fighting his way through the fleeing crowd. Two other officers had made it to the podium where the lawyer was lying in his own blood. His face was covered with it.

Brisco looked back toward the shooter's position to remember what he had seen—a white male, tall, thin, dressed in black track gear, a floppy hat. The spot was empty. The shooter was gone.

He turned back toward the podium. Would McGee live? And if he died ...

He watched as McGee's limp body was lifted to a stretcher and loaded into an ambulance. With lights flashing and short bursts from its siren, the ambulance rolled through what was left of the crowd and headed for Baptist Hospital.

Brisco walked back to his car. As he was putting the key in the ignition, it hit him—McGee had found evidence that Jones was innocent. And the shooter had silenced him.

Fear gripped the reporter as he realized what he had unleashed with his story. McGee could be dead, and in three weeks an innocent man on death row would die. He had to do something. But what? He couldn't undo the carnage from the bullets.

Sitting there in his car, he opened his laptop and began his story. "Famed defense attorney Kent McGee, who recently took over the case of The 9/10 Terrorist, Omar Saddam Jones, was shot today outside his office. Police are looking for the unknown assailant, but in truth the man who actually pulled the trigger will be easy to find. This reporter fired the first shot. I forced McGee's hand. I revealed that he was defending Jones. I put the target on Kent McGee. I wrote the first words that fanned the national hatred that culminated this afternoon in the shooting in Little Rock."

Brisco took a deep breath and reread his words. This was the truth. He was again the reporter he had once been. But at what price?

He again read the lead. It was strong, honest, and clean. It told the real story. But ...

He highlighted all but the first sentence. His finger hovered over Delete.

69

SENSELESS. THAT WAS THE FIRST WORD THAT CAME to Lije Evans' mind as he viewed his friend's lifeless body in the closed-off emergency room. Kent McGee hadn't even made it to the hospital. He'd died on the platform. Mob mentality had ruled. A modern lynching. A man using bullets for his kind of "justice." All over the country were those drinking a toast to the man who had brought down the lawyer defending "the other 9/11 terrorist." Without hearing the facts. Without knowing that McGee was right and they were wrong.

Lije shuffled through memories, the bitter and sweet thoughts of yesterdays. And a slogan from college days: "My country, right or wrong." McGee and Lije had been taught that the slogan didn't end with the word *wrong*, but rather with the word *right*. If only those who lived by the motto knew the rest of what Senator Carl Schurz had spoken in 1872: "My country, right or wrong; if right, to be kept right; and if wrong, to be set right."

McGee had been trying to set it right, and, like so many other great patriots, had been cut down. Senseless! Were they any more civilized than the mob that stoned a man named Stephen almost two thousand years ago? Stephen had been right too.

"You can't do him any good by staying here," a doctor told Lije.

Resting his hand on his friend's arm, Lije whispered, "Say hi to Kaitlyn for me." Then, before tears could find their way into his eyes, he walked out and stood just outside the door. The doctor, he decided, was spot on. He couldn't do any good. He could only harm. And now his friend was dead. Kaitlyn was dead.

Lije couldn't seem to do any good … anywhere. He had done nothing when Arif drove by with the toxin. He'd been missing when Janie was hurt. He hadn't saved Kaitlyn. And now McGee. He was impotent. A spectator. He needed to finally admit it and learn to live with it.

He walked out into the main corridor and was quickly surrounded by the media and curious gawkers. Now McGee would be remembered only for defending Omar Jones, the other 9/11 terrorist. All the good he had done would be swept away, tossed in the trash. He and the innocent man he was defending would never get a hearing and would be forever judged guilty.

Lije pushed through the crowd, got into his car, and headed north. He drove in silence, ignoring the chirping coming from his cell, barely seeing the towns he passed through. He was numb, resigned to his own powerlessness, empty.

He pulled into Salem a little after nine, made a right onto Main Street, a left onto Locust. As if on autopilot, he pulled the Prius into a space in front of his office. He barely noticed the three other vehicles already parked there.

Pushing through the unlocked front door, Lije looked at the faces gathered in the reception area. Heather, Janie, Diana, and Ivy Beals. All there. All knowing the awful truth.

Lije moved numbly down the hall into his office. He sat at his desk, and his eyes were drawn to the framed image of Kaitlyn. A sense of panic, of helplessness took over. Violence was destroying his world, and it had all started on Farraday Road.

"Evans."

The voice yanked him out of the fog. Lije looked up. "Beals. Surprised you're here. Figured you'd been in Little Rock."

The big man shrugged. "I can't do any good there. Besides,

there is work to do. With Kent dead, the game belongs to you now. You have to save Jones. You have to find Arif. And you have to do it before Arif uses the toxin."

"I'm not the man for the job," Lije said. "I don't have the experience, don't have the knowledge. And I don't have the guts. You need to find yourself another hero."

"We already have one," Janie said as she walked into his office, followed by Heather and Diana. The four stood in a line facing him. He took a long, calculated look at each of them and realized they felt the same pain he felt. They'd obviously been crying, but they also didn't appear to be ready to give up. In each face he saw a single-minded determination.

"Moses didn't think he was the man for the job either," Janie pointed out, "but with the right people around him, he managed. We're here. Maybe all of us together don't make up one Kent McGee, but together we can try. I know that life's not about what you can see, but what you can do."

Lije shook his head. "This is so much more than just Jones. Arif has something lethal only Beals and I know about. For the moment, Arif is the most powerful person on earth."

"For the moment," Beals said. "Now tell the rest."

Lije felt panicked. They could all be killed going after Arif. Yet if he did nothing, Arif would kill so many more. He looked again at each face. "The Ark of Death was a Nazi ship carrying a powder that, when mixed with water, is so powerful it can kill millions, even in small doses. The powder had been stored since World War II on a farm in Kansas, where five brothers from Germany had been awaiting orders. I got to Kansas too late to stop Arif. In fact we got to the farm and he drove right past us with the powder in a milk truck. If he mixes that poison into a large city's water supply, it will lead to the most horrific calamity this nation has ever seen. Bleicher died trying to stop that disaster."

"Then why," Heather said, "did so many people want Swope's Ridge if the powder was in Kansas?"

"The powder was in Kansas," Lije said, "but the formula was hidden on Swope's Ridge. It's the formula someone wants and is willing to kill to get."

The room was immersed in tomblike silence as they considered the magnitude of what they'd been unwittingly and unknowingly chasing.

"How would he deploy it?" Curtis asked.

"The Germans were going to use planes, bombers," Beals said. "They were going to drop bombs containing the stuff, probably into lakes that supply city water systems. The poison works slowly, so by the time anyone discovered it, it'd be too late to use an antidote. It takes at least a week for real symptoms to set in. I've been told the toxin slowly consumes the body from the inside out in weeks of horrible torture."

"That's why the verses in Genesis were underlined," Janie said. "Remember, it said that 'all living things on earth perished.' Except it didn't mean a flood; it meant the water we drink. Consider that power in the hands of terrorists."

"Imagine the panic," Jameson added. "Water's the building block for everything. You can't give it up. And if people were afraid poison was in the water, they would be too scared to drink anything. They'd die either way."

"Why can't we call in the government?" Janie asked. "Let them put out the net for Arif. They've got resources we don't have."

Lije looked over to Beals. "I tried," Beals replied. "But even with my CIA background, they didn't believe me. This story sounds far too fantastic to be the truth. My former CIA boss laughed when I mentioned the Ark of Death. The reaction of the FBI and even Mossad was pretty much the same."

"But if they had proof?" Janie said. "Wouldn't having the formula, mixing up a dose, and seeing its power wake them up?"

Beals smiled. "If we had the formula. We don't know what the stuff is made of."

"Actually, "Lije said, "we do. Janie found the formula in one of the page markers in Bleicher's Bible. I had it tested at OBU."

"So you told me," Beals said. "You also told me the chemist destroyed it and all his notes on your orders. He couldn't put it back together if you gave him ten years. We need it now."

"He didn't have the original," Lije said. "It's right here."

Beals grinned. "With that, I can convince the feds. Then we can turn this over to the people with the power to find Arif. And if this can come together in the next three weeks, we can save Omar Jones."

Lije picked up Kaitlyn's photograph. He had checked on the formula that morning and had planned to move it to his safety-deposit box. But when he got the news that McGee had been shot, he'd rushed out. He turned the frame over, spun the clasps, and pulled the back off.

Lije stared at the white back of Kaitlyn's photo.

Someone had been in his office.

The formula was gone!

70

LIJE HAD BEEN READY TO QUIT, TO ADMIT FAILURE. He was now ready to fight. Somewhere out there, on a small piece of yellowed paper, was the most horrible secret on the planet.

"So if we don't have it, who does?" Janie asked.

"I don't know," Lije said. "But first we have to find Arif. He has the powder. Ivy, do you think Arif will try to use the stuff?"

"Probably not," Beals replied. "He's not a fanatic, he's a businessman. His business is just a lot different from ours. Joshua Klasser, who worked with him in the Mossad, said Arif's not going to place himself in danger. He'll play for any team as long as the money's right."

"So he's not much different than a hired gun, a mercenary," Curtis noted.

"His stakes are a lot higher," the detective said. "If he was a fanatic, he would have been on one of the planes on 9/11. He likes living too much to get that involved in any cause. My guess is that he has worked for several different organizations and is smooth enough to have them all fooled."

"Ivy," Lije said, "what did you find out about the truck? Any chance it's shown up somewhere?"

"The truck came from Texas. I traced it to High Top Dairy Products in Fort Worth. The truck you saw is probably one that had been stored in a facility on the outskirts of Weatherford. With the high cost of fuel, the company's experimenting with rail services for large city-to-city deliveries. A few rigs were taken off the road and stored. When I called High Top two days ago, they discovered one of their rigs was not in the warehouse. I got the license number."

"Is there a way to trace its movements?" Lije asked.

"I know he hasn't gotten any tickets," Beals replied.

"What about weigh stations?" Curtis asked. "Aren't trucks required to weigh in when they cross state lines?"

"Yeah," Beals replied, "big rigs are. Adam Horne will work with us off the record. He's the FBI investigator who led the arrest of Jones. I'll see if he can get into the system and at least give us the direction the truck is traveling." He walked across to the conference room.

Lije steepled his fingers. What else could they do? They had to have a location. They all sat quietly, trying to catch words coming from the other room.

"Bingo," Beals said as he walked back into Lije's office. "The truck was weighed in Missouri, Illinois, Indiana, Kentucky, and West Virginia. The last report was yesterday. Klasser was right, Arif's going to D.C. Or at least the truck is. I'm sure of it."

"How'd you get the report so quickly?" Curtis asked.

"Horne ran the tag through the weigh station computerized logs," Beals explained. "The truck's moving steadily east, but Arif's in no hurry. If you look at the dates and times, it appears he's stalling."

"What does that tell you?" Lije asked.

"It tells me he has a meeting scheduled," Curtis said, "and doesn't want to arrive until the appointed time."

"Probably right," Beals agreed. "Hang on, I'm getting a call. Beals here." He waited. "Interesting. That's a whole lot of cash. All in Euros?... Thanks."

Slipping his phone back into his coat, Beals sank down in one of the chairs. "There's a relief group in Dallas that the Mossad believes is a front for supporting radical Islamic groups. This group has offices in all the major American cities. They transferred ten million dollars today to their D.C. office bank account. The full ten million was drawn out today not in dollars, but in Euros. It's now in the hands of an import-export dealer named Hakem. He's supposedly a legitimate businessman who deals mainly in fine rugs."

"Doesn't this all seem too easy?" Lije asked.

"Not at all," Curtis said. "Why should Arif suspect anyone's trailing him or even looking for him?"

She was right, Lije thought. Arif would not know his cover had been blown. The truck he was driving came from long-term storage. The barn he'd looted had been destroyed by a tornado. When Arif passed them on the road, he had no reason to believe he could be identified. Why worry? As long as he didn't get stopped for speeding, he'd be under the radar. A simple plan was always the best, and this one would've worked without a hitch if he, Cathcart, and Lehning hadn't gotten to Schneider's when they did.

"What happens now?" Heather asked.

"Lije and I are going to D.C.," Beals said.

"The office needs a new rug," Lije cracked.

"What about us?" Heather asked.

"Yeah!" Curtis demanded.

Lije looked again at each one gathered in his office. It was time to stop thinking like a hick-town lawyer and start thinking like Kent McGee. He needed a plan. They needed to stop Arif and save Omar Jones. "Heather, go to Waco and find Martin de la Cruz. Ivy can give you the address." Beals pulled out his Blackberry to retrieve the information. "And Heather, I don't care how much cash you have to lay out, get him cleaned up and on a plane with you to D.C. If we catch Arif, we'll need de la Cruz to clear this thing up."

"Lije is right," Beals said. "Arif's slick. He has good contacts in the CIA and other international organizations. Either we tie him up fast in the court system or we lose him. And I know enough about de la Cruz's financial situation to assure you he can be bought."

"Diana," Lije said to the former ABI agent, "someone other than Arif lifted the formula from the picture frame. His truck's route shows he couldn't have done it. Find some leads. Even if we stop the truck and destroy its cargo, the formula is still out there. Getting it back is as important as anything we do. Even if we get the powder, all we've done is postponed death, not stopped it."

Curtis nodded.

"Janie, I want you to go with Heather. I might need your skills in D.C. if we get to see a judge. And locate the prosecutor in the Jones case. We might need him."

"I've already done that," Janie replied. "His name is William Ruth and he's in Washington. He was recently elected to his first term in the House."

"You're a lifesaver. Is everyone set? Realize this, we all need to succeed. There can't be any holes here."

"You got it," Jameson said. "Janie and I'll get de la Cruz if we have to tie him up and drag him in."

"I'll turn this place upside down," Curtis assured the others.

They all appeared ready, but was he? Lije knew he wasn't a risk taker. Yet here he was about to plunge into a fight with a man who thought nothing of committing cold-blooded murder. In spite of that Lije suddenly was itching to get started. Maybe he did have a hint of hero stock after all. "Ivy, I need to grab a few things at the house, then I'll be ready."

"I'll get a private jet. I'll use McGee's connections. The plane will be waiting in Batesville when we get there. We'll be in D.C. before dawn."

71

FBI AGENT ADAM HORNE WAS WAITING FOR LIJE AND Beals at a private airstrip just outside of the nation's capital. "Good to finally meet you face to face," Horne said, extending his hand toward Beals. "Heard a lot of good things about you. Sorry about Mr. McGee's death. What happened was ..."

"There are no words," the private detective replied.

Horne pointed to a black Chevy Tahoe parked along the runway. "There's our ride."

Lije nodded and picked up a small bag. The trio walked quickly to the SUV and tossed their gear in the back. While Horne drove off the landing strip and onto a quiet rural road, Beals pulled out his cell and made a call. As he waited for an answer he said, "Adam, the man in the back seat was Kent McGee's best friend, Lije Evans. He'll be taking over for Kent now."

The agent waved. "Nice to meet you."

Lije just nodded.

"Klasser, what's happening?" Beals asked as he spoke into his cell. "Any movement?"

Lije watched the detective's reflection in the rearview mirror, but he couldn't read anything in the face. The detective never revealed his emotions.

"Thanks," Beals said. He looked at the driver. "You know the rug warehouse I told you about?"

"Know the area well. I can have you there in thirty minutes. Faster if something's going down."

"Nothing yet," Beals said, "but Hakem just left his shop and seems to be heading toward that area. It's the first time he's gone in that direction since Klasser placed him under surveillance. It seems he took a large duffle bag with him."

"The Euros?" Lije asked.

"That's my guess," Beals said.

They drove in silence. The open country became the city and the rural road turned into a congested highway.

"We'll be heading to a spot over by the Potomac," Horne said. "The district's old and almost forgotten. A lot of the buildings are vacant. It's an area where gangs meet. Not someplace you'd want to be after dark."

At the top of Lije's list of places to be tonight was a bed. He was so tired, he could hardly keep his eyes open. Finally, he gave in. Letting his chin sink to his chest, tuning out the murmured conversation in the front seat, he closed his eyes and didn't wake up until he felt the Chevy's motor cut off.

The century-old riverfront warehouses were huge, each surrounded by parking areas lined with chain-link fences. The windows of the old buildings had either been bricked over or were covered by plywood. Broken bottles were strewn over the sidewalks and trash blew across the streets like leaves in the Ozarks on a windy fall day. A sign warned that litterers would be arrested and fined.

"Why don't you check in with Klasser," Horne suggested. "Maybe he can give us a time line."

Beals pulled out the cell. The call was short. "The rug dealer stopped for something to eat. Looks like if he's coming this way, it's going to be a while. You know, eating sounds pretty good to me too."

"Did Klasser tell you how far Hakem is from here?"

"No closer than when he left his shop," Beals replied.

"Then," Horne said, "we can grab something to eat about ten minutes down the road. We'll bring it back here, park over in that alley, and keep an eye on the gate."

The meal was unremarkable, but filling. While they waited, Lije dozed.

Two hours later, with the sun standing straight overhead, Horne said, "I've got a problem. I have a meeting this afternoon. It doesn't look like this deal's going down. Do you want to take a break and go back to the office with me?"

"No," Lije said.

"We'll stick here," Beals said. He glanced over at Horne. "You're not buying the story, are you?"

"I'm buying that there's something on that truck. But I'm not buying into it being what you think it is. That's too Indiana Jones. I don't think what he found in that barn can kill millions like you do." Horne pointed to the back of the alley. "There's some trash cans back there. You could use them for seats or sit on the ground. It's up to you. Call me if something goes down. I'll send someone with supper around six."

"Fine," Lije said. He got out of the car and began the trek to a seat that wouldn't be nearly as comfortable as the Tahoe's well-cushioned bench. Beals followed a few feet behind.

As the Arkansas pair eased to the ground on the shady side of the dirty pavement, their backs resting against an old vacant grocery warehouse, they glanced back to the red brick building across the street. Knowing something would happen but not knowing when kept them prisoners.

"Get some sleep, Lije." Beals checked his watch. "It's one-fifteen and Klasser just told me our man's at a furniture wholesaler's."

Figured. This guy was acting like a small-town dog making his daily rounds, finding out what was in everyone's trash. "How do you think they'll try to get the stuff in the water system?"

"A reservoir is my guess," Beals said. "The McMillian Reservoir has furnished this city with water for well over a hundred years. Logic tells me that'd be the most effective method of distribution, but there are a thousand other ways. We did some studies when I was in the CIA. A terrorist attack on a water system would not be that hard to pull off. The problem is having a toxin that would do a lot of damage before it can be neutralized. Evidently this stuff is perfect for that kind of attack."

If they could stop the truck, Lije thought, then the how and where were no longer important. And the truck was headed right for them. Lije again lowered his chin to his chest. He told himself he needed sleep, he needed to have his wits about him when the truck did arrive. The sleep he prayed for came quickly.

Six hours later, a cell phone roused him.

72

"I GOT IT," BEALS BARKED INTO HIS CELL. "SEE you soon."

Looking over at Lije, the detective said, "It appears he's finally coming this way. Klasser doesn't believe he has any idea he's being watched."

"No activity at the warehouse?" Lije asked.

"None. The homeless are starting to wander back into the neighborhood. I'm guessing they sleep in the vacant buildings. Look down the street. You'll see some teenage boys, probably part of the gangs Horne mentioned. They're getting their kicks pushing around an old man. We live in a pretty sad world, don't we?"

"Yeah. Mine gets sadder every day."

Pushing himself off the pavement, Lije stretched and walked slowly down the alley, hugging the wall to keep from being seen. He watched the boys torment the bearded man, who was pushing a shopping cart filled with trash bags. They knocked the man down and tipped over his cart. He grumbled, picked up his stuff, and moved on. A few feet later they knocked him down again. Finally the kids walked away. They'd look back at the man and laugh. The man said nothing, just pushed his ball cap down over his eyes and kept walking. He was just crossing the street when a black Lincoln Town Car made a left and stopped in front of the rug warehouse.

Lije got his first look at the man he knew only as Hakem. The man was tall, balding, and heavyset. He had the look of someone at the top of the economic food chain. His suit and shoes were expensive. He had a large diamond ring on his right pinky and another on his left ring finger. He seemed unconcerned for his safety as he unlocked the gate, got back in the Lincoln, and drove into the parking lot.

Once parked, he made his way back across the wide expanse of pavement and relocked the entrance. Returning to the building, he punched in a code on a security box beside a small door. He entered the building and closed the door.

"That's part one of the equation," Beals noted as he joined Lije. "I'm guessing part two won't be far behind."

"Just out of curiosity, do you have a plan?"

The detective shrugged. "We play it by ear. There's one way into the building and one way out, at least for a truck. Until Hakem receives his delivery from the High Top Dairy Company, we'll sit here and wait."

"Heard from Klasser or Horne?" Lije was leaning against the alley wall, his eyes locked on the warehouse.

"Klasser found a spot down the street. Horne's still tied up in his meeting. I'm guessing he forgot to send the food."

An hour later it was dark, and dark in the old warehouse district meant pitch black. There were hardly any working streetlights and no traffic. The duo was not alone. A half block away about twenty young men had cranked up a boom box and lighted a fire in a barrel. Probably invitation only.

"Lije, when you saw Hakem lock the gate, was the lock a padlock?"

"I think so."

"Put your phone on vibrate."

Lije complied, and Beals reached into his pocket and pulled out a small cloth pouch. "Come on. I looked for security cameras when you were napping and didn't see any. If that's a simple lock, I can pick it. We'll work our way into the parking lot, and when the truck comes, we can use it for cover and get into the warehouse."

Lije followed right behind the detective. As they crossed the trash-laden street, he whispered, "So this is your plan?" He wasn't surprised when the bald man didn't answer.

Beals quickly picked the lock. A heartbeat later they were inside and the gate was again secure. The detective pointed to a loading dock on the west end of the parking lot. The two set off at a jog to the four-foot-high platform and slid under it, scaring off a half-dozen large rats. For the first time all day, their wait wouldn't be long.

They heard it before they saw it. The diesel motor echoed off the sides of the vacant multistory buildings. Then lights dancing on the pavement signaled the truck was getting closer. Rounding a corner, the milk truck headed for the locked gate and the end of a trip begun in a place called Oz.

The warehouse's big door—twenty feet wide and twelve feet high—cranked open. Hakem, now dressed in casual clothing, walked out of the building and across the parking lot. He unlocked the gate and was sliding it open when the rig arrived. After making a slow, sweeping turn into the lot, the driver straightened the wheel and drove toward the building.

"Come on," Beals said. "We'll jog in beside the tanker. Hakem has his back to us. He's closing and locking the gate. He'll never see us, and the driver'll be looking straight ahead. Let's move."

Rolling out from under the dock, the pair raced along the warehouse wall. The truck was almost halfway into the building when they got to the door and walked in. As soon as they were inside, Beals made another sharp right and ducked behind a long line of rolled and stacked carpets. Lije was right behind him. Hakem walked in, yanked a chain, and the door came down. After lighting a cigar, he strolled toward the truck's cab.

Only one row of lights—those in the center of the building—had been turned on. The dim light and the long rows of highly stacked carpets worked to the uninvited visitors' advantage. Hiding was easy.

The truck stood in an open area under the lights, a full thirty feet beyond the closed entry. Parked in front of the big rig was another large truck that said District of Columbia Water Department.

The truck's driver stepped to the ground and walked toward the back of the warehouse, giving the lawyer and detective a good look at him. Under the cowboy hat lay long, shaggy hair. A big, drooping mustache covered his lower face. This wasn't the guy who'd made the raid on the Kansas farm. Where had the switch been made? Where was Arif?

"So you're the man?" Hakem said.

"I am who I am," came the reply. "Do you have the money?"

The fat man pointed to a canvas bag by the door.

"I was told I'd be given a car."

"Mine's outside. Take it." Hakem fished out a set of keys and tossed them to the driver.

The man studied the keys, then asked, "When will you make your move?"

"I will do it when I do it. No reason you should know. I'll transfer the toxin to this truck, and when the time is right, my crew will put it in the city's system. The plan is worked out. I don't need to tell you."

"I must be well out of the country before anything happens. That was the guarantee they gave me." He walked over to the bag, yanked the zipper, and looked inside. Satisfied, he reclosed it and moved toward the door.

The time had come, Beals decided. He pulled out his nine millimeter. He and Lije still had the advantage. He spun around and in the dim light didn't see the paint bucket. His glancing kick sent it on a noisy journey across the concrete and into a wall. The detective lost his balance and momentarily fell to one knee. In the split second it took to regain his footing, the truck driver ripped a gun from his belt. Now the odds were even.

Tossing his duffle in front of the small door, the driver leaped over a crate and took cover. Slow to react, Hakem finally comprehended the potential for danger and awkwardly moved to join the driver. But his shoe caught in a break in the concrete floor and he was tossed to the ground. His stogie flipped from his mouth and landed on a stack of old newspapers.

Beals stood and fired two rounds, sending wood splinters flying. The driver responded, putting two shots into the carpet the detective was using for a shield, then raced to the small door. He twisted the handle, but the metal entrance didn't give. He cursed and then saw the number pad on the wall. He dove back behind the crate and ripped off two more rounds.

For the moment, both sides were safely out of harm's way. Neither party could get a clear shot. Yet the stalemate was about to be tested by another uninvited combatant. The small fire begun on the newspapers had spread to a shelf filled with paint and cleaning supplies. The ancient wooden shelves were so dry they offered the perfect tinder for the flames. The chemicals, primed to become small bombs, exploded, splashing flaming liquids onto Hakem's inventory. The carpet burned even more quickly than the shelving. Within minutes, flames were leaping a dozen feet into the air. The building was well on its way to becoming an oven.

On the wrong side of the warehouse, well away from the small door, Lije and Beals were trapped. If they moved out from their position, the driver could easily pick them off. If they stayed where they were, they would be cooked by the rapidly spreading fire.

Lije and Beals peered through the smoke and flames. Suddenly Hakem made his move. The detective locked his arm and drew a bead on the big man, but didn't shoot. Instead he let the rug dealer grab the chain and watched as Hakem frantically moved one hand over the other, lifting the large door to its full height.

With the small door so close, why had Hakem put himself in the open? Lije wondered. And why was Beals allowing the rug dealer to get away? But instead of racing out into the parking lot,

Hakem ran toward the center of the warehouse, right toward the fastest growing part of the fire. What was he doing? Then Lije heard the truck's motor fire up. Lije had his answer.

The fresh air from the open door was just what the inferno needed to rapidly escalate its war. Like an army closing in for the kill, the fire was circling its victims. The blaze, with so much dry material to consume and now a strong breeze to drive it, quickly reached every corner of the building. In a matter of minutes, or maybe seconds, the warehouse would be a wall of fire.

The milk-truck driver was the first to bail. Racing to the small door, the smoke now all but shielding him from view, he picked up the bag of money and headed toward the large open entrance. Beals locked his aim, but never got the chance to shoot.

The driver was about fifteen feet from the exit when Hakem yanked the semi into reverse and hit the gas. The big rig moved even faster than the fleeing man. Its back tires caught him and knocked him to the ground. He was barely able to roll away before the eighteen-wheeler's second wave of wheels passed him.

A section of the roof fell onto the vehicle's cab. But nothing was going to stop Hakem, not even the fire licking his windshield. The motor roaring, he cleared the entrance and made it into the parking lot.

Beals grabbed Lije by the collar and pulled him to his feet. They stumbled toward the door as smoke filled their lungs and heat baked their backs. By the time they reached safety, Hakem had shoved the rig into first, made a half circle around the lot, and headed for the locked gate.

The truck's headlights illuminated Joshua Klasser standing in the street. Even as the big rig headed in his direction, the little man stood fearlessly, anchored to the concrete, squeezing off rounds aimed at the cab's windshield. Somehow, even though the shots shattered at least half the glass, they didn't hit the driver. When the rig rammed through the gate, Klasser finally had to roll out of the way.

Smelling freedom, Hakem spun the wheel to the right to head east. It was the prudent move, but he had pushed the truck too hard. The cab's driver-side wheels lifted off the ground, then the tanker trailer tipped and the rig was on its side, sliding toward the far curb. The large section of burning warehouse roof had been shaken from the cab and now skimmed along the pavement right beside the truck.

Racing to the vehicle as it came to a stop, Klasser climbed up on the cab, threw open the door, and, showing incredible strength, yanked the driver out. As he did, the flaming section of roof the truck had brought with it hit diesel fuel spilling out from a ruptured fuel tank. As if following a fuse, the fire rushed back toward the rig. Klasser just managed to drag Hakem into an alley before the truck exploded. The hot shrapnel bounced off walls and flew down the street.

Yet the real show was just beginning. Because of the combustible nature of its toxic cargo, white-hot flames quickly engulfed the truck and leaped sixty feet into the air. The whole district would soon be an inferno. But the danger posed by the lethal powder was over.

Somewhere in the distance, Lije heard the howl of sirens. Help was on the way.

73

LIJE LOOKED BACK AT THE BURNING WAREHOUSE AND remembered something he had read many years before—the difference between those who are heroes and those who aren't is often determined by instincts. Quick reaction.

For as long as he could remember, Lije had always carefully weighed all sides before making a decision. His was a life not built on faith but on the sure thing—what he could see, touch, and hold. He was like those who couldn't follow Jesus out of the boat. As a result, he'd never had the thrill of walking on water.

Now, as he studied the raging inferno, he found himself again locked in a mental battle that dealt with percentages. Yet even as he began to examine the complete equation that made up this horrific situation, instinct kicked in. He knew what he had to do. He'd never been more sure of anything in his life. After a quick prayer, he jumped out of the "boat" he'd always shared with the fearful and cautious and into the one reserved for the bold. He raced back toward the blazing warehouse, vaguely aware of Ivy Beals screaming for him to stop. The old Lije would have done that, but not this one—at least not tonight. This Lije realized taking a great risk was the only way to win a greater victory.

The heat hit him ten feet before he made it to the open door and forced him to duck lower and raise his arm in front of his face. He plunged into what had become a set for Dante's *Inferno.* Keeping low to the ground, he peered through the clouds of smoke to get his bearings.

Flames and smoke were being sucked up through a portion of the partially collapsed roof, giving him a partial sight line. The searing heat made his eyes water so badly he could hardly focus even in areas where he should've been able to see.

What would Janie do? What had he learned from observing her?

If the driver hadn't moved since the truck hit him and he rolled away, he should be fifteen to twenty feet ahead and slightly to the left. If the door was the six on the clock, he needed to crawl toward the ten. He could do that even with limited vision. He just needed to keep his bearings.

For the moment, he was safe. The floor was concrete and nothing was stacked in this part of the warehouse that could burn. Crawling forward, Lije covered six and then ten feet. Staying low, his belly hugging the floor, he looked for the injured driver. He saw nothing to his left and nothing ahead other than burning carpet. To his right was the city utility truck.

Where was he? He should've been right here. Had he gotten out?

Lije heard a loud cracking sound and rolled onto his back. Directly above, a large section of the roof sagged, then let go with a groan. Scrambling across the floor, Lije made it under the utility truck just as the flaming jumble of wood and roofing material hit the concrete.

He'd struck out. The driver was either already dead or had escaped under the cover of smoke.

Crawling toward the rear of the truck, Lije took a final gasp of smoky air, coughed, and crab-walked back out into the open. He was moving quickly past the first section of fallen roof when he saw the hand. The truck driver hadn't made it out. He'd been trapped by part of a rafter. He was alive, trying to push the beam off, but he couldn't do it, not by himself.

Even as he heard another groaning of wood from above, Lije scrambled over to the man. Getting up on his knees, Lije looked into the man's frightened eyes. He deserved his fate. This was an appropriate punishment for his cargo of death.

Then Lije reached under the eight-by-eight section of wood, rose to his feet, and braced himself. He pulled up with his full strength and lifted the rafter an inch, then two, and finally three, but that was all he could manage. "Crawl out!" he screamed. The driver wriggled free and took a few steps toward the door, then awkwardly pitched forward. He rolled over, moaning as he held his leg.

Lije dropped the rafter, grabbed the man by the shirt, and moved toward the door, dragging his prisoner behind him. With fire and heat dogging him with each slow step and smoke threatening to strangle him, Lije somehow staggered the final fifteen feet.

At the door, he stood up, lifted the smaller man over his shoulder, and wobbled out into the parking lot. He hadn't gone far when Beals grabbed the prisoner and Klasser took Lije's arm. They had made it another forty feet from the building when the first fire trucks arrived.

74

"YOU'RE A FOOL!" BEALS YELLED. "IT WAS STUPID to go back in there!"

Wiping his face, Lije nodded. "How's our friend?"

"He'll be fine," the detective replied. "Even if I have to beat him to death, he'll be fine."

Seconds later an EMT rushed up and gave both victims shots of oxygen. His eyes still watering, Lije was vaguely aware of the firefighters charging toward the blaze, but as his vision cleared, his focus switched to the medic and the man he'd just saved.

"Vitals are good," the medic said. "He has a broken leg and a few minor burns. We'll be transporting soon."

"Actually," Lije said, "you won't."

"Excuse me, sir," the EMT said.

"That man to your right is with Mossad," Lije said. "He can show you his identification."

Klasser grinned, pulled out his wallet, and flashed his ID. "This person is one of our agents. I cannot allow him to be treated because it might compromise his mission. We have a doctor at our embassy. I will take him there."

"But—"

"No buts," Klasser replied. "This is bigger than you. Much bigger."

Beals added, "Call Adam Horne with the FBI. I'm sure he's on his way. He'll okay this."

"Yes, he will," a new voice announced.

The paramedic looked over his shoulder and saw a man holding credentials from the Federal Bureau of Investigation. "I'm Adam Horne. The victim will go with Mr. Klasser. And I want to point out that you never treated him. In fact, you never saw him. Do you understand?"

"Yes, sir," the spooked EMT said as he moved quickly away.

With the bright light from the fire as illumination, Lije studied the soul he had plucked from the fire. The charge into the furnace had been worth it.

Moving away from the others, he pulled out his cell, scanned the directory, and hit Send. He waited, then in a tone that was serious and demanding, said, "My name is Elijah Evans and I need to talk to the judge."

"Do you know what time it is?" a woman asked. "Do you know you're asking to speak to a justice on the Supreme Court?" She emphasized the last part, letting the words linger for a moment before adding, "I've never heard of you, Mr. Evans, and I'm sure the judge hasn't either."

"I know what time it is," Lije countered, "and I know what court he's on. You tell him this call was requested by the late Kent McGee. You tell him that, and I guarantee he'll talk to me."

Again she refused. "You're crazy. The judge is asleep. I will not disturb him."

"I'm not crazy," Lije said, "but if you don't immediately give this information to the judge, you'll be looking for a new job. I don't care if you're his wife."

He heard her put down the phone. Soon a male voice came on the line. "Kent McGee?"

"He was my best friend," Lije explained.

"What are those sirens I'm hearing?" the judge asked. "Are you in some kind of trouble?"

"Those sirens mean your life and the lives of a few million others were saved tonight, thanks in no small part to the work of Kent McGee."

"I don't understand."

"You will. I know this is highly irregular, but I need an emergency meeting with you tonight. It can't wait. An innocent man's life is at stake. I have information that can save him. I'm not sure how long I can hold that information until it is taken from me. If you valued your friendship with Kent McGee, you will see me. I know that if he had not been killed, he'd be on the line making this same request. We need to have a hearing in your home within two hours."

"How do I know this isn't a hoax?"

"Justice Carmichael, when Kent clerked for you, he argued in *Sims v. Dehoney* that the latter should have his property restored. You disagreed, saying there was no legal precedent for that ruling. Two weeks later, when Kent pulled out an 1845 case from a New York court, you were forced to change your view. You were the deciding vote in a five to four decision. No one but Kent knew that a ruling over a disputed pig was what changed your mind."

"He told you that story?"

"More than once. And he never gave it away to the press. I could go on about the car wreck in Minnesota on the fishing trip."

"No reason to. You know my address?"

"I do. I need two hours."

"See you then."

Ending the call, Lije dialed another number. This time a familiar voice picked up. "How you doing?"

"Just fine, Janie. Have you got de la Cruz?"

"Right here in our suite."

"You have the address I gave you on Justice Carmichael?"

"Home or office?"

"Home. I need you and Heather to have de la Cruz there in two hours. Can you do that?"

"No problem. We're booked in a hotel fifteen minutes from the address. I made the reservations." She was obviously proud of her foresight.

"Any problem getting Martin to come with you?"

"Money works magic," she said. "He studied racing forms all the way up on the plane. I'm guessing he was figuring out ways to use your cash."

"Did you get hold of our prosecutor turned representative?"

"Sure."

"Need him at the meeting too. Can you arrange it?"

"He's not going to miss the chance to be at the home of a Supreme Court justice, no matter what hour it is. I'm sure Mr. Ruth will bring a camera to record the moment."

"See you at one at the judge's home."

Lije walked back over to the other men. He told Klasser, "I need this man at Justice Carmichael's home in no less than two hours. Can your doctors work that fast?"

The Mossad agent smiled. "Do you need him there alive or dead?"

"Alive, and I mean that. He has to be able to talk. Just get him there. And don't change a thing. I want him to look just like he does now. Complete with the grime on his face."

"Why are you moving so quickly?" Beals asked. "Jones' execution is more than two weeks away."

"You have to trust me on this one. I'm sure Kent would be handling it the same way."

"Okay," Klasser announced, "let's go. And what do I do with Hakem?"

"I'm guessing Homeland Security might want first crack at him," Lije said. "Ivy, ride with our Israeli friend, and don't let that truck driver out of your sight."

"Got it. What about you?"

Lije looked over at the FBI agent. "Mr. Horne, can you give

me a ride? My bag's in your car, and I'm going to need to change clothes. And I also need you to get something for me."

"Sure," Horne replied. "Even though I'm not sure what you're doing, I wouldn't miss it. I can't believe you got Carmichael to agree to a meeting at this time of night. It'll be worth my time just to learn how you did it."

"And just think," Lije said with a grin, "you're going to be part of the floor show."

Lije turned back to study the fire. Seven trucks were now battling the blaze and, even though it was going to take a while to put out, it appeared the fire wasn't going to spread to any other areas. No life had been lost, thanks to his instincts, his leap of faith, and his charge into the burning building.

Now it was time for a plan of action based on logic. He followed Horne back toward the Tahoe. Just before getting to the SUV, he saw the homeless man from earlier in the day. The old guy was pushing his cart toward the fire. Lije reached in his pocket and yanked out a twenty-dollar bill.

Startled, the man took the bill, turned it over, and looked at it.

Lije put his hand on the man's shoulder. "Don't let anyone keep you down. Just keep getting up."

75

LIJE EVANS ARRIVED AT JUSTICE CARMICHAEL'S stately three-story colonial-brick home fifteen minutes before the scheduled appointment. Monique Carmichael, still a bit angry by the way she had been treated on the phone, answered the door and grudgingly escorted the lawyer and Adam Horne to the study. The gray-headed sixty-four-year-old African-American judge was dressed in a pair of navy slacks and a white shirt. He was sitting on the corner of his desk, visiting with the room's only other occupant, a man wearing a brown suit, blue shirt, and conservative striped tie.

"Justice Carmichael," Lije said as he walked toward the esteemed jurist.

"And you are Mr. Evans." Even in casual conversation, this son of a sharecropper had a booming voice that sent chills down Lije's spine. His firm grip, one he had used as a quarterback for Howard University, was as solid as ever.

Lije looked over at the other man. "And you must be William Ruth."

Ruth didn't waste time with small talk. "Your associate asked me to be here, but she gave no reason."

The judge smiled. "And I also was not made privy to why this meeting was so important and why it had to happen at this hour."

"You'll both know very soon," Lije said. "While we wait for the others to arrive—and I know they're on the way—I want to introduce you to FBI agent Adam Horne."

As the men exchanged greetings, Lije glanced over at Ruth. "I believe you already know Mr. Horne."

Ruth nodded. "He was the lead investigator in my—rather, the government's—case against Omar Jones, though the matter was pretty much open and shut."

Lije nodded. "It was laid out about as well as any case I've ever seen. Kind of makes you wonder why a high-powered attorney like Kent McGee jumped on it so late in the game."

The former prosecutor shook his head. "I hate to speak ill of the dead, but most men like McGee love the spotlight. He was itching for some media time and it got him killed. It was all about ego."

Like the athlete he had once been, Carmichael quickly moved away from his desk toward Ruth, folded his arms, and looked down at the man. His voice was assertive and strong as he carefully drew out each word. "Kent McGee didn't care anything about publicity and he didn't crave the spotlight. If he got involved in a case, it was because he was convinced something was amiss. He lived for justice. His death is a great injustice."

The former prosecutor looked like a boy who had just been scolded by his father. Turning his head in an effort to avoid Carmichael's eyes, Ruth stuck his hands in his pockets and stared at his feet. He stayed in that posture until the justice moved away and sat down behind his desk.

"Nevertheless," Carmichael said, "I also thought it was a strange case for Kent to take. Jones was the only one who could've killed that family. That has been pretty well established, beyond any doubt."

Lije nodded and walked over to the bookshelf. He pretended to study the leather-bound works for a few moments. As he did, it struck him that he was actually beginning to act like his late friend. Smiling, with his back to the others, he said, "I agree. On the surface, there's no way Mr. Horne or Mr. Ruth can be wrong. They did their jobs. And, in the incendiary climate of the time, the case deserved the great care they took at each stage of the prosecution. They are to be congratulated."

Turning, Lije walked back toward the center of the room, his hands still pushed deep into his pockets. "My other guests will be here in a few minutes. I'm going to step out of the room in order to meet them at the door. While we're waiting, I'd deeply appreciate Agent Horne giving you an update on the events that precipitated this meeting. I think you'll find them extremely interesting."

Lije walked out of the library and closed the door behind him. He was crossing the home's formal living area when he met Mrs. Carmichael. With her were Janie, Heather, and Martin de la Cruz.

"Hope we're on time," Janie said. As usual, she had somehow sensed his presence before he'd said a word.

"The Old Spice again. Right?"

"That and you're wearing the dress shoes that have a loose heel. You need to get that fixed."

"And Martin. We've never met, but I trust you like the color of my money. Glad you found a suit."

"Your money's fine," the man shot back, "but the story's not changing. What I told McGee will be what I tell tonight."

Lije nodded. "That's just what we want."

"Heather, you ready to grab a bit of the spotlight? This will be moot court on steroids. If we can play in this venue, we can pretty much practice law anywhere."

"That's why I wore the black power suit and white blouse," she said. "I've got everything you asked for, even a few more for backup. Do we stand a chance?"

"It's in the bag," Lije assured her.

Just then the doorbell rang.

"Mrs. Carmichael," Lije said, "I'm sorry for sounding rude earlier. I hope you'll accept my apology."

"Well, I suppose." She looked down at her hands and then toward the front entry.

Lije smiled. "Why don't you take these three into the library and I'll get the door."

He didn't give the hostess a chance to argue. Hurrying to the front entrance, Lije greeted a cleaned-up Ivy Beals, a dapper Joshua Klasser, and a still ragged and dirty wheelchair-bound truck driver, his wrists cuffed to the chair's arms, his leg in an air-filled brace. Behind the trio was a fourth man.

"Lije Evans," Beals said, "meet the tenor in this quartet, Frank Moore. He's with Homeland Security."

"Doesn't surprise me you're crashing the party," Lije said with a grin. "I'm guessing you enjoyed the present we gave you tonight. Hope you're in good voice. You might be asked to perform a solo."

"What?" The thin man was obviously confused. Regaining his composure, he added, "We didn't know Hakem was involved with Al-Qaeda."

"You should have called us and asked," Klasser shot back. "I warned the CIA years ago, but they did not listen either." He didn't bother adding that Mossad had missed the warning signs as well.

"Well—" Moore began, but Lije cut him off.

"Gentlemen. We're going to the library. That is, except Ivy. Did you get a name for this guy?"

"If I hadn't heard him talk at the warehouse," Beals said, "I'd swear he was mute."

"That's fine," Lije said. "You stay with him until I send for you. Wait in the living room outside the library door. Believe me, he'll lead us right to Arif. Let's go, gentlemen."

In the library, after the next round of introductions, Justice Carmichael put his arm on Lije's shoulder and pulled him to one side. "I think I'm speaking for all of us when I tell you how much I appreciate what you did. Your actions saved a lot of lives. Maybe even America as we know it."

"You're overstating it a bit, sir. This whole thing, including what's going on here, was set in motion tonight by my trying to complete a run that Kent McGee began."

Turning to the others, Lije announced, "I see the judge has plenty of chairs. If everyone can find a seat, I'll see if we can quickly push through this rather unusual bit of business."

Lije waited by the door as Carmichael moved behind his desk to his high-backed swivel seat and the others found places on various chairs and couches spread out around the large room. After adjusting the collar on his red polo-style shirt and clearing his voice, a confident Lije said, "We've established in the court proceedings and through our visiting tonight that Omar Jones had to have killed Joshua Klasser's brother and family. Even you would agree with that, wouldn't you, Mr. Klasser?"

"We at the Mossad had no questions about the case. That is, until very recently," Klasser said. "I now believe someone else is guilty, but I do not know where that man is."

"You're wrong for doubting the verdict," Ruth barked. His tone combative, he added, "And if we're here to rehash that ancient case, this is a waste of time and money. I'm leaving."

"Well," Lije said, "it's my money. So just sit down and let me waste a bit more. Besides, you wouldn't have been invited to the party if you hadn't been on the case. And, if I may add, you never would've been elected to the House without that case on your résumé."

Ruth pressed his lips shut and took his seat.

Lije moved to stand behind the gambler, the prosecution's chief witness. "Martin de la Cruz is a remarkable man. Because he has hyperthymestic syndrome, he can never forget anything he's seen or heard."

"That was proven and established at the trial," Ruth said. "There aren't ten people like him in the whole world."

"He's incredible," Lije agreed. "Mr. de la Cruz, if you saw someone ten years ago and had a conversation with him, would you remember that, and could you still identify that man today?"

"Sure. Even if he had aged, I'd pick up things like his eyes, the way he spoke, the way he stood."

Lije walked over to the door and opened it. Ivy Beals wheeled in the injured man.

"The bald man pushing the chair is Kent McGee's chief investigator, Ivy Beals," Lije said. "Ivy's a former CIA agent and Mr. Klasser can speak to his expertise in both his public and private capacities. The man he's pushing, sporting the inflatable cast, drove the truck filled with toxin to the warehouse tonight. So he's our delivery man."

"You didn't tell me about anyone else," the Homeland Security agent said, looking accusingly toward the Mossad agent.

"You did not ask," Klasser replied, his smile revealing much more than his quiet reply.

This was good theater, Lije thought. "You both can have as much time with him as you like down the road. For the moment, he's mine."

The truck driver glared at the Arkansas attorney before returning his eyes to the floor.

"Mr. de la Cruz, please take a long look at our wheelchair-bound friend. I know he's a bit dirty, but just do a quick study and tell us if you've ever seen him before. I have complete faith in your abilities as, I'm sure, does everyone else."

De la Cruz got up from his chair and approached the prisoner. He studied the man from several different angles before returning to his chair. He seemed confused, a feeling he was obviously not used to experiencing.

"He looks familiar," the man who couldn't forget said.

"I can understand," Lije began, "how he could look familiar to any one of us, but how can he look familiar to you? If you'd seen him, no matter how briefly, you'd know him, right? After all, you never forget a face, a name, a date. Isn't that correct?"

"Yeah," came the reply. "But now I just can't remember where."

Lije looked over at Ruth, allowing de la Cruz' admission to

sink in before saying, "Perhaps Mr. Horne can help us out. Adam, I asked you to bring a fingerprint kit." Turning to the justice, he added, "Mr. Horne is one of this nation's top fingerprint experts."

Horne opened his briefcase and took out the simple tools and materials needed to obtain fingerprints. He walked over to the wheelchair. As the truck driver would not cooperate, a not-so-gentle Beals helped Horne obtain the man's prints.

"Heather," Lije continued, "I believe you have in your briefcase something we now need."

Jameson opened her attaché case and pulled out a file. With no prompting, she thumbed through it until she came to the page she knew her partner wanted. Retrieving it, she got out of her chair and moved to the table where the FBI agent was setting up a display. Lije watched as Horne looked from the card to the ten prints he'd just obtained.

"Amazing," the fingerprint expert noted. Shaking his head, he glanced back toward the man whose prints he'd just taken.

"Mr. Horne, you're starting to figure it out?" Lije asked.

"He might be," the judge said, "but I'm not."

"I'm in the dark too," Ruth exclaimed, not seeming nearly as angry.

"The prints I just took," Horne said, "and the ones we took from Omar Jones in 2001 are almost alike except for one pronounced difference. Jones had a scar on his index finger from a cut. These do not. Yet if I were to look at them, I'd swear they came from the same person. There are that many similarities. Except for the scar. Prints at a crime scene are rarely complete or perfect, so we have to make our cases on partial prints."

"You mentioned a scar," Lije noted.

"The prints gathered at the crime scene," the agent explained, "didn't show any scar, but the ones I got from Jones on October 12, a month after the murders, did. You know what's funny?"

"What?" the judge asked.

"The prints we found at the crime scene were almost complete and were everywhere around the bodies. Now that I think about it, it was like the criminal was leaving bread crumbs for us to follow."

"But prints not withstanding," Ruth argued, "de la Cruz saw Jones that night. You can't dispute that."

Lije walked over to the cuffed man, removed the cowboy hat, and put his hand in the driver's shaggy hair. A second later the wig was flying through the air and landed in the former prosecutor's lap. Lifting the prisoner's chin, Lije grabbed the mustache and gave a hard pull. The man yelled as it was peeled from his face.

Lije looked back toward de la Cruz. "Is this the person you talked to that night?"

"Could be," he answered. "I mean, I've always been sure of everything, but now I don't know. He looks just like Omar."

Ruth jumped out of his seat and raced across to the wheelchair. "How did you get Jones out of Texas? This is a trick!" Leaning over Carmichael's desk, he pounded his right fist on the top and yelled at the judge, "This is a trick! They've spirited a man off death row to confuse this issue! They've broken more laws than I can begin to count. They'll pay for this! All of them!"

Janie held up her cell phone and announced, "Mr. Ruth, if you can simmer down and use your inside voice, I have someone on my phone who needs to speak with you."

"Who?" he demanded, his face red, his fists clenched.

"James Ray Burgess. I think you know what he does. He went back to his office at the prison just for me tonight. I have that kind of charm. I'm sure he'd like to get home and get to bed, so talk to him and get this over with."

The former prosecutor grabbed the phone. "James Ray. I need to know why Omar Jones isn't in your prison tonight. And don't think I won't have your head for this."

While everyone studied the rookie member of the House of Representatives, Ruth's expression changed and his voice dropped to almost a whisper. "Are you sure?"

Looking toward the prisoner, Ruth handed the phone to Janie. "The warden is with Jones now. There's no doubt. He's there."

"So this is the man who killed the family," the judge said. "Why didn't we know about him before?"

"No one knew about him," Lije explained, "not even Jones. More than three decades ago, identical twins were born in Iraq. Their mother was not married and died during childbirth. Both boys were adopted, but by different families. Chance brought them together. This man needed someone to frame for the murders and by chance discovered his twin brother living right next door. Omar Jones still hasn't been told that we found his twin brother."

Lije waited for the information to sink in, then he turned back to his host. "Justice Carmichael, I need for you to set in motion the legal steps to get Omar Jones off death row and back home. I want all those who hollered for his blood to realize he was always telling the truth. I want the man who killed Kent McGee to know that he was dead wrong."

"I can move very quickly on that," Carmichael replied. "Mr. Jones should be free within two days, maybe sooner."

"Hold it a second," the representative from Homeland Security cut in. "We can make this a lot easier. We'll have the two men swap places, give Jones a new identity. That'll save the government all kinds of money and justice will still be served. Jones will be free and the Klassers' killer will pay for his crime. That's the easiest way to handle this, and our government will suffer no embarrassment."

"Justice and I have something in common," Janie countered. "She and I are both blind. To me, Mr. Moore's plan doesn't sound much like justice."

"In a normal case," the Homeland Security representative argued, "I'd agree. But we have to have an execution. The nation is banking on this. Judge, if it looks like we screwed up, then consider what it'd mean for national confidence in the very system you lead.

This has to be kept quiet. The switch is one sure way to do that. It's the best way for everyone."

"Except for Omar Jones," Lije pointed out. "His name will be forever linked to this crime. Even if he's alive and known as John Doe, his real name and therefore the real Omar Jones will always be cursed and reviled. He's innocent, and he deserves to be proven innocent. He deserves this nation's deepest apology."

"He's an Arab, for God's sake!" Moore shouted.

"Exactly," Ruth said, nodding in agreement.

"He's an American," Lije said. "And Kent McGee died because too many people see Americans as being only white and looking like you, Mr. Moore and Mr. Ruth."

As the two men glared at the Arkansas attorney, Lije turned toward Justice Carmichael. "Kent wouldn't settle for anything less than what I'm asking. If you give in to the demands of Mr. Moore, you'll not only be cheating Omar Jones and the American system of justice but you'll allow history to judge Kent McGee as a traitor when in reality he was one of the country's greatest constitutional champions. You were Kent's mentor. You are going to speak at his funeral. Are you now going to live up to the standards you taught him, or when Kent died did those standards die as well?"

Carmichael stood up, walked over to Moore. "Is this what America has come to, sir?"

Turning back to Lije he said, "Inform Mr. Jones that he'll be free as quickly as I can make it happen." Carmichael reached out and shook Lije's hand. "I'm guessing this meeting had to be tonight because you knew that if certain people in certain agencies heard about this situation, this prisoner would've disappeared."

Lije nodded. "It had to be tonight. And I believe, if you give Mr. Horne custody, we won't have to worry about Abdul Arif getting away again."

"Mr. Horne will have him. And thank you."

76

KENT MCGEE'S FINAL SEND-OFF WAS BITTERSWEET. One man stood out. On his return to freedom, Omar Jones, as a pallbearer, paid tribute to the lawyer who had believed in his innocence. His presence emphasized the irony of one innocent man dying because he had the courage to stand up for another innocent man who had only weeks to live.

That evening, as the sun set over the Ozark Mountains, a small party of mourners with a special link to McGee gathered at the log home on Shell Hill. Sitting in his living room, Lije Evans listened to his friends put memories into words. McGee, with his keen sense of purpose and honor, had been a star in this group, a leader. They reflected on what had been lost and what gains had been made. The talk eventually evolved into an awkward silence.

"The missing formula."

Beals put voice to the three words they had been avoiding all evening.

Lije stood up and looked at each of his friends, his colleagues. How could he ask them to do more? How could he again put them at risk? Yet if they didn't act, they and millions of others could face a horrible death. He looked from Janie to Heather to Diana, all sitting in safety in sweatsuits and sneakers in Salem, far from terrorists and bombs and death, waiting … for him.

"Tomorrow morning … let's meet at the office at nine. We'll start putting together a plan to figure out who has the formula. We've got to get it back and destroy it or what was accomplished in Washington will mean nothing."

"I'll be there," the private detective said. He stood up and stretched. "I'm going to go to the motel, call the family. This hit my kids pretty hard. Kent was like an uncle to them."

Lije walked Beals to the door. As he watched Ivy walk out to his car, he realized how relieved he was that the detective wanted to work with them. He was a good man. Lije needed him.

When he returned to the living room, he asked, "Anyone need anything to drink?" Before anyone could reply, Diana's cell came alive. The Russian polka she'd set for her ring tone didn't fit the evening's somber mood.

Pulling the phone from her purse, she walked into the hallway. Her words were muffled, unclear.

Silence held the group even after Curtis walked back to the couch. Looking around at his friends, Lije noted an expression on Janie's face he'd never seen before. Something was obviously bothering her. What was she thinking? Was it something about Diana? Was there some unfinished business between her and McGee she'd just recalled? How he wished he could read her like she seemed able to read everyone else.

Instead he had to ask questions. "Diana, did you dig up anything on who might've stolen the formula? We know it wasn't Arif. He was hundreds of miles away that day."

Diana shook her head as she set her cell on the coffee table. "I spent a whole day on it. The office was clean, no prints. At least no strange ones. Whoever was in there probably wore gloves. Arif must have had an associate."

"Doubt it," Lije replied. "He always worked alone. I don't think he'd let anyone in on this job. Besides, why make a copy the first time and come back to get the real thing? He needed the formula and he had it. To steal something twice … makes no sense."

"Diana, could you get me a glass of iced tea?" Janie said.

"I'll get it," Lije offered.

"No, you rest. Diana won't mind getting it, will you, Diana?"

"No, not at all."

McGee's death must have hit Janie hard. It was strange for the normally independent woman to ask anyone for help. Then Lije saw the tears. The blind woman cocked her head a little to the left and, as she did, a tear slid down her cheek.

Lije looked at Heather. She saw it too. Janie was so strong, so sure, so solid. And yet at this moment she seemed so fragile and lost.

"Here's the tea," Curtis said.

"Just put it on the coffee table," Janie whispered. The blind woman seemed to listen intently as the former ABI agent went back to her chair and sat down.

What happened next sucked the air from the room. If Janie had tossed a bomb, it might have had less impact.

77

"DIANA, WHY DID YOU TRY TO KILL ME?"

Heather almost dropped her coffee cup. Lije jerked his head around and stared at the blind woman. The only one who found a voice was Curtis, and though she attempted to sound strong, her tone was high and tinny, like a cheap wind chime.

"Is this ... some kind of joke?"

"No," the blind woman replied, "I wish it were. You were in the office that night. You hit me. You left me. I could have died."

Curtis forced a laugh, picked her purse up off the floor, and placed it in her lap. "The funeral's gotten to you, Janie. There's been so much violence, you're seeing demons everywhere."

Heather looked from one woman to the other, but said nothing. Lije licked his lips, but instead of defending the former ABI agent, he opted to let Janie lead.

"The night before the trip to Mexico, you took me home after the meeting with Reverend Hernandez. Lije offered, but you insisted. After you left my house, it took a bit too long for you to start your car. That's when you left the poison in the backyard, knowing I'd put Harlow out first thing the next morning."

"That's ridiculous," Curtis said. "Lije and I were on our way to the dive site."

"That's what made it so perfect," Janie continued. "You knew everyone would think that. You even convinced him you weren't coming back until the next day."

Curtis glared at the blind woman. "I didn't even know about the formula."

"Oh, but you did. The day Lije went to OBU with Dr. Cathcart, the day I gave Lije the formula right before he left, I thought I heard someone come back into the office just before that. Harlow yipped a little, like she does when she knows a friend is coming. It was you. That's how you knew about the formula. You heard me tell Lije. You just had to find a time when you were alone in the office. You thought you had the perfect setup and the perfect cover. You were sure I'd either be mourning Harlow's death or nursing her back to health. Instead, I was working late. That was where your plan backfired. I stayed late catching up on work because of the time I lost while at the vet's with Harlow. If you hadn't poisoned my dog, I'd have been home that night."

"This is ridiculous," Curtis said. "She can't be serious, Lije. She's delusional. Make her shut up."

"No, I want to see where she's going with this."

Janie nodded, her sightless gaze still aimed directly at Curtis. "Your shoes, Diana. I wouldn't have known you were there if it hadn't been for your shoes. You were so careful. No perfume. You didn't park in your normal spot in front of the office. Your shoes gave you away. One of your shoes makes a squishing sound with every step. It's very distinctive. You're wearing the same shoes now as you did that night."

Curtis fumbled with the clasp on her purse, stuck her hand into the bag, and pulled out her gun. "I never intended to hurt you," she mumbled. "You got in the way. I panicked because you are so darn perceptive. Still, I'm glad you're all right. I want you to know that."

"Diana!" Lije said, getting up from his chair.

Diana stood up and backed away from them, the gun a silent command to stay back. "I had to have the formula. I made a copy the first time, but had to destroy it rather than taking a chance on being caught with it. But I wasn't worried because I knew I could get it again. That's why I came back."

"But why, Diana?" Lije said. "You know how lethal the poison is."

"It's not what you think. I swear to you this was not about personal gain. It's for good."

Lije set his jaw. "You sold us out. You used us! You're Judas in a dress."

"No, I wasn't selling you out, I … what I did was for all of us."

Keeping her gun aimed at the ones she had so deceived, Curtis backed closer to the door. "This is a whole lot bigger than what any of you can imagine, but someday you'll understand … Be smart. Stay where you are."

No one moved as the woman backed out of the room and ducked out the front door. A few seconds later a car started. Lije walked to the window and watched the taillights disappear down the hill. He made no move to follow her or call the police.

"The gunshots and the bomb," Heather said. "They were just part of the cover. But why would she take the formula? Who has it now?"

Lije walked over to Janie, pulled her up from the couch, and leaned his head on her forehead as he held her shoulders. "I'm so sorry about all this."

"Don't be," Janie replied. "Remember, I told you that you can't tame a mountain lion."

Lije nodded, his gaze dropping to the coffee table. Diana had left her cell phone. He picked it up and scanned the most recent calls, both received and dialed. One name was on both. He punched Send.

"What's you need, Diana?" a deep voice asked.

"It's Evans, and I need to talk to you tonight. I'll be at your place in three hours."

"Make it four o'clock. Come alone."

78

LIJE WAS MORE THAN AN HOUR EARLY FOR HIS meeting. The "Make it four o'clock" bothered him. Why the wait? There had to be a reason. Was someone there?

Lije drove slowly past the impressive Lake Maumelle shorefront home of Barton Hillman. His Crown Victoria was in the driveway. An Impala with a rental car sticker in the back window was parked behind it. A meeting was under way. That was the reason for the delay.

After parking a half block from the house, Lije picked his way through a stand of trees and came up on the lake side of the yard. Retrieving Curtis's phone, he scanned her directory. Curtis was methodical. She recorded everything she might need, and this time her compulsive habits paid off. Under Barton Hillman's name were four listings. The first three were phone numbers, but the last one contained only four digits. Odds were pretty good it was a security code. Moving quickly to the back door, Lije noted the coded lock. He tapped in the four digits and heard the sound of a latch sliding free. The pad blinked. He opened the door, tiptoed in, and gently closed the door behind him.

There was enough light coming from an outside security pole to reveal that he had entered the kitchen and the tile floor in front of him was clear. He tiptoed through the room into a long, carpeted hall. With the outside light now behind him, it was time to employ Janie-style thinking. He stood completely still, slowing even his breathing, tilted his head, and concentrated on the sounds of the home. In a room to his right was a ticking clock. Behind the door on his left, a soft popping might be from a water heater. He moved forward.

Five more steps took him past two doors, one on each side. He stopped again and listened. At first he detected nothing, but then, just to his right, he heard voices. A room off the hall was dark, but on the far wall he saw light coming from a partially open door. Holding his breath, he tried to focus. He heard two men. One was Hillman.

He got down on his hands and knees and began to crawl forward, inching along, using his hands to quietly pat the areas in front and on both sides, feeling for any obstacles he couldn't see. He moved around a chair, a table, a potted plant. Halfway across the room, there was now enough light from the half-open door to reveal his path was clear. Rising to his feet, he silently moved forward until he was close enough to listen.

"I didn't come here for small talk. I just want to know if you finally have it."

"I told you I'd get it," Hillman replied. "And I'm a man of my word." The ABI director tapped an envelope. "You know what people call me?"

"Does it matter?"

Hillman cleared his throat as if preparing to lecture. "I'm the Puppet Master. I pull the strings and things happen. I control my world. I orchestrate everything at the ABI. This—" He tapped the envelope. "—gives us a much bigger stage."

"Us? Barton, I thought this was about your patriotic fever. Didn't know you expected me to help you move to Washington and put you on the president's payroll."

"I'm doing this for the right reasons," Hillman said. "I could prove very valuable to this administration. The man running the CIA is an idiot. I would do much better."

"Let's talk about why I'm here," Lije heard the visitor say. "What you get for your services will come later. I need to see what's in that envelope."

Lije held his breath. Finally the man said, "And this is the only copy?"

"That's the original. I know Evans made no copies and neither have I."

Lije leaned against the wall next to the doorway and, shielded by the door, looked through the narrow slot by the hinges. The two were in Hillman's office. The room was lined with built-in bookshelves interrupted only by a door on the opposite side. Hillman was sitting behind his desk. Lije had a side view of him.

The man examining the stolen formula was in a chair directly across from the director. The visitor appeared to be about forty, clean shaven with a military-style haircut. He wore a dark suit, white shirt. His nose looked as though it had been broken at least once and his square jaw revealed a deep scar.

"I trust you're satisfied," the ABI director said.

"If it is what you say it is, then I'm pleased."

"Consider what this will mean," Hillman said. "With this toxin, the United States can control the economic and political balance of the entire world. If we find a pocket of terrorists, we can use this toxin to eliminate them. When others see it work a time or two and word gets out that we have it, no one will challenge us."

"It is great blackmail," the other man agreed.

Hillman laughed. "It's so much more than blackmail. It's power. Nothing scares people like a horribly painful, drawn-out death. This formula redefines the word *terror* in ways even Edgar Allen Poe couldn't imagine. Who knew Hitler would become our savior. This formula will maintain our status as the world's lone superpower. It's like holding all the aces. This will bring stability to the world."

Lije was stunned. Hillman saw himself as the ultimate patriot. By giving their government the deadly formula, he'd actually believed he'd be saving lives and guarantee the U.S.'s position in the world. What he was trying to do was admirable, in a twisted way. But it was dangerous. Suicidal.

"What has the president said?" Hillman asked. He sounded like a kid at Christmas.

"Nothing. He doesn't know."

"He doesn't know? You're in the White House every day. Who have you told?"

"No one."

Lije leaned back toward the crack between the door and the doorway. The balance of power had shifted. Hillman looked confused. He didn't notice the door to his right slowly open or the man who stood in the doorway.

The face from the past had now entered the present. Lije recognized the man depicted in an artist's crime sketch.

"You told me you had orders from the top," Hillman said, rising from his chair.

"What I told you is unimportant."

Hillman reached for his desk's middle drawer.

"Don't try it, Barton. Take a look to your right."

Standing there, holding a gun, was a man Lije knew only as Smith—the man he was now sure had shot Kaitlyn. His mind racing, Lije waited for what would come next.

"What's this all about?" Hillman demanded. Realizing he'd been caught off guard, he slowly brought his hands up and held them out with palms forward.

The guest smiled. "It's about this: in my hand I hold the power of the world. It's worth a fortune. Twenty years in public service netted me nothing. Smith's boss is willing to pay a great deal for this one piece of paper. He's eager to even a few old scores."

Hillman was in shock. He had unwittingly played into the

hands of a friend who had actually been an enemy. The Puppet Master was no longer pulling the strings. "What scores?"

Although his tone remained friendly, the visitor's explanation was chilling. "My generous friend's grandfather invented this formula and created the only batch. He oversaw its loading into bombs that were placed on planes bound for the United States. The planes were loaded onto a ship that came to be known as the Ark of Death. About the time the ship was launched, a man named Bleicher broke into the lab and stole the only copy of the formula, then burned the lab and all the notes. Before General Renfeld could duplicate his research, he was killed by the underground."

Renfeld. Another piece of the mystery fell into place. That's why the Schneiders had never heard from him, Lije realized. That's why the order was never given.

"Renfeld's grandson," the visitor continued, "has tracked down his grandfather's assassin. The name is Klasser. His son became one of the early freedom fighters for Israel. There are wealthy enemies of Israel who will pay for what the Renfelds can and will deliver. They'll get revenge and make a profit."

Now it all made sense, Lije thought. Renfeld's grandson — the unknown foreigner and Smith's boss — knew Schleter had worked with Bleicher. He figured if the formula still existed, it'd be in the hands of someone Bleicher trusted. That meant the best hiding place had to be on Schleter's property on Swope's Ridge.

Kaitlyn had died because of Swope's Ridge, because she got in the way. Lije now knew the why. And Smith was the who. Finally he had the man just a few feet away.

"Barton," the guest continued, his tone still unnervingly friendly, "you've made me a very wealthy man. Tomorrow night, on CNN, the sad news that I died in a plane crash over the Atlantic on my way to a diplomatic mission in England will air. Except I won't be on that plane. And I'm telling you now because you'll never hear that report."

The visitor turned toward the man in the doorway. "Mr. Smith, the money?"

With his foot Smith pushed a large suitcase toward the middle of the room.

"I'm sure there's no need to count it," the dealmaker and deal-breaker said. "And here's what you want."

Smith took the envelope and slipped it into his pocket.

Like a circus ringmaster, the dark-suited visitor announced, "Time to turn the lights out on Mr. Hillman's career. I'm sure the ABI will give you an incredible funeral."

In his push for power and fame, Barton Hillman had put himself on a train to oblivion. He'd misjudged the temptations of money and power. As the signs of recognition traced their way across his face, he seemed to realize he was powerless. He had sold his morals and integrity. He had shamed his office and tossed out his values. He had rationalized it all to make himself into a hero, and now he found himself a fool.

In a way, Lije thought, this final scene was justice. This was the way Hillman should go out. Yet, there was that small inside voice demanding that Lije do something to change the ending. For a brief instant he fought answering that call, knowing Hillman would not have saved him. But doing the wrong thing had created this situation. It was why so many had already died.

Pressing his shoulders hard against the sheet rock, Lije eased his toe against the bottom of the door. He took a deep breath and kicked the door, causing it to fly open and bang against the wall. The noise diverted the visitors' attention, giving Hillman just enough time to fall to his knees and jerk open his desk drawer. By the time Smith turned his attention and his gun back toward the director, the ABI chief had his gun.

Two shots rang out.

79

In a defensive tactic, Smith had moved to his left as he fired a single shot. His blast caught Hillman just as the director pulled the trigger. The ABI-purchased bullet found a fleshy target, but not the one for which it had been intended. Smith's quick move had placed him directly behind his confused business partner. As the lead tore into his chest, the wealthy visitor fell to his knees and crumpled forward over the money-filled suitcase.

The deal was done, but not in the way anyone intended.

The round that caught Hillman had driven him against the wall. Obviously fighting pain, he lifted his gun and fired another shot. But Smith had regained his footing and was out of the room. The director's round penetrated the door's wooden frame.

As he rushed in, Lije's eyes met Hillman's. The director pushed toward the room's exit and fell face forward. Quickly stepping to his side, the lawyer pried the gun from the wounded man's hand and gave chase. Smith was beside his car and reaching for the handle when Lije burst through the front door. The killer quickly raised his gun. Too quickly. Lije's weapon was still at his side.

Smith grinned as he measured his target. "Time to finish it. Your second chances are more than used up."

The big man squeezed the trigger, but the only sound was a

click. As Smith glanced down at his gun, Lije leaped from the porch and raced toward the demon he had been chasing for months. Covering the distance in three quick steps, he drove his shoulder into the big man's gut, knocking him off his feet and to the ground. Smith cursed as his back hit the driveway. Dropping his empty weapon, he reached for Lije's throat. As his fingers found their mark, Lije brought the butt of Hillman's gun down on the big man's forehead. Smith's eyes stared in disbelief for a moment, then rolled back into his head, his hands releasing their grip as his arms fell to his side.

Lije took a deep breath before reaching down to Smith's neck. There was a pulse. He was out, but not dead. Struggling to his knees, the lawyer slipped his fingers into the man's coat pocket. He found the envelope and yanked it out.

This had always been what it was all about. This had taken his wife. This had led to his best friend's death. This had caused Curtis to sell him, Janie, and Heather out. This was what had driven Hillman over the edge.

Tearing the envelope open, he carefully retrieved the onionskin paper. He studied the equation for a moment, then stuffed it into his pants' pocket and moved back toward the house.

Retracing his route, Lije made his way into the office. While he'd been gone, Hillman had pulled himself upright and was leaning over his desk, holding his left shoulder.

"Need to call 911," Lije said and reached for the phone.

With a swing of his arm, the director knocked the phone off the desk. "No. It's not that bad."

"Maybe," Lije countered, setting the gun on the desk and pulling out his cell. "You've been shot, and your guest here doesn't appear to be in good shape either. And Smith probably has a concussion at the least. Let's get some medical help on the way."

Hillman might have been injured, but his reactions were still flawless. In a split second he had the gun and was pointing it at Lije. "Put the phone down."

His tone told Lije the director was serious. In no mood to challenge a wounded man, he dropped the cell into his pocket and waited for the next order.

"Go into the living room. It's just through that door. Turn on the light. The switch is to the right. I'll be a step behind you. Take a seat on the couch."

Lije found the light and moved to the couch. Hillman followed and glanced out the window at the unconscious Smith before easing onto a fabric-covered chair.

"You got taken," Lije said.

"Yeah," came the admission. "I didn't plan on Hoffman selling out. I figured him for a patriot."

"Why?" Lije demanded. "For what?"

"Had to do it. If the United States had that power, just think of what we could do with it. How much good we could do. And thanks to you, we've got it."

"How many wrongs?" Lije asked.

"What?" Hillman's face showed his confusion.

"How many wrongs did you commit in order to try to create your flawed version of right?"

"I don't understand."

"You tossed your job to the side. You let an innocent man die in the execution chamber. McGee is dead. Janie was almost killed. And that's just part of the list. How did you expect all those wrongs to add up to a right?"

"You're an idealist," Hillman barked. "You'd never even consider what I teach my agents—the proven truth that the needs of the many outweigh the needs of the few. I was trying to save America and keep her great. This was a way we could put everyone else in their place."

"Yeah, using the poison Hitler hoped would end America."

"Hitler was a madman," Hillman argued. "In the hands of our president, it would've been used for good."

Lije almost felt sorry for him. He'd been so intent on creating his own version of what was right, he'd lost what had defined him as the director of the ABI.

"Good people do horrible things," Lije pointed out. "They do them because they have selfish needs. You've seen it happen hundreds of times on your job. If you gave this formula to the leaders of our country, how long before one of them used it to satisfy a personal grudge or quench their lust for more power? How easy would it be for them to rationalize every wrong thing they did as being in the country's best interests? Ever since you found out there might be something powerful on Swope's Ridge, that's what you've been doing. You've sold out everything you believed in. You rationalized it every step of the way."

"I don't need your sermons," Hillman shot back.

"Maybe not, but you need to remember your history. Whenever you give a man the power to take lives or save them, you end up with leaders like Stalin and Hitler."

"You know what Renfeld called the stuff?" the director asked.

Lije shook his head.

"The Genesis Project."

"You need to reread the part in that book about the tree of knowledge. This formula might well be the devil tempting you and everyone else who believes it's okay to play God."

No longer fearing for his life, Lije got up, turned, and walked toward the door. Hillman placed the gun on the end table and stood. "Evans, where are you going?"

"To restart my life," Lije said. "At least what's left of it." He reached in his pocket and pulled out a cell, tossed it on the couch. "Give that to Curtis. You taught her well."

"What about the formula?" Hillman demanded. "This country needs it."

"Ah," Lije replied, "the forbidden fruit, the ultimate power, the answer to who is in charge." Pulling the onionskin from his pocket, he studied it one more time.

"I have the contacts to locate Renfeld!" Hillman shouted. "He's the one really responsible for your wife's death. You need to get him for Kaitlyn. She won't rest until you do."

Lije didn't look back. He just kept walking down the steps and onto the driveway, stopping only when he got to Smith's side. The big man was starting to come to.

"You going to take care of him?" Lije shouted toward the house.

"You want me to kill him?" Hillman asked.

Shaking his head, Lije replied, "No, arrest him. Put him away. Get him off the streets."

The ABI director nodded. "I can hang him for several things, including murder, but it would be easier just to kill him now."

"I'm not after revenge. Only justice. So give me your word on this."

"What about the formula?"

"It's mine. I paid dearly for it."

Taking a final look at Smith, Lije turned and started the solitary walk away from the mystery that had haunted him for months. He kept moving down the driveway and stepped purposefully onto the street to retrieve his car. Sliding in, he started the motor and made a U-turn. By the time he passed Hillman's property, the director had Smith in handcuffs and was pushing him into the house.

Two miles down the road, Lije eased to the shoulder and switched on the dome light. Pulling out his billfold, he opened it to a photo of Kaitlyn. She was gone and it was because of words written on a piece of paper. The seconds became minutes as he absorbed the hollowness created by that knowledge. Only the vibration of his phone finally brought him out of a trance.

"Lije!" Janie's voice betrayed her concern. "Are you all right?"

"Smith's in custody."

"And the formula?"

Lije pulled it from his pocket. Unbuckling his seatbelt, he retrieved something from the glove box, opened the driver's side door, and stepped out in the night. His father had always told him to keep a flashlight, a small jar of peanut butter, a pair of pliers, a universal wrench, a screwdriver, and some matches in every car he owned. For years, he had stored these things, and now he finally had use for one of them. Opening the matchbox, Lije took out a match and struck it against the box. As the fire illuminated his face, he lifted the piece of onionskin paper to the flame. As it began to burn, he dropped it onto the road. When all that was left were ashes, he slid back into the car and put the phone to his ear.

"Everything's taken care of. It's gone for good. See you later at the office."

Hitting the gas, he spun the wheel and headed home. Time to rebuild, to regroup, to get on with life. Time to see what tomorrow brings.

Farraday Road

Ace Collins, Bestselling Author

A quiet evening ends in murder on a muddy mountain road.

Local attorney Lije Evans and his beautiful wife, Kaitlyn, are gunned down. But the killers don't expect one of their victims to live. After burying Kaitlyn, Lije is on a mission to find her killer—and solve a mystery that has more twists and turns than an Ozark-mountain back road.

When the trail of evidence goes cold, complicated by the disappearance of the deputy who found Kaitlyn's body at the scene of the crime, Lije is driven to find out why he and his wife were hunted down and left for dead along Farraday Road. He begins his dangerous investigation with no clues and little help from the police. As he struggles to uncover evidence, will he learn the truth before the killers strike again?

Softcover: 978-0-310-27952-5

Pick up a copy today at your favorite bookstore!

Share Your Thoughts

With the Author: Your comments will be forwarded to the author when you send them to *zauthor@zondervan.com.*

With Zondervan: Submit your review of this book by writing to *zreview@zondervan.com.*

Free Online Resources at www.zondervan.com

Zondervan AuthorTracker: Be notified whenever your favorite authors publish new books, go on tour, or post an update about what's happening in their lives.

Daily Bible Verses and Devotions: Enrich your life with daily Bible verses or devotions that help you start every morning focused on God.

Free Email Publications: Sign up for newsletters on fiction, Christian living, church ministry, parenting, and more.

Zondervan Bible Search: Find and compare Bible passages in a variety of translations at www.zondervanbiblesearch.com.

Other Benefits: Register yourself to receive online benefits like coupons and special offers, or to participate in research.